Tersias

G. P. Taylor lives in the shadows of a medieval castle and the rugged North Yorkshire Moors overlooking the cold Oceanus Germanicus. He has spent most of his life in search of the eternal truths and finally believes he has found the reason why he inhabits a tiny space on this planet. In his spare time he enjoys looking at the stars and eating at The Ivy. G. P. Taylor can be emailed at shadowmancer@btopenworld.com.

Praise for *Shadowmancer*:

'The new C. S. Lewis.' BBC *Heaven and Earth Show*

'The biggest event in children's fiction since Harry Potter.' *The Times*

'The adventure unfolds at a vivid and breathless pace.' *Observer*

'A magical tale of vicars and witches.' *Daily Telegraph*

'A compelling and dark-edged fantasy . . . highly recommended.' *Independent*

Praise for *Wormwood*:

'Wormwood is breathtaking in scope . . . an extraordinary achievement told by a master storyteller. The book is, quite simply, marvellous.' *Guardian by the same author*

Shadowmancer
Wormwood

Tersias

G. P. Taylor

faber and faber

First published in 2005
by Faber and Faber Limited
3 Queen Square London WC1N 3AU
This edition published in 2007

Typeset by Faber and Faber Limited
Printed in England by Mackays of Chatham plc, Chatham, Kent

ISBN 978-0-571-23608-4
ISBN 0-571-23608-1

2 4 6 8 10 9 7 5 3

*To Kathy, Hannah, Abigail and Lydia
who give me the joy of life and to Maddy,
at The Whitby Bookshop, who was the first
person ever to buy my book.*

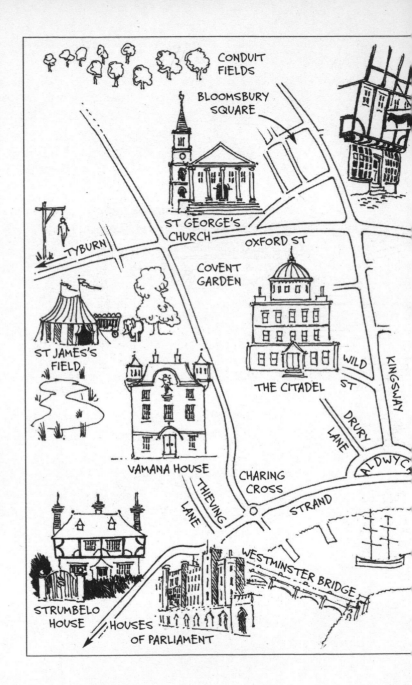

YE BULL AND MOUTH

CLERKENWELL

LONDON WALL

HOLBORN

NEWGATE

ANGEL ST

MALACHI'S STABLE

LONDON

circa 1730

FLEET PRISON

CHEAPSIDE

ST PAUL'S

FLEET ST

LUDGATE HILL

BREAD LANE

CANNON ST

RIVER THAMES

Tetragrammaton

In his malcontent, Magnus Malachi paced the dirt floor of the old stable, then walked slowly to the open door and peered warily around its edge deep into the night sky. He leant on a long staff, stroking its whalebone handle with his thin, grubby fingers.

'It still comes, Tersias, the star is upon us,' he squawked as he looked at the approaching comet and fretfully plucked pieces of his thin black goatee beard from his chin. 'Astound me with your predictions. The comet has to be repelled before it destroys the world and my little piece of the kingdom.' He snarled as he turned and looked across the dark stable to the small boy who sat quietly behind the bars of his cage. 'I was right to buy you, the best guinea I have ever spent,' he muttered as he stalked about. 'Who would pay that for a blind beggar? they said. The man must be a fool, they said. Now who's the fool?' he shouted. 'I have me a prophet boy, an oracle beyond oracles. Ask him a question an' he tells no lies . . . the secrets of the universe are lodged between his cabbage ears and all for a guinea piece.'

Tersias sat on a small wooden three-legged stool next to his tattered bed. Holding on to the thick metal bars that made up the walls and roof of his painted gold cage, he peered out through his blind eyes into a black world. He knew Malachi was nearby – he could smell the heavy scent of myrrh that was pressed into Malachi's long beard to make it glisten. He could hear the rubbing of his boots against the hard ground and sense the dragging of Malachi's foot as he clumsily paced up and down.

Tersias had endured twelve winters, and for the last month he had been locked in his cage with only enough room to walk five blind strides. He had grown frailer with each day, and his once fitted jacket hung like a ragged cotton sack across his hunched shoulders.

'So what do you say, boy? Will my charm work, will it stop the heavens crashing to the earth?' Malachi sniffed and dribbled as he spoke. 'I have to know . . .' He croaked like a thin crow perched in the dead branches of a witch tree.

'It will not destroy the city,' the boy said slowly, rubbing his soft white thumb against the bars of his prison. 'I cannot lie to you. Your spell is useless, there is no one to hear your mumblings.'

'*Mumblings?*' growled Malachi in reply as he wafted his tattered coat back and forth and lashed out with his bone-staff, smashing it against the side of the cage. 'I don't mumble . . . This is an art, a profession of the highest degree. It isn't a mumble – mumbles are for fat old hags that charge a penny for a wart cure. I paid seven guineas for these grimoires, they have curses that were spoken by the ancients . . . You say the comet will not strike the earth but my charm has no effect. How can it be?'

'You asked me the future and I know what is whispered to me, but how or why are not of my understanding,' the boy said quietly.

Malachi stormed about the stable, throwing logs onto the fire. They crashed into the flames, sending bright red sparks up the smithy chimney and scattering hot coals in the hearth. 'Then I will chant it again and cast the spell once more,' he declared. He reached into the large, tatty leather bag that hung

2

from his shoulder on a long strap. He rummaged deep inside, feeling into the corners, his hand quickly searching amongst bones and claws, string and hair.

'Got you!' he screamed merrily as he pulled out a long thin dried finger that had been severed at the fattest knuckle. 'I will make the charm with this, Tersias,' he said, and he scurried to the large table that stood like an alchemist's altar by the far wall and dipped the tip of the wizened finger into the candle flame. Malachi carefully burnt the fingertip until the fire charred it deep black, then, taking a large pewter plate, he scratched a circle into its centre.

'Severed finger, drownèd man . . . Catch the Hekat if you can . . . Come hither, spirits, from near and far . . . Work my desire, destroy the star . . .' He hopped and pointed the smouldering digit from earth to sky as he danced clumsily around the room casting the spell.

He rummaged in the bag again, took a scoop of black powder and sprinkled it with a shaking of salt over the etched circle. He then slowly scratched seven deep gouges from the centre of the plate to its rim, filling the furrows with the powder as he tipped six large drips of thick oil from a chipped pot jug. Three drips of hot wax were dribbled precisely into the hub of the powder, splattering and sizzling as they hit the mixture. Malachi settled the plate in the middle of the long table, then, taking the finger again, scraped a hole in the centre of the mound of powder, lit the fingertip with the candle and ignited the plate.

There was a sudden blue flash as the essence exploded, sending a cloud of dense sulphurous smoke high into the roof. The plate glowed red-hot as the embers fizzled across the table, shooting out sparks in every direction. The powder bubbled the metal with an intense, blinding heat, sending claws of hot pewter burrowing into the oak table.

'So mote it be . . .' Malachi stuttered as he brushed the

3

burning glimmerings from his beard, wiped the smoke from his eyes, then scratched his head with the stump of the severed finger. He slowly walked to the door and peered outside into the night.

For several long minutes Malachi gazed nervously at the comet as it grew brighter and brighter, its long white tail flicking from side to side as it twisted and spun towards the earth.

Tersias sat quietly, picking the loose thread from the sleeve of his coat and singing to himself. He tried to remember life before his kidnapping, a time when he could see reality and not just the faces of the secret visitors who arrived unannounced and invisible to the world, whispering the future to him. They would come most often when he was falling to sleep and murmur his name. In his mind he could see them – vague, drawn faces that seldom smiled. Bitter, caustic voices that rasped against the ears in words. Now they would come on command: as soon as a question was asked they would whisper their reply and he would give it as if it came from his own lips.

'Best he be blind . . .' The words echoed through his mind over and over again, spoken by his mother before he was taken away. 'A blind beggar is better than a lop foot or cacky hand. Earn more money, blind boy – blind man, better for sympathy when begging be done.'

They were the only words spoken by his mother that he could remember. His memory allowed him to see her face before the blast of white burning light gouged his sight and plunged him into darkness and the shadow land he had walked since that childhood day. Again and again he built the sour picture in his mind, pondering on what had happened after he woke from his shocked sleep and felt the thick cloth swathes wrapped around his head, keeping out the light and sticking to the thick, scaly scabs that covered his eyes.

It was when strange hands pulled the cloth roughly from his

4

skin that he knew he was blind and alone, stolen from his home. He could never forget the childish panic that ran through his legs and quivered his lips before spilling out as fresh tears and breath-stealing sobs. His infant words had screamed for his mother, shouted her name, but answer came none. In the maddening thoughts that raced through his mind he thought she was there, hiding from him just out of sight, somewhere very near. Hide and seek, that's all he could think of – that she would take off this dark mask and he would see her face and not know her betrayal.

Instead it had been dark corners of stinking rooms, picking lice from his skin and eating the crumbs from another's table. Rough hands and harsh words from a stranger who gave neither love nor name and tied him to the begging post in Covent Garden were all his young days knew. Long hours of beating rain and biting cold had stripped tender flesh almost to the bone as he held out his hands for the grace of passing strangers.

His sightless, scarred face had brought the pity of the hardest heart. He would beg, blue-lipped, for a widow's mite or fop's shilling. He was a favourite of the nighthawks who bustled in their thick skirts and passed him pleasantries and half-eaten sops of bread. Then, as the last lamps were snuffed out, Rough-hands would return and take him back to the garret, dragging him through the damp streets, up two flights of narrow stairs and into the high loft, taking from him the begging bag and silently counting the money, penny by penny.

Then on Walpurgis Night, when Rough-hands slept, the creature came for the first time. Between long drunken snores, Tersias could hear the cracking of the floorboards as the room filled with a dark oppression. As he huddled into the shabby blanket and wrapped his feet from the nibbling rats, it slowly and purposefully encircled him with its deathly presence. He could sense through each nerve and breath that something hovered over him, filling the room with its foul stench. Tersias squeezed himself into a tight knot, hoping to become so small that he would not be seen. He pulled his knees to his chest and covered his blind eyes for fear that they would somehow see what was before him.

A dark voice beside him quietly spoke. 'I am the Wretchkin. When you dance with me, it's always to my tune.' He felt a velvet hand stroke his face. 'Creatures of power always need their little pixies and dryads to do their bidding and you can be my dryad. In return I will give you a perfect gift that will astound the world and make you great . . . Nothing I give will be nugatory.'

In a brief moment a sharp spike seemed to rip through his face, throwing back his head and twisting his neck as he was thrust against the damp plaster and pressed to the floor by an unseen power that rushed through his mouth and swirled in his head. Then, suddenly, the presence was gone and the room echoed again to the snoring of Rough-hands, propped in a chair by the dampening fire.

It was then that the voices of the Wretchkin came like the first faint whispering of confessional conversation. Tersias thought he was surrounded by a scornful crowd of gawpers, that the room was filled with people laughing and cajoling him. He answered the mocking and was quickly told to be silent by the gruff voice of his faceless keeper speaking in his sleep as he slobbered and bibbed back and forth.

The voices continued to whisper news of tomorrow, great events, pageants and hangings. He was surrounded by their babble. They filled his mind, echoed in each sinew. Sometimes the voices of the Wretchkin would talk together, bringing rumours from far off places for him to overhear. It was as if the voices were in his head and only he could hear them, that they were messengers that spoke only to him. The next night he spoke back to the Wretchkin. At first, he thought they couldn't hear him, but as the image of their faces grew in his mind he spoke boldly. From then on they would come like attending angels proclaiming the future.

'Don't tell them who speaks to you, Tersias,' they would call in one voice as they left him alone as the dawn broke. 'He'll think you're mad, lead-lipped and mercury-minded.' They laughed and quipped like a choir of Minster boys.

In the days to come, Tersias was sold on from Rough-hands to a Limehouse noose-maker, then lost in a match of French Jack, a wager in a game of cards. He was left by London Bridge, forgotten by his drunken master, and fell for a guinea into the hands of Magnus Malachi, dealer in treatments, purveyor of the darkness and caster of curses. The Wretchkin followed him to the stable, where he was locked in a caged manger. They were always ready to speak, always near and without name.

It was by an irresistible compulsion that Tersias unwittingly uttered his first oracle. Malachi had been bent over his pot, scrying the dark waters for a foresight of the future. He had muttered his oath and his questioning was overheard by the Wretchkin. They whispered the answer to Tersias, who could not contain his voice and shouted out Malachi's desire and what fate would befall him. It was then that Malachi double-locked the cage and set up his bed in the stable. He lit the smithy fire and kept Tersias from begging in the street.

There had followed countless questions and exhortations that had tested the Wretchkin in their devotion to Tersias. Each time Malachi asked, they answered, uttering through the lips of the youth the precise reply that Malachi wanted to hear. In the four long weeks of his confinement, Tersias had spoken the words of these creatures many times.

7

Malachi had leapt with joy as his newfound prophet surpassed his wild dreaming. Tersias had spoken of the coming comet time and again as it had secretly approached through space. Malachi had stomped his whalebone staff unbelievingly into the ground and called him a meddler, scraping one foot against the dry ground like a raging bull. Then all suddenly changed when he found the tattered pages of the *London Chronicle* and read for himself of the great discovery. Tersias could feel the rising convulsions of awe and panic that overflowed from Malachi, making him virtually speechless other than repeating the words louder and louder – *the comet, the comet*.

Now the comet was here, stretching from one side of the dark night sky to the other. The spectacle had come and London was deserted. The rats had fled the houses after the first bombardment of sky-ice that had cracked the atmosphere and burnt its way into the earth's crust. Tersias and Malachi were the only ones to still inhabit the stable yard that clung to the back wall of the Cross Keys inn to the north of Cheapside. Every lodging lout, guttersnipe and vagabond had abandoned the city; all that could be heard was the cry of dogs and the rustling autumn leaves.

Malachi edged his way further and further into the night air, his eyes fixed on the approaching star. Everywhere the crashing of ice crystals invaded the atmosphere, falling to earth around the city and beyond. Silver meteors plunged into the river, boiling the water and sending skyward an explosion of hissing gases. The comet grew brighter in the eastern sky as it plunged nearer to the earth behind the moon. From the east a howling wind lifted the water from the river as the comet arched towards the moon, its orbit pulled towards the lesser light. The whole earth shuddered as the comet smashed into the moon's dark side, sending plumes of lunar dust high into space. It fractured in the surface of the moon and exploded towards the earth in a million fragments of ice that twisted and spun as they crossed the sky.

'I did it,' Malachi shouted, dancing from the doorway to the cage and peering in at his little prisoner. 'My dear soothe-tooth, you were right, the comet has crashed into the moon and will not strike the earth and my alchemy prevailed.' He reached in through the bars of the cage and took hold of Tersias by the chin, nipping the flesh until the boy squealed.

Tersias could smell the scent of burning sulphur and fried onion that laced Malachi's fingers in thick grease. His eyes watered and rolled with tears that fell across his cheek as the pungent vapours filled his senses and his twisted skin pulsed with pain.

'My little boy cries for Uncle Malachi,' his master cajoled, pretending to cry. 'See how his splendid tears fall from his blind eye – what a testimony of love!' His voice wailed like a sea siren. 'I will buy you a golden cage – for your protection, of course. When the city is rebuilt we will go to Tyburn and you can prophesy at the hangings for a shilling a time. I will be rich, and you – you can have a blanket, washed every week,' he exclaimed excitedly, his voice rising higher and higher.

'I will not speak,' Tersias said, backing away from Malachi. 'I am not a creature from some menagerie.'

Malachi walked quietly to the other side of the cage as Tersias searched for a telling sound. 'Why is that, Tersias? Do you not want to please me? I have given you warmth and food and shelter, have I not? Is this how you repay your friend Malachi?'

'Have I not paid off the guinea you gave for me?' Tersias asked as he fumbled around the cage. 'I have begged for you and told you the future, what more do you want? Shall I be a public spectacle to be ridiculed?'

'Who would care for you, Tersias? Bring you water and clothing, serve your food and change your bed? I am your eyes in a world of darkness, your ears in a world so deaf that it cannot hear the truth. The debt to me is greater than a guinea, I bought a life not a lease, on this the law is clear. You are my apprentice until you are twenty-one and then you will be free.' Malachi paused and slowly ran his staff from bar to bar, clanking the metal menacingly. 'If you want your freedom now then the ransom price is two hundred pounds, the cost of your keep until you come of age. Then you will have the key to the door and you can walk free.' His voice sharpened like his face. 'Until that time you are mine and you will speak for me to whoever I want. Just be glad you will never see the circumstances of your utterances or the faces of your enquirers . . .'

'What if I refuse, what will you do then?' Tersias asked as he wrapped himself in his blanket and sat in the middle of the cage, awaiting the onslaught of the plunging staff that he knew would bite at him through the bars. He could hear Malachi walking away from the cage to the fireplace, dragging his cumbersome leg stiffly behind him. And then he heard the sound of metal being thrust into the fire, slithering across the stone hearth and poking deep into the ashes.

Silence was a fearful thing to Tersias. He strained his ears to listen for what Malachi was doing but all he could hear was the deep rise and fall of his own laboured breathing. The smithy ashes were turned again as the poker was thrust deeper into the fire, surrounded by white-hot embers. It was then slipped quickly from the sparking cinders and the dragging foot gathered pace towards him.

'What does he do?' Tersias cried fearfully under his breath to the Wretchkin, somehow knowing within him that a great evil would be done.

'He brings a fire-stick glowing hot, burning as bright as the hatred in his eyes,' said the voice in his head that echoed through him. As the creature spoke, Tersias was overwhelmed by a deep sickness that twisted his gut. The smell of the Wretchkin filled his nostrils and bubbled in his throat.

Tersias suddenly began to distinguish the dark image of Magnus Malachi, pressed upon his mind by the Wretchkin. He gave a gasp of complete surprise as he could clearly see him for the first time, his long coat sweeping over the dirt floor. It was like a lucid dream unfolding at dawn, played out across his mind like a dancing mist that slowly cleared. Malachi was much taller than he had thought, thinner and drawn in the face, his goatee beard long and black with sticky buds of myrrh glowing in the light of lamp and fire. Tersias could make out that the Wretchkin was behind him, out of the cage, watching Malachi from over his shoulder. It was as if they were joined in thought and whatever the creature saw was pulsed into his mind for him to see.

The creature's stare was fixed on the fire-rod that Malachi carried in his hand. It glowed with a white-hot tip that sparked and oozed a thin and constant wisp of blue smoke. Tersias could see the hand that gripped the poker, each finger tipped with a thick black nail that clawed out of a long, stained finger.

'I have a surprise for you, Tersias. Are you sure you will not speak for me?' Malachi said as he got closer. 'If you don't speak for me then you will be mute as well as blind . . .'

'A fire-rod to still my tongue?' Tersias asked as he got to his feet and backed away.

'You guess well . . . You are no use as a beggar, but as a prophet and seer you are unique. Do that for me and your life will change. You will have a golden cage and silk sheets. I will tell the world you are my own, my adopted son. I will teach you the way of alchemy and the secrets of the world will be yours.'

'And I will perform like some dancing bear as a party trick?' Tersias asked, as in his mind he watched his master draw closer.

'You will astound and amaze, I will be your guardian and you my apprentice,' Malachi said as he lifted the fire-rod and pointed it through the bars of the cage towards Tersias, who pushed himself further away, squeezing his back against the thick metal rods.

Malachi pushed the hot poker slowly towards him, inch by inch. Tersias turned his face away from the fire-rod. 'Feel the heat, Tersias? All you have to do is say yes and you will have no fear. We can seal our friendship, so mote it be . . . Better to be a quick-tongued friend than mute enemy. BLIND AND SILENT,' he shouted.

'I will not speak.' Tersias shouted, as the blistering poker got nearer.

'Then you are brave or stupid. Be my oracle and live with a loose tongue, refuse and I will singe it to the roof of your mouth.' Malachi pressed the fire-rod closer.

'Speak for him, boy,' a soft-voiced Wretchkin said quickly. 'He will kill you.'

'I will prophesy for you,' Tersias said reluctantly. He pressed himself against the metal bars and gasped as the heat from the fire-rod began to singe his skin.

'A wise boy will always keep his tongue,' Malachi said as he slipped the poker from the cage. 'Tomorrow we will take to the streets and you will speak to the people. There has been much madness, and they will want to know what comes to them. I will prepare you a carriage fit for a king and you shall be driven by the finest horse in London.'

2

Black Mary's Well

In the thick bright moonlight, the broad lane that led out of Rag Street and across Conduit Fields was etched with a vivid silver thread that picked out the branches of the small snarled trees against the sky.

Jonah Ketch lay huddled in the remnants of a stack of summer straw, wind blown and dalliance scattered across the grass near to a pile of weathered stone that encircled a surging wellspring. In his hands he gripped a quart gin pot that he had wrapped in the tails of his dirty white shirt and warmed against his thin body through the night. He moaned to himself and twisted the curls of his bushy black hair in his melancholy as the growing cold seeped through his coat and breeches. In his belt an old rusted pistol pressed awkwardly against the ground, clashing against a long knife that had slipped its leather sheath. He groaned with each cold breath and tried to open his eyes to look up at the night sky and the comet from which he had tried to escape. But sleep snared him with its grip and held him to the living dream in which he re-lived his waking moments like some bitter torment.

Jonah had run from his lodging in Goose Alley when the meteors from the comet first struck. He'd watched fearfully as a fireball smashed through the dome of St Paul's, then danced with frantic steps through the mud of Fleet Market. The streets had been packed with people fleeing the apocalypse as stone upon stone had fallen from the sky, burning blood-red hail on the city. As he had run along Saffron Hill he saw a man torn in two by a fragment of blistering sky-rock that had roared from the heavens like an avenging angel, spitting black sulphur as it cut through its victim before crashing through the wall of Bullhead Yard. He had run even faster, clutching the quart pot of gin and keeping to the narrow alleyways of Clerkenwell Green until he reached the open fields and was greeted by the woeful cries of the hysterical inmates of Lord Cobham's Mad-House, locked away and left alone by the fleeing matron.

Far in the distance he could see the pile of stones that was Black Mary's Well. Jonah had walked the last mile in the company of a thousand people who streamed north towards Islington village and the fire at Hampstead that burnt brightly on the dark skyline.

At the well stones he had decided to stop, to rest his feet and sup gin from the fat-necked jar until its numbing warmth had dragged him into a deep sleep. He knew this place well. Here two lanes came together, lined by a thick gorse hedge. It was the ideal place to lie in wait, covered by the first black of evening gloom. Here he could patiently hold fast until he could trap a lone traveller or tired carriage as, approaching the outskirts of the city, they lapsed into a false feeling of security.

In his fifteen years he had already killed one man – though it was more an accident than an act of murder, as the old pistol he carried had almost of its own wanting discharged lead into the belly of a fat man with false teeth. Jonah had pulled the gun from his breeches on the man's approach, and as he shouted for the man to stand, there had been a blinding flash. He had stared hopelessly as the shot ripped into the man and he crumpled to the floor, belly split and torn like a Whitby whale. In the half-light Jonah had looked around but could see no one. He knew he had time to empty pockets and without panic or fear had walked the three paces and stared down at the wide-eyed face before quickly rifling the man's pockets of a fob watch and leather purse.

The highway had provided for him. He was a footpad without club or cloak. A common robber and thief doing the only work for which he was able and with no one to tell him different. In his heart he dreamed of being a highwayman, free to wander as far as Lincoln or York, and not trapped to London lanes. Black Mary's Well was his holy place. Drink from the water and it would take away the pox, cure a fever and flush out the gout. Now he prayed in his sleep to Black Mary to take away the stench of gin from his throat and lift his legs from the ground. But as he opened his eyes from slumber he knew she had not listened. The pain of the gin tore at his head and swelled his eyes to bursting; the solace of drunken sleep now gave way to a fire that burnt brightly behind each eyeball.

He breathed deeply, taking in the cold night air and laying on his back in the deep straw as he looked up to the clear sky. The comet had gone. In its place the embers of its dust floated to the earth like a myriad of tiny stars bursting to red, green and purple flames as they were sucked into the atmosphere. To Jonah they looked like a billion tiny candles spluttering and sparking on the crest of heaven. He smiled to himself . . . He was alive.

Like the whole of London, Jonah had thought that the coming of the comet was the start of the apocalypse, the end of the world and the final judgement. He knew he had much to stand charge for. He was a debtor of the greatest magnitude and his sins consumed his every moment. So far he had escaped punishment for the crimes he had committed, but he knew that at the end of time he would answer to a power from which even he could not escape.

Jonah sat up and pulled the gin quart from his shirt-tails and rattled the pot. It was empty. His tongue cleaved to the roof of his mouth, dried by the bitter juniper berries. He looked around before crawling to the wellspring and plunged his face into its cold water. It burnt the skin and set fire to each nerve, shuddering his spine with its chilliness. He wiped the water from his face and listened. From somewhere in the distance came a familiar sound: through the crispness of the night he heard the turning wheels of a boneshaker rattling down the lane with the common trot of two drawing horses. The metal wheels struck against the stones and slopped through the ruts of mud. A carriage approached – a gentleman, a noble, a woman of grace, a pilgrim to the well, a priest from Court with a gold cross or Bishop's ring . . . all to be relieved of their pride and their purses.

Jonah's mind raced, he felt his heart swell with the urge to take from the rich and keep it for himself. It was an overwhelming desire, like an inner force that he could not resist. He smiled and checked the pistol. With one click it was ready and with one hand he scooped a drink from the well, spilling the water from hand to mouth.

'Bring me luck, Black Mary and I will never forget you,' he said quietly, then began to crawl towards the lane as the carriage rattled towards him. He kissed the pistol. 'Once more, my friend, once more.' He spoke the words like a prayer. 'Never let me down . . . never.'

Jonah searched the deep pocket inside his tattered frock coat. Quickly, he found the flour sack with its rough-cut eye-holes and charcoal-painted smile. He slipped the disguise over his head, peering through the slits into the night.

In the distance he could see the outline of the carriage against the red glow of the Hampstead firestorm. There was just the driver, no musket-man or plate-boy, and two fat horses quickly pulling the covered trap. A woman, he thought to himself as he stole through the gorse that picked at his coat. He waited . . . The excitement fretted his brow and twisted his gut, ridding him of the gin fever and pounding his heart. With one hand he held the hem of the flour sack to his neck, twisting it tighter and tighter. This was all he loved: waiting for the time to pounce and take what should rightly be his. Jonah could see the silhouette of the driver, a small thin man, his hat pulled tight to his ears and cape drawn round against the night chill.

As the carriage approached he made ready to jump. In his haste he slipped down the bank and into the lane, landing in the mud. Then Jonah jumped to his feet. 'STAND! Your money or the lead! Give me what is yours or end up . . . dead!'

A horse reared and twisted the carriage to one side, pulling it into the ditch and trapping the wheels in the thick November mud. The driver fell from the seat and vanished into the darkness. Jonah strode towards the carriage, steadying his pistol towards the small window and door that flapped open.

As he walked he held his breath, his eyes searching the murk for the carriage man.

'Come out!' Jonah shouted as he tried to discover where the driver was hiding. 'It's no use veiling yourself with cow grass, I can see your eyes. Come out or you'll have one pistol and your passenger the other!' He spoke quickly as he tried to fool him.

'Leave him be,' the driver said as he crawled from under the carriage, still holding his long whip as he got to his feet. 'You make a mistake robbing us, you'll be hunted from here till Christmas.' The driver stared at the mask with its charcoal smile. 'Lord Malpas will have you hanged for doing this.'

'He'll have me hanged if I don't. Out of the way, my good fellow, I am a highwayman of distinction.' Jonah aimed the pistol at the man's head. 'Turn to the carriage and you will see nothing. Ask no questions, tell no lies. Now turn your head or take the lead.'

'You're a footpad and a thief. Nothing but a lad with half a yard, fresh from his mother's arms. You walk the road in stained breeches stolen from a hanging. Find a horse, then you can be a highwayman.' The driver cursed as he turned to the carriage, taking hold the rim of the wheel and looking to the ground.

Without warning, Jonah took the pistol by the barrel and viciously whipped the stock across the back of the man's head. 'Never turn your back on a stranger,' he said calmly as the man slumped to the floor. 'I am a highwayman and not a thief.'

From inside the carriage Jonah could hear two men in deep conversation. They spoke eagerly in hushed tones, just above a whisper. Jonah waited, and in the glow of the carriage lamp saw a man lean forward towards the dark shadow on the other side of the coach. The talking continued, as if nothing in the world could halt the desperation of the spoken words. Then the lamp was hastily snuffed out and the carriage plunged into darkness.

'Come out! No tricks! I have a pistol primed and ready for each of you,' Jonah shouted, his voice tinged with apprehension. There was no reply, but the conversation in the carriage stopped abruptly. In the eerie silence Jonah waited. 'I'll tell you again. Come out or I'll fire and you'll take your chance with the lead.'

'You can fire what you like, boy, but the rope will stretch your neck like any other and I'll have you drawn and quartered with your heart black-tarred and put on a stake in St Giles yard. That'll show the world what happens to thieves who stop a Minister on his way to Parliament.' The words shot at Jonah with breathless speed. 'And if you make me get down from my carriage then I will chase you through Conduit Fields myself and whip your backside all the way to Tyburn. Do you hear me, boy?' The voice billowed from the dark of the carriage into the night.

'Step down and stand. I care not for who you are or for what power you serve,' Jonah replied, pressing his finger to the cold metal of the trigger. 'I listen to no authority but my own and it is to me that you will answer.' He stepped away from the sight of the door and raised the pistol ready to fire. Quickly, he looked back up the lane and listened for any sound of approaching horses. But the night was empty, as if the whole world was a vacant place and all life had been scourged from the earth. The coachman lay in the long grass, arms out-stretched as if dead, steam from his nostrils rising up like mist-angels as he panted. 'This is your last chance,' Jonah continued as he held the pistol steady. 'Stand down and let me see your faces.'

The carriage gently rocked as a man stepped into the night. He wore a long French coat, and white ruff sleeves covered his hands as he attempted to conceal the fine, gold ring he wore on his right thumb. Jonah stared from behind his disguise into the jet-black eyes of his victim. He was a small, thin man with pinched cheeks and thick bushy brow with a voice that did not fit his frame.

'Tell your companion to step down,' Jonah said. He looked around edgily, fearful the militia could be near at hand.

'I travel alone,' Lord Malpas said curtly as he looked at Jonah. 'I take it this is what you want.' He held out a small leather purse.

'I heard you talking to someone, saw his shadow in the carriage. Tell him to come out.'

'There is no one there, your eyes deceive you. I am alone, I always travel alone. Now take the money and be off into the night to your molly.'

'I don't want your false money, one purse for your gold and another full of painted lead weights. Do you think I am that stupid? You lot are all the same, carry two purses for fear of being robbed, always wanting to keep your hands on your gold. Now tell your companion to stand down.' Jonah stared at Malpas, aiming the pistol at his head. 'I mean it, tell him to stand down.'

'How many times have you to be told that I travel alone?'

'I heard you talking, saw the shadow,' Jonah replied.

'Then see for yourself. Search the carriage, you will find no one. What you heard was the wind rattling around in the emptiness of your head.' Lord Malpas brushed the falling white particles of dust from his coat.

'And when I look you will run off, bleating like a January lamb. First, your purse. Throw it to the ground.' Malpas threw the purse to the ground and slowly folded his arms as he calmly looked around. 'Now the other. The one with the real money in and not the lead.'

'You've done this before, haven't you, boy? You're hanging will certainly be well attended by everyone you have fleeced in your young life. Such a waste. I could always use someone as talented as you.' Malpas slowly took a fat purse from his waist-band and threw it to the floor.

'Now tell your friend to come out of his dark hole and stand before me,' Jonah insisted as he stepped towards Lord Malpas.

'How many times do you have to be told? I am *alone*,' Malpas shouted in frustration, his voice echoing across the fields.

Jonah stepped even closer to him and put the pistol to his temple. 'Quiet! Face to the dirt, my Lord, and then I will see if you tell the truth.'

'And let you shoot me in the back of the head?'

'I may shoot you in the side of the head if you don't do what I say,' Jonah hollered as he pressed the gun deeper into his temple.

Malpas meekly dropped to his knees and buried his face in the damp of the soft brown earth. Jonah Ketch stealthily edged his way to the carriage door, one eye staring at the crumpled body of Lord Malpas snorting in the muck of the Highgate Road.

'Last chance,' he said as he crept closer to the door. 'Out now or I'll fire.'

'It's empty, fool,' Malpas muttered, his mouth filled with the dust from the road. 'There's nothing in there for your kind.'

'Then I'll see for myself,' Jonah replied, and he quickly spun on his heels and pointed his pistol into the dark void of the carriage. For several long, black moments his eyes tried to search the gloom. Within him, his instinct told him that there was another presence close by, as if he could feel the energy of a sullen dark life near to him. But though he looked again and again, his eyes scourging each corner of the carriage, there was no one to be seen.

It was then that Jonah saw a thin black case nestling on the fine red canvas seat. In the light of the moon he could clearly see the gold dragon clasp that pulled the two sides tightly together. The tight marbled skin that covered the case shone like the back of a flattened snake, its white ivory handle burning bright against the black leather.

Jonah felt drawn to snatch the case and run into the black of the night, yet as he held out his hand towards it a sudden feeling of fear darted across his mind. Like a chilled nightmare, several long red tongues flashed before his eyes in a waking dream. The voice of a stranger spat the words again and again in a deep, dark voice as Jonah reached for the ivory handle: 'LEAVE . . . ME . . . ALONE!'

'What's in the case?' Jonah asked warily as he turned to Lord Malpas.

'Nothing for you, boy. Just some papers. Now take the money and go, there is nothing else for you here.'

'That's too fine a case for papers. Something tells me there's more in there.' Jonah turned to look into the carriage.

'It'll do you no good, boy. Take that case and you'll have more to fear than the gallows,' Malpas said. He slowly got to his feet, slipped his hand into the back of his frock coat and edged his way, inch by inch, towards Jonah.

There was a sudden flash of bright steel as Malpas lurched at Jonah, stabbing a long thin blade deep into his arm. Jonah uttered a shrill scream and gasped with pain, then in one movement lashed out at Malpas with such force that the lock of the pistol embedded itself in his thin cheek.

Malpas fell to the floor, clutching the bleeding wound as he desperately tried to wipe the blinding blood from his eyes. There was another blow and another as Jonah hit out again and again, the pain from the knife wound pounding through his body.

Then he stopped and looked to the ground. Malpas lay face-down in the road, his long raven hair scattered like thick twigs in the mud. He made no sound; his bloodstained hands gripped the thick ribbons of dead grass that clung to the deep ruts.

Jonah grabbed the black, jet handle of the knife and tried to pull it from his arm. It dug even deeper, as if it had a mind to bury itself into his flesh. At his feet the two purses lay humped together; he swiftly picked them from the floor and put them in the pocket of his coat. Then he stopped and listened, unsure if he could hear a jangle of horse-metal in the distance. Quickly he leant into the carriage and took hold of the ivory handle of the black case, lifting it from the seat and into the night air.

Jonah turned to run, scrabbling up the gorse bank and over the pile of stones at the Well. Instinctively he stopped, put the case on a large stone and bathed the knife, still embedded in his arm, in the water from Black Mary's Well. The cold chilled his flesh as it ran along the polished steel of the blade. Again he tried to pull the blade form the wound and again it gripped tighter, pulling itself deeper into his flesh. Again he heard the voice as he struggled to vanquish the pain that fired through each nerve: 'LEAVE . . . ME . . . ALONE!'

The voice spoke as if it came from all around him and within him at the same time. A voice that made each hair on the back of his head rise from its place and stand terrified at the sound. It was a voice that shuddered his spine and turned his feet to lead, the frightening voice of childhood that would lurk in dark corners and beneath his bed. He grabbed the case and tried to run, forcing one foot to fall in front of the other as he picked his way through Conduit Fields towards the lights of the city.

The Bull and Mouth

The faint echo of footsteps followed Jonah like a dark shadow as he ran feebly through Bloomsbury Square and into Hart Street. The last stragglers of the sky panic huddled on the steps of St George's like a pack of ravens squawking in the morning rubbish.

Jonah stopped and looked back, convinced that the militia were nearby, that Lord Malpas had somehow raised the alarm and called out the troops. He rubbed his eyes with a bloodied hand, wiping beads of salt from his brow as he panted into the cold night. The knife throbbed and burnt in his flesh, slowly pulling itself deeper so that the black jet hilt forced the threads of his jacket against his skin. The silver blade caught his chest with each step he took, so now he held his bleeding arm away from his body and his mind raced with the pain that fevered his thoughts.

It was then, as he looked back to the north, that he saw what appeared to be the shape of a large dog sniffing at the road outside the iron railings of Bedford House. It stalked up and down, its snout ferreting amongst the piles of fallen leaves as it shivered and twisted in the bright glow of the moon. It fixed itself on a scent and then, without warning, stood on its hind legs, shook itself and began to walk across the square towards him.

Jonah stared in amazement as the figure got nearer and nearer. He stepped back into the shadows and watched. The figure stopped every few feet and sniffed the air, first from the north and then from the south, then slowly paced through the trees and passed the sheep that scurried out of its way.

Jonah knew he was being followed. Stepping from the darkness, he walked painfully down the street. Everywhere was the debris of the sky-quake: upturned stalls littered the market plac and empty barrows, tipped and twisted, filled the road with splintered wheels and broken shafts. The sign for the Bull and Mouth blew gently back and forth, squeaking on its rusted hinges. Jonah walked faster, turning every third step and casting a long glance to see if he was still being followed. Far behind, skirting a shadow of a stable yard, was the figure on all-fours, its face buried in the earth. Quickly, Jonah ducked into the doorway of the baker's shop. He saw the figure get to its feet, then stoop again and place a hand on the ground as if feeling for the heat of each step that Jonah had taken.

There was a loud clatter as the door to the Bull and Mouth suddenly swung open. Jonah turned as a man rushed towards him, arms outstretched, staggering and about to pounce, his large whiskered face covered in white froth. Without thinking, Jonah leapt to his feet and pushed the vagrant forcefully towards the glass-panelled window as he sidestepped and pelted towards the door of the Inn. Behind him he heard the crash as the man staggered into the glass and crashed through the brittle crystals.

Jonah slammed the door of the inn behind him and slid the short wooden beam into its keeper to prevent its opening. He twisted his coat from his back, hanging it over his shoulder to cover the knife. His fingers entwined in the weave, hoping to dry the drops of blood from his hand. Then he turned, not knowing who would be behind him or what welcome he would receive.

Several candles flickered on the fireplace. In the far corner an old man slumped into an empty plate, his long grey beard soaking up the remnants of a spilt beer. The fire glowed in the grate as three decrepit rats blindly scampered along the skirting and disappeared into the dirt and darkness. Jonah felt his feet sticking to the floorboards, which were dried in patches with small piles of fresh wood shavings. The thick smell of tobacco and beer seeped into every corner.

The warmth of the fire eased Jonah's heartache and melted his concern. Sleep filled the inn – restful, drunken sleep that he knew well. He stood silently and listened to the old man snoring long bellyfuls into his pewter plate.

Then, looking through the glow to the dark, eerie shadows that encircled the room, Jonah saw Maggot curled up on a fresh mound of sawdust like a thin mouse under the table by the fire. His face was covered in an old cloth, his hands curled around his head, knees to chin. He was a small boy, withered in height by years of lack. He had a weathered face with wise eyes that had seen sufficient misery for thrice his eleven years. He slept fitfully, warm-backed and cold-fronted, unaware of the visitor who stared at his slumber and slumped against the window seat, resting the case beside him and carefully pulling back the curtain to look into the street.

In the distance, by the broken market stalls, Jonah saw the dog-stalker walking in the shadows, carefully picking his way closer. Jonah drew the pistol from his belt and pulled back the hammer . . . The man dropped to the floor again and sniffed the dirt, lifting a piece of earth to his lips and tasting it with the tip of his long blue tongue.

A sudden sharp dart of pain brought Jonah to his senses. 'Maggot, wake up, you dirt bag,' he said quietly. 'Wake up or I'll stick you with my knife.' Jonah looked to his belt – his knife had gone, lost in his escape.

'Call me by my proper name,' Maggot said as he stirred,

unsure if he was dreaming. 'You never call me by my proper name.'

'There's only one name for a Maggot. Now wake up and bolt the doors and whatever happens don't let anyone in here.'

Maggot crawled out from his nest and wiped away the sleep from his eyes as he peered around the inn. He looked at the old man slumped across the table. 'He'll be sad today, Jonah. Old Bunce thought the world was going to end so he gave all his gin and beer away. Said he'd never enter heaven the landlord of a liquor palace.' The old man snored heavily as he spoke. 'He'll have a gin head and be mad as Hades when he wakes up. He was calling you a coward for running away, said you'd be out looting the molly houses looking for a quick guinea.'

'This place will be looted if you don't bolt that door,' Jonah interrupted.

'What's stopping you doing it?' Maggot shouted back louder than he thought possible. 'Got the devil after you?'

'More like a madman from Lock's Hospital. He's followed me like a dog for the last mile, crawling and sniffing like a bloodhound. And if he gets in here he'll eat you up, Maggot.'

The boy ran to the door and slid the thick bolts quickly into the grimy frame. Old Bunce stirred from his plate and sleepily stroked his greasy beard. He slowly opened the wart-covered folds of skin that covered his eyes and looked about the inn. Without saying a single word he yawned and fell again into a deep snorting sleep.

'How much did he drink?' Jonah asked as he peered through the chink in the curtain into the night.

'A gallon of ale and a bottle of gin, then he ate a whole bottle of vinegared eggs and drank the sups from every flagon left on the tables.' Maggot gestured with his hands and pretended to stagger about the room. 'It was enough to kill a man half his age.' He stopped and looked at Jonah, and for the first time he

27

saw the hilt of the dagger sticking out from the cover of his coat. 'So they got you?'

'A lucky blow . . . from behind,' Jonah replied painfully.

'And he follows you?'

'Not he, but something or someone else. I left him face-down in Conduit mud, bubbling like an old toad. Picked up this tail in Bloomsbury Square, thought it was some kind of dog . . . Could be a night-watch late back to Bow Street.' Jonah spoke nervously, still unsure as to who was really following him. He had always got clean away before, melted into the dark of night, but something told him that this pursuer was in some way a consort of Lord Malpas and that his escape had not been complete.

'Did you bring anything back for Maggot?' the boy asked hopefully, his eyes devouring the luscious snakeskin case.

Jonah reached into his pocket and threw the two bags of coins to the floor. 'Take your pick, right or left. One's gold, the other's lead. Choose.'

Maggot stared at the bags of coins, his eyes trying to pierce the leather to see which contained the false money. He waited for a signal from Jonah.

'Go on, Maggot, take your pick. You can have a third of what you choose – then some for me, some for Tara,' Jonah said as he thought of her. 'Go wake her, tell her I'm crock. I'll keep an eye out for the watch-dog. Take 'em both, I wouldn't want you to go away empty-handed and turn me in to the Justice.' Jonah was panted, and beads of sweat trickled over his forehead as his face winced with the deepening pain.

Maggot ran in his heavy boots across the dirt-stained wooden floor and through the kitchen door that led to the stair-way and the rooms above the inn. Jonah smiled to himself, and a feeling of smug satisfaction rushed through him. His mind danced back to the day he had stolen those boots at a Tyburn execution. When the man had dropped, Jonah had rushed to be a hanger-on and speed the work of the rope, for which he had been paid a sparkling shilling. As he had gripped the wet, kicking legs he had slowly slipped the fine black boots from the dangling man and stuffed them one by one into his frock coat. Maggot had worn them from that day. He packed the toes with old paper and hobbled around, showing the world what a fine gentleman he really was. It was also on that day that Jonah had spoken to the Man in the Stars, begging that Maggot would die an old man with memories of many summers and that the rope would not stretch his neck.

Outside, the watch-dog still edged his way closer to the inn. Jonah eyed him through the crack in the thick, crisp curtains, watching as he stooped to the ground and peered through the darkness. The shadow got closer and closer. From where he sat, Jonah could also see the drunken vagrant asleep in the broken window of the baker's shop, his legs dangling over the ledge of the window into the street. By his feet was a small pool of trickled blood that stained the flagstones like a crisp treacle cake.

The clatter of feet on bare boards turned Jonah's head to the kitchen door, which swung open with the force of an October gale. It had been a day since Jonah had last seen Tara, but there in the red glow from the fire she gave nothing of herself but a thin wry smile.

'They stuck you?' she asked as she crossed the room, carrying a small bundle of torn cloth and a pot of thick, green nettle salve. 'Maggot tells me it was a knife. Rich man or poor man? A rich man's knife is always sharper and cleaner and leaves a better wound. I may be able to save your arm . . .'

'Would I rob the poor?' he asked.

'You would rob your mother, if you had one, and –'

'Tara would share in the takings as she always does,' he said, finishing the sentence coldly. 'Anyway, I wasn't got. The man I was robbing sneaked up like a coward and got in a lucky blow, nothing more, nothing less. I can't get the knife out, every time I try it digs itself deeper.' Jonah peered out of the window, then looked quickly back into the room as Tara took hold of the knife by the hilt and bathed the blade in nettle salve.

'This'll hurt . . . and you deserve it,' she said. Then she smiled at him before pulling the dagger as hard as she could.

There was a tearing pain that electrified Jonah's arm and burnt through the muscles of his face, standing his hair on end. He let out a long deep groan as blackness fell around him, fading the fire's glow and plunging him into another world. He could feel the blade gripping to the twine of muscle as it was slowly pulled from his arm. The blackness got thicker and darker as the candlelight blurred.

A faint muttering and the smell of nettle salve mixed with hawthorn berry were all he could bring to mind. The darkness was utter and complete. It enfolded him like a shroud that tightened by the second. Slowly, the pain ebbed away, and he became aware that he was resting by a large, warm rock that towered above him and cradled him like a cupped hand. Far in the distance he could hear Tara calling his name over and over. In his mind he could see her long dyed-red hair, white powdered face and beetle-juice lips. Jonah looked up, as if swimming upwards from the depths of dark water to the light of the sky. He slowly opened his eyes as the door to the inn was rattled frantically from outside.

'Leave it be,' he said in a whisper. 'It's the man who followed me.'

Tara looked at Maggot and made a sign with her bloodstained fingers covering her lips for him to be quiet. The three sat in the light of the fire and waited. The rattling came again and Old Bunce stirred in his sleep. Tara's eyes flashed from door to window. Maggot quietly got to his feet, stepped the four paces to the chink in the curtain and peered out. The watch-dog sniffed a drop of blood that had fallen on the doorstep. He then slowly dipped his crooked white finger into the blood, lifted its tip to his nose and sniffed it again before slowly licking the drip from his finger like the lees of a fine old burgundy wine. Maggot was deathly still as the man's red eyes searched every inch of the inn, looking for some hidden way of slipping inside. Suddenly, as if called from far away, he turned and walked away into the night.

'He's gone,' Maggot said quietly as he returned to the fire, placing a seasoned elm log on the flames. 'Never seen the likes of him before, never want to again.'

Tara wiped the blade of the dagger on a ragged piece of cloth, then turned the sharp steel in the light of the fire. 'Sharp blade, sharp as anything I have ever seen,' she said, looking closely at the dark engravings that ran along the blade. 'Your man had a taste for fine things. Who was he?'

'Best you didn't know. There was something about him that wasn't . . . normal. He was as quick as the devil . . . and he spoke to himself in the carriage as if he were talking to someone else. He picked on the wrong man when he tried to kill Jonah Ketch.'

'Man?' she asked almost laughing. 'You're a boy, two years younger than me, so that makes you fifteen.'

'You're a man when your father's dead, no matter what age you are,' he snapped back.

'That makes Maggot a man and he's younger than you,' she replied, brushing her spiked hair back with her fingers and flicking the long strands over her shoulder. 'You'll soon be like Old Bunce, running an inn and getting drunk.'

'When I'm healed I'm getting out of London. Should have kept on running and not stopped at Black Mary's Well. I could have been in Highgate by now. I could've walked to Lincoln or York, stole myself a horse and been a highwayman.'

'And be hanged by the side of the road and someone would steal your boots.'

Jonah didn't reply. He looked sullenly into the fire and stared at the sparking embers huddled tightly around the smouldering log. Tara continued to stare at the knife blade, trying to understand the runic scribbles that covered the steel. Her fingers traced the outline of a setting sun and a coiled snake that appeared to be sinking into the hilt – the long golden rays and scaled tail formed an intricate finger guard that met with the jet handle as day meets with night.

'This is a fine thing. All that gold, he must have been quite a dandy.'

'Now he's a dandy who sucks mud, a dandy robbed of both purses, his fancy case and a knife to replace the one I lost in Conduit Fields.'

'So we'll be going three ways on all you've got?' she asked him as she tightly bandaged his arm.

'What would life be if you didn't have friends to share it with? I may even give some to Old Bunce to replace the gin he gave away last night. End of the world? This is just the beginning. I can feel it in my bones, something special will happen and we, dear friends, will be the beneficiaries of London's wealth.'

Maggot toyed with the leather case, rubbing the gold catch and the soft black leather with his grubby fingers. 'Have you seen inside, Jonah?' he asked, his voice trembling at the thought of what such a fancy case could contain.

'You're the best lock thief in London, see if you can get into it. See if you can lift the catch in the time it takes Tara to get me a drop of hot-pokered beer.'

'Done,' shouted Maggot. He rummaged in his pocket for a broken hatpin and with it fumbled at the lock. 'Ain't nothing I can't break in the whole of town, and this one's nearly gone . . .'

Tara took three steps to the door and Maggot let out a squeal of satisfaction as the hatpin twitched the crude spring and the lock snapped open. 'Done it,' he cried triumphantly, smiling at Jonah, looking for approval.

'That's my Maggot. Look inside and tell me what was worth him trying to kill me for.'

Maggot slowly opened the case. It had a strong musty smell, like Traitor's Gate at low tide. He lifted the lid on its stiff hinges and as he did so all around him began to be drawn into a deep iciness, as if the hands of winter wafted against their legs and kept away the heat from the fire.

Jonah shuddered with the sudden draught. A shiver ran down his spine as Tara walked back with a pot mug of warm beer.

'Another log for the fire,' he said. 'What have you found in that box, Maggot?'

The boy stared into the case, his eyes searching every inch of the solid green slab of glistening stone that lay framed in the black velvet lining. 'It's . . . It's a stone,' he said in a whisper.

'Then bring the stone by the fire before Old Bunce sobers up and we'll see what it's worth. Could be a piece of solid topaz or an emerald. We could be rich.'

Maggot carried the stone to Jonah. He lifted it from the case and turned it around in his hands as he looked at each polished surface and rounded corner. 'Knew it wasn't papers. The lying old dog had me believing it was papers. Nothing of value, he said . . . Told me I'd regret taking it, he said. Now I know it's worth something, but what it is I have no mind.'

The stone box glistened in the firelight. Tara reached out and took it from Jonah. She ran her hand quickly around the edge, the cold stone chilling her hands. On one side was a thin slit edged in solid gold. She held the box in front of the fire; the light penetrated the stone, casting her fingers in an opaque outline against the glow. Inside the gold band she could see the outline of a lock.

'Can you open this?' she asked Maggot. 'This is a box, an empty box, and it's made of alabaster. I have seen this before. Best get rid, it'll do us no good to keep it.' There was a sound of concern in her voice as she quickly handed the box to Maggot. 'I met a man who had an alabaster ring, he told me how every time he wore the ring he felt as if a cold hand was gripping his throat. He gave it to a girl in Covent Garden . . . They found her dead, the veins in her neck frozen. The man got the ring back from the Justice and gave it to the priest at St Clements. He wore it to Mass and as he supped from the chalice the wine turned to ice and choked the breath from him. They buried the priest and hung the ring around the neck of the Virgin and Child – only safe place they say. Alabaster – devil's fingernail, I call it.'

'A story to frighten children,' Jonah said as he sipped the warmed beer. 'It's worth money and tomorrow we sell it and dine out on the profit. I'll take you to *The Beggar's Opera* at the Haymarket, we can sit with the gods and throw eggs at MacHeath as he starts to sing.'

Maggot wasn't listening, his mind was cocooned in the task of breaking the mortise. With nimble fingers he felt the lock and eyed up the gold band that clung to the opaque alabaster. 'If we could get this from here we could sell it,' he said as he picked up the dagger and dug at the gold band. 'No use,' he said, and placed the stone box on the table by the fire. It was then that he slipped the tip of the blade between the band of gold and the cold stone, and with no further aid or action the box began to open by itself. The room chilled as Jonah got to his feet and looked on as the two sides separated like the opening of a Billingsgate oyster.

'This is a spectacular trick,' he said as he giggled to himself.

'No wonder that the man didn't want me to take it from him. What else will it do but open?'

They looked on transfixed as the green box opened to its fullest extent and laid itself out on the table before them. It had been cut to the thinness of a host. Inside, the two halves shimmered as if coated with the crispest of mercury. In one glance, Tara was charmed by its beauty.

'A looking-glass,' Tara said as she pressed her face closer. Her reflection glowed, her red hair and beetle lips shining brighter than ever as the coldness grew around her. 'See how my face moves in the glass, I flicker and gleam . . .'

'Already mad with the mercury, are you, Tara?' Jonah asked. 'This is a late hour and we have much to sell in the morning. Hide the case in your room. Maggot and I will sleep by the fire and wake Old Bunce as I ease my sluice in the morning. Put the box away and get some sleep.'

Tara didn't reply. Her mind was engrossed in what she could see.

'Put the box away and get some sleep,' Jonah said again, pulling harshly on her sleeve.

'I have slept enough. Stack the fire and rest your wound. It's you who need to sleep and in your dreaming find some manners. I want to think. This is such a beautiful thing, the best gift you have ever brought to me.'

Maggot crawled under the table and curled up in the pile of shavings and Jonah hunched himself against the warm hearth. 'It's to sell, not to keep,' he said as he closed his eyes and cradled his wounded arm.

'Well, for one night it is mine. A looking-glass for the soul.'

'Thought you said it should be got rid of?' Maggot mumbled as he curled tightly into his coat and stretched his toes to the end of his boots.

'That was a ring, this is the most curious thing I have ever seen and tomorrow it'll be gone for ever,' Tara said fretfully. 'So tonight I will rest with it close by.' She sat at the table and looked into the glistening mercury as she held her face in her hands and closed her eyes.

All was quiet as sleep filled the room. The mercury began to tremble and from the box a moon-silver hand broke free, reached up and lightly stroked Tara's face like the touch of a fly. Without waking, Tara brushed it away. The box slowly closed and sealed itself from prying eyes.

The Prophet

In the murky half-light of dawn, a long procession crossed the square, threading through a crowd of those who had been unable to flee from the comet. As he strode out two yards at a time, the leader of this procession pushed passers-by out of the way with one hand and knocked them to the ground. He waded through the mob as if they were a spring surge of a Streatham sewer. He looked around, towering over them, two feet above the head of the tallest man, grim-faced and weather-gnarled. A small thin smile showed he had filed his teeth into a row of sharp brown fangs. He was a giant, orphaned at birth, who was named after the flowers that filled the wicker basket in which he was found. Now Campion, the 'Human Bear', was known for his large size and the thick brown hair that covered him like a winter coat.

'This way Mister Solomon,' he said gruffly as he downed a man who stood before him and stepped over his writhing body. 'The steps are here . . . You can speak to the people.'

In his wake waddled a small man dressed from head to foot in a rough purple coat and tight breeches. On his head sat a squat round hat with tassels which clung to the white tufts of hair that sprouted from the side of his baldy head. The man didn't reply as he stepped onto the back of Campion's victim, wiping a sod of horse muck from his shoe as he paused and looked around him. In a long file, a following of men and women snaked their way through the crowds, eyes fixed on Solomon as if they were unable or unwilling to remove their gaze from him.

Solomon muttered to himself as he strutted like a cockerel on a spring morn. His appearance in the square had silenced the mundane muttering of the mob, and everyone turned to watch the trailing procession wind its way across Covent Garden market to the white steps of the church that rooted itself by King Street corner.

Campion hobbled breathlessly to the top step. As he turned, the first light of the dawn sun broke across the city. Solomon, followed by his disciples stood before him. Together they turned to face the east, slowly bowing their heads as the light fell upon them.

Without command, Campion raised his hand to the crowd and beckoned them to draw closer. 'People of London . . . We have survived the coming of the comet and the wrath of the powers of the universe . . . Mister Solomon has a word for all of you. Given to him are the secrets of what is to come. LISTEN – or die in your ignorance.' He panted and spluttered out the words that had gone through his head time and again, rehearsed and to him without meaning.

The crowd jostled, leaving their silence behind as they gawked and moaned at the array of purple-clad devotees clustered around the prophet.

'Do a trick for us, Solomon,' a feckless ostler shouted scornfully from the mass, and he tossed an old dried bread loaf at the gathering. 'We want to hear what will happen to us now the comet has gone.'

'Let's hear what wisdom you can dream for us today, Solomon. You come here every day with your ranting and quaking,' screeched an old woman leaning on a handcart as she picked the dirt from her fingernails.

38

Solomon coughed and cleared his throat, filling his chest and raising himself to the occasion. The crowd fell silent, charmed by some unseen spell or hypnotised by Solomon's waving of his large white handkerchief. Not a sound or murmur was heard, only the soft wingbeats of street doves, the clatter of carriage wheels on cobbles and the hubble-bubble of a far-off street fayre. Every man and woman waited in anticipation as they stared at Solomon and his followers in their purple coats and sour faces.

'Who feared the comet?' Solomon shouted angrily at the crowd as he danced from foot to foot. 'Who thought they would die and be cooked in their own beds? Come on – I can see it in your eyes . . . Fear is a pitiful thing and all of you fear something.' He stopped speaking and glared at the people, trying to catch them eye to eye as if to look into their souls.

'None of you, not one, will escape the wrath, for a time is coming when you will all face your end. A bitter, twisted end when blood shall boil and the fat of your bones shall seep from your flesh and the teeth from your head will fall like rain from the sky.' He searched the crowd for a faint heart. 'YOU!' he screamed as he pointed to a thin man with a frost face and pox-pitted chin. 'Survived one plague to die in another. The pox took your sister and your mother. Didn't it?' he said, guessing the man's fate, while his followers shivered and shook and moaned and wailed as if they clung to the precipice of Hades. The man nodded fearfully, shocked that his past was on display at such a time as this.

'Now look at you, a monster of the London streets, not fit for a menagerie, but even one as ugly and pus-festered as you could come and be a part of Solomon's kingdom. All you have to do is have faith in me. For a time is coming when the earth shall grow cold, black locusts will engulf the city and everything that all of you has held dear will be *snatched from your hands!*' Solomon ranted on, spitting as he shouted out the words before falling silent. He looked at the crowd and sucked in a deep breath of cold, damp morning air as he drew them closer like flies to his web. 'Listen to Father Solomon,' he said quietly, as if he spoke only to each individual. 'I am the answer, the way to follow, a path through the rugged mountains. I have seen the heights of heaven and depths of hell.' He raised his voice, then let it drop low. 'There is nothing my eyes have not beheld, nothing my ears have not heard, not a word my tongue cannot understand. I can speak in the language of angels and devils. I am the only one who can save you from what is to come.'

His listeners turned to one another as those that surrounded Solomon on the steps shuddered and moaned. A ripple of panic tremored through the congregation of bystanders. There was a sudden crack high above them like the pounding of a canon. The sky filled with bright stars that burst from a cluster of sky-crackers and fell to earth, showering the market in fine silver-paper medallions.

'Look!' Solomon shouted as another explosion danced across the dawn sky, flickering in the first glow of sunlight. He held out his hands for all to see, and there dancing on each palm was a ball of blue flame that flickered over each finger. 'Fire that does not burn and a sky that gives forth wedding charms,' he shouted. Pox-face dropped to his knees, wringing his hands as he looked to heaven.

'Why do these things come?' a fishmonger shouted as he cowered beneath his stall.

'As a sign of his power,' Campion replied as he fell to his knees.

'Fire-crackers and circus tricks,' shouted the ostler as he threw yet another stale loaf, hitting Solomon in the chest and sending him reeling backwards. Campion grabbed him by the collar to stop him falling. 'Follow you? I'd rather chase a crack in a louse ladder . . . At least you'd get something at the end of it.'

The crowd laughed. They had grown bored with the daily spectacle and began to walk away. Not even the comet had dampened their desire to live their meagre lives. It had come and gone like fire and plague before it.

The disciples stood their ground, surrounding Solomon as he brushed the rotten crumbs from his chest. Pox-face knelt sobbing in the dirt.

'You've charmed the crowd, Solomon,' the ostler sneered as he rolled up his sleeves and looked around him. 'Only that broken wretch from all these people? No one to listen to your ranting and shaking? We've seen too much, too many words. Look at me, you merry men – an ostler without a stable or an inn and yet I have more than all of you with your purple coats and quivering lips.'

'You will have even less than that if Campion tears your arms from their sockets,' Solomon whispered as he walked down the steps, taking pox-face by the arm and lifting him to his feet. 'Here is a man broken by the world, with no hope. I will be all he has. In me can he trust.' Solomon raised his fist and shook it at the sky. 'Nothing or no one will stand in my way. I will be the father of the nations and all men will come to me.'

'Then the man's a cockle-head with mud for brains . . . just like you,' the ostler said, rubbing his rough hands on his coat front, and he turned his back and walked away.

'Campion, take our brother to the Citadel and . . .' Solomon paused as he watched the man walking into the distance, the sun glistening on the damp of his coat. 'Make sure our ostler friend finds somewhere to rest his head . . . for ever.'

The giant smiled and pulled the fingers of his bear-like hands, clicking and crunching the bones one by one. He

41

pushed through the ranks of disciples and lifted pox-face from the ground, casually draping the man over his shoulder like a rolled-up blanket. Then he set off to follow the steps of the ostler from the square.

Solomon nodded his head and he set off at a pace across the cobbles, rubbing his long pointed chin with the tips of his tobacco-stained fingers. A line of dreary disciples fixed their eyes upon him and followed without flinching as he picked his way through the barren market place of Covent Garden towards the Strand.

Every street and alley where the pilgrims trod as they slithered through London was scattered with the debris and disorder of the comet. Carriages were overturned and horses lay dead like large swollen-bellied flies, their feet upturned, bodies twisted and harnessed, the stink of corruption and decay billowing like an early-morning fog.

Solomon pulled his large white handkerchief from his pocket and flapped it several times in the breeze before filling it with a handful of dried rose petals and then covering his nose. 'This is what I said would come,' he shouted out, knowing that the procession of followers would hear his every word. 'Death has come like a thief in the night. They will mock us and ridicule us, but time will tell and Solomon proclaim and truth will out.' His disciples squawked in agreement, frowns of smug satisfaction cast across their faces.

The sun, so weary it could hardly lift itself from the horizon, cast long shadows into the Strand. They swayed back and forth as the stiff November breeze blew the torn canopies that hung over the empty shops. Solomon stopped and looked to the ground at his feet. There before him were the charred remains of a body outlined in grey dust, nothing remaining but the sole of one boot, as if the man had been burnt from the inside out, spontaneously combusted by the act of some foul fiend.

'This', he said to his followers as they gathered around, 'is what I said would come. Look, he has been totally destroyed in his wickedness – ashes to ashes, dust to dust, nothing left but one bad sole.' Solomon laughed feebly as he set off again at a trot, scurrying across the road and disappearing into the labyrinth of roads that skirted the river towards Westminster. 'Come on, come on! You need to keep up. We have work to do and the lost need to be found. We must search them out of every street and lodging house in this city, from the highest to the low they have to be found.'

He turned back to the Strand. Hearing the sound of a large crowd cackling and screeching by Charing Cross, he stepped out, his leather-shod feet dancing across the rough stone pavement and over the morass that ran like an open sewer down the middle of the road. The noise grew louder – shouts from acrobats and buskers merged with the thrilled squeaks of children who gazed merrily at tumblers throwing themselves into the air, stacking higher and higher on one another to the height of a house. When the pinnacle was reached they would collapse the pyramid and fall without pain to the ground, tumble in the dirt and spring to their feet, caps outstretched to welcome all that was thrown their way.

Solomon gathered pace, drawn quickly on by a desire to be immersed in what he could see. He ran, leaving behind the crawling purple meander, and giggled to himself as the sound of pleasure filled the street. All about him people laughed and stared at fire-eaters gripping burning coals and spurting jets of flame from grease-black mouths. A snake-charmer sat cross-legged as he played the chanter and mimicked the head of the cobra that reluctantly drew its head over the tip of its wicker basket in the cold morning air.

From every corner of London had come an impromptu fayre of bedraggled clowns, monster-mongers and actors to gather where the Cross once stood. To Solomon's side a blonde-haired street musician strummed a bow-backed guitar and crooned the chorus to a children's rhyme. The faint smell of fatted calf gently teased his senses as the scent of the luscious fat of blistering flesh on the roasting fire by Crag Court wafted from White Hall to the Royal Mews. Solomon gasped for air as the excitement of all that was around him took his breath and in one moment returned him to his childhood. Cast aside were all thoughts of himself and cares for today as each sound and sensation evoked within him a feeling of sheer joy. Gone were the thoughts of disciples. Solomon stood alone, a man overtaken by the thoughts of boyhood and lost in the divine spectacle that surrounded him. His eyes gawped, and he could feel his boots shivering as he quivered with joyful anticipation.

But then, from the centre of the crowd, there rose up the strangest creature he had ever seen. Towering above the people, a wrinkled grey beast the size of a whale reared up on its hind legs. What Solomon thought was a long arm stretched down from its head and swung between two thick, round, gold-tipped teeth that came from the mouth, each the length of half a lance and curved like a dragoon's sabre. A tiny eye the size of a sparrow peered back at him as a drummerboy beat out a tune for the beast to hop back and forth until it dropped to all fours and shook its rump like a fat Drury Lane dancer.

Solomon was spellbound as his mind raced to find the name of the creature that curled its thick hairy lip and wafted its immense grey ears back and forth like the flags of a foreign country. Smiling to himself, his mind plucked the name from his memory. He had seen the beast in the *London Chronicle*, sketched to appear twice its real size. This was Ozymandias – the elephant from Africa. Now it stood before him cold and hungry, half a king in a hostile land, majestic yet unloved, noble yet forlorn, half mad from the shackles that were clamped to its grizzled stumps.

Ozymandias stared at Solomon, rocking its head from side to side and moving from one foot to the other to avoid the cane of the young boy that tapped its callused legs. As their eyes met, the joy drained from Solomon and the dismal purgatory of the world returned. It was as if in that moment of malice he saw the world in its true light. His frivolity seeped away as the bitterness bubbled from the depths of his hardened heart. A scowl came back to his face and his eyes narrowed and lips tightened. He looked around for his disciples, feeling strangely aware of his sudden loneliness in the great throng of people that swirled about him. The fickleness of these pastimes stuck in his gullet and his eyes peered meanly at those around him. He took one final look at the creature and he turned away, leaving it to its chained misery as he pushed through the crowd towards the centre of the circus.

Solomon looked up at the large wooden cross hastily made from the beams of an old house and defiantly forced in the ground where a stone monument had once stood. The arms of the cross were festooned with gold streamers that blew in the wind. He chuntered to himself of its arrogance, bickering loudly at all that it stood for, searching within for the strength to smash it to the ground and crush every slither of timber to dust. From the remnants of the monument's stone steps he looked out over the heads of those gathered around as jugglers tossed balls of fire from one to the other and a large black monkey the size of a man, dressed like a Spaniard with a rope around its neck, danced to the strained sounds of the minstrel.

In the fresh morning breeze he surveyed the crowd, hoping to see the familiar sight of a purple coat and pilgrim face. But it was the glint of gold that first caught his eye and then the

45

sight of the long, flowing black cloak that wafted out behind the tall bearded man who ungainly pushed a hand carriage topped with a golden cage. The sound of the fayre was silenced in his mind as every thought was concentrated on what he could now see coming along the Strand. Within the tight confines of the cage he could make out the shape of a small boy wrapped in a thick blanket, topped with a fine sprout of bright white hair. The man had a soft felt hat that drooped down the back of his head, and from where Solomon stood he could clearly see that he was singing to himself.

The boy held tightly to the bars of the cage, unsure as to where he was being taken or why he was without liberty. As they approached, the large circus crowd parted like an ancient sea to let them pass, then formed a tight circle as the man rested the cart on its spindle legs, drew out a long staff and stamped it to the ground whilst pulling on his beard.

'I, Magnus Malachi, magician and seer, bring to you the people of London – TERSIAS THE BLIND. His eyes may have been rooted from his head, but his sight goes beyond our understanding. For one shilling he will answer any question and tell you the secret of your soul.' Malachi shouted dramatically, as loud as he could above the noise of the rabble.

Intrigued, Solomon stepped down from the broken steps of the monument into the mire of the street and forced his way through the crowd towards the magician. He squinted through the armpit of a soldier who stubbornly refused to stand aside and let him through. Reaching up, Solomon took the long pin from his tasselled hat and plunged it into the soldier's rump. There was a loud scream as the soldier looked around, turning to see the face of his attacker and lashing out at a podgy-necked man with red cheeks. Solomon sniggered as he stepped by safely, returning the bloodied pin to its place. In several steps he stood before Malachi and the boy.

'Think of it,' Malachi protested loudly, 'think of it as the wisest shilling you ever invested. You are not giving your money away but buying a glimpse of the future. Not only will he tell you what is to come, but what is already here.' Malachi filled out his chest and stomped the whale staff against the stone. 'I need no stooges, this is not a pantomime,' he said as he wagged his long finger under the soldier's nose. 'The gods will speak to you today and all for the price of a shilling.' Malachi stopped speaking and looked intently at the gathering. Tersias twisted and turned in his cage, aware of the crush of people that pressed in around him. He couldn't feel the presence of the Wretchkin – he was alone, trapped. He could hear the groaning of the crowd as Malachi continued to draw the mob. 'I will give one free consultation to prove to you all that what I say is the truth and that Tersias of London is the first true oracle this town has seen since the days of Saint Tara. Now, who will that be?'

A man stepped forward flanked by two tall militiamen and a small squat man in pince-nez glasses. 'I will,' said the man, and he stepped closer to Malachi. Solomon watched intently. He had seen these men before and knew their names from the *London Chronicle*: this was Lord Malpas and his secretary Mister Skullet. Somehow Malpas looked different, his face was deeply scraped and at the back of his head he wore a bandage as if it were a small white hat. To Solomon, Malpas looked every inch a man who had been dragged through a forest of hedges or fought with the Spanish monkey.

'Ask him what it is I desire back and where it can be found,' Malpas demanded, his voice strained with the pain of his cracked skull.

'Tersias hears you himself, he will answer,' Malachi replied, hoping to stimulate a quick retort from the boy.

Tersias kept his own counsel. The Wretchkin made no

sound, all he could hear was the muttering of the mob as it grew in its discontent.

'Tersias, the man needs an answer.' Malachi spoke strongly, urging him to speak out.

A sudden rushing came, as if the spirits were carried on black wings that beat through the streets from another place. The picture of a dragon came into his mind as he felt the Wretchkin growing closer. The creature spoke, and Tersias felt that in some strange way it was different – powerful, older, with a hint of hostility in its voice.

'His name is Malpas,' the spirit said, whispering in his ear, its breath chilling the back of his neck. 'Lord Malpas, a politician . . . He has lost a box and a dagger.'

Tersias cleared his throat. 'You have lost a box . . . and a dagger. You are Lord Malpas.'

The crowd recoiled as Malpas stepped back and turned to Skullet, surprise emblazoned across his face.

'Is that true?' Malachi asked loudly as he pulled the cap from his head and offered it for filling to the crowd.

''Tis true,' Malpas replied, staring at Tersias. 'I was robbed by a thief on Conduit Fields. There is a reward for his capture. Two hundred pounds.' Malpas paused, allowing the bounty to take effect. 'Tell me, Tersias. Where is my property to be found?'

'That will cost you a shilling,' Malachi shouted as he pushed himself towards Malpas, his cap outstretched, only to be pushed back by the militia.

Tersias spoke out, relaying the creature's whispered reply. 'It is still in the city, out of sight of man, and there it will stay. Ask again in two nights and I will have the answer. But you should take greater care of other people's property.'

Lord Malpas stared at Malachi. 'How much for the boy? I must have the boy. I will make you a wealthy man.'

'He is not for sale, Lord Malpas. Not for all the gold in the world. He was a gift to a man in his dotage, a pension from the gods to a man of poor means.'

'Then bring him to my chambers tomorrow evening at seven o'clock and we can complete this consultation without prying eyes.' Malpas didn't wait for a reply. With a bandaged hand he motioned for the militia to force a way through the crowds.

Solomon watched eagerly as a throng of people pushed forward, babbling their questions to Tersias and filling Malachi's hat with shillings.

'Father Solomon,' said the voice of a disciple who pulled on his sleeve. 'We had given you up for lost.'

'*Lost?*' replied Solomon, half shouting, 'I have found what we have been looking for all this time. This was no coincidence, our separation was foretold and planned. I have found *him*, the one we have been waiting for. He is here, a blind child led to us by a charlatan. To have him as a disciple was ordained. We must do all in our power to encourage Mister Malachi and the child to part company . . . And tomorrow they will be visiting Malpas.'

Solomon thought on as he and his followers turned their backs on the sun and scurried into the dark alleyway that led to the Citadel. He rubbed his hands as he walked quickly into the ever-growing gloom.

Thieving Lane

The iron-braced wheels of the handcart rattled loudly against the glinting wet cobbles of King Street. Magnus Malachi breathed heavily as he pushed the cart through the night the last mile towards the home of Lord Malpas in Thieving Lane. Every turn of the wheels echoed from the far walls of the darkened houses, sounding crisp in the deep gloom. The streets were ominously empty. Gone were the chestnut carts and braziers, lamplighters and street-sellers that would usually inhabit the streets until the old Warden called the midnight curfew.

Malachi squinted in the dim light from the lantern strapped to the front of the cart that failed to light his path. From far behind came the howl of a dog as it cried to a moon that struggled to be seen in the cloud-patched sky. His wizened eyes darted back and forth and long strands of his hair blew across his lined face. For Malachi, every alleyway was the home of a robber, every shadow cast by some villain. Thieving Lane took its name from the footpads and vagabonds who would stalk the unwary, cut purses and throats and make off with your money. Here in the dark street, Malachi felt like a sacrificial calf waiting for the wolves to strike.

Tersias sat in the dirty cart, holding on to the shabbily painted gold bars of his new cage as the cold mist from the river swirled about him, touching his face like an unseen hand, leaving drops of dew across his soft, pale cheeks. He showed no fear; his world had no day and no night. The blackness of his blindness hung like a dark shroud over him. In the safety of his cage he listened to the turning of the cart's wheels as it crunched the stones and cobbles into the dirt, rolling ever onwards into the silence.

'How much further?' he asked Malachi quietly as the wheel of the cart dropped into a deep puddle, throwing him from one side to the other. 'I hear no people, where are we?'

'Quiet, lad. Soon be there.' Malachi grumped his reply as he listened out for night noises, not wanting any sound to break his concentration. He dug his heels deeper into the mud and strained against the cart, pushing it deeper into the darkness of the street. The cobbles of the road ahead were traced in silver and silhouetted in the light from the Hangman Inn. To the side was a cavernous alleyway that reached up like a narrow cathedral; at its very height the two sides touched each other, as if the fronts of the houses rested face to face. Malachi stopped pushing the cart and took a long deep breath as beads of cold sweat slowly trickled down his spine. He shuddered as if a ghost had whipped his back, frantically trying to make sense of the black shapes that danced before his eyes in the darkness of the alleyway. He rested the handcart and rubbed his face with his hands, peering into the night through his fingers.

'Lord Malpas will pay you for this?' Tersias said, breaking the silence. He wrapped himself in the thick blanket. 'He's a worried man. I don't trust him.'

'Trust? You say such as that and he'll have us hanged. Malpas is the man behind the Crown, everyone knows that. This is my golden opportunity, boy. I could find favour at Court. Find a friend in high places, a man with power and influence. Don't talk of trust, trust doesn't matter – what matters now is finding his house before we are robbed by the villains that haunt this street.' Malachi's words echoed coldly through the alley. 'Now bury yourself in that blanket and keep silent, the less sound we make the better our chances. Why a man like Malpas should live here is beyond me – surrounded by thieves and murderers, not a place for a man of reputation.' Malachi stopped as if to bite his tongue and silence his own outburst. He looked around, fearful that his rage was overheard.

From far behind he heard the stealthy tap, tap, tap of metal shoe plates pitted against the stones. He looked back along the dark street and made out three figures walking slowly towards them in the gloom.

The sound of footsteps followed him through the night as he fought the fear that told him to leave the cart and run for his life. Each step was echoed from far behind as his distant pursuers kept time and pace. When he stopped they stopped, and the night fell silent but for his breathing and the heavy pulsing of his frail heart.

'Quickly, Tersias, we are being followed. Hold fast, we will move quickly.' Malachi frantically pushed and pulled at the handcart in a vain attempt to speed it through the night and down the slope to Thieving Lane. His feet slipped in the vile, putrid muck that washed over the cobbles. The cart rolled slowly, as if held back by the blackness of the night. The sweat glistened on Malachi's brow as he panted and gasped in the cold night, chastising himself for his stupidity and vanity in setting a gold-painted iron cage on a rickety hand cart.

Slowly the cart rolled down the slight incline, squelching through the mud and muck. Malachi waded ankle-deep through the festering mass that oozed like a flowing blanket of swill across the street. He faltered as his feet crunched against discarded bones that appeared to have clawed their way to the surface from hidden graves and now lay scattered across the street like the contents of a robbed tomb.

Malachi looked back up the slight slope to the narrow alley

opposite the inn. There on the corner the three figures stood looking back at him through the night, their bodies outlined by the faint light of the door lamp that shone out its feeble welcome.

'We are to be robbed!' Malachi muttered as he forced the cart on to its destination. 'I have nothing to steal but you, Tersias. Hide yourself away and say nothing.' He handed Tersias a bag of silver coins wrapped in a silk cloth. 'Sit on these, and if you are found don't speak.'

The slamming of the door to the inn broke the sullen silence of the street. Malachi looked back again – the road was empty, the dark figures had departed. He laughed to himself. 'Wine-bibbers, Tersias. Inn-lovers desperate for gin, and I thought they were out to rob us.' He snorted as he pressed on through the mud. 'When you get to my age the mind plays tricks with you. But then again, you are a precious gift to an old man and not one to be lost so readily.'

Tersias didn't answer. He slowly poked his head out from the blanket that covered him like a fall of black soot. His small hand gripped the cage to steady himself and his head jostled from side to side as he rocked over the mud-covered stones.

'Soon, Tersias, you can speak for Lord Malpas. Mark you well to answer his every question. He's a powerful man and not one to be crossed. We could both end up with a week in the stocks or a month in Newgate. Speak well, my blind oracle, and he will favour us kindly.' Malachi wheezed as he spoke, his hands gripping tightly to the cart.

'Then you will not mind if we take from you anything that you are finding hard to carry?' The voice spoke firmly, and Malachi stared in horror at the three hooded figures in sacking masks who stood before him in the gloom.

'Stand and deliver!' the small voice whispered from the shadows to the side of the street. The words were quickly followed by the click of a flintlock pistol.

The magician turned to face the muzzle of a gun pointed upwards at his head. 'You are nothing but a boy, put that gun away and leave me be,' he scolded.

'Not one boy, but three men, out for the night and ready to kill. I suggest you give us anything that may make us go away and we will leave you with your life.' The smallest figure prodded a pistol into his stomach. 'We want what you've got and quick,' he said briskly as the taller robber pushed Malachi to one side and looked at the cage.

'What do we have here?' he asked, leaning over and rattling the gold bars. 'A caged magpie ready for supper?'

Malachi noticed the dried bloodstain on the sleeve of his frock coat. 'You are injured, my friend, and I am a man of medicine. Leave me be and I will help you.'

'Just a clip from a lucky man who was fated to eat the London dirt,' the robber replied, and again he rattled the cage. 'I am strong enough and all he damaged was my pride.'

'Then fear not. I am Magnus Malachi, a pious man not concerned with money but the human heart. I have nothing to take, silver and gold are of no use to me.' Malachi spoke quickly, his lies falling easily from his lips.

'No money? Then what shall we take? Your cart is of no use to us.' The robber paused and looked at Tersias. 'Why is he caged? Does he bite?'

'He . . . he has a disease.' Malachi thought feverishly. 'I keep him caged so that the world will be safe. He went blind so quickly and now he can only speak. He's quite mad, he says the strangest things, words drop from his mouth like honey from the comb, yet not one letter can be trusted for the truth.' Malachi twisted his beard with his fingers as he rambled.

'A poor old man out with a Bedlam boy, is that what you would have us believe? A strange old man pushing a mad boy in a golden cage in Thieving Lane? Who do you come to see?'

54

'No one . . . We are out for the night air, it helps me to sleep.' Malachi breathed deeply, sucking in a lungful of coal smoke and London smog that was tinged with the bitter taste of tanning acid. 'The best air you can breath.' He coughed. 'A remedy for many a sickness.'

'And what of you?' the highwayman said softly as he shook the blind boy in his cage.

Tersias lifted his head from the safety of the blanket and opened his empty eyes. The robber gasped as he peered at the lifeless white gaze that fixed upon him.

The boy tried to smile at him, sensing him near as he held out a small frail hand. 'We are as Mister Malachi says. He cares for me and gives me a home in this cage and a blanket for the cold.'

'Cage?' The robber turned to Malachi, pushing him against the wall. 'Do you keep this child locked up like a thief, Mister Malachi?'

'Only when we are out, it is for his own good . . .'

'So what does he do for you that is so valuable? I can see that he is not kept for his own good.'

The magician thought for a while, studying each mask as he looked the robbers up and down in search of some hidden clue as to their identity. 'He's an oracle, he speaks of things that are to come and I charge a sh . . . shilling.' Malachi stammered as he stood on his tippy toes – the robber held him up with one hand, pressing him firmly against the damp stone wall of an undertaker's shop.

'So, where do you take this oracle on a dark night?' he asked as he prodded the thick blanket with his fingers, searching each fold.

'To a friend, a friend who lives in these parts,' Malachi replied cautiously. He slid his hand into his pocket and took hold of the golden guinea that he had kept for so long tucked away in the depths of his tattered and torn frock coat.

'There is never a straight reply from you, is there, Malachi? I want an answer or my little friend will place the pistol up your nostril and cover the walls with your brains, if you have any.' The small thief pushed the flintlock towards Malachi's head. 'He doesn't have a steady finger. The slightest tremor will set the lock and you will take a snort of the hottest snuff in London.'

'My friend's name is Malpas – Lord Malpas, if you must know,' Malachi said reluctantly. He looked back along the street, hoping that someone would come from the inn or the fat old Warden would pass by.

The robber stepped back as if stung by the words. He looked at his friends, his hot breath steaming from the eyeholes of the sack mask. 'And this Malpas, what business do you have with him?'

'A demonstration. He wants to know his future and little Tersias is the only oracle of his kind in the whole world. Tersias speaks the truth and many men will pay a fine price to hear the truth before they turn it into lies.'

'What things do you say, boy?' The robber stepped forward and spoke to Tersias through the gilded bars of his cage.

'I could give you a demonstration,' Malachi replied as he tried to edge his way between them. 'I'm sure that among you there would be a shilling?'

'We will have an exhibition, but there'll be no shilling.' The robber paused and looked at his two collaborators. 'What do you say, our futures for his life?' The masked figures silently nodded, their sack masks sodden with the thick mist that swirled around their feet and wafted in dark spirals through the flickering light from the inn. 'Well, Malachi, it would appear that your generosity has saved your life. Our future for yours . . . But if we don't believe you then I will part your throat and you'll sing through your stomach.' The robber pulled out a long thin silver blade with his left hand and held it under

56

Malachi's nose. 'This was a gift from a gentleman, sharper than any knife I have ever known. Pray that your oracle speaks the truth, or else his blind eyes will be witness to a murder so foul that he will never dare speak again.'

Malachi stared at the blade glinting before him. His eyes were drawn to the mystical symbols that were encrusted in the bright steel. He looked, then looked again, sure that the snake that formed part of the hilt had shivered its silky scales and momentarily unfurled its long coils before freezing back into the solid metal.

'I think you will be pleased by what Tersias has to say to you, if not . . . astounded,' he said, his voice fading in his spit-dry throat.

'But not here,' the robber said, and he glanced to his friends and nodded for them to go ahead. 'Follow them, they know a safe place and not too far from here, out of sight from the world. An ideal place to listen to your oracle . . . or cut your throat.'

Malachi walked on, pushing the handcart behind the two thieves as the other walked closely behind, the tip of the dagger sticking into the back of Malachi's coat.

Tersias buried himself in the dirty blanket. His ears began to burst with the sound of the wingbeats of the spirit, summoned by his unconscious thought from far away. In his mind he could see the creature rising from the black water of the great river, climbing from the foot of London Bridge as if its home was deep in the murky waters. Tersias dreamed he saw the beast crawl higher up the stonework of the old church, then shake its wings and set forth into the night sky. Now he could plainly see the features of the creature, its long hair trailing through the night sky, its face torn and half rotted. It held out a thin white hand that reached towards him as it swooped through the night alleys, following each street and ginnel, darting in and out of open doors stirring the houses from their sleep. Closer and closer it came as he was pushed through the night into Angel Court then into the open night of St James's Field.

For the first time since he had felt the presence of the Wretchkin, Tersias began to fear the presence of the approaching creature. This beast wanted more than just to talk through him and conjure with human minds. There was a malice to its thoughts that left him feeling weak, as if the beast had sucked from him a heartbeat and a hope.

Tersias took his hands from the warmth of the blanket and covered his eyes, wanting to shut out the sight of the creature that flashed through his mind. The handcart stopped. He could hear the rustle of dry leaves in autumn trees and the babble of winter geese on moon water. The thoughts came faster and stronger as the spirit drew closer. Tersias held his breath, fearful that the beast would consume him, entering his body never to leave.

'Now, Malachi, this is the place. Tell Tersias to be an oracle for us.'

'What is the desire of your heart? Is it something precise that you would like to enquire of him?' Malachi prodded Tersias with the long stick that he pulled from the side of the cart.

'Tersias, tell me . . . What life will I live? Will I die in bed or will the hangman have my clothes?' The robber laughed as he spoke.

From the lake came a sudden sound of screaming as a multitude of terrified geese rose from the still water, beating their frantic wings against the night air. They soared as high as they could, as if to escape some unseen beast that had fallen into their midst. Their fearful cries echoed across the city as they swirled around and around the treetops. Then, from the darkest point of the heavens, the Wretchkin fell to earth, diving and spinning across the great lake, dipping the tip of its long dark wing into the mercurial water. Seagulls and street doves spiralled with the fleeing geese as they tried to escape the dark presence that flashed over the water, then came to rest several feet away from Tersias.

The spirit slowly walked towards the cart, its eyes fixed on the robber's knife, its stare captured by the glinting blade. In his mind Tersias could see it slowly approaching him as he buried himself deeper into the blanket.

'Tersias!' Malachi moaned as he prodded him again. 'Our friend wants to know what will be.'

Tersias heard the voice of the creature and spoke forth his words as it put its hands upon the robber's head and slowly stuck a long finger into his ear as if to feel his mind. 'He has stolen much and pleased himself, he has no concern for the rope or anyone but himself. In life so it will be in death. I can see the noose around his neck but not pulled tight enough to take his breath.' The creature stopped speaking momentarily and Tersias saw that its long thin fingers gently caressed the blade that the robber held in his hand. 'This knife shall be your downfall – it is not yours and never shall be,' he repeated as the creature spoke. 'Take it back to the fields where it was found and leave it by the well.'

'He speaks gibberish, gobbledygook and poppycock. I was given this knife fair and square. It's mine to keep.'

Tersias ignored the robber's protest as the beast spoke on. 'There is one here who shall be taken from you. They shall be transformed and changed from the street. Their life shall be as a piece of jacaranda, rare and fragrant. Then a living grave will consume them and the locusts will eat of their flesh . . .'

'Words, stupid words,' the robber blurted out, and he pushed Malachi back with one arm. 'You are lucky to leave here with your life. Go to your friend Malpas and lie for him, Tersias. May he take pity on your blindness and not decide to cut out your tongue as well.'

Tersias didn't look up; in his mind he saw the beast take to its wings and fly off across the night sky, running across the roof of Buckingham House like Spring-heeled Jack as it vanished into the night.

'I won't leave here empty handed,' the robber ranted angrily. He grabbed the pistol and held it towards Malachi. 'Empty your pockets and pray to whatever god you follow that you have enough gold to buy off my lead.'

Malachi stepped backwards, pressing himself against the small ornamental trees that encircled them by the lake, his hand quickly rustling in his pocket as he groped for the guinea piece. 'I only have this and nothing else,' he said, feebly holding out the coin while his mind raced for a way of escape. 'Take the boy – he is nothing but trouble and I admit to being a charlatan and an interloper. This is nothing but a circus trick and I a failed magician.' He got down on one knee, holding out a shaking palm with the coin trembling in the moonlight.

'Take it!' the robber shouted to his small collaborator, who dashed forward and grabbed the golden guinea from Malachi's palm, checking its soundness by biting the metal through his hemp mask. 'Good job it's real or else I would blow you across this park and the geese could pick out your entrails. Now go, leave us be and don't walk these streets again.'

Malachi looked up from the ground. He and Tersias were alone – the robbers had gone, melted into the dark wood of the park. He grasped the cart with shaking hands and pulled Tersias back along the deserted track into Angel Court and towards Thieving Lane.

In the park the dew settled like a covering of fine silver droplets as the villains huddled in the undergrowth by the great oak that had looked over London since the time of fat Henry. They watched Malachi struggle to pull the oracle along the track, his journey lit by the silver abundance of the clearing night sky.

'A golden guinea, Maggot. Enough to keep us in beer and bread for a month,' Jonah said as he pulled the sweated mask from his head. 'Did you enjoy the chase?' he whispered to Tara as she unbuttoned the frock coat she had taken from Old Bunce.

'He knew about the knife,' she said as she pressed a piece of thick cloth into the opened and bleeding wound in Jonah's arm.

'The boy knew many things and we got them for a guinea,' Jonah replied excitedly.

'Will you take it back as he said? I have a feeling there is more to that knife and the alabaster box than we will ever know. A bad feeling – as if it knows about us and wants to tell the world.'

'You're a dreamer, Tara. Look what we got tonight. Soon we will have enough never to steal again. More money than we have ever known.'

'Did you see his eyes?' Maggot asked, rolling on his back and looking up at the stars. 'He's a boy, even younger than us. We can't leave him as a slave to that old man, you don't know what he'll do to him. And if he can tell the future then think of what he could do for us. He was right about the knife, he knew it was from Black Mary's Well – how did he know that if he wasn't an oracle?'

'Maggot's right, Jonah,' said Tara. 'We can't leave him with Malachi. A boy like that could tell us where all the money is hidden in the city. We'd know where the militia were hiding out and what was on every carriage.' She felt a coldness in her flesh, an icy embrace, the same as she had felt when she had opened the alabaster box.

Jonah turned the concern round and round in his mind. He thought of knowing and of having. His every sense was consumed by the desire to possess. Jonah hated clawing in the dirt for every penny, and under the stars he began to understand what he wanted. He dreamed he saw himself seated in a carriage like Lord Malpas, stopping outside a fine house and stepping onto white polished steps.

'A double dare!' he said, getting to his feet and brushing the dew from his breeches. 'Follow them to Lord Malpas and kidnap the boy when they leave – and what's more, we take whatever money Malachi fleeces from the good lord.'

6

The Logical Mister Skullet

The distinct smell of rotting flesh that pervaded the hallway of Vamana House went unnoticed by Skullet as he shuffled his way along the long oak-panelled room to the beating at the front door. In his left hand he carried a long black rod tipped with a golden wolf's head. He tapped out each pace on the stone floor in time with the frantic banging and shouting that sounded through the heavy fortifications.

In his other hand Skullet carried a small candle dressed in a shabby wooden holder that allowed the wax to dribble and spit over his fingers. The light burned with a blood-red flame that cast the shadow of his thin face across the high ceiling and dank, stained wood. With every step another thump, thump resounded against the blackened oak door that stood the height of two men and the breadth of several. The sound filled the hallway like the beating of a failing heart. From the street, Skullet could hear the bleating and complaining of a shrill voice, like the whispered words of a dying man. His pace stayed the same, unhurried and resistant to the protestations that beckoned him onward.

'Quiet, man!' he shouted, his voice trembling with the force of his bellowing, 'Lord Malpas is trying to dine and your whining will not make me open the door any faster.' Skullet placed the candle on the rest by the door and began to unfasten the six bolts and slip the thirteen locks that held the entrance fast against the night.

Vamana House had stood against rebellions and plagues, every stone shaped by bloodstained hands, every doorway forged in pain and misery. For three hundred years it had been the home of a Malpas. From the dwarf lord who first put stone on stone as a refuge for his thievery in the deep marshes that flanked the Thames to Pious John, who scourged himself every hour with a whip of coarse rats' tails. Now, surrounded by houses, its land consumed as the marshes were drained, it was the town house of Lord Trigon Malpas. With its twin towers and slit windows the house grew like an old gnarled tree from the mud of Thieving Lane.

As the last bolt slid from its keeper, Skullet paused and looked back along the hallway to the wide flight of stairs that led upwards to the library overlooking the narrow street. His father had been the scullion to Trigon's father. For every Malpas there had been a Skullet to comb their lice-ridden hair and polish their muddied boots. He had been born on the same day, at the exact minute and to the very second as Trigon Malpas. Skullet had breeched his way into life in the deep lead-lined cellar far beneath the house, whilst high above Lady Malpas had moaned that her servile drudge was farrowing a piglet in the bowels of hell.

From that day, Skullet had kept pace with the life of his master, watching him grow in riches and malevolence. He had endured many things as Lord Malpas had made his life in Parliament, puppeting the King, manipulating and spellbinding everyone on whom he cast his piercing black eyes.

Placing the black cane by the door, he took hold of the large iron handle with both hands and pulled the door from its frame. There was a momentary pause as the tight seal was broken and the large oak door softly and silently glided open on the thick metal bands that hinged it to the stone wall.

The night gushed in, street mist flowing up and over the

64

marble steps and into the hallway. There before him was Magnus Malachi, tightly clutching the hand of a small boy who cowered beneath him.

'Robbed!' Malachi shouted as he let go of the boy and waved his arms back and forth as if to beat away some unseen spirit. 'Came out of the night, seven of them with knives and cutlass, pistol and blunderbuss. Never stood a chance, they took my money, all I had.' Malachi collapsed to the cold steps and sat snivelling with his face in his hands. 'What shall I do?' he moaned through his fingers.

'You will get to your feet and come in,' Skullet said firmly. He took hold of Tersias by the collar and lifted him from the marble step and into the house. 'Lord Malpas will not look kindly on your snivelling, he hates weakness and your moaning has already disturbed his stomach. If you want my advice, Malachi, and desire to leave this place with your innards still in place, then wipe away your fop's tears and get inside. There is only one fire in the whole house and it will not warm the street as well.'

Malachi got to his feet, wiping his face with his sleeve as he pushed Tersias further into the hallway. He looked around at the fine oak panels that ran into the distant shadows, his eyes darting from the soot-darkened portrait of Trigon Malpas's father to the shocking similarity of Mister Skullet. 'A fine man,' Malachi said as they ambled by the dirt-encrusted painting that looked menacingly down from the immense gilt frame. 'Lord Malpas?' he enquired meekly, pulling Tersias along behind.

'They are all Lord Malpas. Every generation. Not a single painting of anyone or anything else. Since the time of the great Lord Homuncule Malpas they have hung in this place. Every generation has always provided a male heir, not one single female was ever born . . . alive.' Skullet stepped on to the

65

stairway. 'Let me tell you this, Mister Malachi. In this house there are rules that have to be obeyed. Never look Lord Malpas in the eyes, keep your gaze at his feet. Tonight you may answer directly, but do not ask any questions, Lord Malpas does not like questions. Do I make myself clear?' He lowered his voice to a whisper.

Malachi nodded in agreement as his eyes searched the faint details of the canvas that dominated the wall at the turn of the stairs. The flame of Skullet's candle flashed shards of light against the image of Homuncule Malpas, clutching the severed head of a wolf. 'Is this the founder of your fine dynasty?' Malachi asked, stepping back and looking up at the painting that towered above them.

'There has been no finer man than this,' Skullet said, and he raised the candle higher to illuminate the face that stared down at them. 'He was a knave to the King. They were hunting in the deer park when they were attacked by a mad wolf. With two cuts from his dagger he beheaded the beast and saved the King's life.'

'The hand that grips the dagger is bandaged?' Malachi questioned him as they turned the flight and walked higher. He stopped momentarily and looked again – the knife was familiar, he had stared at this blade before.

'Bitten by the wolf in its last breath of life. A wound that never healed. Some say that the commingled blood drove him mad, and wolf blood has been in the family's veins ever since . . . Mention it not. Lord Malpas will not take well to it.' Skullet lifted the cane and pressed the wolf-head against Malachi's cheek. 'Be warned, Malachi. You will be paid well for your oracle's voice, but any trickery and you will have me to deal with and I know only one thing – violence.' Skullet gave out a gentle laugh, turned and led on up the stairs.

Tersias remained silent as Malachi led him along the landing

66

towards the open library door. A shaft of amber light flooded into the hall, illuminating the cracks in the wooden floor and the backs of the scurrying mice that ran across the landing.

'Wait,' Skullet ordered briskly as he stepped into the room and bowed his head. 'Your guests have arrived, Lord Malpas.' Skullet turned to Malachi and nodded for him to enter. 'Remember what I said,' he whispered, giving him a sullen smile.

'Malachi, Tersias . . . How wonderful for you to join me in our dowsing of the elements,' Malpas said excitedly as he stepped from the library ladder and opened his arms in welcome to his guests. 'I often tell Skullet that we don't have enough visitors to this place, we should get out more . . . But I never have the time or chance for such frivolity.' As he spoke he twisted a small posy of red flowers in his hands. He smiled at Malachi and bade him sit by the fire.

Malachi glanced at Skullet, confused by the warmth of the welcome as he obeyed Lord Malpas and sat by the large open fire, watching the glistening flames dance up the chimney. He held Tersias close by and brushed imaginary dust from the shoulders of his tattered coat that in such fine surroundings seemed even more ragged and dishevelled than before.

Scattered on the woven fire-rug were golden tipped arrows that appeared to have been strewn purposefully across the floor. A long green shaft had settled across two purple darts that pointed to the door. Malpas noticed that Malachi was carefully studying the design.

'They are Rhabdomanteia . . . I can see they intrigue you, Mister Malachi.' Malpas stepped forward and settled on one knee before the fire. 'You and I are both seekers of the future. In my own primitive way I consult the unseen in the hope that I will be guided. With these arrows I dowse for knowledge. I cast them before the fire as I ask a question and, to the trained eye, the pattern of their landing reveals the answer.' Malachi didn't reply. As instructed he kept his gaze fixed to the floor. 'It may be primitive, but it does convince me that this world is not all we will inhabit . . . But Tersias is a real oracle and getting a name for himself in high places. Only this afternoon the King himself asked if we were to meet. As his guardian you may soon find yourself in important company.'

Malachi bristled with pride. He patted Tersias on the back of his steaming coat, the night damp evaporating in the heat of the fire, his face reddening with the flames. 'I hope you will feel free to ask whatever you desire of my little companion. We are somewhat dishevelled, having been robbed by a gang so vicious that we only managed to escape with our lives.'

'Robbed, Malachi? And you never saw this event before it happened?' Malpas sniggered and the side of his mouth curled with amusement. 'Did they take you for much?' he asked as he rubbed the bruise on the side of his face.

'Everything I have ever had – a golden guinea, my beautiful timepiece . . . It was only the fact that they would have to feed Tersias that stopped them from stripping him from the carriage and making off into the night.' Malachi looked up, catching a glance of Lord Malpas eye to eye.

'There has been a scourge of robberies in this city. I myself was victim of a foul fiend who took from me something very precious, and it is for this that I have called you here tonight. If you answer me successfully I can make you a rich man. What the boy said at the Charing Cross intrigued me. So let him speak and later we will have supper . . . Skullet, snuff the candles and let our oracle be lit by the firelight.' Lord Malpas shuddered with pleasure as he scooped up the Rhabdomanteia and placed them carefully into a green felt bag that hung like a Christmas sack from the large stone fireplace.

Fussing around the room, Skullet snuffed out candle after

candle. Darkness flooded in. With a steady hand, Malachi cajoled Tersias into the centre of the rug and faced him towards the large chair that Malpas had sunk into like a broody rook. The firelight reflected off the boy's face and lit his empty white eyes with a bloom of deep red light that seemed to surge from his soul.

Malachi looked suspiciously around the darkened room, check behind each piece of large furniture for any inquisitive spirit that might lurk unseen in the dark corners. He swished his long coat back and forth, muttering a forgotten charm under his breath, the glistening of incense smeared into his long beard. The fire cracked and spluttered as Skullet fed the flames with tinder-dry husks of ash and holly, and the scent of the sweet wood began to fill the chamber.

Tersias felt the hot glow of the flames fanning across his face. Already he knew the Wretchkin would find him. Since the coming of the Wretchkin into his life he feared little. Tersias felt he was like a leaf scattered on a lake, blown by the wind, its only hope being to soak up the cool water into its dry flesh and then slowly sink into the depths of the murk and become absorbed by the sodden mulch. With each calling of the creature, the reality that he once knew was being gnawed from him. Every time the spirit left, it was as if the creature took something from him, a piece of his soul or sliver of his spirit; every trance and vision robbed him of another spark of existence. Tersias now felt a deep tiredness consuming him as the will to live was slowly stolen from his soul.

'Now, my Tersias . . .' Malpas spoke softly to him as he and Malachi huddled towards the light of the fire. 'I need an answer to my question. As you said before, I have lost a box – something that was entrusted to me by my father. It has been in my family for many generations. Tell me, dear Tersias, where can it be found?'

69

Tersias listened for the familiar sound of the approaching Wretchkin, but there was utter silence. Malpas waited impatiently, scratching the palms of his hand with his pointed knuckles. He looked at Malachi, trying to catch his eye, then nodded to Skullet.

'What my master is saying is –' Skullet paused as he gulped his breath. 'Do you know where the box has been taken and by whom?' He banged the black rod against the wooden floor.

'I cannot speak yet . . .' Tersias replied. He turned his head quickly about the room, hoping to see a sign of the spirit in his mind. Not a sound stirred in his head, not a word was whispered to him.

'By what power do you speak?' Malpas asked.

'By the voices that come into my head.'

'And they are not with you now?' he asked quietly as he scanned the boy up and down in the light of the savage fire.

'No, my lord. I am alone.'

'Tell me, boy . . . these voices, are they from a creature that visits you?'

'Not even I would ask him that,' Malachi argued, looking Malpas in the face.

'Then you are a fool, Malachi. For this oracle is a seer of spirits. His blind eyes have been surpassed by a vision that can see what mankind has desired since Adam fell by the treachery of that woman.' Malpas turned to the boy and took hold of his hand. 'Do not be afraid of me, Tersias. I too have desired your gift. Do the creatures visit you, and is it their voices that you hear?'

''Tis as you say, Lord Malpas. For some time now it has come upon me, each time getting closer and closer. I can see the spirit in my head and hear the voice like a dawn bell.'

'Do you fear them?' Malpas asked as he rubbed his hand.

'Just one . . . A strong voice, older and wiser than the rest.

70

When this comes I feel a shiver run down my spine.' Tersias shuddered in remembrance.

'Call this voice, Tersias. Ask it to come to you, there is something that I need to know.'

Tersias muttered to himself as he pictured the creature in his mind. He groaned within, begging for it to come to him. 'Open the window,' he said quickly, stepping back from the fire. 'I can hear the creature calling.'

Malpas sprang to his feet and ran to the narrow window. He quickly opened the half-light and allowed the stench to flood in from Thieving Lane. He looked around the room in expectation, his eyes searching for sight of the creature. Skullet stood by the fire, wand in hand, outstretched as if to protect himself from what was to come, as Malachi dug deep into the sack he carried, looking for the wizened finger with which to cast a spell.

'Is the creature here?' Malpas asked as he paced back to the fire, his gaze fixed on the narrow window.

Tersias shuddered as he heard the call of the beast as it rose up from the waters like the leviathan and came to him. Over the houses and rooftops it beat its wings and then, forcing its way through the window, burst into the room.

'Powerful company you are keeping, boy,' the creature said as it stroked his face. 'I know this house well and Malachi will be lucky to leave with his life. What does this Lord Malpas want with me?'

'A box, the box you spoke of before is still missing.'

'Is the creature here?' Malpas asked as he looked about the room.

'Be quiet!' the creature screamed, Tersias repeating the words.

'It can hear us. Skullet, ask the creature if it can hear us.'

'I hear you, Malpas, but you are deaf to my words. The boy will speak for me and I will answer only that which I want.

71

Over me you have no command. I am not a slave like others you control.'

'So you know my name and my intentions?'

'I know much of your family and that which you seek has been close at hand. Ask Malachi, he sniffed its presence by the lake. The Alabaster isn't far away. The street-robber fills his belly with the guinea he stole from Malachi. Find him and you find what you desire.' The spirit was momentarily silent; it stepped towards Malpas and looked into his eyes. 'Tell me, Malpas, do you feel death crawling through your bones, is that why there is an urgency to find the Alabaster?'

''Tis as you say, dear creature, as you say.' Malpas sat sullenly in the chair by the fire and stared at the floor. 'I am the last in a long line of a fine family. My wife, Griselda, sits in the country house at Strumbelo and fills her mind with pure thoughts, never wanting to lie with me, and in the Alabaster is my legacy and my chance to live on.'

'Cast your net to the north. You have spies who can find this villain in a day, but act quickly. They intend to sell your green box and flit with the money. They tire of London life and seek the country air. As we speak plans are being made and the Alabaster sits under a flea-ridden bed next to a full privy pot.'

'Where? Where is this?' Malpas called out as the creature let go of Tersias and stepped towards the doorway.

'I have nothing else to say to you, Malpas. Call me again, it has been a long time since I have stood in this place.'

There was a sudden, forceful blast of air as the creature sped from the room. Tersias was thrown towards the raging fire. Malachi leapt towards him as he stumbled blindly against the hearth and began to fall into the blazing brazier. Skullet pushed Malpas from his path as he jumped from behind the leather chair, taking hold of Tersias by the coat and pulling him to the floor.

72

'A child like this is too good to be burnt, Mister Malachi. You should take care of your charge, else others take him into their consideration.' Skullet got to his feet and brushed the singe from Tersias's sleeve.

7

Skandalon

Maggot hid behind the smoke-blackened, broken statue of Saint Sebastian that peered down from under the dark eaves of the empty steeple-house on the dried marshes across from the front door of Vamana House. The boy smoothed his hand back and forth across the grimy, white carved marble and felt the broken arrows that pierced its cold flesh. Maggot was idling away the minutes of the night, waiting for Malachi and Tersias to appear. He wondered why the saint had died this way – shot through with thirteen arrows whilst still fresh-faced and just out of youth.

From his hiding place at the height of the house roof, Maggot stared shakily to the ground. He had climbed the rickety wooden scaffolding higher and higher, from statue to gargoyle and finally up the laddered arrows of the marble saint. He sat there like a black crow brooding on what was to come. This was a view of London he had seen many times before. Maggot had climbed chimneys and swept the soot as he made his way to the clay smoke-pots of the fine houses of Curzon Street. Some were big enough for him to climb out of and gulp the air, taking in the sunlight and looking over the rooftops to the edge of the city. He would wait and wait, staring at the scene before descending into the hot, black hell with its blinding stench and blackened bricks. Then he would appear into the room, soot-black and white-eyed, his small size and strong limbs dowsed in crusted carbon.

Now he looked down upon the gloomy stone façade of Vamana House with its grey buttresses and narrow windows that gave out glints of light through their murky leads. The high door bled a crease of light onto the marble step, and inside the house vague shadows moved back and forth like thin spiders webbing the gloom.

As Maggot clung to the back of the saint, the marsh mist rolled in from the river and filled the street to knee height. He thought of Tara and Jonah eating their way through the guinea in the Bull and Mouth as they waited for him to come and tell them that Malachi was marching back to Cheapside. His belly groaned like an old man as he thought of food. In his mind he could smell the roast meat and fresh bread, tinged with the malted brew. Maggot licked his lips and closed his eyes, imagining the taste of the feast he would never eat.

They had drawn lots as to who should eat and who should bleat. The bleater would stay behind and keep watch whilst the eaters would dine on Malachi's stolen money. Maggot always pulled the shortest straw, every time without exception it would always be him. Yet in his high nest he felt safe. No one could see him here, no one ever looked up. The gaze of the world was firmly fixed to the mud, eyes down and shoulders hunched.

The sound of voices and the slow opening of the door pulled Maggot back from his daydream.

'Stay, Malachi. My home is your home,' Malpas protested as Skullet held Tersias by the hand, not wanting to let go.

'We have stayed too long, my dear lord. But I will return tomorrow and Tersias will speak again for you,' Malachi said anxiously as he tugged Tersias towards him, trying to free him from Skullet's grip.

'I insist, it would be my pleasure. This is a fine house with soft beds and good food. I will even light a fire in your rooms. Imagine, your own fire and breakfast served by Skullet.'

The words loosened Skullet's grip. Malachi managed to prise Tersias from his twisted, bony fingers. He opened the cage door and bundled the boy onto the carriage, then snapped shut the lock and twirled the key before sliding it into his pocket. 'I have horses to attend to and the boy likes his own bed,' Malachi said, then paused as his mind flashed to find another falsehood. 'There are duties that I have to do for the oracle that can only be done in secret.' He smiled as he spoke, his thin lips pulled tight against his crooked, stained teeth.

'Then you will be back tomorrow?' Malpas urged him as he picked his way along the narrow step, fearful to tread in the dirt of the street.

'Tomorrow,' Malachi replied, and he took hold of the long handles of the cart and pushed as hard as he could, squelching off into the mud.

Malpas gave a shallow wave as the cart made off into the night street. He stood and watched as a feeble Malachi made heavy progress along Thieving Lane, the sound of the vibrating carriage echoing from the cold stone buttresses.

'Take the militia and follow them,' Malpas whispered to Skullet, unaware that his murmurs floated upwards on the night breeze. 'Make sure they go to Cheapside. Leave the guard all night and as the sun rises have them arrested and taken to the Fleet Prison. Search the house and bring me anything you find.'

'With what shall they be charged?' Skullet asked as he rubbed his hands together.

'Robbery. I slipped a silver spoon into the boy's pocket as we came down the stairs. Malachi was too busy trying to escape from us that he failed to notice. It carries my crest.' He sniggered. 'I know every judge in London and on my word they will have the old dog hanged. I shall step forward and plead for the boy's life, begging the court to spare the blind beggar, and

76

he will be given to my care. Griselda has always wanted a son. Now she can have one and earn her keep.'

As Malpas turned and scurried like a rat up the steps and into the bleak hallway, Skullet stopped and looked up at the front of the old broken-down church. He felt as if he was being scrutinized, inspected and dissected by piercing eyes . . . that God himself was staring down in judgement. For several moments he looked at each of the statues that lined the high eaves. From the roof a host of street-doves bolstered from their sleep and rose up high into the night sky. They swirled and twisted ever upwards to the bright moon, taking Skullet's gaze towards the crest of stars. He gave a shudder; the cold mist shivered his heels as he turned from the night and into the house, unaware that he was being watched.

Maggot glided down the marble saint and edged his feet towards the large stone gargoyle. It sat, squat and fat, on a small ledge overlooking the shuttered church door that had been nailed up when the congregation had wilted into extinction. He pushed against the statue as he stretched the tip of his toes to the ledge, holding his weight on the ends of his fingers. Above him he heard the sound of wingbeats like those of an eagle wafting the air steadily as it circled unseen above his head. As he stepped on to the gargoyle, Maggot looked around, sure that a creature had quickly rushed by, cutting the air with its crisp wings. There was nothing to be seen; in the distance he could hear the call of the geese as they took off from the lake.

He pushed harder against the statue as he tried to grip on to the gargoyle and pull himself to the safety of the ledge. It was then that his back was struck by a sudden and forceful blow. Maggot jumped to the gargoyle and clung on as beat after beat rained down upon him. Cowering, he turned around to see his adversary, his hands slipping from the cold stone of the carved demon as he was slowly forced from the ledge. He could see nothing – it was as if he was being struck by an invisible creature that hovered above him. Far to the north a flash of deep red lightning fired the night and in a brief moment he saw the terrible outline of the Wretchkin, its face of torn flesh staring down at him, wings outstretched and clenched fists hammering at his body.

In fright, Maggot let go of the gargoyle and he began to fall between the stone face and the old scaffolding to the street below. His leg struck a wooden brace that held the scaffold to the church, sending him spinning down towards the statue of a Templar knight, its long lance upstretched towards him. Suddenly, from all around, shafts of wood began to cascade about him as the wooden bracing lifted from the building and began to collapse to the floor, dragging with it the stone gargoyles and saintly statues. In a brief moment that seemed to be frozen in time, he glimpsed the Wretchkin silhouetted by the full moon high above him. The beast glared down from the pinnacle of the temple as it pushed the final strands of scaffolding from the stonework, and then suddenly vanished.

The falling wooden struts clashed against the stones as Maggot fell earthward, the Templar lance getting closer with each second. He screamed as the shaft thrust towards his face. The lance ripped his tatty frock coat and pierced the collar, shredding the frail cloth and dragging him to a violent halt. Maggot dangled like a caught summer trout from the tip of the shaft as the scaffold gave way. Thick swirls of dust danced in and out of rods of moonlight as the debris of the scaffolding smouldered like the remnants of an earthquake.

Terrified, he kicked and twisted against the lance, trying to shake himself free. His coat ripped and Maggot fell to the ground, crashing into the rubble. Without hesitation he jumped to his feet and began to run. The pain of the fall shot through his body and his leg gave way again and again. Maggot hobbled as fast as he could, tears of pain welling up in his eyes as his leg twisted and bent with each step. As he got to the corner of Bell Alley he rested against the wall and looked back to the steeple-house. Skullet was in the street, dragged from Vamana House by the crashing of the scaffold. By his side were three stocky militiamen, summoned from their sleep and half-dressed in their long red tunics.

Maggot pressed himself into the safety of the shadows and scampered like a long-tail on his hands and knees, dragging his leg agonizingly behind him. Knowing he had to continue, he gritted his teeth as the pain of each movement took the breath from his body and bone grated bitterly against bone.

Never looking back, eyes fixed firmly ahead, face set like flint, he crawled through the muddied streets and dingy alleyways by the banks of the Thames. There was an eerie emptiness. The fear of another comet forced the people who had returned to the city silently back into their houses. At the Charing Cross the circus celebrations had gone, leaving only the dung of Ozymandias lying in a cold pile upon the monument steps.

Yard by yard, Maggot hobbled and crawled through the silent streets. To relieve his searing pain he pulled a broken plank of wood from the doorway of a boarded shop and stuck it into the pit of his arm, where it took the weight from his leg that hung limp and dead. He was driven on like a maddened animal by the memory of the beast that had attacked him. Constantly he looked back, fearful that the creature silently stalked him through the pitch-clad streets. Every nerve in his body shot sparks of fury through his skin, and the sensations of fear and pain twisted his gut.

It was the sound of laughter that took away the pain. He could hear Jonah singing, music spilling from the door of the Bull and Mouth into the empty street. The words of the bawdy

79

song carried along Lyon Row to the corner of Holborn, where Maggot slumped against the door of the cook shop. He looked towards the light that flooded from the inn as if it were the only place in the whole world where life carried on. He felt a dampness smothering his hands and in the half-light looked down to see them covered in blood. A voice in his head cried out for him to stop, not to take another step. Wave upon wave of cold shudders flooded up from his feet, engulfing him as if he were being drowned in ice.

From Bloomsbury Square came the shrill call of a large dog. The moon beat down its hard blue light, casting shadows across the street and giving life to every stone and blade of grass, transforming them into fragments of the beast that chased Maggot in his mind. He couldn't move; the cold, overwhelming passion of his fear rooted him to the ground. Across the street was his sanctuary, a warm and welcoming place of music, tepid beer and the handshake of friends. But between Maggot and the inn stood a chasm of darkness that boiled with every lonely terror he had ever known.

The baying of the hound came again, its shrill echo leaping from building to building. Maggot looked up, sure that the spirit from the church would appear on the rooftops and chase him through the streets like Spring-heeled Jack. His mind leapt ahead and took him from chase to capture and then to the torment he would receive before being treated by the creature to a long, miserable and painful death. His heart pounded and cold sweat trickled across his ruddy cheeks that stung with the itch of the cold night air. In the darkness the noise of his breathing led him to fear that someone stood close by, waiting for him to make a move. Maggot was trapped by his own fears, caged by his imaginings. A dread voice told him to hide and take shelter until the light of morn cast away the shadows of his dreaming – but then he thought of Jonah and what he had to tell him. If he didn't act soon, Malachi and Tersias would be well on the way to Cheapside.

Maggot got to his feet. He looked frantically back and forth, peering from the safety of the doorway. The pain from his leg made every bone tremble as he wedged the wooden crutch under his arm and made ready to run. The voice came again, shouting for him to stop, to give in to sleep and wait until dawn.

'*No!*' shouted Maggot as he burst from the doorway, staggering upon the stick as he lurched across the street to the inn.

The hound cried out again, this time closer than before, and Maggot's fear flashed the image of the winged demon into his mind. In terror he threw the crutch into the shadows, hoping to scatter whatever tormented him. Maggot fell towards the door, arms outstretched, screaming as the ground shot to meet him. 'JONAH! JONAH!' he shouted fearfully, the words erupting from his mouth.

Jonah rushed outside as screams filled the street. In the moonlight he saw a large black dog galloping towards him from the shadows of St George's church. In the mud, Maggot tried to scramble to his feet, then fell to his knees, calling out in pain as he held out his hand for Jonah to save him.

A sudden and overwhelming panic stopped Jonah dead. He looked at Maggot and then at the approaching hound, a low, harsh growl rumbling in its guts. As the dog got closer, its teeth snarling, Jonah hesitated as if held fast by hands that pulled him back to the safety of the inn. He turned away from Maggot and looked to the light that flooded the street. Maggot screamed again – 'JO-NAAH!' – his voice fading in terror as the panting creature paced upon him.

The black dog stopped three feet from Maggot and sniffed the scent of steaming blood that rose from the boy's broken body into the night air. It looked at Jonah, who stared back, unable to move, and then to Maggot. It took another pace towards him, bending its head as if about to take him into his mouth and drag him into the dark night.

'LEAVE HIM!' Jonah shouted at the dog, struggling to pull himself from the grip of fright that froze his bones. The animal stared at him with its piercing black eyes, moaning and growling, and suddenly Jonah's eyes closed to the world as the entrancing glare of the dog took over his soul. A deep, hidden memory exploded, bringing with it the exact same sight: Jonah was looking up, staring into those very eyes. He was a child of four months old, wrapped and swaddled, in a room lit by a meagre fire. He could smell the dog's breath as the beast panted above him, drooling long fat dribbles of spit on to his face. Then it came – the heavy paw with its dirty brown claws that tipped the cradle onto the floor and sent him spilling into the straw. It growled and nuzzled him as it tried to pick him up with its mouth. Jonah saw again the fireplace of his house as the memory filled his mind, dug from the depths of his unthinking, provoked by his fear. No one came, he was alone. The creature pulled at the rags that tightly wrapped him as it dragged him face-down across the floor. Clumsily it lifted him across the threshold and into the lane, gripping him with its long brown teeth. Jonah heard again the shout and the screams of his mother as she sat entertaining outside the gin-house. Frantically the dog shook him up and down as if to rid him of his swaddling and make off into the twilight.

Jonah found himself choking as he gulped the night air.

From behind him came a sharp, brittle click as a pistol hammer fell. The shot rang out and the burning lead sped past Jonah's head, narrowly missing his right ear. There was a scream as the hound was knocked backwards through the air, spinning and turning as it fell to the ground. Jonah watched helpless, falling to his knees and fearing he had been shot, as the beast smashed against the broken market stall. For several seconds the brute lay silent as the echo of the blast rumbled from street to street.

Tara pushed Jonah out of the way as she ran to Maggot, the pistol in her hand. The dog stirred to its feet, growling. It turned and looked at her, blood trickling from the wound in its right hip as the fur matted. It snapped a loud bark like a human cough, then quickly ran into the black grime of the market shadows.

Without hesitation Tara pulled Maggot from the mud, dragging him to the inn and laying him by the fire. Jonah didn't move, he stared into the moonlit night as the baying of the brute shouted out from distant streets. All he could see were the bloodstained wrappings and his mother's shawl as she picked him from the dirt, wiping the drool from his face as she remorselessly placed him by the fire and went back to her trade. Jonah was left in the night alone, tears filling his wide eyes. No one to comfort him, no hand of kindness, as the mad staring glare of the wild dog burrowed in his mind.

'You staying there?' whispered the voice of Old Bunce as he rattled the door to the inn, trying to bolt the wood against the night. 'The madness isn't over yet, Jonah.'

Jonah looked about him. The shadows shimmered with every passing cloud as the night grew darker with each moment of the fading moon. He turned and walked wearily to the inn. Old Bunce stepped to one side as Jonah pulled himself through the doorway and looked for Maggot. He ignored the sea of faces of the ragged mob that stared, drooling in their beer, bedraggled and half mad.

Tara had cleared the tables from the fireplace and thrown a dirty overcoat to the floor and laid Maggot upon it. She looked up as Jonah made his way to her, rubbing his face with his hand as if to wipe away the vision that had plagued his mind.

'It could have killed him, Jonah, and you did nothing – *nothing!*' she shouted as she held the boy in her arms.

Maggot looked up, trying to smile. 'I fell from the scaffolding. Something . . . something made it fall down. They've gone to Cheapside.'

Jonah looked at Tara. She stared at him, her face etched in anger. 'We can't leave him. He's broken his leg.'

He didn't reply. His eyes flashed around the room, his face burning red in the glow of the fire. Maggot squeezed Tara's hand.

'You have to go, Tara,' he said as he tried to lift himself up. 'Old Bunce'll take care of me. You said it once – whatever happens, we carry on. It's all we've got.' He paused and looked at Jonah. 'I heard them say that Tersias has a silver spoon in his pocket, slipped in unaware by Lord Malpas. They will declare he is a thief and have Malachi hanged.'

8

Poculum Caritatis

Bread Street echoed to the sound of an old clopping horse that clattered its hooves against the wet stone cobbles. A thick leather leash held it fast against a narrow wooden strap, fastened to the side of the empty stone-built bakery. High above, several sacks of flour, left behind when the people had fled from the comet, dangled from the hauler. They swung gently in the Thames breeze, twisting like a Tyburn beauty that had only just given up kicking.

From Cheapside, the clamour of the turning metal wheels of Malachi's handcart sung out into the night, keeping tune with his crooning. He stomped against the slight incline of the road like a horse dragging a dray the last few yards to the safety of the stable. Tersias gripped the cage with both hands, holding fast to the cold metal bars that kept the world at bay. Malachi stopped and rested the cart on its two frail standing legs as he looked back along the empty street.

The broken crown of St Paul's stood fractured against the black night, lit by a crescent of moonlight that crept from beneath a pillar of dark cloud reaching upwards from the horizon. He rubbed his stained hands together and pulled his sticky beard into a long spike of coarse hair. The breeze blew against his lined face so that his long locks of hair billowed out from under his hat. Malachi sniffed his fingers, then picked his nose. Something nagged at his thoughts. In the silent night he was restless and unsure. He wiped the snot from his dew-stained fingertip, then pulled on the cart handles and began to pace to the corner of the street and the narrow alley that led to the stable yard.

As he walked, his long cloak wrapped itself tightly around one leg, bringing in his stride to a short shuffle. He stopped and kicked out, muttering under his breath and damning the maker in a long curse. 'Will you not leave me alone?' he said angrily, jangling his leg back and forth as he tried to unravel the material that had swirled itself into a tight knot around his knee. 'I have but fifteen yards until my home fire and you plague me with your grasping.' He jigged as he spoke, turning around and dancing from foot to foot. The leather on his shoe suddenly split, spilling his bare, callused toes into the mud, and his foot became trapped in the mouth of a boot-dog. 'Blast you and curse your maker! Said he was a mender of bad soles and yet the skin he pulled over these weighty feet was but a membrane of a bat's wing.'

Malachi leant against the wall of a merchant's house that stood in the stream of slop that was Cheapside. He pulled at his boot, dragging the muddied leather over his throbbing toes. 'Oh Tersias, if those blind eyes could see the travesty of my life, your heart would never want to leave old Malachi,' he sighed. He was tired to the bone and worn out through his hopelessness.

The boy held stiffly to the bars of his cage, rocking back and forth, his small head jerking from side to side as he grunted and squealed to himself. 'Sa-comin . . . sa-comin . . . sa-comin,' he said over and over as he shuddered and rocked, his white eyes staring at Malachi as if they could see his every detail.

'Coming? Who's coming?' Malachi asked quickly, looking around the street to see if they were being followed.

'Sa-comin for me, sa-comin for you, Malachi – the puppet on a Newgate tree.' Tersias barked like a deck-hound as he frantically rattled the cage. 'Biting . . . biting as they fly. Eating everything that walks in their way . . .'

'What you talking of boy? Cold sent you mad? Speak to me with sense on your tongue and not in your dreaming.' Malachi pressed himself into the shadows and looked back to St Paul's. 'Are we being pursued – is that what you can see?' A growing panic trembled in his legs.

'Sa–comin, Mister Malachi . . . You have to go, leave me in the street, don't go back,' Tersias said urgently as he stared at him.

'Bodgepigs and poppycock,' he snarled. 'You are a feckwit. I have nothing to fear from what you say, you're ranting. I've starved you for too long and you've gone mad.'

Malachi grabbed the handles of the cart and hobbled quickly towards the entrance of the alley that led to the stable yard. The houses edged in over his head, coming together in a tall arch as shutter met shutter high above. They formed a high, vaulted cave that dangled with long strands of dirty cobwebs formed from fragments of discarded skin and horsehair, trailing down like rats' tails. Tersias ranted on as he rattled the cage and shook himself from side to side. In the distance a single candle feebly lit the window of the house that clung to the stable.

'See, Tersias, you were wrong,' said Malachi merrily as he pushed the cart deeper into the darkness. 'We have nothing to fear – a light to be a lamp to our feet, to welcome home the weary traveller and be a salutation to its hearth.'

'*But we got here first!*' The sudden words were spoken by a shadowy figure, and two dark shapes stepped before Malachi.

'*Again?*' Malachi asked as he saw the outline of the hessian masks. 'What more do you want from me? Robbed twice by the same villains, and they even break their promises.'

'I have come for the boy,' Jonah said. He pushed Malachi out of the way, knocking him to the ground and into the black pit of shadow that edged the alleyway.

'You take a great chance, boy,' Malachi said as he looked up. 'I could have sold your hide to Lord Malpas. The dagger you carry belongs to him. I kept my mouth shut and the secret to myself and this, *this* is how you repay me?'

'Then we are equal in our debt, for I shall save you from a hanging. If the boy looks in his pocket, even his blind eyes will see that which would have you dangle like a Newgate doll.'

Tersias rummaged with his small hands and grasped the crested silver spoon. He flashed it before Malachi.

'The crest of Lord Malpas, the wolf-head and dagger, slipped into his pocket so that you would be found and hanged and the boy would become his.' Jonah grabbed the spoon from the boy and slipped it into his own pocket.

'How did you know of this – did you put it there?'

'Not I, fool, but Malpas. To indict you as a thief and have one of his black-capped friends judge you as guilty,' Jonah said as he helped Malachi from the mud and gestured to Tara to unlock the cage and free the boy.

'You never steal alone?' Malachi shrugged in rage as he was pushed against the wall.

'Never. Safety in numbers and a lookout at all times,' he replied quietly as Tara slipped the catch and pulled the boy free. 'One more thing, Malachi – the money.'

'You took my last guinea, everything I have ever had,' he barked back, hoping to be left alone.

'Then you won't mind if my friend searches the cage?'

Tara quickly pulled the blanket from the carriage. A black felt bag fell to the ground at her feet with the familiar jingle of bright coins.

'That is all I have. You would take the boy and every penny to my name?' Malachi said as he swung out to grab at the moneybag.

'Give him the first five coins from the bag and we'll take the rest. Is that fair, Malachi?'

'FAIR? I'll take every penny back from your soul, boy. You will dread the day that you ever heard of Malachi. Lord Malpas will search you out and with one cut of his dagger turn you from a cockerel to a hen.'

'Then I will learn to cluck and lay eggs. But first we shall live well, and I await the day he has the guts to stand spur and scrap with me.' Jonah turned to Tara. 'Give him what he is worth and we'll be off. Let's hope the boy can run.'

Tara silently threw five coins into the mud at Malachi's feet and dragged the boy into the shadows of the alleyway.

Tersias couldn't protest. He looked back to Malachi and smiled a thin, cold smile, as if his eyes could see him grovelling in the mud, looking for the money that had sunk into the dirt. He plodded on into the blackness behind Tara, unaware of the night that soaked up every candle of light. All he hoped for was a warm bed and a sup to take the dry bark from his throat.

The boy no longer moaned to himself of his misery, which had become a long-forgotten feeling. The blindness had made him a puppet, dragged like an old man from place to place, fed on rot that he couldn't see, never allowed the grace of time to sit on sunny summer banks and taste the breeze. No foolish games of ball or chance, or childish merriment of the winter dance. His lot was sitting wrapped in lice-ridden blankets and squalor. This was just another passing on, he thought, as the pain of Tara's tight grip dug into his arm, pulling him onwards.

But a thought stirred in him like a fleeting pleasure as he remembered the smell of the fire that filled the grate of Vamana House. Tersias turned in his mind the planted silver spoon and deep within he knew he had momentarily hoped that they would be captured and Malachi hung and he returned to the promised soft bed.

Then, before Tara had time to cry out or make a sound, a large dirty hand suddenly fired from the doorway and grabbed her, covering her entire face. The firm folds of the life-hard-ened palm pressed against her soft skin, smothering her breath as it dragged her into the alley that butted onto the stable yard. For a brief moment, Tersias stood alone, aware that his companion had gone. He patted his hand outwards, feeling for her coat, wondering why she had stepped away.

Jonah turned and looked towards the street, not knowing-where she had vanished. 'Tara!' he whispered. 'Stop hiding and come out!'

Malachi chortled. 'Given away the name of your accomplice – a girl . . . You shouldn't be hard to find now, boy. Maybe she's run off with someone else, the stink of your treachery too much for her pretty white nostrils.'

'Shut up, Malachi,' Jonah shouted at the old man. 'Maybe you won't live to tell her name to anyone. I still have –'

His words were cut short as Tersias was plucked from the alleyway like a brand from the fire.

Jonah instinctively grabbed for the knife that he kept strapped to his belt. He held out the blade to ward off the unseen hand that had stolen Tersias from before his eyes. A lit-tle way ahead, in the darkest part of the alley, he could hear the muffled call of his companion. It was the sound of someone choking to breathe as the smothered coughs and groans feebly called news of her doom.

Malachi grovelled in the dirt, still searching for the gold coins that had fallen at his feet. He turned and saw that the small shadow of Tersias had gone. 'What tricks do you play on me?' he asked as he shook the dirt from his hands as he got to his feet. 'Where is the boy? He's valuable and he's mine.' He stepped towards Jonah.

Without warning Jonah lashed out at Malachi, slashing the front of his coat with the knife. Its blade shone in his hand as if each grain of steel was made of moonstone. 'Not one more step!'Jonah said ferociously. 'We are not alone in this place and I want no trouble from you,' he said as the sound of footsteps closed in on his words.

'We are surrounded,' Malachi muttered as he stepped back into the shadows, hoping they would cover his fear. 'They are ahead and to the side . . . LOOK!' he gasped as a giant shadow filled the entrance to the alleyway, blocking their escape to the street.

The outline of a gigantic figure seemed to fill the entire space, rising up from the mud to the height of the window lintels and silhouetted in deepest black by the moonlight that filtered in from Cheapside. Jonah looked back towards the stables. Several men swelled out of the gloom and walked towards them as if they had risen up like corpses from the mud. In the half-light he could make out the tight caps pulled over their heads, the stiff brims jutting out like curled bacon. Each one carried a double cosh linked by a short length of metal chain that jangled with each step. From this he knew they were Solomon's disciples.

Malachi edged his way closer to Jonah as the silent, ominous figures got nearer. A sea of half-faces danced before them – each was wearing a gold opera mask that glowed eerily . . . Jonah backed against the wall as the men formed a solid rank. The giant shadow of Campion ambled towards them, puffing and panting with each step as he dragged Tara behind him on a long lead tied around her neck. Jonah could see that her hands were bound and a thin gag of ragged material was wrapped tightly around her head, keeping her shouts for freedom to a low moan. Not far behind, Solomon pulled Tersias from the shadows, his hands tied and mouth gagged.

The giant got closer and closer, his bright eyes staring through the slits in the opera mask that was pressed tightly against his fat face, held by two lengths of thin black cord. He smiled a bright smile, laughing through his pointed, filed teeth. 'You two will come with us,' he said. 'Put the knife away or I'll snap off your hand.' He spoke with the voice of a man half his vast size.

'Leave them to me,' Solomon croaked as he dragged Tersias along behind. 'They cannot run, they are outnumbered and know they are completely overwhelmed.' He giggled as he spoke, lifting one hand to his head and scratching his ear. 'You are Magnus Malachi, the magician?' He looked at Malachi and smiled, his face etched in shadow. 'I am taking the boy. I will be his father. This child was foretold to me in a dream. He will bring London to its knees. Both of you will either come with us and be my disciples . . . or we will bury you in this mud and no one will ever know or mourn your tragic passing.'

'You can get away and take the girl,' Malachi tried to whisper to Jonah, his voice trembling like a lark.

'There is no point or chance of escaping,' Solomon said. 'We would only find you and in the dead of night sneak into your lodging and cut your throat. Come with us, become one with us. It is the only way you will see your friend and you, Malachi, your blind oracle.'

Jonah looked at Tara. Her mask was stripped from her head, her hair was messed in strands across her face and tangled in the swath of material that gagged her voice. He tried to catch his breath as his heart leapt up his throat, and his fingers curled tighter around the handle of the knife. He could feel a reassuring, pulsating glow coming from the dagger that warmed his hand and slowly spread up his arm like new blood being pumped through his veins. Jonah stared at each figure eye to eye, searching for some hidden weakness.

'What will your answer be?' Solomon said as he stepped closer, dragging Tersias behind. 'Freedom with us or the captivity of the grave?'

'Run, boy, run!' Malachi whispered again as he allowed the tattered spell-bag to fall from his shoulders. He grabbed the long strap and swung the sack back and forth. 'If you're going to take me, then you'll take me dead,' he said through clenched teeth.

'Dead or alive is of no concern to me,' Solomon replied sternly, nodding to his small band of disciples.

At his command they began to swing the wooden chain-linked coshes around and around their heads. The sound of the spinning wood and twisting metal buzzed back and forth in the dark alley faster and faster. Whirring and whirling through the night air, the noise grew to a deafening pitch.

'There will be no second chance, Malachi,' Solomon said. 'Not for you or your hooded friend. If you come with us, he will have his crime put to good use and you will find all that your soul has cried out for. You can drink from our loving cup and be made immortal.'

It was then that the giant stepped forward and lashed out with one hand as he tried to swipe the hood from Jonah's head. The knife sprang to life, taking Jonah by surprise as it lifted his hand into the air and slashed the palm of the colossus, sparking blue moonstone flashes as it sliced across the flesh. Campion cried out and recoiled into the shadows as if bitten by a viper.

The disciples stepped back and looked to Solomon for a signal. Campion held his slashed hand to his chest, still clutching tightly to the leash fixed on Tara's neck. 'YOU!' He shouted with such force that it rattled the glass of the windows above them. 'You will pay for that!' Anger spilled from him as he put his hand to his mouth and licked the dripping blood, sucking it through his filed teeth.

'One more step and I'll take you as well,' Jonah said to Solomon before he could say a word. 'Give me back the girl and you can have Tersias, he's nothing but a blind fool.' He flashed the blade back and forth, trying not to show the panic that told him to run and leave her behind.

'I don't make deals with fools in raggy masks or old men who live in hovels,' Solomon said calmly above the noise of the whirring batons. 'TAKE HIM!' he shouted.

Malachi dashed forward, head down, and dived into the throng that stepped towards them. 'RUN!' he shouted as he pushed against three disciples who, taken by surprise, dropped their wooden staves to the ground. Solomon jumped quickly out of the way into the shadow of Campion and pushed him towards Jonah.

'NOOOOO!' screamed the giant as he lunged towards Jonah's neck. He grabbed the sack mask and pulled it viciously away. Jonah turned and saw Malachi being beaten to the ground as stave upon stave fell upon him.

'Run! Get away!' Malachi called feebly to Jonah as the blows beat upon his back like the sounding of a child's drum.

Instinctively, Jonah lashed out in the blackness, hoping to strike Campion with a fatal blow. The giant dodged the blazing flashes that cut the night before his eyes, leaving a fiery trail like a sparking brand from a bonfire. Then Jonah grabbed for Tara, his hand grasping the long lead that tied her to her captor. Campion pulled the lead, jerking the boy towards him, and with a blow from his clenched, bleeding fist, smashed Jonah in the face as Tara kicked and kicked to free herself.

Jonah reeled from the blow, his head swimming with the sudden pain that churned his mind. Towering above him was Campion, who took on the appearance of a large bear that was about to pull him limb from limb. Without thinking, Jonah stabbed the knife into the beast as hard as he could, then took to his heels and ran towards Cheapside.

Back the blade back and forth, trying not to show the panic, forcing him to run and leave her behind.

9

Mens Sana in Corpore Sano

The long line of purple–clad pilgrims edged its way through the empty streets of Covent Garden. Campion sauntered ahead, checking each shadow and alleyway as he looked for signs of the night militia. All was quiet. The marching feet squelched through sticky, black mud that stuck to their boots like blood. Tara and Tersias were dragged like two broken donkeys, unwilling in their gait yet pained and obedient to the tight cords with which they were pulled along. The gags around their mouths bit into their skin, pulling back their faces into tight smiles.

Solomon pulled Tara on a short lead and with every third step he turned to her and grinned, hunching his shoulders and shuddering with glee at the same time. 'Soon be at your new home.' He drooled as he spoke. 'I have something for you . . . something special. I have kept it for a long time for one such as you.' Solomon stuttered, choking on his words. 'A bridal gown of fine purple – rich and perfect, fit for a queen. Will you be my queen?' He faltered as he pulled sharply on the leash.

Tara turned her face from him and stared at the dirt. She thought of Jonah, hoping that he lurked somewhere in the gloom and would burst forth from the black shroud and slice her captor from ear to ear. It was a vain, hopeless thought that in its passing lost any sense of joy. She knew Jonah too well. He would be away, hiding behind a pewter cup in the Bull and

Mouth, joking with Old Bunce as he forgot about her. She remembered the first day they met when he had barged his way through the doors of the inn and stood before her. In his belt was an old pistol; it forced its way from his torn waistcoat for all to see. Tara knew his name; his reputation had slithered ahead of him. He was the son of the hangman Jack Ketch and was dressed from head to foot in the discarded clothes of those dispatched by the gallows.

His first words had been in mockery, chiding her for wearing riding breeches and boots and saying how he needed a new boy to carry his pack from town to town. He had boasted as he always boasted of crimes he had never committed. Recounting the stories given to him by his father, he gave his own name as the scoundrel and embellished the achievements of his imaginary villainy. Yet there had been an ounce of charm that had bonded her as a friend, his bad company corrupting her good character. Her eyes had been taken in by his warm smile and the strength of his voice that filled the room.

It was nearly a year ago to the day, on St Martin's Eve, when they had gone to Piccadilly as the moon had set. Together they had waited by the entrance to the park and as a fat man bade farewell to his carriage they had leapt from the darkness to rob him of his gold spectacles, wallet and watch. It had been the most exciting thing she had ever done. Her whole body had pounded with thrilling quivers as they ran through the streets, chased by the night-watch who coughed his way far behind them. From then on she had grown in her compassion for Jonah, until like brothers they stalked the streets picking pockets and mugging the weary.

Tara tried to picture his face in her mind, but somehow as he had run off from the alleyway so had his memory begun to fade. Her thoughts turned to Malachi, beaten and left in the mud for dead as the pilgrims stormed a torrent of blows upon his back. Then, at the word of Solomon, they had sheathed the bludgeons in their purple coats before forming a line and meekly following their master.

Solomon pulled on her leash again to drag her from her dreaming.

'We are here, my dear girl,' he said gently as they turned from Drury Lane into Wild Street. 'The Citadel – your new home.' He stood on the bottom step in front of a tall, newly built stone building with a fine pavement that edged onto the muddy street. 'The pilgrims give everything to me. Each stone was purchased with their blood, sweat and fear,' he whispered to Tara as hand by hand he slowly wound up the leash, jerking her closer. 'There is no turning back. As soon as you step across the threshold you will never be the same again. Life starts here – the boring, mundane drudgery of your plebeian state is at an end and your erudite education begins.'

She snarled at him, biting on the gag which choked her words, pressing her tongue to the back of her throat. Around her the newly cut stones and sharp black doors were outlined in blue moonshine and crisp shadows. Breaking free of the London mud, they were stacked stone upon stone like grey coffins piled higher than any of the surrounding buildings. Tara could clearly see hand-cut marks on the corner of each stone that resembled the outline of large beetles crawling along the white mortar line.

Campion pushed open the two black iron doors that screeched over the red tile floor of the hallway. He groaned in pain as the wound to his palm gaped open. Solomon dragged Tara in from the street, grabbed her by the hair and twisted it into a tight knot in his hand. 'You can be a part of this,' he said, pulling back her head so she was forced to look up at the ornate carved ceiling high above them. 'I find art such a powerful force. It invokes so much emotion – love, joy . . . pain, suffering.'

97

As the iron doors slammed shut behind them, the bell-like clanging resounded through the high vaults and along the long corridor that led into a cavernous blackness that appeared to go on and on for ever. Campion dragged Tersias out of sight, holding him like a puppet by the scruff of the neck as he flopped from side to side, bound and gagged.

To Tara's right was a vast staircase, each tread the width of a stretched cat, crusted in shining brass. From somewhere above, Tara heard the distant sound of softly-sung words calling to them.

'They are singing in welcome,' Solomon said as he began to untie the gag. 'If you scream it will take away the moment.' He looked at her intensely, eyeing every inch of her face and smiling smugly to himself. 'Remember, this will never happen again. Life has to be lived, each second enjoyed and not endured.' He stopped and turned back to the doors they had entered by. His shaking hand drew Tara's stare as he pointed to them. 'See, there is no escape. One way in and one way out. Each door weighs as much as a carriage and not even someone with your criminal intent could force those locks. Don't think of escape – it would be futile, even a ghost would need a key to escape from the Citadel.'

The singing grew louder, filling the domed hallway with the sound of shrill voices. 'Take my hand and I will guide you to a place of delight and splendour. I'm sure not even you could resist its charm.'

Several faces appeared on the long white balcony that ran from the staircase around the vaulted chamber above them. They mouthed the words of an old song, but it was as if other voices, hidden within them, sang the words that jarred and clashed from stone to stone. Tara spat the gag from her mouth and took a deep breath, thinking that this was her chance to lunge at Solomon and bite the apple from his thin turkey neck with its folds of hanging skin.

He looked at her and smiled. 'It would be a worthless gesture,' Solomon said, reading her thoughts. 'This is part of your fate. Do you think all this happened by chance? You have been brought here by a force far beyond your imagination and our lives will be joined for ever.' He began to walk higher, a step at a time, each pace falling to the rhythm of the words sung by the heralds. He pulled on the leash and Tara followed on, her eyes scanning the faces that looked down enviously towards her. 'You are here to be one of us, to leave behind the crime and grime and to be enchanted by higher things.'

Tara looked at the bleakness of his lined face and in the candlelight saw faint patches of powdered skin on his withered cheeks. She could also make out a thin streak of black kohl etched under each eyelid that stood out against his yellowed eyes. She followed his every step, climbing higher as the singing grew louder, and as they ascended she became aware of a thousand faces staring out from the balcony, each lit by a single candle clasped in bright white hands etched in purple bands. The singing became intense, churning her insides and chiding her to free her voice; the choir entranced her, she had to swallow back the desire to join their singing. Then the words suddenly vanished and the song was more a gathering of voices, rising and falling as if conducted by hidden hands. Second by second she could feel the voices pushing deeper and deeper within, as if each note was a small finger probing her skin.

Tara wanted to scream, to break the spell that was being cast over her and run from the Citadel and into the streets. In the whole of her short life she had never felt a feeling like this as both fear and joy urged her on, surging through every part of her body, twitching each nerve and sinew in a magical yet fearful dance.

She looked at each face as she stumbled from step to step, now just two treads from the top of the stairway that led to a passageway tiled with jewelled marble that glistened in the candlelight. A boy caught her eye with a bright smile on his ruby lips. She could see him mouthing the words as the song flashed through her like a summer storm. He held out his hand, offering her the candle, and she reached out with her bound hands, hoping to touch the flame.

'It's this way,' Solomon said sharply, his voice breaking the spell and pulling Tara back to her captivity. 'There is something far more exciting here than the offering of a candle. You mark my words, I will show you something that will illuminate your very soul.'

The singing stopped. The final echoes went back and forth through the chambers of the Citadel like the running of frightened feet escaping into the distance. With one breath, the choir snuffed the candles, and wisps of deeply scented smoke billowed to and fro, rising in black spirals. At the far end of the passageway, Tara could see a shaft of light pouring on to the bleak slabs from a half-open doorway. The beams danced over the cold stone floor and etched shadows against the white stone walls.

'We shall walk this journey together,' Solomon said as he untied her hands with his long, cold fingers and took the leash from her neck. 'You are amongst friends, or should I say family?'

'Let me go, old man!' She spat at him and stepped back away from his beady, glaring eyes. 'I have friends who will come for me and cut you to pieces for what you've done . . .'

'You mean the boy who ran away like a scalded cat?' Solomon laughed, his voice echoing through the Citadel. 'You have no idea what you have let yourself in for, have you, dear? You will never be allowed to leave, there is no going back. For you the world you left is over. You will either follow me as a disciple or be sweet meat for my greatest experiment.' Solomon scratched his chin as he looked her up and down and thought deeply to himself. He gazed at her mud-soaked boots and boyish breeches and smiled. 'I think I can trust you. Something tells me you are different from the rest, you have a flame about you that makes me think the desire of your heart is the same as mine.'

'My desire is to get away from this place and see my own again,' she replied curtly. She pulled the fragments of the gag from her teeth and rubbed the sores on the side of her mouth. Tara had promised herself not to speak, to remain silent and not convict herself with her own tongue. But the desire for insult grew in her throat and the words spilled from her mouth. 'The boy needs to be set free. What do you want him for, you poisonous dwarf? Has he ever harmed you?'

'Such spirit becomes you. Thinking of others? Such an open heart for one so young. The boy is needed for our future and I need to know the right time and place for . . .' He paused and looked at her again, his eyes searching her face as he explored each feature. 'You are such a strange girl, and my inner voice tells me there is more to you than meets the eye. Tell me, what is your secret?'

'I have no secrets,' Tara said sheepishly, looking down to the cold marble to hide her eyes from his gaze. She swore herself to silence, never wanting to speak to him again, and having passed through fear she felt wrapped in the calm of the condemned man. Many times she had wondered about a moment such as this, knowing that somewhere in her future her death waited like a stalking nightmare that would coldly step into her life and demand it from her.

'Everyone has a secret,' Solomon said. He took her by the chin and lifted her head and stared into her eyes. 'Even Solomon in all his glory has a secret. I'll share it with you if you want. Give me a penny for my thoughts and I'll give you the secret of the universe.'

He let go of her face and took her by the hand, holding it upwards towards the light and examining it intently. 'Strange . . . Almost as big as my own, hardened by work from an early age and nails bitten to the quick by worry. Look at the lines,' he exclaimed mockingly as he leapt a step backwards. 'A life that will end tomorrow, run over by a carriage full of Ottomans – is that your future, my dear girl? You had better stay here with us. Leave the Citadel and you will be in great danger. You'll never be able to cross the highway again for fear of being minced into the mud by a cart of mad Moors.'

Solomon cackled, dropped her hand and turned away. For several moments he stood silently looking towards the shafts of light that shone into the blackness of the corridor from the doorway.

Behind Tara, the choir had dispersed and silently disappeared down the stairway into the labyrinth of corridors that filled the Citadel. Only one was left – a boy holding a candle. His purple gown that hung like a cowl from his shoulders. Tara looked around her as she felt his cold stare burrowing into her mind. The boy gestured for her to be silent by putting his finger to his lips and opening his eyes like a peering owl. He pointed to the passageway as if to tell her that her future was before her, then without speaking he turned and was gone.

Solomon spun on his heels, unaware of what had taken place. His face was burning red, intoxicated with a desire that had overtaken him. 'I shall show you . . . I have decided to place my future in your hands. Something tells me that you are the one to know.' He rubbed his hands together and spat out the words. 'Mad, I must be mad – but then again, the whole world is mad and I am the only sane and rational mind in the whole of the city,' he said quietly, as if he spoke to himself. 'Oh yes . . . You must have a name. The name from the world is no good here. I will think of a name, something to describe you. When I get to know you better I will christen you with a new word and write it upon your forehead for all to see. Your head will be wrapped in purple bands for three months to stop your escaping and then it will be time.'

There was a sudden clomping sound that grew closer and closer, climbing the stone steps from the hallway below the balcony. Solomon shook off his dreaming and lifted his head, freed from the trance. He peered towards the steps as if awaiting a messenger, someone he knew well.

Campion staggered up the steps, picking thick, slimy wax from his ear and then licking it from his thick hairy finger before rubbing the remains into the creases of his forehead. He stood before Solomon and hunched his huge frame as if to give a bow. 'Needed . . .' he said in a hoarse whisper. 'They need you.' Campion tried to speak secretly, not wanting the girl to understand as he rubbed his bandaged hand against his breeches and glanced sideways at Tara. 'Time for feeding, and no one knows who to give them next. What about – what about the girl?' Campion looked at Tara and gave a half smile as he drooled an inch of spit from the corner of his mouth.

Solomon ignored him and took Tara by the hand and pulled her towards the stairs. They passed Campion who stood motionless and dribbling like a fat hound, his bloodshot eyes and cracked lips burning red against his bright white face.

'Come, child,' Solomon said quickly as he ruffled himself in his purple coat and preened the tufts of his hair with his hand. 'I have worked for years to see this night and all that I have ever wanted has been given to me. Now I will share it with you.'

Together they walked quickly down the long flight of stairs to the entrance hall with its large black doors and high ceiling. Solomon turned quickly, pulling Tara into a long dark corridor with no light. On and on he pressed, slowly descending into the depths of the earth. The echo and clatter of his town boots against the cold marble made the passageway feel as if it had been cut from solid rock.

They gathered pace, Tara almost running to keep from being dragged along by Solomon. She quickly realised that on both sides of the passageway were narrow doorways; they were lit by a small flames encased in through black holders made of tanned leather that looked as if they were made from hollowed-out hearts dipped in vinegar and dried by an embalmer's fire. They allowed only a chink of light to illuminate each handle, hanging from the dark oak doors like dried apples.

Tara could hear the sound of faint crying as she passed each door. To the right and left she counted more and more heart-lights as Solomon dragged her further and the smell of damp straw and rotting meat began to fill her nostrils.

'Not much further,' Solomon said excitedly as his hand argued with a long strand of hair that wisped around his ear in a thick clump. 'Soon be at the growing-room, soon you'll be able to see what all the fuss is about and see my answer to a world that doesn't want to listen.'

The heat grew more intense and the atmosphere became humid and dank. As the passage levelled out there were no more cell doors, and the sound of crying faded. Far ahead and lit by a flickering lamp was a wooden door with rust-red hinges. In its centre was a large metal plate that hung from a thick nail and swung gently back and forth as if vibrated by the door to which it clung.

As he got nearer the end of the passageway, with each step Solomon made a sharp, high-pitched squeal like a large bat returning to its cave. He let go of Tara's hand and gestured her to follow with his curled fingers. 'This way . . . Now we are here.' Taking in a deep breath of the hot dank air that filled the passageway, he snorted and sniffed as he raised a trembling hand to the metal plate that hung from the door. 'You shall see what I have inside.'

Behind the plate was a thick, round glass window. Tara stared at the door, not wanting to take another step. She glanced at Solomon. In an instant she thought of running, and she slowly and cautiously took two steps backwards to give her a chance to turn before she started to flee.

'Campion guards the entrance so it would be pointless to run and would only anger me even more,' Solomon whispered as he fumbled in his pocket for a key to the door. 'You saw the cells that we strode by? They are filled with people who made this journey and decided to run. They are the fools I plucked from the streets and who turned down my offer of kindness and wouldn't even look at what I wanted to show them. Behind that glass is what is to come. If you follow me then you will be safe and secure in my love – but if you turn and run then I have a cell for you and your prospects will be on the other side of this door.' Solomon found the key and placed it in the lock. 'As the key turns you can decide from which side you view the future.'

Tara hesitated, quickly looking for any sign of Campion. In the distance she could make out the sound of wailing from behind the locked doors. From the pained noises she knew that it was a mortal fate that awaited each of the unknown, unseen inhabitants. Solomon saw the dilemma that flashed across her white face, now stained with the beetle juice that had smeared from her lips into an operatic smile.

'You are such a silent creature, and yet your eyes speak more than a million words and your hands tell of your hidden secret.' Solomon banged the wooden door. 'Look through the glass and make me a happy man!' he shouted angrily, before looking at her and calming his voice. 'That's all I ask, nothing more. Then we will talk and eat. Please look.' He screwed up his thin face and whimpered like a dog as he held back the metal plate that protected the glass. He beckoned Tara to step forward. 'Look at the glass . . .'

In the half-light, Tara stepped towards the glass and stood on her tiptoes to peer into the room beyond. She gripped the door with her fingers, holding the ledge of the glass to steady her, as her eyes grew accustomed to the amber glow that filled the room.

It was as if she stared into an underground garden with sunlight filtering down through the leaves of a tree that stood in the centre of the room. Its bark shone with a silver glow as peels of its thick skin rolled back and fell to the ground. On every branch the brightest, greenest leaves, each the size of a large hand, dangled gloriously and oozed luscious drops of golden sap that ran across their leathery skin and fell like gigantic tears to the floor below. On the highest branches was the finest red fruit she had ever seen, bowing the tips of the branches and making them bob back and forth, wafting the leaves like the strands of an eastern fan. Hanging from the branches were ten golden plates tied with thick red cords that had been wrapped so tightly that they cut deeply into the bark.

It was then that her eyes were taken to see the first of the creatures that hung from the lowest of the silver stems. Each one was the size of a small bird, with a small head capped with a spiked horn. She could easily see the long, folded black wings sleeked back against the large back legs and barbed feet that gripped tightly to the bark.

'These are the first,' Solomon said proudly. 'I have been waiting eleven years to see this day. Soon there will be a million of my little locusts and when the day is right I will release them into the night air and they will do that which has been fore-told.'

'They will die in the London fog and starve like the rest of us,' Tara replied. She gawped at the creatures as they crawled sleepily from branch to branch.

'My locusts have taken many years of breeding and are now used to the cold. They have been . . . modified. As for what they will eat –' Solomon paused and looked to a wooden barrel by his feet. He lifted the lid and slipped his hand into a slush of rotting meat, picking out a piece of pig rump and holding it in his bloodstained hand as the stench leached around them. Without saying another word he slipped the lock and opened the door, throwing the handful of meat to the base of the tree and then quickly slamming the door shut and locking it as fast as he could.

Smiling to himself, Solomon stood back and let Tara watch alone. One by one the creatures dropped from the tree and grabbed frantically at the meat, fighting each other and pulling and biting at the strands of flesh. Tara gasped as more and more of the beasts appeared from the branches of the tree, buzzing and rasping like choking hens before falling to the feast and fighting ever more frantically for the meat.

'They cannot resist, it happens every time,' Solomon said cheerily as he took Tara's hand. 'Imagine if I allowed you to step into the room . . . Stripped of your flesh in less than fifty grains of the hourglass, all that would be left would be your clean white bones . . . It is a sobering thought and one that I know will help you change your mind as to your future.'

Pressing her nails into the palms of her hands, Tara stared at the creatures as they tore at the quickly disintegrating piece of pig flesh. She tried to speak but the words stuck in her gullet.

Solomon read the concern that veiled itself across her face. 'I think a night in a chamber with two of my other guests might sway your mind and take away any doubt that lurks within you,' he said, wringing his hands over and over.

From the far end of the long passageway the lumbering steps of Campion echoed towards them, filling the darkness with a dark cadence. Tara looked towards the dark, looming shape of the bear as he jangled a set of large brass chamber keys in his squat fingers.

Lex Talionis

Jonah burst in through the doors of the inn as if the devil himself was hanging from his coat tails. The knife wound in his arm had broken open and blood now seeped through his coat sleeve, forming a dark stain that ringed his arm like a mourning band. Fear still gripped him, and thick beads of sulphurous blue sweat dripped from his forehead, soaking his long black hair and chilling him to the bone. He felt as if he had been chased, hunted through the night like a frightened fox back to its lair.

He looked around the room, searching for a friendly face and the comfort of the fire. The inn was empty, except only for Old Bunce, propped up against the sticky, pitch-coloured bar, and the black-draped carcass of a drunken fop who snuggled in his coat with just the tip of his muddied boots staring at the world. Bunce gripped tightly to a large flagon of foaming beer, squeezing it with both hands as if he never wanted to let go of something so precious. The reddened veins stood up in his cheeks and his bulbous rouge nose rested on the rim of the pewter flagon, settling in the yellow froth like a winter red-breast on melting snow.

'Maggot?' Jonah shouted in panic, not seeing him in the inn.

'Not here,' Bunce replied sternly, opening one eye and peering across the room. His nose twitched and sniffed, tickled by the froth. 'Not that you'd be bothered – leaving the boy in the street to be eaten by a mad dog. Good job Tara was there to save him. Left to you he'd be chewed to pieces.'

'You can't blame me,' Jonah shouted at Bunce. He crossed the inn, snatched the pewter vessel from the old man and poured himself a drink. The fragrance of the warm beer clung to his wet night clothes.

'Where's Tara?' Bunce grunted as he snatched the flagon back from Jonah and cuddled it in his arms like a lost child.

Jonah paused and looked around the room, his mind racing as he tried in vain to grasp words that would cover his folly and deny his cowardice. He drew in a deep breath, then took a mouthful of the warm beer, wiping the froth from his face as his eyes flashed back and forth and his tongue cleaved to his mouth, unable to utter an explanation.

'She's . . .' He stopped and looked to the fire that grizzled in the grate, its quenched embers covered for the night with a stack of fresh birch twigs. Jonah watched the smoke twine in and out of the stems as the heat slowly roasted the wet bark, sending bright sparks up the blackened stone chimney and spewing an incense of the forest into the room.

'So where is my Tara? She has work to do other than following you around London. If you were a woman I would say you were a witch who had charmed her. So – what have you done, with her?'

Jonah edged his way towards the fireplace and the large oak chair with its hand-worn wooden frame and spindled legs. 'She's . . . lost,' he said in a whisper, hoping the old man would fall into a drunken sleep and never wake until Jonah had put the world to rights.

'LOST?' shouted the old man as he slammed the flagon to the counter, sending a shower of beer high into the room. 'How can she be lost? She is not a handkerchief or a watch, you blaggard – she is a woman, flesh and bone. You cannot say she is lost.'

'We were attacked by the Solomites. They took her and a boy . . . I managed to escape.'

'You ran away, tail between your legs like a scalded cat,' Bunce shouted at him as he scrabbled under the counter for the fat black truncheon he would use to soothe fighters to sleep. 'I've a good mind to wrap this around your head, lad. Give you the hiding that you deserve. Lost? Tara *lost* – and you calmly stroll in here as if nothing has happened?'

'We were attacked and I escaped. They were set to take Tara and kill me. I saw them beat the magician to the ground until his face was smothered in the mud and one of them was the size of a mountain with hands like a shovel. How could I have fought them off?'

'You think more of yourself than you do of anyone else, don't you, boy? I have watched you and cursed your coming here with your fancy ways and tales of thieving. Foul-tongued and feckwitted, never to be trusted, just like your father, and you smell twice as bad.' Old Bunce swung the truncheon back and forth with one hand while with the other clutching the flagon of beer. 'You can keep away from this place. I'll go and see old Solomon and pay the price to get her back and I'll take it from your thieving, every penny.' With that he crashed the truncheon on the oak counter and drunkenly threw the flagon at the wall. 'Maggot's in the back room. He has a visitor. Someone to heal his leg, an old friend and one I trust not to leave him to the dogs,' he slobbered, daubed in beer froth.

The words stung Jonah like a cold frost; they brought home to him his selfishness and his betrayal.

Bunce kept his stare fixed to the floor, not wanting to cast his eye on Jonah. 'Back room,' he barked again and pointed to the door with his long stained finger that looked like the talon of an old hawk. 'Go say your goodbyes then get out. There's nothing here for you any more. Get back to your lodgings and dine with the rats.'

Jonah shrugged his shoulders and slowly paced towards the

door. When he looked back he saw that Old Bunce had folded his arms and fallen into a beer-sleep against the bar, and now snorted like an old sow, chuntering to himself in his shallow dreaming. And he saw too the eye of the fop, staring at him from the folds of his hunting coat that was wrapped around him like a cowl. It was a momentary glimpse of a lucid, sharp eye peering like a wolf's, blood-red, hungry and cold. It gazed deep, searching Jonah for any sign of weakness. But when he looked again the fop slept peacefully, wrapped in melancholy.

Jonah pushed gently against the panelled door that slowly opened into the back room. This was a private place, entered only by Old Bunce. It was always locked, its treasures kept from prying eyes, never to be shown to the world. He felt a rising sense of excitement as he pushed the door further, the light from within flooding through the ever-growing opening.

Suddenly, a hand, long and white, grabbed the wood and quickly opened the door. 'Hiding, boy?' the voice said from inside the room. 'He's here if you care to see him. Broken leg – snapped doing your business.' Blinded in a whirl of candlelight, Jonah felt a hand take him by the jacket and pull him through the doorway and into the room. He scrunched his eyes to shield them from the brightness as he tried to look for Maggot and take his first glimpse of Old Bunce's private chamber.

'I'm Griselda,' the voice said, as Jonah covered his face with his hands and peered through his fingers to protect his sight from the blinding multitude of candles that lit the room with the heat of a summer's day. 'I'm a friend of Old Bunce,' she said, and she gave a half smile. 'Maggot will come and live with me and his leg will mend. I live in the country . . . You can come visiting if you have the mind.' Her voice suggested a knowledge of Jonah that he didn't like. He thought it was as if everyone had been talking about him, burning his ears with their gossip. Prattling to each other in idle chitchat about how he had frozen with fear at the sight of the hound, unable or unwilling to help his friend.

Jonah took his hands from his eyes. In the intense brightness he could make out the face of the woman who stood before him, her powder-white skin shining in the glow from the fire and the mass of candles that burnt around the room. She was dressed like a man with her hair tied back and wrapped in a brigand's black head-band; she wore riding breeches and black country boots. As his eyes grew accustomed to the intense light he stared around the dark-panelled room. To his right was a large stone fireplace with a black grate filled with tinder-bright logs that burnt with the fragrance of a pinewood. The room towered above him, and from the high ceiling were garlanded war flags and suits of silver armour. The walls were hung with old wreaths and ancient swords, bows and majestic war bands. This was the secret chamber Old Bunce had kept from the world. Jonah screwed up his eyes. Every wooden panel was lit with a large white candle and from the ceiling hung the largest, brightest chandelier that Jonah had ever seen; each glass jewel glistened like a diamond with the flame of a thousand candles.

Finally, there before him was Maggot, wrapped in a thick red blanket and snuggled before the fire, his head resting on a plump cushion with tasselled corners, his eyes closed and a contented grin smothered across his pale face.

'I gave him some valerian to make him sleep and take away the pain. I have called my carriage to take him to Strumbelo. It is not far.' Griselda smiled her icy smile, then looked at the bloodstain on his frock coat. 'I have heard much about you from Old Bunce, but he never mentioned that you had been injured.'

'A lucky blow, by a coward who took me from behind, not a man to stare you in the face whilst he stabbed you,' Jonah said as she pulled on his sleeve, making him wince and his eyes fill with pained tears. The woman pulled back his shirt and unwrapped the folded cloth that had formed a sodden bandage around the wound, stained with the deepest green of nettle salve.

'It doesn't heal,' she said. She took a cloth and wiped the mess from the bloodied hole in his arm. 'By what weapon were you run through?' Jonah saw a look of concern cross her face as she searched the wound for any trace of metal. It was as if she looked for a sign, something that would tell her who had attacked him.

'A dagger with cold steel and a liar for an owner,' he spat back as the woman pressed a wad of cloth into the wound and a sudden, intense jolt of pain shot through his entire body.

'This is no mortal wound and by no liar's dagger,' Griselda said. 'The hands that forged this blade were not of this world, and if I am right then I know the owner of the knife too well.' She looked up and saw a tear cross his cheek. She smiled and wiped the bead of salt away with her fingers. Jonah was sure that as she touched his face, his skin tingled with ecstasy, as if new life had been spread upon him like thick golden honey. 'You have the knife – it is here with you and smeared with someone else's blood.'

'How did you know?' Jonah asked, suddenly ashamed to look in her eyes. 'I took it fair and square, he lied to me and this was the debt of his lying. Anyway, he buried it so deep in my arm that it had to be forced out. It had stuck to me like a horse in a glue pot, dug itself deeper and deeper.'

'This is what it will do. You have carried on the curse and used it again. It will make you fight and kill in every circumstance.' Griselda held out her hand, nodding for Jonah to hand over the blade.

'It's mine and I won't give it away, it's all I have to defend myself and I have to free Tara.' Jonah stepped back from her and into the doorway, hoping to find sanctuary away from the light of the room in the darkness of the inn.

'So she is lost?

'Captured by the Solomites. They took her and a blind boy, an oracle called Tersias who says he can see the future. I say he's listened too much to Magnus Malachi, the old fool. But he won't listen to him any more – Malachi was beaten to death in the alleyway. Saw it with my own eyes, beaten like horsemeat and squelched into the mud. That's why I ran . . . I am not done with this life and don't want to face the next – if there is one.'

Jonah looked at the woman, surprised that she was listening. He wanted a chance to stand in his own defence, to put right all that had been said and justify himself and give good reason. 'Don't listen to Old Bunce, he's a fool,' he went on. 'It was the dog, it took over my mind. I could've saved Maggot . . . I was lost in my own head, a dream gripped me, blinded me . . .' Jonah was unable to think of what to say next as all that had gone before came flooding back; it was as if the gates of his mind had been broken in some ancient siege and the enemy now rushed in.

He looked to the woman again, trying to meet her eyes, before allowing his gaze to fall sullenly to the floor. 'Do you understand? Do you believe me? You have to believe me.' Jonah gulped back his tears. He felt ashamed, broken and tormented. He had allowed himself to be drawn in by this woman's smile, to surrender himself to weakness, and in his heart something had broken as he realised how easily he had given over his friend Tara to an unknown fate. 'If I knew the future I would surely try to change it,' he gagged, wiping his face with the back of his dirt-stained hands. 'I should have stayed and tried to save them, but I couldn't. I had to run – it's all I know. I've been chased so many times it comes so easily. The first time I ever stood up to anyone was the night I was stabbed.' Jonah put his hands to his face and covered his eyes. 'Don't tell anyone I've said this. I've never told anyone before, nobody has ever really listened.'

'Your secret is protected with me,' Griselda said kindly as she stepped towards him, taking a cotton bandage from a large black leather bag by her feet. Jonah looked into the bag as she wrapped his arm in the thick white cloth. He could see it was packed with strange wooden boxes etched in dark ink with long words and symbols he couldn't read or understand. Lying on the very top was a dried snakeskin threaded on a silver chain; to one side and slightly hidden in the depths of the case was a jaw bone of a long-dead animal, its white fangs and jagged teeth protruding from the worn mandible.

Jonah hesitated as he reclaimed his thoughts and dried his salt tears. 'Are you a witch?' he asked quietly, just above a whisper, as the fire spat and cracked in the stone hearth. Jonah pointed to Maggot. 'He looks like you've tranced him. Saw it done once at the spring fayre. Looked just like that.'

'Do I look like a witch?' The woman smiled at him as she tied off the bandage with her long fingers, taking a slither of red thread and wrapping it around his arm.

'It's all them things in that bag – snakeskins, jaw bones and potions. Isn't that what witches have?'

'I don't know because I'm not a witch,' she said, looking at Jonah with eyes that could penetrate the soul. 'I am someone for whom there are no boundaries between the worlds – dreaming and waking, night and day are the same to me. There are things that we know little about. In every tree there is a cure, every plant a remedy. That is the way in which the world was made. The apple brought man's destruction and the vine has brought our redemption.' Griselda laughed as she saw a look of puzzlement cross his face. 'Maggot is not tranced, he is in a curing sleep. I will take him home and he will stay for a while as a favour to Old Bunce.' She looked around the room as if she was listening to another voice that Jonah couldn't hear. 'Before I go I ask for one thing . . . Show me the dagger.'

'"Tis mine to keep?' he asked warily, as if she would steal it from him.

'If you think it will do you good and you can control it and not it control you . . .'

'How can I be controlled by a piece of metal?' Jonah asked as he rummaged in his pocket and took hold of the warm handle of the knife.

'There are things that you don't understand. If I am right then what you carry was forged many years ago on the Hill of Zion by the magician Hiram Abif. Long ago and in a faraway place it was the blade of the spear that pierced the side of a king at the Battle of the Skull. It was held by the Roman, Longinus, who knew too late the nature of the one whom he pierced. With the blood still fresh upon the metal it was taken and fashioned into a dagger. The blade is known as the Mastema. It has been handed down from generation to generation and everyone who has held its grip has been seized by its spell.' Griselda looked at Jonah and lifted his face so that they met eye to eye, her bright blue stare piercing his. 'Did the dagger travel alone or did you take an alabaster box from its possessor?'

'No, there was nothing . . . Not a thing. Just the knife.' Jonah pulled the knife from his pocket; it throbbed in his hand as if pulsating with life. 'Is this what you speak about?' he asked, hoping she had been mistaken, that even one who spoke so wisely would be proved to be wrong.

'Ah . . . It is the Mastema,' she said with no hint of surprise. 'This is the knife and I know the keeper is Lord Malpas.'

'His carriage had broken down by the old well in Conduit Fields,' Jonah said quickly. 'I went to help and we got into an argument, he stabbed me in the arm and I ran away. The knife was stuck in my arm, it could've killed me . . .' He flustered as he looked around the room, desperately seeking some way of escape.

'That is a frightening story, but you survived and are here to tell the tale so well. But what you have is very dangerous. It will seek its master and keep alive the curse.'

'If you believe in curses, then that's your superstition. I believe in what I see,' Jonah snapped back as he rolled the knife backwards and forwards in his hand.

'Not believing in something doesn't make it untrue. Sometimes it is only with knowledge that we can come to believe. Hiram Abif was a great man, a builder of a fine house, its dimensions laid down to echo the halls of the universe. In a secret place he forged the Mastema out of the finest metals. Every day he carried it with him and as the morning star rose from the sea he would point it to the heavens and speak to the sky. Then three men came who demanded Hiram to speak out the words so that they could listen. When he refused, they killed him and cut out his future from his forehead. Since that time the Mastema has carried a curse. All who clutch it will be broken down and turned to dust.'

'But you don't take it from me and yet you know I took it from Malpas,' Jonah said.

'I wouldn't touch such a thing,' she said curtly, pushing out her hand. 'As for Malpas, then his future is like burning coals in his own lap – as is yours. We in this world have a freedom to choose: good or bad, right or wrong. Each path is laid before us and yet we let our feet tread the path to perdition and our only thought is about the nicety of the shoes we wear for the journey.' Griselda laughed as she folded the two sides of her leather bag and shut it tightly. Jonah looked at her again; she seemed to be blurred and indistinct from the light that surrounded her, as if she was melting before his eyes, being absorbed into the brilliance of the candles.

'Life is not as we think. You will keep the knife until it is time for you to do what is right. Upon your forehead is written your future, every path you should take and every lie and twist you make of it.' Griselda stopped and looked about the room. Her face changed, the smile fell from her lips and her deep blue eyes suddenly narrowed as if she looked into a different world. 'Tread carefully, young Jonah, for you are being stalked and a wolf roams about, waiting to kill and destroy. It'll take more than a knife to save you from its treachery.' The words chilled Jonah like some dark prophecy uttered by a Greenwich hag.

Suddenly, without warning, Griselda pushed him away from the door and dashed through the opening and into the darkness of the inn. 'Quickly!' she shouted. 'Old Bunce . . .'

Jonah turned and gave chase, knowing he had to follow. A shadow flashed across the wall as Old Bunce clutched his throat with one hand and frantically waved the other back and forth, as if trying to push something from him.

Griselda lashed out through the blackness that covered Old Bunce, a dark smog that appeared to be consuming him. 'Leave him!' she shouted, stepping back from the writhing shadow. She reached into the pocket of her frock coat and pulled from it a long silver chain fastened to a thin wooden vial. Quickly she twisted the cap and flicked the vial. In the darkness, Jonah saw several drops of glistening crystal fly through the air towards the black mass that hovered over the old man, who shuddered breathlessly on the floor.

The door to the upper rooms slammed shut and heavy foot-steps beat on the treads of the stairs that led to the sleeping rooms. Jonah looked about the inn; there was no sign of the fop in his long black coat.

'Upstairs! Run quickly, what he seeks must be there!' Griselda looked to Jonah as she spoke, her eyes telling him that she could see his thoughts. There was a blinding flash as the crystals hit the dark mist that choked Old Bunce and held him to the floor. Without hesitation Jonah ran to the stairway and tried to pull the door open. Then he stepped back and kicked out the panels, squeezed himself through the opening and into the stairway, and undid the bolt that had held the door firmly shut.

Above him he could hear the frantic searching of Tara's room as her simple wooden bed was thrown across the floor and glass was smashed. Jonah scrambled up the stairs and turned into Tara's room. There in the darkness he could see the image of a man outlined in the light of the moon.

Jonah drew the dagger and held it before him. 'Want some of this, do you?' he shouted at the man, swishing the dagger back and forth. It sparked blue and gold shards in the darkened room, cutting the air as it pulsated in his hand.

The man stepped back, sensing the blade had some power over him, something which he knew he could not conquer. He shook himself and stepped quickly towards the broken window, whose frame was torn from its hinges.

'One more pace and I'll run you through,' Jonah said as he slowly moved toward him.

'I had you once before, boy,' the man said in a low growl. He pointed a long hooked finger at Jonah. 'Tore you from your bed and dragged you across the floor and into the street. Remember me, lest you forget. For one day I shall have you again, and this time . . .'

It was then that Jonah saw the man's eyes change from a lifeless dull white to a bright glowing red that lit the darkened room, and his finger was transformed into a thick black claw. The man smiled a dark smile, his lips parting in a thick grimace to reveal his sharpened fangs.

Jonah froze in terror as the image of the face churned his mind. He knew he had stared into the depths of those bloodied eyes long before. Dread reached into the pit of his stomach and an urge to scream a warning to Griselda, but his throat was gripped with terror.

The man laughed as he reached for the window. 'You have what I was sent for and before this moon has waned I will come back for you. Jonah Ketch, guttersnipe, I will eat of your flesh and not even that knife will stop me.'

The man leapt from the window and into the mud below, his laughter echoing around the empty streets as it changed into the baying of a hound. Griselda burst into the room and Jonah fell to his knees, as if his life had been stripped from him by the baying hound.

'Lycaon,' Griselda said quietly, sniffing the air and lifting Jonah from the floor. 'I should have known that old dog would be in this.' She looked out of the smashed window with its tattered wood and broken glass. 'It would appear that he came for something that you told me you didn't have.'

Jonah bowed his head. He felt a wave of fitful remorse sweep through him as he picked the alabaster box from under the mattress and held it close to him. 'I wanted to keep it for myself, there was something so beautiful about it.'

'Beauty can be deceiving and even the tormentor will come clothed in light. Lycaon's presence here meant the Alabaster was nearby. The dagger and the box are never separated for long.' Griselda paused and looked in the street. 'Now you must do something for me. You must go to the place where you last saw Malachi, hide yourself and see if he has any visitors.'

'But he's dead,' Jonah argued, not wanting to leave the inn for fear of Lycaon.

'Dead or alive, he has been the cause of much in this city and all this has fallen into our hands. There is a price on your head and the dagger will bring the dead looking for you.'

Trismagistus

In the Citadel, Campion slammed the cell door firmly shut with his thick-fingered hand and clomped up the narrow flight of stairs that led into the darkness. His fat tongue dribbled over his rough, spiked chin, and with the dirty nail that stuck out from the crooked little finger of his left hand he scraped his pointed teeth. He stopped and listened, turning his head in the thick black of the dark tunnel and cupping his ear. The sound of sobbing, soft, gentle and deeply tinged with true grief, danced like a golden butterfly to his ear. He had succeeded, he thought to himself as he turned back to the steps and laboured each leg upwards. The mournful sniffle followed him higher as with each stride he distanced himself from the tears.

Tara sat grasping the thin tallow candle that she had grabbed from the entrance to the cell before Campion brusquely pushed her through the narrow door and into the darkness. She wiped tears from her face with the sleeve of her coat, clumsily spilling the hot, burning wax on to the back of her hand. She dropped the candle to the floor. It rolled across the cold stone slabs, the wick burning brighter and brighter.

Instinctively she reached out, trying to grab the candle before the light was extinguished, her hand snatching at the flame as it rolled away from her. 'No!' she screamed as she slumped to the floor, her outstretched fingertips gripping the candle just before it slipped from view down a long flight of stone steps that fell away into the blackness.

There was a dull thud and the clunk of something dry and dead falling to the stone floor. Tara gripped the candle and began to roll it slowly back towards her. She could hear the grunting of a voice struggling to free itself of an impediment that choked its speaking, as if it had never uttered a welcome for many years.

'You?' asked the voice hoarsely, coughing out the word. 'Is it you?'

Tara was silent. She held the candle away from her, hoping its light would not give away her presence.

'Too . . . too bright for me to see,' the voice hooted like a gruff, old owl. It was a man's voice, and now it coughed and spat out luminous phlegm. 'There is only me left, everyone else has . . .' The man paused, sighed and took a deep breath. 'They have gone. They are but grateful dead, and I a passenger of absolute tragedy.'

For several seconds there was complete silence as Tara peered deeper into the cell that stretched out before her in the candlelight like some vast marble cavern. Then the sound of wrought-iron chains being dragged over the cold stones filled the chamber as the man hobbled back and forth. Tara got to her feet, holding the candle as high as she could and letting the hot wax drip down her fingers and across the back of her hand.

In the pale glimmer, surrounded by thick black shadows, she saw him. He looked up towards the light, covering his pitiful eyes with his hands to protect them from the brightness, his ragged clothes hanging like torn sails from his frail bones. He wore the remnants of a frock coat, silk trousers and a once-white shirt that now draped over him, tattered and torn, as if he were covered in rotting garlands that hung down around his feet. She stared at his thick black beard that had grown two years in length from his bony chin. By his feet was a bed of torn cloth, swirled into a stained and bloodied nest. He was tragic and pathetic; she thought he was like a lost boy or street urchin, starved and grubby, dishevelled enough to move even her heart.

Tara stepped towards the stairway that led two flights down to the floor of the cell.

'Who comes with the light?' the man said as he backed away from her, his hands taken from his eyes and made ready for a beating. 'I have nothing left but my mind and that you cannot steal.' He spoke fretfully as in the cold corner of the chamber he took on the form of a cowering child.

'I want nothing,' Tara said calmly as she held the candle before her, now realising she had but one hour of light left in the wick. 'I too am a prisoner. We share a fate. I fear mine will be worse than yours.'

The man laughed scornfully at her words. He bristled to his feet, screwing up his eyes and running his hand through the mass of long black hair that grew like rat-tails from his bruised and bloodied head. 'My fate you will never share. My friends are gone. Solomon took us to make us his own but we refused. We knew his secret, what he would do with London. The key was turned in the lock so long ago that my mind cannot remember when. I have lived in darkness, licked the water from the walls and for my food I . . .' The man looked around the cell, his feet shuffling away a pile of bones that lay cluttered about him. 'Now I am sent an angel to share the light.'

Suddenly the man turned and looked at her as he squinted through his fingers. A dark force seemed to grip his mind and sharpen his tongue. 'You have no right to bring that here. It'll take me a week to see again when it is gone. In this place you see through your fingertips, you let the light of the mind shine out through your eyes – for what they are worth.' He paused. 'Eyes without the light have no use. They are frustrations, they pollute the mind with images that you can never be rid of. They remind me of what I have lost.' He slumped mournfully to his bed of rags and covered his feet with his dirty clothes. 'I have a mind to pluck them from my head, for they have offended me. And to eat them as some morsel to nourish my guts, as they no longer feed my soul.'

'You could escape. We have an hour of light from this tallow. I could take you with me.'

'We tried that at first. In those days I had a friend, a companion to share the darkness. We would sit for hours and work out a plan to rid ourselves of this torture. It was fun to catch the mice and nibble their bones one by one, sharing all we caught.'

'Did they set him free?' Tara asked as she sat on the step.

The man laughed again, rolling his tongue around his mouth, then biting with his teeth against the strands of beard that tickled his lips. 'He found freedom. Not that Solomon would ever let him go. We refused to be changed. Refused to give in to his demands and wear his colour purple.'

'Did Solomon kill him?' she asked, trying to weigh the intentions of her keeper.

'He had an accident. He fell where you now sit. Cracked his head and spilled his wits across the step. All because of hunger. We ate the mice, consumed the rats and picked the legs from every cockroach that scampered its way across the floor. Then it came like a spectre, dark and cold, rising in the pit of the stomach and churning the guts. It gnawed at you from the inside and . . .' The man got on his knees as if to pray. 'You have to understand, please . . . It started as a joke, a wild word whispered in vanity.' He cleared his throat and coughed again and again, pulling the mucus from his beard. 'All I asked for was a game of pitch and toss. I had sewed a golden guinea in the lining of my coat, the first one I had ever earned. I took it from the lining and asked him – heads or tails. He enquired as to the wager. My life or his, his life or mine. There wasn't enough food for two of us and the cold creeps in and I needed an extra coat. If he'd have won I would have done the same thing.'

'What did you do?' Tara asked as she moved back one step of the stairway.

'*Let me finish!*' he snarled through the mass of hair that covered his face. 'Why do women always interrupt? They never listen – gossip and knitting, that's all they're good for.' He looked around the chamber as if to search for the thoughts he had lost. 'That's it . . . I tossed the coin and he shouted heads, it clattered to the floor and we chased it round and round. He caught it first and then together we traced our fingers over the outline that was uppermost. It wasn't a head but a tail. He'd lost fair and square. Do you know,' the man said slowly in his melancholy, 'he was my best friend . . . ever?'

'Where is he?' Tara asked as she looked around the darkened cell for a trace of their friendship.

'Nothing would ever be wasted, I promised him that. He went up those steps and then fell to the floor. Head first, cracked like an egg at Easter. I shouted for Solomon to take him away, but he left him here, goading me through the slats in the door to clean up my mess. Do you have a name, girl?' the man asked, as if he didn't want to pursue his thoughts any further.

She looked at the candle flame and hoped against hope that it would burn slowly to give her more time in the light. She cupped her hand to one side to save the flame from the cold draught that swept in from the door.

'What does my name matter in times like these? I am no longer who I was and I await an uncertain future.'

'In polite company you always know the name of the one you will . . .' He stopped and looked to the flame, his bloodshot eyes now accustomed to the glare. 'My companion has been gone for many days, weeks, years . . . So many I don't know. I can tell neither night nor day and all I can hear is the whispering that plagues me through the walls. I have kept something of him to keep me from loneliness. I find myself talking to him in those dark hours when sleep has gone. He is the most marvellous company.' The man panted, as if short of breath. 'My very own manikin,' he muttered. 'If only I could move the lips . . .'

Tara took another step further back, aware that the man oozed a madness that consumed his mind. She looked around the cell for a weapon, hoping that she could escape before his insanity grew even further. By her feet she saw a long thick bone picked dry by teeth that had even gnawed at the marrow. She grabbed it quickly and held it behind her back as she stepped further away from him.

The man then frantically rummaged in the depths of his ragged bed, pulling at long strands of rotting fabric as he burrowed his face into the dank cloth. 'It must be here, I was speaking to him only hours ago . . . Must be here, must be here,' he said again and again as he dug into the bed like a scavenging rat.

The chamber was filled with a sense of his lunacy. Panic started to shake Tara's body: first her feet tingled with tiny spikes of heat that jabbed at the flesh like a million burning spines, then the numbness edged its way higher and higher, twisting her stomach and shouting at her to run. She knew that at any moment she would have to face something diabolical.

Without warning the man turned quickly and like a gleeful child thrust a severed head towards her, his hand stuffed in the neck hole. 'This is it!' he said, smiling, his voice echoing around the stone chamber as he jangled the severed head before Tara like some tattered puppet. 'In death as in life, Mister Moab keeps good company.'

Tara moved further away, edging herself higher up the flight of steps and clutching tightly to the long thick bone that she held behind her. She stared into the one open eye of the severed head that bobbed up and down on the man's hand, its tongue slobbering in and out with each jerk. She held tightly to the tallow and thinned her lips to a tight smile.

'Mister Moab is pleased to see you,' the man said as his eyes widened with a sense of affection and he grinned at the head of his friend. 'Say good morning to the lady, Mister Moab . . .'

Neither Tara nor Moab spoke. She stared at the head, knowing that madness gripped the man even more, and the head stared back through its one open eye and smiled a soft blue smile with its rotting lips. The man giggled as he pulled Moab's beard and watched his lifeless jaw go up and down. He mimicked the dead man's voice, bringing the sound of life to dead lips. 'Good morning, my lady,' the man squeaked in a high-pitched voice, still pulling on the beard to move the jaw. 'Give Mister Moab a kissy-kiss-kiss . . .'

'Mister Moab keeps you well,' Tara said as she stepped back even further away from the man. 'I have never been one for kissing a stranger, even one so handsome as Moab.' Her voice quivered, giving away a sense of panic that now filled her heart and numbed her face. 'Perhaps some other time . . . when we have gotten to know each other more.'

'Lady's frightened Moab,' the man said, lifting the head to his face and conversing with it eye to eye. 'Doesn't like the look of you, afraid your beard will ruffle her pure white skin.' The man held the head of Mister Moab up towards the light of the candle that shone down from the top of the stairway. 'She's hiding behind the light, afraid of the dark.' He began to whisper in a low gruff voice that echoed in the cell like a hoarse bark. 'Why do they always think the light will protect them, Mister Moab? Solomon sends them to see me, every one with a candle and they're all the same. Stand up there, candle in hand, brave as Punch. Oh, to see their faces as they hang on to the last seconds of the wick before they are consumed by blackness.' The man looked at Tara and saw that the candle had burnt to a short stub in her fingers. 'Not much of the light left . . . Then Mister Moab can sneak up in the darkness and steal that kiss. What do you think she'll taste like, Mister Moab?' He shook the head back and forth. 'The thin ones are always salty – brine for blood, brine for blood.'

The stub of the candle began to melt in Tara's fingertips. She looked around her, trying to see the layout of the chamber, striving to memorise every detail. She knew that at any moment she would have to face the madman and the darkness alone.

'I know every inch of this cave,' the man said as he dropped Moab's head to the floor like a worthless trinket. 'My eyes are comforted by the darkness and like a blind man I am aware of everything around me. There is no stumble in my feet or fear in my beholding of what is to come. But what of you?' he asked, looking at the light that flickered in her hand. 'What do you fear of what is to come?'

Tara held the light as close as she could, hoping that she could absorb its rays into her heart, that she would be filled with its light for ever.

'A matter of minutes, seconds even. Then the blanket will return and we shall be one and old Moab will have his kiss.'

'Moab will have to wait a long time for his kiss and so will you,' Tara shouted as she quickly tossed the remnants of the tallow towards the pile of cloth that the madman used for a bed. She could wait no longer for the wick to expire; she had to have power over this final act. This was her choice, her chance to change her fate. If the light were to flee then it would be at her choosing, she would not wait for time to take it from her.

For a brief moment there was darkness, smothering and complete. The man wailed like a baying hound at the moon, his voice echoing around and around as he fell to his hands and knees and scurried like a rat on the floor of the cell. '*My time, my time*,' he moaned as he rustled through the old straw that littered the stone slabs, searching for Moab with blind hands that darted left then right.

Tara pressed herself against the cell wall as close to the doorway as she could go. She held the bone in her hand like a large bludgeon, waiting to lash out should the man come close. The heavy oppression of poisoned blackness fell around her like the thickest, blackest night of all. Overcome with tiredness, she closed her eyes – they were useless, just as he had said. She listened, aware of the madman somewhere nearby, below her, to the right, scurrying and scratching through straw and tinder cloth.

In her mind Tara pictured the man's drawn and bearded face. She listened even harder, her hands trembled and the numbness grew deeper and more intense, gripping her like a barrel band and pulling each rib tighter and tighter. It was then that she heard the scratching of his long fingernails against each stone step as he groped his way through the dark oppression.

'Mister Moab comes for his kissy-kiss . . .' the man said slowly as he held out the skull before him and slowly crawled up the steps. Tara kept silent, trying to control the panic in her breath so he could not hear the rise and fall of her chest. 'Very clever not to reply,' he said, stopping on the stair and sniffing the air. 'But you won't have gone far from where you were. Too frightened of the dark to move about – they always stay near the door, never move or stray, always in the same place. Even until the last breath they cling to the door, hoping salvation will come.' The madman laughed as he spoke to the skull, holding it aloft by its long hair and running his fingers over its loose skin to find its mouth. 'We are waiting . . . Mister Moab doesn't like to be kept waiting.'

Tara fought back the urge to run, her legs quivering and jumping as the numbness darted through each nerve. In the darkness she moved her hand over the bone and measured its length. She felt the thick joint that hung from one end, then gripped the femur with both hands and waited, listening for a breath or a sigh. For what seemed like a dark eternity she waited – but all was quiet, so quiet that the darkness hissed like an old snake too frail to move yet venomous and deadly, filled with unspent poison, waiting for her to step upon it before it would bite.

'Girlie . . . Girlie . . .' came the low whisper from her right. 'Speak to Mister Moab . . . please.'

The voice was barely three feet away, at waist height and coming towards her a step at a time, dragging the long chain behind it like the unfolding coils of the serpent. Tara held out the bludgeon, her eyes tightly shut, listening with a myriad of burning nerves. She could feel him close by as the clunk of his metal tethers slipped across each stone step and the stench of his unwashed grave clothes filled her nostrils. With every step his breathing rasped and wailed as he gasped at the cold air.

Tara opened her eyes, hoping for a glimpse of the man, a meagre outline at which she could strike out – something to show her that he was near. Below, there was a flicker of amber light that bobbed like a Thames nymph over the pile of scattered clothing and straw. For a fleeting moment it lit the chamber, then vanished as if it had never been. Then again and again, this time brighter as the flame jumped from strand to strand of Moab's old coat. In the black, grim darkness the tallow had smouldered, unseen and in secret, growing in power as it fed from thread to thread with its wax-fed flame.

In that second the madman struck at Tara, swinging the skull by its long black locks and landing the blow to her stomach, doubling her up with the blow. She gripped the bone and lashed out at his silhouette as flames danced on the floor below him. He dropped Moab, who clattered down each step, rolling and smiling his grim, one-eyed smile. The madman then fell face down against the steps, struck unconscious by the blow from the bone, growling and gurgling in a soup of mucus that dripped from his nostrils.

The cell glowed with burning embers that lit each corner and every crevice. For the first time Tara could see the gore-stained walls and bone-scattered floor that seemed to go on into the dark distance for ever.

'FIRE!' she shouted as she banged the bludgeon against the door, demanding to be heard. The room filled with black sooty smoke. In seconds she could hear the clattering of the bear as his footsteps pounded towards the chamber door along the narrow passageway.

Campion ran as fast as his fat legs would waddle. He slid the lock from the door and pushed against the heavy beams. Smoke billowed from around the frame as he pushed it further to peer inside.

Seeing her chance and her victim, Tara lashed out again, thrashing Campion over the back of the head. He paused, not knowing what had happened. As he slowly turned his head and looked at Tara, she struck again, this time across the forehead with a powerful, hate-filled blow that screamed out from her soul.

Campion buckled at the knees, falling forward majestically like a toppled tree as he collapsed onto the madman, compressing his starved frame to the floor until it took the shape of the stairway. Tara did not wait – she jumped onto the pile of flesh, digging her heels in as hard as she could, and then, chased by wafts of dark smoke that reached out to grasp her bloodied hands, she leapt into the passageway and ran like a Beltane mare towards the stairs.

12

Feckwit

The light from the fire crept under the stable door and into the muddied yard where Jonah stood ankle-deep in dung. As he peeked through the dingy broken glass, the stable beckoned, warm and inviting, and stirred in Jonah a yearning for a home he had never enjoyed but had always wanted. To him its poverty was as rich as any palace, its horse manger fit for a king.

In the alleyway, where he had searched for Malachi, the broken ground spoke of his beating with its churned mud and single gold coin sparkling against the ruddy black, the leftover from the thrashing by the Solomites. Jonah picked the coin from the dirt, rubbed it clean and placed it in his pocket – not to keep it for himself, he thought, but to hold it as a reminder of what had gone before. The night was dark and cold; the chill from the river was icy and cruel and nipped the feet through his thin boots. He leant against the door and rolled the gold coin slowly in his hand, wondering why it had such a power over him. It stirred his heart and made him want even more. He held the coin in the palm of his hand and looked at its glistening edges. There was nothing finer, nothing more desirable, he thought. This was worth dying for . . .

With a shiver, Jonah shook off the unwelcome thought. He shrugged his shoulders, pulled up his collar and pressed his ear to the wood. His hand slipped to the lock and gripped it slowly as he carefully pulled back the long wooden handle. Inside he heard the catch leap with a quick rattle as the wooden bar jumped the gate and the door sprung open. He slid his fingers slowly through the narrow opening. His heart raced and he could feel a flush of excitement thrill through him, pulsing blood to his fingertips.

Quickly he stepped inside, pulling the door shut and sliding the wooden lock. It gave a deep and satisfying thud as the catch dropped home. He looked left then right, checking to see if he was alone. Just a few feet away, standing defiantly by the fireplace, was the carriage that Tersias had been carried upon and the boy's cage. It had been pushed close to the wall; the door to the cage was open, dangling on broken hinges. The remains of the boy's bed were scattered on the cart. Jonah hesitated; he rolled his bottom lip between his fingers, pinching his nail into the skin until it hurt. It was my fault, he thought to himself, as the weight of all that had gone before came back to him. Tara lost . . . Maggot injured . . . Malachi murdered . . . the boy Tersias captured . . . The thoughts swirled through his skull, with Jonah firmly in the middle of every calamity. He closed his eyes and rolled back his head as he leant against the wall.

It was then, in his private shadows, that the sight of two red wolf-eyes blistered through the darkness. In the depths of his imagination Jonah saw the haunting face of Lycaon. He scrunched his eyes, trying to blank from his mind their burning gaze.

In panic he looked around the stable. The walls shone with the glow from the fire that gave a golden edge to poverty and turned the stable into a glimmering chamber. But even in the half-light of those warm and gentle fire embers, even in that sheltered ambience, Jonah could see the face of the half-man half-creature leering a smile of welcome. This, it seemed, was a matter of blood that tied them as brothers. They were kindred spirits bound and weighted like the legs of a mutineer before being cast to the ocean.

Jonah shook his head. 'Not my fault,' he said to himself in a voice just above a whisper. 'These things happen and I can't be blamed . . .'

Then the voice of Griselda came to him like the calling of a ghost that only he could hear: 'Tread carefully, young Jonah, for you are being stalked . . . A wolf roams about, waiting to kill and destroy. It'll take more than a knife to save you from its treachery.'

Jonah instinctively grabbed for the Mastema in the pocket of his frock coat. He gripped its warm handle and sighed a deep fretful sigh that left him cold and empty. Taking the knife from his pocket, he put the blade to his lips and kissed it against his flesh. As he placed the sharp tip inside his mouth his eyes closed as if pressed shut by the corpse-washer, and Jonah fell into a deep slumber.

The sound of horses thundering across damp ground, kicking up the clods and sods of tree mulch and bark, filled his head. Jonah opened his eyes as he was thrown to the ground of a clearing in the depths of a large forest. To his left and right other riders jumped from their horses and gathered around him, forming a tight phalanx.

'It comes for the King!' one shouted as he drew his sword, beating the hilt against his small shield, then wiping the sweat from his brow with the back of a chain-mail glove.

'Let me stand and fight!' shouted a man who gripped Jonah by the shoulders, trying to pull him out of the way.

Jonah turned and looked into the man's bloodied face, 'No, my lord – we fight for you,' he said as if he knew who the man was and why he should be prepared to give his life for him.

Looking down, he saw the Mastema in his hand. At half a league he could hear the cry of a beast as it ran through the forest.

It growled and cried as it broke from the undergrowth and into the fog-engulfed clearing, the mist swirling and choking like smoke from an October fire. Jonah looked up at the mat of grey clouds that filled the sky above the fog. It seemed so plain, ordinary and everyday – and there in the clearing by the fallen oak the beast prowled. It stalked the phalanx of four warriors and the solitary King, probing their weaknesses and waiting to strike. The hunters had become the hunted, chased like squawking geese through a grasping forest of elm and ash and broken yew that clawed at their faces.

'When will it come for us?' shouted a man with his back to the King.

'It is me it seeks,' said the King as he tried to push through his guard to stand alone before the beast. 'When the tormentor comes we shall raise up a banner against him.'

'Then I shall take it,' Jonah cried as he broke from the phalanx and charged the beast, clutching the knife in his hand. 'In the name of the King you shall die,' he screamed, running headlong towards the large grey wolf that bared its bloodied teeth in anticipation of his folly.

Jonah spoke no more. Before he could strike one blow the hound had leapt upon him, taking his arm in its teeth and tearing at the flesh. It tossed him from side to side and when the essence of life had left him it dropped him to the floor like an unwanted morsel of meat.

The beast turned towards the King and licked its bloodied lips as it stood panting, spewing out deep cold breaths of steaming mist and staring through its blood-red eyes. The phalanx grew tighter to save the King, swords drawn and shields proud yet without breastplates or helmets. For half a day they stood, never moving, always facing the beast. The wolf lingered, staring through its wild eyes and waiting for the fall of darkness.

Jonah lay nearby in a brash of nettles, the breath shattered from his body, one arm tattered and torn, the flesh ripped by wolf-teeth.

He turned his head away from the beast. There, a finger's length from his hand, was the dagger. It begged him to reach out. Silently, inch by inch, he moved his hand through the painful spikes of nettles towards the blade, until he could grasp it with his fingers.

It was then that the beast saw him move, as life returned to his body. The wolf turned and leapt upon him, snapping and biting against his neck. Without hesitation, Jonah plunged the dagger into its chest, and blood trickled through its thick coat. Again and again he plunged the blade home, deeper and deeper with each strike, and with every thrust the beast screamed like a scolded child. With all his strength Jonah pierced the creature with a final blow, looking into eyes that beseeched him to stop. Then it fell upon him, soft, warm and moist. It stared into his eyes as they lay together in the cool, wet grass, cheek to cheek, in a gentle embrace. Jonah could feel the beating of its heart as it pressed against him. Yes . . . yes . . . yes . . . It sighed a final sigh and dropped its head against his chest as the ghost was given up.

'Malpas!' cried the King.

Jonah opened his eyes and thought he was dead. There before him was Malachi, smiling.

'Feckwit,' shouted Malachi as he leant against a home-made crutch and balanced on one leg. 'You frightened me half to death standing there tranced and muttering away like a lunatic. I was sleeping in the back room.'

'I must have dreamed . . .' Jonah stuttered. 'You're alive?'

'Ah! But they left me for dead. Stole the boy and the girl, beat me into the mud and then made off. Takes a lot more than a bunch of Solomites to kill old Magnus . . .' Malachi brushed the dust from Jonah's coat as the thought of how close to death the beating had taken him was cast across his bruised face. 'At least you're unharmed. Come and sit by the fire. It has been a long night. I have lost everything and from the look of it so have you.' There was warmth in his voice and kindness in the hand that pushed Jonah towards the wooden chair by the fire.

Malachi watched the boy take the seat and shrug off the cold night. 'We could be friends, companions and fellow villains. Couldn't we?' He twittered on, not waiting for the boy to reply. 'Are we not thrown together by malicious circumstances? A single willow whip will always bend, but two yoked together can never be broken.' Malachi smiled at Jonah and offered a hand. 'To what is to come,' he said, the tone of his voice tinged with hesitation as he thought of an uncertain future.

Here they were, magician and thief, a strange unholy union of need and not trust. Malachi realised for the first time that he had no one to call to, no one in his life whom he could call a friend. A chill shivered his spine as he was rippled with the shades of loneliness. I am but a beggar of amity, he thought, and as he looked at the boy he could not help recalling the other boy, the blind oracle Tersias, to whom his fate had bonded him but whom he had treated so callously. Perhaps this boy, Jonah, had come to his stable to offer him another chance, a chance to make amends.

Jonah offered his hand. The wrist dripped with blood. As he looked at his blood-sodden shirt cuff a sudden realisation of the unsuspected wound flashed across his face. Malachi saw his concern and pulled back the sleeve of Jonah's coat, exposing the gnawed flesh.

'You have been bitten, a dog I would say . . . When did this happen?' Malachi reached to the bag of talismans strung from his shoulder.

'It didn't . . . It was but a dream,' Jonah said as he wiped the hair away from his eyes and stared at the torn skin.

'A dream with fangs . . . that bites so deep it rips your flesh. This looks more than a dream to me,' Malachi said softly as he took a long piece of crimson cloth from the bag and wound it around Jonah's arm. It had the smell of chocolate and hawthorn berries, mixed with the pungent aroma of damp old women who leave their tell-tale wetness on coffee-shop benches like the trails of fat slugs. 'This dream of yours, did you feel as if it were alive?'

Jonah looked at the glowing embers of the fire, hoping the light would warm his chilled heart. 'I could see everything, I could feel the breeze on my face and the sweat running down my spine, it was as if –'

'As if you were there?'

'You know of these dreams?' Jonah asked as he winced, the pain thumping through him like firebrands. 'There was a wolf. I was with the King and I had to protect him from the beast. It had chased us for miles.'

'And you were the one who felt a call to stand between the two of them?'

'I killed the wolf with the dagger I stole from Malpas. It is the Mastema.' Jonah looked at Malachi as he finally finished binding his arm and tying off the stinking cloth with a small bow.

'That is a name to conjure with . . . the Mastema. I heard of it once, but never knew that Malpas carried it. Who told you that name?'

'It was a woman called Griselda, I met her tonight – she told me . . .' Jonah stopped speaking and looked to the floor.

'I have heard of this Griselda, she lives at Strumbelo House, by the Thames at Chelsea,' Malachi began as he laughed to himself. 'There is a rumour she is a witch. Too many strange things take place under her roof. Not one to be trusted . . . or listened to by the likes of you. All you need now is Magnus Malachi.'

'Then you better have this back,' Jonah said as he reached into his pocket and pulled out the silver wolf-spoon that he had taken from Tersias. 'I had a mind to sell it and laugh at you even more, but after tonight . . .' Jonah paused, uneasy in his manner, not knowing what to say. 'Something . . . something inside me has shouted at me to give it you back.'

'Then I shall have a trinket from Malpas to make up for the loss of Tersias . . . That boy would have made my fortune. He truly was an oracle, never before seen in this city. I should have taken better care of him, but he frightened me. He'd look at you with those cold, lifeless, blind eyes and they could see the depths of your soul. No secrets can be kept from that boy and Solomon will have his heart exposed to all the world if he keeps Tersias from me.'

'And how will you get him back?' Jonah asked as he pulled the chair closer to the fire to let the crackling coals warm his cold bones.

'Don't ask me how, it'll come later. All I know is that I want the boy back and the boy I will have.' Malachi paced the floor and twisted the silver spoon in his hand, his fingers scratching at the crest of the wolf-head. 'My life has always been a travesty of despair,' he said, entwining the stem of the spoon in his beard. 'When I found Tersias I knew I had found my future and my fortune – to have him stolen from me by a madman in a purple coat makes my blood boil!' Malachi picked up the fire poker and furiously rattled the glowing embers.

'What does the prophet want with him?' Jonah asked as he pulled off his tight boots and rubbed his feet, picking the dead lice from between his toes.

'Solomon has plagued this city for two years. At first he cleared the streets of the vagabonds and scoundrels. He preached of transformation, of how he could take a broken man and turn him into a gentleman. The purple fool believed we were not to be left in our impoverished state and that only he could save us. As time went on, anyone who spoke out against him simply vanished. The rumour was,' he whispered, looking around the stable as if he was being overheard, 'he had creatures at his control that could rise up from the ground and drag the detractors to hell.'

Malachi stepped closer to the fire and stared into the flames. Jonah joined him in his gaze as they watched the flames dance through the wood and cinders. 'Soon no one dared say anything against him. Solomon and Campion would go from shop to shop asking for charity. It was never a good thing to say no. Those who did lived to regret it. There were accidents and always nearby would be Solomon to preach to the wary of the follies of humankind. He wants Tersias because he needs to know what his place will be in the future of this city. Solomon wants to build a bigger temple and it is he who will be worshipped.'

Jonah shrugged his shoulders; he had no concern for the ways of Solomon. Life was to be lived; it was hard enough just stealing the tattles and knick-knacks and avoiding Newgate Jail and the hangman. He didn't want his head filled with the twisted thoughts and philosophies of purple-clad zealots gone astray in the fantasies of their deranged minds. Jonah held out his hands to the soft blaze of the fire, and then, looking up at Malachi, was surprised to see a crystal tear roll slowly across his grimy cheek.

Malachi fumbled clumsily in his pocket as he tried to grasp the dirty, slimy cloth he had used for the last year as a handkerchief. He pulled it slowly from his pocket and examined the contents before lifting it to his face to wipe the emotion from his eyes. Quickly Jonah grabbed his hand and from inside his frock coat took the fine, blue silk kerchief that he had stolen from a Piccadilly fop the day the sky had broken open. He looked at Malachi and wondered why the magician was crying. Something of his grief stirred Jonah as he got to his feet and tenderly wiped several drops from Malachi's wrinkled eyes.

'That was a kind thing to do for an old man,' Malachi said as he turned away from Jonah and stared into the fire. 'I don't know what tricks my mind is playing or why my heart should be bursting from my chest. The thing is, Jonah . . .' Malachi stopped speaking and looked around the room as he bit his grubby fingernails and pulled on his beard anxiously. 'The thing is, I can't stop thinking about the boy. When I bought Tersias he was just a chattel, something I thought I could trade. But the more time I spent in his presence the more I knew he was different. I am not a man of compassion, but even I would find myself in the dark hours wondering what the boy had gone through and why one so young should have such misery thrust upon him. What god would allow such an innocent to suffer?'

Malachi held out his stained hands towards Jonah. 'See these?' he said shakily. 'These hands bruised that boy many times and never did he complain. Once I held a burning fire stick to his face to torment him and all he did was look back with those dead blind eyes that showed no emotion. This is my lament, my guilt . . . and the cause of my tears. Today I had a beating that taught me so much. With every blow I thought of what I had done to him, every bruise speaks of my anger. I had been so quick with my wrath, my tongue was like a sharpened blade, and yet when I lay in the mud left for dead it was his blind eyes that stared back into my mind.' Malachi threw another log into the embers of the fire as he looked at Jonah and searched his face for some sign of sympathy. 'I know many a man like me, common brutes with only themselves to satisfy. It is not a station in life that I now desire, and the calamity of it is that I have lost the only thing I really wanted – the company of that small, helpless waif. My life has been like a long winter without the joy of Christmas to console me through the dark days.'

Malachi took the wolf-head spoon and breathed upon it before wiping it against the cuff of his coat and burying it deep in his pocket. He staggered to the makeshift altar that was pressed against the far wall of the stable. It was littered with the conjurings of his alchemy: dried frogs, a living toad locked in a large glass jar, the dried tail of a pig, several cups of fermenting stomach-broth and a large flour sack filled with saltpetre.

'Somewhere here I have a remnant of my magic,' he said as he searched the nitty-gritty that cluttered the altar, moving to one side a crumpled sheet of lead that he had once tried to turn into gold. 'I know it is here somewhere and I would like you to see it. Maybe then you would understand why –'

There was a sudden frantic clattering at the door and the wood began to bubble and blister with each blow. Splinters of jagged elm leapt across the room like jags of lightning, and seconds later the metal-strapped beams gave way and fell to the floor.

Several scarlet-clad militia burst in through the smashed-open stable door. Jonah leapt across the room to Malachi and pushed him to the floor, his quick fingers picking clean every pocket of his frock coat. Malachi sought sanctuary under the altar and cowered like a cornered rat against the wall, his whiskered, tear-streaked face peeking out from the darkness.

'MALACHI!' shouted Skullet as he pushed aside the militia and stepped into the room clasping his wolf staff. 'You're a thief, a villain and a liar. I warned you of the cost of your trickery and now I come as your judge, jury and executioner . . . Search him!' he shouted to the guards.

Malachi was dragged from under the altar by his beard and spread-eagled on the cold floor.

'What do we have here?' Skullet asked warily as he looked at Jonah hiding under the table. 'A street rat, an urchin, a conspirator? Come out, boy, or my men will rip off your ears as they pull you from your hole.'

In the shadow of his hiding place, Jonah took the Mastema and plunged its glowing blade into the horsehair plaster that loosely covered the wall, burying it to the hilt so it would not be found. Then he crawled into the light of the room and got up from his knees to stand before Skullet and his guards. Taking the wolf-stick, Skullet pressed it firmly against his cheek. 'A boy, a fine boy without blemish or wrinkle . . . A little dirty and in need of his yearly bath but still a nice specimen.' Skullet barked out an order to the militia, who gripped Malachi firmly to the floor, pressing his face into the dirt. 'Search him! He has stolen from Lord Malpas and for that he will be hung by the neck and dangle from a Newgate branch from dawn till dusk.'

'He has nothing,' Jonah spat back as a guard grabbed him by the scruff of the neck and dragged him to the door. 'It's me you want, I stole the wolf-spoon, not Malachi.'

Skullet turned towards him as a red rage crossed his face, burning his cheeks like a blood moon rising from the sea.

'Then you are a double thief convicted in the presence of all these witnesses and for that you both will hang.' Skullet laughed as he signalled for the militia to take the boy away. 'No one makes a fool of me, boy. I know Malachi took the spoon when he came last evening, and you have never been near the house.'

'Malachi isn't a thief. You stuffed the trinket in his pocket and no court in the land will believe you. There's more to your accusations than a silver spoon pinched from Malpas,' Jonah sneered as he was dragged away. 'Newgate won't keep me and your chains will melt upon my wrists and I will call it a great joy to plunge a dagger through your heart.' His voice wilted as he was taken into the alleyway and shackled to a cart led by a small fat pony with a bloated gut and pinched feet.

'Magnus Malachi, magician and *magus extraordinaire* . . . whatever shall be done with you?' Skullet enquired as he pushed him in the face with his stick. 'Gave the evidence to the boy,,, did you? That won't get you off the gallows.' Skullet stopped and looked about the stable, his eye catching the empty cage. 'Where do you hide the oracle? In a cellar, perhaps?'

'You are too late. The boy has gone, stolen from me but three hours ago, taken by the Solomites. Your loss is their gain and from them, not even Lord Malpas could retrieve his goods.'

'A hearty story to deceive me from the truth, perhaps?' Skullet said as he began to twist the wolf-stick and pull the black-lacquered shaft away from a bright silver blade. 'Perhaps this will loosen your tongue . . . or cut it from your head.'

13

The Giaour

Deep within the Citadel, Tara stumbled with feeble steps along the smoke-filled passageway, looking for her escape. Somewhere in the distance she could make out the dim glow of a heart-lamp hanging to light the doorway to a cell. Clumsily she trotted on, her feet skipping to the beats of her heart, as from far below in the labyrinth she could hear the screaming of Campion as he called the alarm of the fire.

In the hot half-light the choking fumes billowed around her head. She fell to her hands and knees and crawled beneath the dense cloud of smoke that was sucked higher by an icy draught, dragging with it the stench of the cells. The whole of the Citadel had been brought to life as from every direction came the clanging of hand-bells and the clattering of feet running towards her in a maelstrom of smoke and harsh voices. She pressed herself against the stone cold walls as a troop of devotees ran past her towards the calls of Campion, who was shouting louder and louder for water to quench the flames. To her complete amazement, not one of the Solomites saw her in the thick smoke as she huddled like a starving, frightened hedge-pig escaped from a gypsy fire. She crawled on, higher and higher, as the bells clattered and clanged, their calling and clanking dulled by the thick fog of Moab's burning bed. Again she pressed herself to the wall as a gaggle of choking Solomites ran by her, slapping and spilling their wooden buckets as they ran to quench the flames and the screams of the madman.

It was then, at the point of blindness and suffocation, that Tara felt the doorway with her fingers and, reaching up to the handle, found a thick iron key that had been left in the lock as the keeper had fled in panic. She quickly turned the lock and pulled on the handle. Pressing the door open with her foot, she peered inside the brightly lit cell.

There, surrounded by several lampstands lit by long white candles and tied to a large oak chair, was Tersias. He was draped in purple cloth and upon his head was a golden helmet that looked old and well worn. It covered his eyes, pressing tightly against his flesh, cutting into his cheeks. It was like a crown, a coronet for a prince, studded with green gemstones that sparkled in the bright candlelight. All around him were offerings of the finest foods set on silver platters and perched upon small oak tables that seemed to have sprung up like thin brown mushrooms from the dark stone floor that was covered in a scattering of rose petals.

Tara got to her feet, took the key from the lock and slammed the door shut. She grabbed a cloth from Tersias's throne and stuffed it between the wood and the floor to keep out the black, sooty smoke that now filled the passageway outside. Then she turned the key in the lock, sealing them both in the room.

Tersias didn't move. Something held him firmly in another world as a deep sleep gripped him to the throne.

'Tersias . . .' Tara whispered as she untied the leather thongs and shook him by the shoulder, trying to wake him. The boy didn't move, his fingers holding tightly onto each arm of the oak throne. 'Tersias!' she shouted in his face. 'Wake up! We have to escape!'

The boy began to stir. His thin lips mumbled as his hands lifted from the throne and touched the front of the helmet.

Tara grabbed the metal helmet and began to twist it from his head. Tersias cried out as if in deep pain, his hands reaching for the golden dome to keep it in place. 'NO!' he shouted as he tried to push her away. 'Leave it be! It is a part of me, never to be removed.'

'Tersias, it's Tara – I have come for you, we can escape,' she said, still trying to free the boy from his golden hood. But in the midst of his gruntings and protestations she saw a trickle of blood that glistened in a lock of hair hanging down from the coronet. She felt under the rim with her smallest finger, now realising that the helmet was pinned to the boy's forehead and his temples by four golden thorns pressed through the metal and tipped with large green gemstones. 'Tersias, this will hurt, but it is for your freedom,' she said as she twisted the first thorn from the rim of the coronet, pulling it from his head.

The boy winced in pain as she dragged the thorns from his skull one by one, throwing them to the floor. 'Who ever did this to you was a madman,' she said as she looked at the final thorn in the palm of her hand. Rows of sharp flickers edged each side of the twisted pin. Looking closely, Tara thought how they resembled tiny stars set on the edge of a far galaxy.

A scream from Tersias grounded her thoughts as he thrust the golden helmet from his head and let it crash to the floor. 'Why do you come for me?' he asked as he got to his feet and gripped the arm of the throne, not knowing where he was.

'We have to get out of here. They will come for us, they will kill us.' As Tara spoke the words she realised the true danger of their predicament. Until that moment she had hidden her fear for the future, hoping against hope that Jonah would be there for her. 'Tersias, tell me what is to come,' Tara asked as she took him by the hand to lead him to the door, wanting the oracle to prophecy kindness and long life.

'I know nothing,' he replied. 'When they brought me into this place the voices couldn't follow. The creature that speaks to me, the Wretchkin, it cannot find me. As soon as the crown was placed upon my head every forethought was stripped from me and I was doubly blind. Solomon sang and chanted around me. I could hear him lighting candles. I was made to sip from a chalice, wine that burnt my tongue and took me to another place, filling my head with sleep and dreams. He told me that as long as I was in this circle of light then the voices would stay away. Then they tied me to the throne and left me alone.'

'We cannot stay with these people,' Tara protested as Tersias sat down on the floor and fumbled with the great candlesticks, tracing his fingers through each crack and crevice. 'Stop your games, Tersias, and come with me. I lit a fire in my cell and clubbed Campion so I could escape. It will not keep them for long and he will come for both of us.' She tried to pull his hands from the lamp holder and get him to his feet.

'I know it's here,' Tersias said, gripping the thick base of a large golden candlestick that was somehow embedded into the stone floor. 'I heard him, I counted the footsteps and here he paused. There was a loud click like the cocking of a pistol and a sudden gust at the back of my neck. Solomon left the chamber and I heard the stone slide back. There is another way from this place, different from the door you entered. All I have to do is find the key and we will have our escape.' He fumbled further, his fingers sliding along the cracks and round the thick feet. 'Use your eyes, girl. What can you see? I'm the one who is blind, remember.'

'If I knew what I was looking for I could help you, but in this search I am as blind as you are,' she snapped in reply.

'A spring, a lock, something that is different. It has to be here, this was the place he walked to, I heard it and have never been wrong.' Tersias spoke angrily, the desire to escape growing in his heart as the cursed trance of the coronet ebbed from his mind.

'Did your voices tell you or was it your imagination?' she replied, unsure where to look, resentment in her voice.

'If you lived as me for one day you wouldn't have such a tongue. If you endured an hour of my life then your heart would have sympathy for who I am. I once had my sight, but it was taken from me by my mother's greed. She blinded me and sent me to beg, that I now know. Sold me for a mug of gin and forgot who I was by the time night fell. When I was imprisoned in this place with the crown upon my head and the linctus seeping through me, I saw what she had done.'

Tersias looked up at Tara and for a brief moment they stared eye to eye. It was as if he could see her face, that his deep white empty eyes were for that moment fully sighted and able to penetrate her every thought. 'I have been a floating reed for too long. I have been moulded by the hands of men to do their bidding. They have plundered my flesh with their desires and stolen from me my childhood. Even the voices had their way with me, with no care for who I am. An empty vessel to be filled by whoever cared to take control, a lap dog to a lady.' Tersias got to his feet and staggered across the room, slumping himself in the throne and pulling his legs to his chest, curling himself tightly against the darkness that surrounded him. 'When I slept I saw it all. My life danced before my eyes. I heard every word and relived each blow. In those dark hours I lived again my short life.' He paused, raising his face from his knees and looking about the room. 'It is all very clear to me and for that sleep, Solomon has my thanks. But he will have nothing more. I would rather die than be his puppet.'

Tara couldn't reply. She looked at Tersias, a boy who had the understanding of a man. Until that time she had cared little for his condition. He was a brand to be plucked from the fire, a chattel to impress Jonah, a feckwit who muttered the future. As he sat upon his throne draped in the purple coat and breeches, dressed as a disciple of Solomon, Tara knew that she looked upon a boy. He was flesh and blood, not just a circus trick or a Mayfair freak but a child, just like her.

'You can be with us, one of us, a friend for Maggot. We can be your family,' she said as she grabbed the crown that lay at her feet and held it before his sightless stare. 'We will take this, it will keep the voices away. We could find a priest who will rid you of their haunting. You could be well again.' She spoke quickly, her mind racing. 'I once heard of a man, a teacher, who could cause the deaf to hear and the blind to see. I was told his desire is that we are all made well. We could search for him and when he is found ask him to do that for you.'

'And what would we give such a man? If it were true then he could ask for the world in exchange for my sight,' Tersias said quietly. His voice was muffled by the sleeve of his coat, his face pressed into the thick fibres that bristled against his skin, reddening his cheeks.

'They said he asked for nothing, but I would give him all I had,' Tara said as she frantically thought of what, poor as she was, she could possibly give.

'All of nothing is nothing,' Tersias replied. 'Neither of us have riches. You are the molly of a thief and I the puppet of a magician and now the prisoner of a madman.' The boy gave a deep sigh. 'I miss old Malachi,' Tersias said mournfully as he thought of the old man. 'There was a meanness and a roughness to him but he was still the kindest of all my masters. He would talk to me for hours, tell me all he would do. Once he called me a son. Now I will never see the fool again.'

'If we don't go quickly we will never see the light of day again,' Tara shouted as the thud of footsteps beat along the passageway and the clanging of bells ebbed away. 'They have conquered the fire and now they will come for us.'

A heavy banging on the cell door vibrated the whole wall, sending a shower of dust cascading from the ceiling like a fall of fresh snow. 'You have the key, boy?' Campion shouted as he beat against the door. 'Locked yourself in, did you? It's safe now, the fire is gone. Solomon will soon be back and he will not be pleased to have the key gone missing.'

There was a long silence as no one spoke. 'Don't make me knock down the door, I can see the key is in the lock . . . Now, open the door and let us tend to your needs.'

'He thinks you are alone,' Tara whispered. 'Keep him at bay and I will look for the catch – if there is one . . .'

'I am safe,' Tersias said as Campion poked at the lock, hoping to push the key from the chamber. 'I will wait until the master returns, then when Solomon is here I will come out.'

'He is in the city on important business, why wait for his return? Come to the door, turn the key and LET ME IN!' Campion shouted, his voice so powerful that it rattled the door on its hinges.

'I am but a blind boy and know not how to get to the door, so how can I turn the lock? If I could find it in my perpetual darkness then I should call it a miracle,' Tersias teased.

'The same way you . . . The same way . . .' Campion faltered – he remembered strapping the boy to the chair and placing the gold coronet upon his head before leaving him, and he realised now that there must be another person in the room with Tersias. 'Neither of you can get out of that place,' Campion blustered. The deception stung him like a September wasp. Furiously he poked at the lock, trying to jiggle the key from the hole. 'I'll have you both, and as for the girl, she will have a beating far worse that what she gave to me . . .' He kicked against the door.

'I'm alone, what do you talk of?' Tersias said. 'The girl has long gone, I heard her screams as she fled the fire.'

'You are a liar and for that I'll punish you,' Campion shouted as he beat his fist against the door and stomped his feet back and forth, knowing not what to do next. 'Open the door, girl, or I'll have you blinded like your friend and never again will you gaze at my pretty face.' He wiped his sooted brow with the back of his dirty hand. 'What I have seen today, you will see for the rest of eternity . . . Open the door and have done with it!'

'What did you hear Solomon do when he stood by the candlestick?' Tara asked quickly, unable to find any catch to open their way of escape.

'I heard his heels click upon the stone, then there was nothing for a second, then another click and then the gust blew the back of my neck. The door is in the wall behind me, that's where I heard the stone sliding and grinding when he left the chamber.' Tersias spoke quietly, not wanting to be heard by the brute at the door.

'Then he must have done something with this one here,' Tara said as she pushed against the candlestick, tilting its base from the ground and spilling a gill of sizzling wax on to the stone floor.

There was a quick, loud click, and beneath them a whirl of ratchets shuddered the stones as the far wall was dragged to one side, stone scraping upon stone. A gust of dank breeze bellowed into the room, wafting the candlelight and flickering the flames that cast warped shadows like grasping hands on the high ceiling.

'We have a magic that will vanish us from this place, Campion,' Tara shouted as she pulled Tersias from the throne and dragged him towards the opened wall. 'You will never find us, and I doubt if you have the strength to take down that door, fat man.'

Her taunting inflamed the beast. Campion rose up, took in a long deep breath and clenched his hand into a giant fist, lifting

153

it as high as he could, as he prepared to strike the wood. 'No one gets away from Campion!' he screamed as he beat on the door again and again. The wood blistered and the key was knocked to the floor. He raised his fists again for a final blow, lifting his hands high above his head and sucking in a deep breath of acrid fumes.

Screaming, Campion plunged his fists towards the door, cracking them against the thick oak beams. He stepped back, his narrow, beady eyes examining the door that now hung loosely upon its hinges. Then he took a sudden step forward, pulled back his head and butted it against the wood. The beams gave way, splitting the door in two as they cascaded into the brightly lit cell.

'Campion's come for yer!' he shouted, a smug smile upon his face. His eyes searching the room for the children, he pushed his way through the broken mess of the smashed doorway to stand in the room. 'No tricks, Campion hates tricks . . .' he said as he hunted behind the throne for the children, unaware of the existence of the tunnel just feet from where he searched. 'Whatever you've done, you will pay for it boldly – there is no escape, no one leaves the Citadel, *never*!'

From behind the stone wall, Tersias and Tara heard his brash shouting. They stood together in a tight passage lined with shimmering white stone and lit with the heart-lamps as far as they could see. Blowing towards them was a gentle breeze that smelt of lavender and fresh figs. Tersias sniffed at the breeze.

'I smelt that before, when Solomon left the cell. I would never forget a scent as lovely as that,' he said as he held tightly to Tara. 'I have known it before,' he said longingly. 'There was a girl in Covent Garden who would always bring me bread when I was begging, and if she had many favours she would give me a slice of meat. She always carried a garland of lavender, it would spice the cold air and –'

'Kept the smell of her dirt-filled life from her nostrils,' Tara said cuttingly as she looked back and forth, wondering which way would give them freedom. 'Are you sure you have no sight of the future?' she asked Tersias, her voice faltering as she spoke.

'None. The voices cannot find me here, Solomon has a power to keep them from his Citadel. I have called upon them many times but they are silent. When I was Malachi's servant I would beg the voices to leave me alone as they taunted me, now they are gone I long to hear them again.' Tersias spoke softly, his voice chilled and strained like the failing cords of an old man.

Tara set off at a pace, her feet deciding which path to follow as they ascended into the growing light. 'I heard Campion say that Solomon was away from the Citadel. When he returns they will surely come looking for us. Campion may not know of this tunnel but it will be the first place that Solomon looks.' Tara squeezed her companion's hand; it was wondrously soft and warm, his skin tickled her palm as it oozed heat through her veins. 'Warm hands, cold heart, that's what my mother would say. No good for baking bread, not hands like that. Made for mischief and milking cows.' She laughed, the sound echoing down the tunnel and into the far shadows. She felt warm towards the boy and responsible for his safety – she would be his eyes, a good shepherd to lead this lamb through the dark valley and into the light.

The tunnel got narrower and narrower. From all around them they could hear the chanting and singing of the Solomites that pierced the hard stone walls and shivered the candles in their heart-shaped lanterns. The sound became like the mournful groan of a white whale, pierced and bleeding in a cold sea.

The floor to the tunnel was overlaid with a crisp white powder like fresh snow that crunched with each step. It sparkled

155

and glimmered tantalisingly as they walked on. Tersias smiled to himself, forgetting his fear and enjoying the closeness of Tara's company. He lifted her hand to his face and held it against his cheek as she led him slowly on, step by step, and in that brief encounter a dark thought struck him. As Tersias met Tara in the honesty of a kissed hand, shared in gratitude for her company, the power of her long-kept secret came to his mind..

'When will you tell Jonah your secret?' he asked gently, in a matter-of-fact way.

'Secret?' Tara asked, turning to one side to look at the boy in the narrowness of the tunnel. 'What secret?'

'I felt it when you took hold of my hand. Felt that you had kept something to yourself that you would not share with the world. Something that you think would break your friendship, if he knew.'

Tara bristled, giving Tersias a cold, icy stare that he could never see but only feel through her tightened fingertips. She swallowed and gulped back her surprise. 'No one can ever know. Promise me that. It'll harm no one and its keeping has no consequence for your life. If Jonah were to find out then he would soon become a forgotten friend who would find himself a far worthier companion than I. Do you know what I hide from him?' she asked quickly, hoping that whatever power had plundered her heart had not divulged the true depth of her secrecy.

'All I know is that you are not who you would first appear to be. You have compassion and kindness.' Tersias stopped and held her hand again to his face, touching it against his cheek. 'You can be whoever you want to be. We do not have to follow the fate of our birth – look at me, the blind beggar of Stepney, now chased by kings for what I know. Such is life. Our fate can spin on a farthing and our life itself be snuffed out like a candle. That's what Malachi told me.'

They tramped on in silence, Tara pondering on the condition of her soul and the reason for her secrets. Tersias counted his footsteps and ran his hand across the tunnel wall, feeling for the slightest notch or crack which might be a marker should he return alone. He tried to memorise every touch of his fingertips. As they climbed ever higher, they no longer heard the Solomites, all was silent except for the crunching of their footfalls on the crisp white crystals.

The tunnel made a sudden, sharp turn, then levelled out and opened into a large room with an oak door against each wall. In the centre of the room was a great table adorned with two freshly trimmed candles set on silver sticks, and on the table was an outsized brass clock covered with a bell jar. The pendulum swung back and forth, counting the seconds and pushing the sword-shaped hands.

'What do you see?' Tersias asked as they stood at the entrance to the room, the sweet smell of lavender stronger than before.

'There is a table, a clock, candlesticks and three doors.' Tara said. 'Which shall I take?'

'Let us try them all and when we see what is ahead then we can choose our escape.'

'How do we know which one will be the safest? Campion could be behind it, dining on one of his guests, or Solomon, or —'

'For me every step is taken in darkness. You have eyes, use them well.' Tersias took her hand. 'Take me to each door, I will tell you which one we should go through.'

She did as he said, leading him across the room and standing him in front of the first door. He put out his hands and touched the wood, then slowly ran his little fingers against the beams, touching each grain of the wood, listening with his fingertips.

From door to door he went, feeling for what was beyond, silently connecting to who had been there before as his fingertips

157

searched out their testimonies traced in each oak fibre. Then Tersias pulled Tara closer and whispered softly. 'The first door is locked, beyond it are people. The second is a passageway, no one has been that way for a long time. The third door is the strangest of them all. It is as if it is just a door with nothing behind – the hinges have never been opened and it has no lock or latch. We have but one choice.'

'Choice?' said a voice from behind them. 'You have every choice in the world. We cannot choose when we are born, but I can choose when you die.'

Solomon stepped into the room from the first door. 'You may have fooled Campion but alas, you could not fool me.' He looked at Tara. 'Magic – is that how you escaped? I was the only one to know of my secret way in and out of every room in this building and you have found me out. I take it you didn't appreciate the company of Mister Moab. I have always found him frightfully entertaining . . . . But now I will unearth you a more suitable guest to share your time with.'

Solomon grinned darkly and crossed the room towards them, a horsewhip twitching in his fingers.

Sons of Prattlement

In the light of the breaking dawn, the two high towers of Fleet Prison grew like tall oaks from the mud of the dirty street, rising through the dank smog and into a crisp, clear sky above. The six o' clock watch swapped the keys with the night-men, who sallied quietly back to their beds, wiping off the dew and grime of eight hours' listening to the chokers and moaners hanging from their cell bars, desperate for a breath of fresh air to take away the stench.

Prison fever gripped the walls and lined the throats of most of the inmates. Their retching echoed across the courtyard, through the portcullis and into the ears of the approaching militia, who were escorting the cart in which Malachi and Jonah were jostled to their captivity. Skullet picked his way through the dung. To keep his feet from the dirt, his fine leather shoes were perched on a pair of the finest iron risers, which clip clopped against the stones like metal stilts. With each step he defiantly prodded his long black staff into the mud and shouted at the guards to pull the fat donkey faster.

Mrs Devereaux ran out in welcome, wiping bacon grease from her warty face and quickly folding *The Times* in her bosom pocket. Jonah knew her well: she was his father's third wife, but would never take his name. She always said she had married beneath herself – 'on the bounce,' she would squawk, meaning it was more out of sympathy than love. As for Jonah, he had quickly departed the household, gone within the day of her arriving and with no love lost.

Malachi saw Jonah grimace as Mrs Devereaux fussed about the guard, thrusting a white linen sack into his hand. When Skullet came into view, she jumped upright, straightened the skirt over her fat rump and coughed several times to attract his attention.

'You dying, woman?' Skullet chortled as he walked towards her, Malachi and Jonah listening to his every word. 'Can't be canoodling with someone with jail fever, can I, Lizzy?'

She giggled like a child and put a hand to her face to cover her crimson blushes. 'Everything's ready, just like you wanted. Both in the same cell, no windows and near the gallows.' She looked at Jonah, her face changing from the soft smile that she had given to Skullet to a look that spoke of cringing resentment. 'Thought I'd told you never to come back, Jonah Ketch. I never wanted to see your face in here again.'

'So you know the ruffian, do you, Lizzy?' Skullet handed her his staff and wiped his hands on her sullied apron.

'Knew his father better. Married him when he was the jailer here. Took up and died on me within the month, he did. Never was reliable, could never hang 'em straight, always left them to dangle.'

'You poisoned him, you old hag,' Jonah shouted as he attempted to jump from the cart, only to be pulled back by Malachi. 'He had so much lead in him that he could have been rolled out and spread on the church roof. You can't deny that, can you, Lizzy?'

'Never did. Mister Skullet will bear me out. Your father died in my arms of jail fever. Loved him with all my heart . . .'

'Loved him from the depths of your wallet. Got his job, got his money, threw me out and bought a quart of gin. Strange how all your men die . . . Didn't one choke on your dumplings. Were they made of lead?'

'I think you boast with the voice of a dead man,' Skullet said as he waved the cart on. 'Take them and lock them away. There will be a court tomorrow at eleven. The indictments are ready and so is the rope. Feed them, give them wine and let them fester. Mrs Devereaux and I are going to share breakfast . . .' Skullet grinned at the jailer, giving her a sly wink as he turned from the gate and followed her to the hostel. 'Make sure they are comfortable. Lord Malpas wouldn't like any mishap to befall his friends.'

'What about my lawyer?' shouted Malachi as Skullet began to walk away. 'I have the right of an advocate.'

'No son of prattlement will do you any good. Your case was sealed when you stepped into Vamana House. Enjoy your last meal and kiss this life goodbye.'

Skullet and Mrs Devereaux disappeared together into the warm glow of the hostel. The smell of roasting nutmeg and ginger mixed with baked piglet billowed from the doorway and into the street.

Malachi sniffed the air, an unexpected joy that wetted his tongue and stirred his memories. He slumped back into the cart, resigned to his fate. With one last glance he looked back on London and his lost life as the cart rattled over the broken cobbles of the prison yard. Two large black gates swung quietly together, blocking out the world with a long slow thump.

'Never see it again, Jonah,' he whispered hopelessly to the boy. 'But I don't mind my fate. I have trod this earth for fifty years, but you – you are just a poor boy. There is malice abroad and I have been the one who has dangled the sprat on the hook. I have caught a malevolence that has infected your life and brought you to this.'

'When you were my age, did you ever wonder how it would

all end?' Jonah asked as the cart drew up to the small door that led into the deep dungeons beneath the prison.

'Never . . . I thought I would live for ever. But in a strange way it is good to know it will all be ended tomorrow.' Malachi chuckled to himself. 'November the 5th . . . A night of mischief and bonfires will light my passing to the stars. We can rise up together like brands from the fire and go on our journey hand in hand.'

'There is much I wanted to do,' Jonah mused. 'I wanted to rob the King as he travelled to York. To see his shrivelled face as I stuck my pistol up his fat German nose and demanded everything he had. Imagine that! And then I would escape, ride to Edinburgh as fast as the wind and dine in the Witchery and deny I had ever been to London. Such would have been my life . . .' Jonah laughed as a militiaman grabbed him by the arm and pulled him from the cart.

Together they were marched into the depths of the dungeons. Down and down they spiralled, along cold dark landings hemmed in by rough-hewn stones braced with iron straps, and through a dank sewer that spilled out of the wall and vanished again down a flight of stone steps into an unused passageway.

As the clatter of their feet echoed in the all-consuming darkness and the air got colder, the chattering of the militia dwindled. A jack-lantern lit their feet, casting the meagre light and criss-cross shadows of the metal candle cage across the walls. The men visibly drewing closer, and shudders of trepidation danced across the back of their necks, standing each hair on its end.

'Where do you take us?' Malachi asked the guard.

'To the royal dungeon. It's not been used since the time of King Richard. You both must be special guests for Malpas to keep you so secure. Not the usual place for a man who stole a spoon. Must want you out of the way for good.'

'I am the man who sold the world, and right from under his nose,' Malachi replied. They marched quickly on into the glow of a fresh torch of burning tar-cloth that lit a large doorway.

'This is your lodgings,' the guard said abruptly, stepping to one side and shuddering as he turned his back. 'We'll be glad to get out of this place too, many rumours of what has gone on down here.'

'The ghosts?' Jonah said, stepping into the cell.

'You know of them, lad?' asked the guard cautiously as he slowly began to close the door.

'My father would never come down here when he was the jailer. One night he and some other men had a bet. Got a boy inmate, strapped a side drum to his chest with a candle mounted on the top and sent him down here alone. They told him to beat the drum with every step he took. He wagered on how far the boy would get.'

'How far did he walk?' The guard tried to make a hasty count of each stride he had taken into the dark depths.

'Two hundred and ninety-nine and he beat no more. Then they heard his screaming. None of them would dare come for him and the lad was never seen again. Father said that the ghosts would let you in, but they would never want to let you out again.' Jonah drew them closer with each word that he whispered. 'It is said', he went on quietly, 'that the boy haunts the steps, and someone, one day, will have to pay the price to see his soul set free.'

A broad silence descended upon the militia. One nervously held the grip of his pistol, whilst another pulled up the collar of his coat against his shaved and sweated neck. They looked at one another and a growing nervousness passed from eye to eye.

Dry-mouthed, the guard attempted a reply. 'Best be going,' he quivered. 'Once you're locked in there'll be no need for a door-man. There will be no escaping from here, will there, boy?' The guard thrust a linen bag into Malachi's hand filled with a fresh ham and flagon of wine. All the militia nodded anxiously, none of them wanting to be left alone with the prospect of a childlike spectre beating their way to hell with a drum and candle.

'No, sir,' said Jonah, covering his mouth with his hand. 'I would never dare leave the cell and face the drummer boy . . .'

The guard quickly slammed the door and turned the lock. There was a scurry of feet as the militia ran along the corridors in double time.

Jonah turned and smiled at Malachi. 'Terrible thing, this fear of ghosts,' he said. The gasps of the guards could be heard echoing along the landings as they clambered back to the daylight.

'But what of the boy?' Malachi asked nervously. 'This is not a laughing matter.'

'If it were true then I would be afraid as they are, but the ghost began its haunting when I saw that guard shudder. It is a haunting of my imagination. Now they are the ones with fear in their bellies and sweat on their backs and we, Magnus Malachi, are in the safest place in London. We have a day before the trial. No one will come down here. The ghosts are but a legend to keep prying eyes away from all the wares that were stolen from the prisoners. What better guard than a terrible spectre to keep the nosy old hag Mrs Devereaux at bay?'

'You're a villain through and through, Mister Ketch,' Malachi said, 'and one that I like very much. It'll be a pleasure to spend my final hours with one such as you.' He plumped himself upon an old wooden bed next to a large empty stone fireplace.

'Then you will have my company for a long time, for I am not planning on dying,' said Jonah, still smiling at his good fortune at being imprisoned in such a place as this. 'We have light and soon we'll have warmth, and when darkness falls we will have our freedom. This was once my home; there is no better place to be imprisoned than this. I know every inch and every stone and tonight we shall be free.'

With that, Jonah set about the transformation of their captivity. Pulling Malachi from the old bed, he took the wooden frame and smashed it to pieces, piling the broken wood into the cavernous fireplace. He then tore the cover off the old straw mattress and wound it around his hand; reaching through the barred window of the cell door, he took a light from the tar lantern in the passageway.

Quickly the dried wood burst into flame and the fire took hold, filling the dungeon with a warm tender light that made bright their circumstances. Malachi squatted like a fat old owl, saying nothing but the occasional grunt of pleasure as Jonah smashed a large table and stoked the fire even higher so that the flames leapt violently up the wide chimney.

Soon they had enough tinder wood to keep a burning in the hearth for a day and a night. Jonah thawed his backside against the flames, then leant back and settled contentedly on the warmed stones next to Malachi. Together they broke the flesh and shared the wine from the linen bag.

Jonah sniffed the flagon before he put it to his lips. 'She has a poisonous way with her, does Lizzy Devereaux,' he said as he smiled at Malachi and took a mouthful of the wine.

'A wicked and poisonous tongue and one that hopefully she will impale in Skullet's ear and suck out what little brains he has,' Malachi replied. The thought of Skullet and Mrs Devereaux sharing breakfast soured the taste of the wine. 'I take it you have some plan to magically transport us from this place?'

'I have something that will take your breath away and is far better than any of your magic: something that'll leave Malpas and Skullet wondering what power has been at work in our lives.' Jonah chewed a large piece of meat from the ham bone and gripped it with his teeth like a mad dog. 'By the time of the trial we'll be long gone. We'll be supping chocolate with Lady Griselda at Strumbelo and working out how to get Tara and Tersias from Solomon.'

'As easy as that?' Malachi asked as he watched Jonah begin to gnaw on the bone.

'As easy as that,' Jonah mumbled through his meat-filled mouth, spluttering pieces of chewed ham over Malachi's sleeve before taking a large swig from the emptying wine bottle. 'I heard that this jail was a palace,' he said thoughtfully, swallowing the chewed mixture of meat and wine. 'King Richard lived in this very room. They say that something horrific happened, something so terrible that he never came back and turned the place into a dungeon.'

Malachi smiled, his heart warmed by the wine and also by the thought that he might soon be seeing Tersias again. Since they had parted, he thought of the boy with affection and not simply as a means to rake in the shillings. 'I suppose this is another of your stories,' he said to Jonah, and laughed as he took the bottle and finished the dregs with a laborious gulp. He looked around the dungeon's thick stone walls that held up the large vaulted dome above their heads. The flames from the fire lit each stone as Malachi tried to imagine the King dining there. ''Twas a little drummer boy,' he said sarcastically as he wiped the dregs from his lips, 'that frightened the King and he got on his horse and ran away into the day's end?'

'It's the truth, I tell you,' Jonah protested as he threw more wood on the fire. 'There's bad blood in these stones. It has never been a happy place, too many dark corners and forgotten passageways. That's why they built the new jail, couldn't get a guard to stay here overnight – too many noises, too many things went wrong.'

'More stories?' Malachi chuckled as the wine numbed his lips.

'I tell you, it's the honest truth. My father told me that one day he cleaned out a cell and put the bed by the wall with a fresh mattress of straw. He filled a bucket with water and emptied out the slop. Then he locked the door and took nine paces . . . . He said it was like the sound of a madman, some-one gone berserk thrashing the wood and ripping the straw. He ran back and the cell had been destroyed. Everything had been ripped to pieces, like some dog had chewed everything. Whatever had done it had been so strong that it could bite through bed wood. There were teeth marks, but nothing was seen of who did it.'

'And that's what your father told you?' Malachi said. 'Sounds like more stories to keep you away from what he was hiding down here.' He snuggled into the warm hearth and pulled his long coat around him like a blanket. 'It has been a long night and Malachi needs time to dream of what he is to do. Wake me when you have your plan ready – and if not, let's approach our judgement without the curse of tiredness hang-ing from our eyelids.'

The magician quickly fell asleep, snoring and shuddering in his dreaming. Jonah watched him, fascinated by his twitching and moaning and the way he curled his thick, dirt-encrusted beard in his fingers and dribbled over the back of his hand.

Far in the distance he heard the jail bell call the ninth hour, its dull thumps rumbling through the passageways and down the landings to the deep dungeon. Jonah lay back against the fireplace and looked about the room. It was stark yet warm, hostile yet with a strange sense of peacefulness. Dungeon, palace or monastery, it mattered not, all he knew was that they had to escape. He turned to look at Malachi again. All fear of him had waned; he stared simply at an old man dressed in a long black coat and magician's hat, his curse-bag strung tempt-ingly from his neck.

167

As the thought of fleecing his companion for what he had in the bag invaded his mind, Jonah pleaded with himself to leave the man alone. Malachi had pledged friendship – on the other hand, the consideration of what treasure lurked a touch away made him drool. After all, he thought to himself, wasn't he going to set the old man free? Surely this could be a down payment for freedom, a small price to pay rescuing him from the gallows.

He reached out towards the bag then stopped, pulling back his hand and squeezing it into a tight fist, hoping the desire to rob Malachi would leave him. Again his hand reached out towards the bag, getting closer and closer. He wanted to shout out to wake the man from his dreaming so he would be stopped.

The battle raged in his heart. Still willing himself to prevent his fingers from slipping the clasp and furrowing through the sack, lightening it of every precious stone and trinket it might contain, he touched the bag. Malachi didn't move. Jonah edged his hand close, his fingers instinctively making their way to the clasp. It was as if Jonah was watching someone else, a hand like his, yet not his own. Not wanting to take part and yet loving what he did – this was as much a part of his life as drawing his waking breath. His fingers took hold of the tiny clasp that had been warmed by the glow of the fire. It felt flesh-like in his touch, as if from within it he could sense the beating of a heart. Jonah stopped and looked at Malachi – he slept on, moaning and drooling like a small child, unaware of the fleecing taking place under his long sniffling nose. With three fingers, Jonah lifted the catch, slipped the flap and delved into the depths of the bag.

It was fire-warmed and freshly moist with a lining of smooth, velvety mould that stuck to the back of his hand. Jonah could sense a multitude of offerings with his fingertips.

Suddenly he caressed the cold metal of a thick, stone-encrusted ring. The tip of his finger smoothed its way around the edge, counting the cut stones one by one. Carefully he picked it from the bag, sliding his hand softly and quietly so as not to disturb the magician.

Malachi didn't move; he snored on, panting and moaning, clutching his beard and rubbing flakes of incense from each greasy strand. Jonah picked the ring twixt thumb and forefinger, holding his breath as he slipped it silently from Malachi's curse bag. He cared not for the potions or amulets that brushed against him as he retrieved the heavy signet from the dark depths. It was strangely heavy, and snagged as he lifted it from the bag and pulled it into the light of the fire.

He gave a sudden fearful gasp and fell from the hearth to the cold stone floor, dropping the ring and the dried finger to which it was set. It rolled like a giant's claw towards the flames. For a split second he thought to leave it to be engulfed. His eyes darted from Malachi to the ringed finger and back again, checking the depth of his slumber. Jonah's hand darted towards the flames, picked up the finger by its long black nail and firmly plunged it into his coat pocket. Then he slumped back to the fireside and pretended to be asleep.

Cautiously he opened one eye to look at Malachi – the magician slept on. Jonah pulled the finger from his pocket and examined the nicotine-dried skin and crusted fingernail that had been cut from the hand of some poor, unfortunate woman.

Tabula Rasa

Solomon danced from step to step of the spiral staircase as he led a procession of seven favoured disciples high into the tower that dominated his Citadel and overlooked the city. He smiled blithely as he looked out through the grubby arched windows that were etched into the golden dome of the roof. Below him was London, squalid and begrimed, veiled in a layer of damp grey ash that coated every rooftop as the last drops of the morning rain splattered against the buildings.

To the east, the sun feebly edged its path higher, vainly trying to break through the thinning mist as the strands of a glistening rainbow bent from the sky and lit the pinnacles of Fleet Prison.

Tersias and Tara followed on behind Solomon, their hands now tied and the golden crown pushed firmly upon the boy's head. Dragging his weight, Campion struggled on behind, panting and gasping as he pulled each cumbersome leg up each step.

'Quickly,' begged Solomon. 'We have to see our city, speak out upon it and command it with our hearts.'

The seven disciples followed, running to the windows, raising their hands to heaven and babbling like madmen in a language that Tara could not understand. She looked around the lime-washed room. From the high vaulted ceiling, long, hooped chains dangled down. She saw that they were attached to large round baffle boards that could be opened to let in more light along with the London smog. In the centre of the room was a large crystal dome that appeared to be balanced on what was once a wooden barrel. By one of the principal arches was an oak throne, the match of that to which Tersias had been tied in his cell. It was garlanded in fresh lavender and ivy; red petals were strewn about it. By the throne was a long wicker basket woven of yew wands into the shape of a thin sarcophagus; the lid of this coffin was decorated with sorrel leaves and rue spikes. A suit of purple clothes was dressed upon a headless manikin that stood stiffly by the throne. All was meticulously prepared, neatly pressed and ready for her to wear.

Solomon looked at Tara as he ran his hand down the rough fibres of the purple coat sleeve and smiled. 'Soon, my dear, this will all be yours.' He crossed the room to the crystal. 'Come, see . . . the like of which you may have never seen before, nor ever see again.' He beckoned to Tara to follow him. His disciples were still babbling and chanting as they looked out over London, speaking to the spirit of the city.

Tara slowly crossed the room. It was cold and smelt strongly of lavender. Solomon held out his hand as Tara looked into the large dome-shaped crystal that magnified all around it. She could see a bright light far below that lit the branches of a tree. Suddenly she realised that she had seen this before. The recognition of what she saw crossed her face as she clenched her teeth and fought back a swirling dizziness that spun in her head.

'That's right, my dear, you remember well,' Solomon said as he began to untie her wrists. 'It is the room of the locusts and that which you see is the tree of life. Soon they will be ready and from this place they will begin their journey across the city. They will cleanse it of everyone who does not follow me. From their judgement there will be no salvation.'

Tara didn't reply. Her eyes were transfixed on a single swirling locust that spiralled upwards towards her, fixing itself upon the crystal and staring at her through a gigantic black compound eye that glistened at its edges in a multitude of colours. The creature appeared to glare at her, following her movements as she edged around the crystal and away from Solomon.

'It likes you,' Solomon said as he took hold of a baffle chain and began to pull a wooden board away from the high vaulted roof. 'See. When the time is right the locusts will rise up from the tree and I will open the panels of the hypnoscope and they will fly up and out of the baffles, from the tower and over the city.' He raised one brow and smiled tightly. 'Remember what they can do. No one will escape them. The city will be plucked bare, but we will be safe. The fragrance of our robes will keep them from us.' Tara saw that the cask holding up the crystal had slatted panel doors that ran around the circumference, each locked with a small brass catch in the shape of a shrivelled hand.

Solomon toyed with one of the catches as he stared at her. 'So quiet, so thoughtful and never complaining,' he said as he moved towards her. 'Look at the creature, see how beautiful a beast it is. I found them myself, searched the known world and for many years have changed them little by little until they are made by my design. In ancient times they would eat the flesh of the field and plagued mankind by stripping the land bare. Now they will plague mankind again, and this time I have given them a taste for different flesh.'

'A man can't do that,' Tara blurted out. 'You're not the creator of the world, you didn't set the stars in their place.' She pinched her own hand sharply, so the pain would give vent to her growing anger as her stomach twisted and churned. 'How can you change the way in which a creature lives? It's not right.'

'Right and wrong are just different perspectives. There will soon come a time when we will not need an egg for a chicken and you or I can live on for ever by growing a new heart. I have discovered the foundations of life, and with these locusts I will bring an end to the decay of this world and herald the new.' Solomon scoffed as he strutted about the room. 'The King has no power and Parliament lines its own pocket. Politicians and princes, they are both the same, men of ignoble birth clambering for recognition. Their time has passed, the clock is now set for the empire of Solomon.'

Tara could see that he was convinced by his own words. Around her the chanting grew louder and louder as the disciples called upon the sun to shed its rays upon the rooftops. Campion gripped Tersias by the collar, and from the corner of her eye she saw the brute dragging the boy across the floor and placing him in the oak throne, strapping his arms to the wooden rests.

'Is she going to join us?' Campion asked abruptly, wiping the slaver from his flaking skin.

Solomon turned and looked him up and down as if the question should never have been asked. 'Dear Campion appears to be concerned for your future. As you can see, we have a pilgrim suit for you to wear. Taking the purple will signify to the world that you are one with us, never to leave. It is not just an outfit of clothing but a sacrament. In taking this you will denounce who you are and what you once were, it'll be a new birth with a new family. Come girl, now is the time.' Solomon took a small silver goblet from his coat pocket and, unscrewing the tight lid, offered the vessel to her. 'One sip and an oath and all will be well. You will be dead to the past and alive to the future. All I have will be yours, there is a kingdom waiting and you will be queen.'

Frantically Tara looked around the room for a way of escape.

The disciples turned from the windows and gathered about her, chanting and wailing with dark words that tore at her heart. She thought of Jonah – lost, unknown, in a different world. She saw Solomon's smile contort to a rough grimace as his stunted limbs jerked towards her, the light flashing from the chalice. She could hear Tersias grunting in the chair, his mouth gagged by Campion, and she began to drown in the mass of disciples who now filed up the spiral staircase and into the chamber.

Pressed to the wall by the throng of faces, Tara held her hands to her eyes, covering them from the blank stares that she now faced from all the disciples. The noise grew louder and louder, turning her mind so that she found it hard to keep to her feet. Before her was Solomon, always a yard away, holding out his hand, offering her the chalice.

'Do this for me, little girl,' he said calmly. She looked towards Tersias, whose screams beckoned her help. 'He will be safe. All you have to do is drink the cup and all will be well. Campion will hurt him no more and our protection shall be upon you.' Now Solomon was excited, stumbling over his words, one hand shakily grasping the chalice and the other fumbling with the purple band around his neck. 'Please, my dear,' he said. He swallowed hard, gulping back his drool as he stared upon her.

'NO!' she screamed. She lashed out with her arms to push back the disciples, her mind spinning faster and faster as the room swirled about her.

'Don't make us hurt him any more.' Solomon coughed harshly as Tersias let out another deep and painful groan. 'Campion has desires towards the lad that he will want to fulfil. He is a cruel man who was born to this work. Please don't allow him the satisfaction of his heart.'

Tersias screamed again as a disciple took hold of her arm and twisted it stiffly up her back. '*Drink* . . . *Drink* . . . *Drink*,' they began to chant, and they pushed her towards the crystal dome and the staring black locust that looked as if it were desperately scratching at the surface of its prison, trying to break through to her.

Engulfed by the power and the presence of the people, Tara fell to her knees, sobbing for relief from the torment. She held out her quivering white palms towards Solomon, tears dripping into her cupped hands as the disciples stood around her, wailing in words she could not understand but which had the power to force her further to the floor.

'YIELD TO ME!' Solomon screamed, his face red and his hands shaking and his eyes bulging from their sockets with his desperation.

Tara could no longer think nor hear. Magic lanterns of bright blue light began to quickly flash through her mind. Her head spun faster as from all around the brightness was sucked from her vision as if a thick, dark blanket was now cast about her. In that moment she was savagely cut from the world. She was forced back into a darkened corner of her soul. All about her was torment and chaos as her body twitched and convulsed, but there in the darkness she was utterly alone.

Dully, she could feel her head being held back and the pressing of cold silver against her foaming lips. Only the sensation of stale wine dribbling over her stiffened tongue and the picking of a myriad of sharpened fingernails against her skin kept her tenuous linked to the world. There was no noise, no struggle. The ranting and shaking of Solomon's disciples ebbed in her mind to a sound like the rustling of leaves on a winter day. His voice was a dull irritation somewhere in the darkened sky high above her head. She could make out vague commands and felt her body being twisted and moulded by many hands. There was no pain – not in this place. Here was the room to which she had been

175

dragged many times when the world had threatened her with its intolerable madness. This was her enforced hiding place, a sanctuary of the mind and a bastion for her troubled spirit.

Tara gulped again. As if from far away she could sense more drops of the foul vineous liquid dripping through her clenched teeth and trickling like hot vinegar down the back of her throat. She coughed out her tongue as her head thrashed from side to side, freeing itself from the many hands that grasped her hair.

From within her she heard the sound of a snake, hissing in the blackness and drowning out the world. As the spasm left her, this creature would always come, a reminder of what she had endured and a harbinger of her future woes. In the darkness she was aware of the ebbing of the paroxysm as the last sensation of trembling shook her fingertips. Then came a deep and sourly doleful sleep that completely closed her mind to the world.

Slowly and painfully, Tara opened her eyes to the brightness of the morning. Sunlight flooded into the room. Before her stood the dwarfish frame of Solomon. In his hand he carried a shard of broken looking-glass in which she caught a dim reflection of her face. The numbness of the fit held her for a moment as she tried to lift her hand from the floor. Somehow there was a difference. Her body felt larger than before, her arms seemed to stretch out into the distance and across the room like long branches. Clumsily she tried to gain her footing, but found that her right leg was bound back by a sharp contraction that held it fast as if the bones were forged of iron. Her eyes were clouded and in the mist of her vision she realised that she had been dressed in the pilgrims' clothing, the rough purple jacket itching her skin.

Solomon stared at her. He flashed knives of sharp sunlight across her face with the mirror, sweeping through the mist like a summer beacon. 'You are back in this world?' he asked quietly as he got on one knee and peered closely into her face. 'The wine will make you drowsy for two nights, but on the third day you will wake as a new creature, transformed, changed from a cygnet to a swan.' He deepened his voice, speaking slowly and glinting the bright sunlight across her face. 'Listen to me, child. You are dying and I can save you and I can take away the convulsions. Solomon and only Solomon can do this for you. I mean you no harm and in this there is no trick. Listen to my voice, hear my words. I am the only one you can trust, no other. It is I, Solomon, your saviour, your healer, your redeemer. I am the master of your soul and the focus of all your thoughts. When you hear my name you will rejoice. For me there will be no disobedience. Listen to my voice.'

Tara could not escape his words; they were like pounding fists that hammered the mind, beating her resistance further away as the hissing of the snake grew louder and louder. 'Tersias,' she asked softly. 'What of the boy?'

'He is safe. The boy is by your side. No harm will come to him. I, Solomon will save him.'

'Solomon will save him . . .' She repeated the words over and over, knowing them to be true, knowing them to be the only words that would ever matter. 'Solomon . . .' she muttered to herself, and the word sounded through her body like a shimmering light as a heavy dark slumber climbed through her veins, numbing every muscle and enveloping her in a bruising blackness.

'Sleep, my child, and wake to a new life.' Solomon spoke in the tone of a prayer, and he summoned Campion to help him lift Tara into the yew coffin. Together they bundled her clumsily into the long basket that had been lined in purple silk and strewn with goose feathers. Tara didn't stir; she was gripped by the trance and the vile potency of the linctus from the chalice.

Solomon roughly took a clump of her red hair in his hand, pulling the long strands through his fingers. 'This is not right,' he said as his voice trembled. 'Have someone shave her head and wipe the paint from her face, then she shall be . . . perfect.' He laughed as he closed the lid to the basket and tied the leather thongs at each end, securing them tightly. 'Such a boyish face, there is a difference to this child more than in her manner. She was a good choice, Campion, a good choice.'

Campion grunted as he was left to drag the coffin across the room and lift it upon a long window ledge at the far side of the chamber, away from the passage of the sun. 'What about the boy?' he asked. He waddled back to the crystal and watched the locust eating its own leg. 'Are we to do the same with him?'

'I cannot meddle with his mind,' Solomon replied as he put the shard of looking-glass into his pocket. 'He is far too precious, an oracle as has never been seen before, and he is mine.'

Solomon walked across the room to the oak throne and tapped the boy on the shoulder. 'Tersias . . . Tersias, can you hear me?' he said, then tapped loudly on the metal crown that was pressed upon the boy's head. 'It is time for you to perform for Uncle Solomon, to call upon what powers you desire and tell me no lies.'

Tersias remained silent, his eyelids firmly shut and his lips sealed. The golden crown squeezed his head, pressing against his face, moulding it to the shape of the metal. He had heard every one of Solomon's words and listened to Tara as she had been drugged and metamorphosed before him. He knew what would come, not through some celestial knowledge but through experience – experience of desperate men and the desires of their hearts. First would be the pleading for him to speak, then the threats and finally the beating. As sure as night would follow day and swallow the summer sun, he knew that

178

Solomon would beg, urge and then coerce him to speak. This man was no different; the pious were noted for their cruelty.

Campion came to him first, grabbing him by the neck with one hand as he peeled the helmet from him and then prodded him in the eyes with his short fat fingers. 'He is definitely blind,' he said to Solomon as Tersias howled in pain. 'How can he see the future if he has no sight?'

Solomon cackled and rubbed his hands. 'He does not need eyes to see, Campion. His sight is not from this world. There are eyes of creatures we know little about. They can see the future, tell of what will happen. They listen to the ramblings of kings and nations. Every court has its own spirit, every city a fallen angel. These seraphic beings know the ways of men and ordain our future. Tersias can hear them speak, he can talk to them and they share with him what many would die to hear.' Solomon looked around the room anxiously; his shoulder twitched several times as if to rid itself of some invisible creature that sat upon it. 'For all we know, we could be in the presence of a legion of such beings. They could be all around, listening to our words and guiding our thoughts. Think of it, Campion – we could be puppets to a far higher master. All that I desire could be the whisperings of some devil.'

Campion looked about him, wiping his arms as if to rid himself of invisible demonic strands. He glanced at Tersias and then across the chamber to the wicker coffin, rubbing the tiredness from his face and wrinkling his brow in deep frustration. 'Why do we not speak to them ourselves and have done with the boy?'

'If only that were possible,' Solomon replied as he took hold of Tersias by the chin. 'If only . . .'

Tersias opened his eyes and looked up. From far away he could hear the wingbeats of the Wretchkin flying over the city towards the tower as it wafted gently through the smoke and mist. 'Tersias . . . I can see you,' it called softly as it spiralled above him. 'I can see your face.'

'It comes to me,' the boy said unexpectedly, taking Solomon by complete surprise. 'Let us both go free or I will tell the Wretchkin of what you have done and ask it to rip out your throat.'

Campion looked about him, not sure if he could hear the creature above the pinnacle. Solomon saw his panic and laughed heartily. 'Tell it what you want, but if any harm befalls me I am sure Campion will take great pleasure in sailing his basket upon the Thames . . . However, I do not think your friend is ready to be transformed into a fish.'

'I will tell the Wretchkin whatever its asks of me. Touch the girl and I will kill you myself.'

'I think, Campion, that the boy has lost his heart to our latest disciple. Such is the power of love. But in this case it will never conquer all.' Solomon rolled back the sleeves of his coat and untied the purple scarf from around his neck, folding it neatly and placing it in his pocket. 'Love – such a strange thing. I remember once, as a child, loving a dog. Whatever I did to it, no matter how cruel I could be, the creature never remembered my transgressions. Unconditional, all-forgiving love. Fit for dogs – but I pride myself as being far more sophisticated than a canine wit.' Solomon looked at Campion. 'Make ready, my friend. If the creature that visits us causes any harm, kill the boy. His death will send the beast away and it will harm us no more.'

It was then that the Wretchkin slipped silently into the room. For several moments there was complete quiet as it looked closely at Solomon, staring into his eyes and examining every inch of his frame. The creature stroked his face and Solomon, feeling the touch like a shallow breeze but unable to see the spirit, shivered suddenly.

'Is it here, boy?' he asked Tersias anxiously, stepping back to the crystal.

180

'I am everywhere,' the Wretchkin replied suddenly through the boy, the sound of his voice altered to that of the creature. 'You are a brave man, playing with my oracle. Either that or a fool.'

'I am neither fool nor braggadocio. All I want from you is to know my future. Tell me and the boy can go free.' Solomon stood his ground, his hand gripping the broken looking-glass, ready to cut the life from the boy. His eyes flickered one way then the next, hoping to catch a glimpse of the creature. 'That is not much to ask, is it?'

'It is more than many men would ever dare to think. Why are you so obsessed with your future? Is there no contentment with the life you have?' Tersias convulsed as the words of the Wretchkin shuddered through his mouth. 'For the past three thousand years I have come to the likes of you and shown them the way. Your kind is the worst. Tell the world you are the saviour, trick them into following you, and when what you said was the truth doesn't come to pass you'll slope off and hide or poison your disciples. You'll tell them that the only way to get to the Promised Land is by dying to this life. Is that the truth?'

'It was something that had crossed my mind. Only you can tell me what is to come.' Solomon clutched the glass shard in his hand, his heart telling him to end the boy's life and despatch the creature back to the darkness.

'That is a wicked thought, Solomon,' the creature said as it prowled around him and pinched his ear with its thick claws. 'Do not even think of harming the boy. I have not done with him yet.'

'Then tell me what I need to know and I will be done with him,' Solomon snapped at the Wretchkin, angry that his thoughts should be so transparent. The spirit looked at him intently, watching the quiver of his eyelid and the twitch of his mouth. Solomon wetted his lips, his tongue flickering like a frightened snake.

'Listen and this will be done,' the creature spoke slowly as Tersias thrashed from side to side, his heart pounding and thick beads of sweat dripping across his face. 'Never blind the boy with your talismans. I will speak to him when I want. Nor imprison him where he cannot be found.' The Wretchkin paused, as his consideration was drawn to the crystal and the locust that had now begun to feast upon its own legs, hanging to the glass by the slightest barb.

The silence of the creature drove Solomon to distraction. 'Do you still stay with us?' he asked, his voice fraught with panic. 'Whatever you want, I will do. The boy shall lodge with me and never wear the crown again, or be placed in the circle. That I promise, but *please*, tell me what is to come . . .'

The Wretchkin laughed, his mirth apparent on the lips of the boy as a thin grimace that contorted his innocent face. 'So mote it be, Solomon. From your mind I gather that your concern is for your plans and what will happen when you release the locusts.' Tersias groaned as the words were whispered from his lips. 'The way for you is not as you desire. Tell Lord Malpas you have the boy, he too searches for him. Malpas would wish to be Emperor, to lead a revolution and do away with the King. In him you will have a companion for your quest. Do this and all you could ever imagine would be yours.' The Wretchkin stalked across the room and stood over the interlaced wands of yew that formed the wicker coffin. 'Find the friend of the girl and you will also find what Malpas searches for. Her companion has a knife and an alabaster box that he stole from Malpas. It is vital that these are found soon. In that I will have my desire. Give Tersias food and treat him well, Solomon. I will be watching. Every breath you take may be your last.'

Foscari

In the royal dungeon in Fleet Prison, Joanh emerged sullen and resentful from the long sleep that had held him throughout the day. He wiped the grit from his eyes with the back of his hand and studied the fading red embers of the fire. In the hearth light he felt the warmth of the embers against his face. But the cold night air fell from the wide chimney, wafting the glimmers and sending puffs of swirling smoke and ash spinning around the hearth like tiny whirlwinds.

Malachi slept on, his head nodding back and forth, his lips quivering with each and every breath as if uttering a silent curse. Night was here, soon it would be time to leave the dungeon far behind and escape. Pulling up the collar of his coat and wrapping the wide lapels tightly around himself, Jonah huddled closer to the flames and looked up the cavernous, black chimney. High above he could hear the chiming of a distant bell. Five long carillons and then silence as a cold gust blew down a fall of black soot. It fell upon the glimmers of fire like black snow.

Jonah took a deep breath, the smell of the soot filling his head with thoughts of childhood. He remembered the chimney boy with his badger brush and harsh cough that would echo down the smokestack and into his room. The boy's master would shout *Climb higher, Brush faster*, as showers of black dust fell in thick clumps and beat against the dirty blanket that was wedged against the fire-breast with a long black brush. Then the boy would appear, blackened and choking, from under the blanket and he would be brusquely brushed down by his master and wrapped in the old blanket and carried from the house spluttering, and not a drop of dust then fell to the floor.

Malachi stirred, the cold creeping through his feet. He opened one tacky eye and stared at Jonah. 'Still here?' he said, his teeth chattering. 'Thought you would be long gone by now, leaving old Malachi to fend for himself and dangle alone.'

Jonah took hold of the old man by his fingers and wrapped them in his palms to warm them through. 'Promised I would stay and that together we would leave.' He blew a soft warm breath upon his hands. 'I said we would escape and together we will. I have a plan. When they come for us it will be as if we have vanished without a trace.'

'Then we'd better be quick, I don't think Skullet will leave us here for long without having someone check upon us. Ghosts or not, they'll be down and have us manacled before night is out. He'll have breakfasted upon the delights of Mrs Devereaux and when he's done picking over her bits his mind will be back to our fate.'

'We'd better be on our way then,' Jonah said, and he got up from the hearth and began to stack the broken beams of the table against the back of the deep fireplace, far enough from the flames so they would not catch alight. Malachi watched as Jonah busied himself back and forth, pulling long beams of old dried wood and breaking them in half. One by one he interwove them, stacking the planks higher and higher. Malachi, intrigued by the boy, raised one eyebrow and watched him work like a young bee building a hive.

'Should I ask what you are doing?' Malachi enquired as he got to his feet and painfully stretched out his arms towards the ceiling.

184

'No,' replied the boy.

'Are you going to burn down the prison and we walk from the ashes like a pair of fat phoenix?'

'No.' Jonah was lost in what he was doing.

'Then we are to tunnel from this place and what you are preparing is a celebratory fire?'

'No.' He smiled. 'But soon you will see for yourself.' Jonah busied himself stacking the wood against the sidewalls of the fireplace, linking them together to form a wooden web. 'Tonight, Malachi, we will make our escape through the roof and emerge into the city.'

'Climb? Do you expect me to climb?' Malachi asked incredulously as he looked at his frail, worn hands.

'If you could fly, then that would be an option. We have but one way and that is through the chimney, onto the roof, across to the wall and then into the night. Skullet won't find us and we will be free.'

'I can't . . .' Malachi said as he turned quickly from him.

'You can't give up before you try,' Jonah snapped. 'I am but a lad and the thought of having my neck stretched is not one I wish to entertain. You can come with me and together we can escape. I can't leave you.' Jonah grabbed the man by his coat and pulled him back. 'What would you do, stay here and die?'

'You wouldn't understand. Any other way and I would join you, but this – it is too much to ask.'

'There is no other way. Do you have some magic to melt the stone, a spell to soften the locks and dazzle the guards? Speak, Malachi, or else follow me,' Jonah shouted. ''Tis an easy climb, every chimney is made that way. It'll be like climbing the steps to the cathedral and any old hag can do that.'

'It is not the climb, but the cavern itself. The blackness, the pressing of the stones, the narrowness of the tunnel. It is these things I fear – more than hanging from the end of the rope.'

Jonah laughed, his face exploding in a bright smile. 'You would rather die than go into the dark?' he asked as he picked a broken table leg from the floor. 'I'll be your light, a step ahead all the way. I'll keep the stones from falling upon you.'

'But you don't understand,' Malachi argued, his face contorting as the small flickers of the sooty fire cast shadows across his every line. 'I cannot go up the chimney . . . I would have an eruption, an explosion of grief that would cause my head to burst. It's not just the darkness, it is the enormity of the height. I am glad to say that my feet have never left the ground, not even a jump or hop would I ever make for fear of the height to which I could be taken.'

'Fear is a prison that will keep you for life, it is only hope that'll set you free – that's what Uncle Shawshank told me.'

'And what happened to him?' Malachi asked as he crossed the dungeon to the door and peered into the flickering darkness of the passageway.

'He was a circus performer, a rope-walker who would cross the skies from building to building on a tightrope. He was a fearless man . . .'

'And?' interrupted Malachi.

'Shawshank went to the Mayfair, tied a rope from the roof Mr Hatchard's bookshop across Piccadilly, stepped out and . . . fell to his death.' Jonah sighed as he suddenly realised the stupidity of his words. 'But he didn't fear anything, not even his final step, and neither shall you. I thought Magnus Malachi was a powerful magician, not a snivelling coward.'

'Magician I am, coward I am also,' Malachi stuttered, pulling nervously on his beard. 'I once cast a flying spell, hoping from that day I would be able to soar over the city and amaze the world. The more I thought of this the more I became frightened of what would happen. How would I get down from such an exploit, what would happen to me if I was always to remain in the air?' Malachi gripped the bars on the door as if to root himself to the earth. 'I thought the spirits that I had tried to enchant would come at a moment's notice and levitate me from the ground, never letting me go. So I stay on the ground, feet firmly planted. Climbing in deep darkness is for others and not old Malachi.'

'Then I go alone,' Jonah said as he stepped into the fireplace among the smouldering coals and peered up the chimney.

'You'll burn, boy,' Malachi shouted as he scurried across the room. 'The walls will be red hot.'

'Where you and I are destined to end up will be even hotter and I have no time for redemption,' the boy shouted as he wrapped the cuffs of his coat around his hands and looked up to grasp the first stone he could reach. The wound to his arm gave a sudden sharp bite that sweated his brow. 'Come on, Malachi, follow me and we shall escape this place and Skullet. If not for me, for Tersias. I know your heart misses him and I fear he will need you more now he has fallen into the hands of Solomon.'

Malachi looked about him, looking for something to show him the future. In his excitement he shuffled from one foot to the other, his mind torn apart by his fear of the chimney and his resignation to the hangman's rope. 'Jonah, don't leave an old man in this misery,' he whimpered.

'Then follow me and I will help you climb. I promise your feet will be on solid rock, there are more steps here than in the Tower of London.' Jonah gripped on to the first stone and pulled himself from the ground. The stone seared his grip like a hot loaf picked from the oven. He climbed quickly and in several steps found the first ledge. It was crammed with decades of thick black soot that swirled around him as he got to his feet and looked back down the chimney to the smouldering fire that lay in the hearth.

There, peering back at him like a large bearded owl, was Malachi. 'Where is my first footing?' he whispered, his words floating upwards on the hot thermals of the fire as he feebly grasped a loose stone.

'Higher, Malachi, and to your right. Look how they are set in the wall ready for you to climb.'

Malachi looked up. In the glimmer was a stairway to heaven made of stones projecting from the wall and spiralling the chimney. He could make out the ghostlike darkened figure of Jonah, now edged in the black soot that whirled about him in the updraught. 'Pray for me, boy. My throat is already burning like these coals and my heart beats so loudly I am deaf to the world.'

Malachi picked his way to the first ledge as Jonah pressed on above him. The steps got wider as they climbed, each the width of a double span; flat stones three inches thick and set deeply into the walls. Soon his beard was coated in thick black soot. Around him, swirls of smoke smouldered upwards, biting at his throat. As he climbed he kept his eyes tightly shut, groping for every stone and telling himself he had nothing to fear. He muttered as he went higher, trying to remember the words of some old spell to protect himself from the crushing blackness and the scorching heat that chased him.

From high above, the whispering of Jonah urged him onwards. Malachi looked up and opened his eyes. In the darkness he could see the glow of a faint light that emanated from the wall of the chimney. Jonah had stopped, and he gestured for Malachi to be silent. The magician pulled himself on to the ledge where Jonah stood, looking through the back slat of an empty fireplace. His soot-blackened face was lit by the dim light that came through the narrow chimney flue. The sound of men talking in a room, their voices competing with one another to be heard, filled the smokestack. One scornful voice cut above the others, piercing the darkness and setting Jonah's mind on edge.

'Militia,' Jonah whispered into Malachi's ear. 'We are at the level of the ground.'

'Hear that?' said an anxious voice from the room.

'What?' asked another.

'Whispering, right beside me, as if someone was speaking in my ear.'

'What did they say?' another said scornfully. The sound of a metal tankard being thrown across the room echoed into the chimney. 'You've drunk too much, you'll be telling us that you can see the ghost of that drummer-boy young Ketch was on about.'

'I tell you I heard something whispering. You're not getting me down in those dungeons again – you'll all go together, but not me. It's me he's after.'

Suddenly the man stopped speaking as a door was flung open, smashing loudly against the wall. Jonah and Malachi heard from within the room the sound of Skullet's voice.

'Captain!' he shouted loudly, his voice muffled by the fire-back to a loud grunt. 'Take your men and bring the prisoners to the yard. They are to be taken to Vamana House. Lord Malpas has prepared a trial for midnight in the Great Hall. Judge Dobson has been dragged from his dotage – he is a gentleman more willing to judge the hearts of others than himself. Even the creator has more pity on a bad soul than the Honourable Dobson.' Skullet scoffed loudly. 'When he finds them guilty . . . they are to be executed in the morning.'

Jonah sensed there was a hesitation in Skullet's voice, as if something whispered to him that he was being overheard. There was then the sound of the door slamming and several men pushing over wooden chairs and running from the room. As they ran they clattered their sabres, frantically fighting with one another so as not to be the one left behind.

'They are coming for us and soon will find that we are gone,' Malachi said. 'The militia will know the only way out is to the roof, and then they will catch us again and have done with us.' He gripped the stones above the ledge, steadying himself as he looked down to the dim glow.

Jonah didn't reply as he pulled at a stone above his head. It came away in a great cloud of black dust and cobwebs and a blistering of bolting spiders, and with one hand Jonah threw it down the shaft to the smouldering fire below. It crashed against the neatly intertwined stack of wood that Jonah had patiently built around the walls of the chimney. There was a clattering of broken boards as one by one the pieces of wood fell into the centre of the fire. This pile of tinder-dry firewood quickly burst into flames, the bright light illuminating the heights of the chimney and sending blasts of hot smoke towards them.

'It'll keep them off our backs for some time,' Jonah said. In the half-light he beckoned Malachi to follow him higher. 'Keep climbing behind me, quickly we will lose our breath as the fire grows, our only hope is to get to the stack before we dry like kippers.'

Malachi didn't relish the thought of dying in the smokestack and being slowly dried by the dense fumes that now sucked at his throat.

'I hope . . . you know . . . what you are doing, Jonah.' Malachi coughed out the words. The smoke began to sting his sore eye-balls as they climbed hand over hand towards the stars and the ever-brightening opening above their heads.

'I can't go on,' Malachi said. He felt the walls hemming him in, pressing closer and closer like the jaws of a giant sprung trap.

'Look to the stars,' Jonah shouted. 'There you will have your freedom.'

'I have looked to the stars all my life and they have been like lying wives, never telling me the truth and squandering all I have. What good will they do me now?' Malachi asked as a billow of sulphurous fumes engulfed them both in thick blue smoke.

Within a minute they had reached a large ledge that stuck out from two sides of the chimney to form a small balcony. It was littered with the dried carcasses of long-dead crows on which the crawling red mites appeared to glow in the starlight that flooded through the four chimney stacks above their heads.

'Three feet and we'll be free!' Jonah shouted as if to wake the dead, his words falling and spewing forth from the fireplace in the dungeon below just as Skullet and the militia burst into the room.

'Find them!' shouted Skullet. His command billowed upwards with the flames and smoke as his men scoured the dungeon for any sign of the *foscari*. 'They cannot be far, Mrs Devereaux told me that no one could ever escape from here. We are below ground, there is no way out . . .' It was then that he saw the blazing fire, and a sudden realisation of their escape span through his mind. 'Spring-heeled Jack!' he said to himself as he ran across the room. 'They've escaped up the chimney . . . You, stay here,' he said, pointing to the Captain of the Guard. 'The rest of you up to the roof. There'll be hell to pay if either one of them gets free and mark my words, one of you will take their place on the gallows if they escape. *Quickly . . .*'

The militia ran to the door, not one staying to guard the fireplace, leaving Skullet by himself with only the flickering glow of the flames to give him light.

'Come back!' he shouted. But the sound of their clambering footsteps beat away into the distance, up the passageways and dark stairwells towards the surface and the starry night. 'I want one of you with me . . . What if they return?' Skullet realised that they did not want to hear and would never come back. He looked to the fire, a dark thought quickly shooting through his mind like a blaze-blackened arrow. 'Roast pig,' he said to himself, and he began to scurry about the dungeon picking up the leftover pieces of the broken tables and chairs and piling them upon the heap of broken wood that Jonah had stacked by the fire. 'You may escape the gallows, but from this there will be no freedom.' Skullet shouted through the fire, knowing his words would carry up the chimney as he threw more and more wood upon the fire.

High above, Jonah looked up to the narrow stacks that were wedged in against the capping stones on top of the chimney. 'We'll have to break out of this place,' he said.

'Is it wide enough for us to climb out?' Malachi asked as the smoke from the growing conflagration billowed around them with its choking fumes. 'I cannot stay in this tomb a moment longer. If the smoke doesn't kill me then the pressing of the walls within will tear my soul apart.'

Jonah scrambled from the balcony up to the chimney pot. He held his breath, grappled his way through the opening and squeezed himself out of the smokestack. Far below he could see the militia running around the courtyard of the prison, looking for a way to the roof. The noise of their escape had woken Mrs Devereaux, who bustled about the prison gate, looking up at Jonah and shouting curses as she wiped her mutton-dripping hands upon her apron.

Wildly, Jonah pulled at the chimney pot, hoping to pull it from its base, knowing that Malachi would never be able to escape through it. The powder-dry cement broke free and the thick, hard-baked terracotta shattered into splinters that scuttled over the tiled roof and cascaded to the courtyard below, showering the militia with shards of red pot.

Their screams echoed out from the prison and into the city.

Mrs Devereaux fulfilled her duty as jailer by frantically swinging from the prison bell to warn the world of the escape. Jonah laughed as she dangled from the rope like a fat pigeon hung by its feet. Her shrieks and caterwauling raised the prisoners from their lice-filled beds to stare down at her as she swung back and forth, fearful of letting go of the rope.

As the choking sounds of Malachi came from deep inside a thick cloud of smoke that swelled up from within the stack, Jonah grabbed another chimney pot, then another, tearing them with his bare hands from the capping stones. One by one he threw the terracotta pots to the ground far below, caring not for who they rained upon. Then there was a sudden clattering of a ladder against the roof tiles and, turning quickly, Jonah saw that the militia were about to scale the rooftop.

With one hand he reached in to Malachi. 'Quickly, take my hand and I will pull you free,' he said. He tried to drag more debris from the capping stones to make the hole bigger for the magician. 'If only your spirits would raise you through the roof and hear your spell.'

'I fear I have been talking to myself.' Malachi coughed as he took Jonah's hand and heaved himself upwards towards the starlight.

Jonah pulled and pulled and at last Malachi squeezed himself through the hole and into the fresh air. He choked as the cold night breeze throttled his lungs, burning them with its chilling gasps.

'Run, Jonah, make good your escape,' he said, wheezing breathlessly as smoke billowed from his beard as if he were a tired old dragon. 'I cannot go on . . . no further . . . It is finished.'

'You must!' Jonah shouted back above the screams of Mrs Devereaux, the clanging of the prison bell and the shouts of the militia mounting the ladder. 'I will not leave you behind.'

'In this you will have to. I am stuck like a rat in the trap. Wedged by my indulgences to the iron-bracing strap that encircles every pot and I cannot be free of it,' the magician said, resigned to his fate, and he pulled his curse bag from inside his coat. 'Here, take this. It is my spellbinder, the only thing of value I have, it'll be yours. Live in the stable – look after the boy and forget this night.' Malachi grovelled in the bag, unable to find what he sought. 'It has gone . . . I must have . . .'

'No, Malachi. When you were asleep I lightened your sack and for that I am ashamed. But as the stars bear witness to my words I will come back for you. Lord Malpas will not have his way.'

'Then run like Spring-heeled Jack and frighten the children as they sleep with your devil's feet. Leave Magnus Malachi . . . This is a good place to say goodbye.'

'Not goodbye – but till the morning,' Jonah said. 'I will come back, fleet-footed and with friends.' He ran quickly across the crimson tiles, vanishing in the darkness as the first militiamen cautiously edged their way higher towards the rooftop.

Stabat Mater

The high tower of the Citadel stood against the strong breeze that blew in from the west, lifting with it the pungent smell of the street as it swirled higher. Solomon stood in the lofty archway, his hands raised to the sky, his eyes closed as he whispered to himself. The wicker coffin had been dragged to the middle of the room and placed on a rough-hewn bench by the side of the viewing crystal. A bright red candle set on a tall candlestick lit the room, shining on the limewash in a soft, amber glow, colouring the ceiling with a spectrum of light that shone from the hypnoscope. The locust had gone; all that remained was the barb of a chewed foot caught in a tiny fissure in the surface of the glass, as if the creature had consumed all but this tiny fragment of itself.

The ornate, intertwined lid of the wicker coffin had been placed to one side, its twisted yew wood shining like the thick, dark veins of a beast fresh from labour. Inside the sarcophagus Tara lay motionless, her face whitened with powdered lead, her head shaved, her lips freshly painted with beetle juice. The top of her head was wrapped in tight purple bandages that gripped the skull and squeezed the bones. She smiled softly, dribbles of red lip-ink trickling from her maw as if she had feasted on fresh meat.

The room was crowded with disciples who jostled to scrutinise the corpse, rubbing against each other in their coarse jackets and stiff trousers, men and women alike, all the same, every ounce of uniqueness made bland by their baggy, drab garments and shorn heads. Campion stood in the dark shadows, crunching the bones of each finger and whispering to Tersias. The boy never replied. His hands were tied to the oak throne, the blinding crown placed on his head to serve as a caveat to his compliance. Upon his face were fresh scratches torn deep into his skin, and his cheeks were swollen and bruised with the marks of Solomon's fine gold ring. The bindings upon his wrists were tight to the point of bleeding.

Campion addressed the boy quietly as he waited for his master to speak. 'It'll be my pleasure, boy, my pleasure to take from you your blind eyes and then your life if you don't come with us.'

Solomon turned and in one fluent, cat-like movement stepped from the window and dropped to his knees. As if by sleight of hand he brought forth a golden cylinder spiralled to the shape of a fat snake with jewelled eyes. He untwisted the cap and proffered the contents to the gathering.

'Scaramouch . . . Scaramouch,' he muttered. 'The girl is dead. For three days she has lain in the tomb, the tendrils of decay wrapped about her. But I, Solomon, can bring her back to life. Remember I saved you all, took you from the streets and gave you a new life. So will I for this child.' His voice squeaked as it trembled from his lips, his body shaking with excitement. 'Now is the time.'

The gathering stepped back as Solomon got to his feet and stood before them. He looked at each disciple eye to eye, studying their lined faces and searching out their allegiance as he reminded them of past favours with a glint of his eye. It was as if he gauged some hidden consensus of what they desired as he stood over the coffin to administer the thick beverage that trickled from the serpentine flask. He dripped several large drops onto Tara's reddened lips and then rubbed them into her dried and flaking skin with the tip of his finger.

'So in death, so in life,' he said, gasping between each word in gleeful expectation of what was to come. 'Child of death – dying and knowing what is to come – be set free from your old life!'

There was a flash of Chinese powder and a blue flame danced over Tara's porcelain white skin. Several of the disciples gasped as an exact image of the girl's face appeared to leap from the coffin and be projected upwards to dance before them in mid-air.

'See – life returns. My gift to this child as it was to each of you.' Solomon paused theatrically, a faux tear trickling across his face as he sobbed the words as though they had come from the depths of his heart. 'Life . . . Child,' he said as more powder exploded from his hand. The disciples echoed his words: 'Be raised up and live!'

Tara coughed as the linctus lifted her from her dreaming, bringing warmth and life back to her gelded muscles. Each drop buried its way deeper like strong acid tearing down the veil of darkness and sleep.

'Rise, child, to new life! Come from the grave, leave behind the death of life.' Solomon smiled as with one hand he gently lifted her head from the soft purple pillow.

Tara opened her eyes and looked upon all those who stood before her. A soft voice whispered inside her head, telling her she had not truly been dead. Her eyes flickered, grasping at the light and trying to understand the looks of sympathy that confronted her. A pox-faced, shaven-headed girl of her own age smiled peacefully at her, a rough purple hat pulled to one side of her head and resting on the jagged, rat-chewed flesh of her right ear. It was as if the girl's smile leapt from her face and floated across the room to land upon Tara and fill her with joy.

Suddenly Tara realised that all the expressions of love in this place had left the dimensions of internal emotion and were

197

translated into a physical presence that had mass, colour and reality. Even thoughts were given shape and expression as they pulsed towards her like a solid wall. It was as if the sleep she had endured had transformed her mind, taking her to another realm of understanding where the feelings of the heart could take life and speak for themselves.

Solomon nodded slowly, as if he knew what she was thinking and shared the grace of the experience. 'This is life,' he whispered to her, and she saw the words forming on his lips as black sparrows that leapt from his mouth and flew sharply into her heart.

To Tara his voice sounded like that of a father, gentle and strong, warm and lovely. 'Solomon,' she replied. 'Yes . . . This is life . . .'

The prophet took Tara's hand and helped her to stand. Campion stepped forward, placing his huge hands around her waist and, in one movement of strength, lifting her up and placing her feet softly upon the criss–cross stones.

'Today, before your eyes, you have seen another miracle. Believe in Solomon! I am the only one who can do this. To this Citadel, many will flock to be set free from the chains of life.'

Turning from them, he took Tara by the arm and led her to the window overlooking the city. She could see the cathedral of St Paul with its broken dome and the lights of the houses below. The sky was cut in two by the small crescent of a bright new moon that razored across the clouds. In the distance the glowing embers of the faltering Hampstead fire lit the horizon.

Solomon cupped his hands and whispered to her, pausing between each sentence to cast an eye on the disciples behind him. For several moments he muttered to her and stroked her hair as she looked out over the meagre streets. There was a lantern outside the inn on Duke Street that cast its shadowy fingers on a dog that cocked its leg and scurried off into the darkness. All was quiet and still, a perfect reflection of Tara's heart.

Without the need for a word to be spoken, Solomon and Tara turned to face the disciples. Solomon grinned, his face filled with mirth as he wrung his hands and shivered his shoulders gleefully.

'On the day we give ourselves to the Citadel, we are given a task. Each one of you left this place and went into the wilderness of the city and returned with a gift. Tara is no exception – she too must now leave and go forth. She has been given her trial and in that she mustn't fail me.' Solomon looked at the girl, gently pushing her with his hand as if to give the signal that she must leave and take up her quest.

Tara looked around the room, unsure what to do. She looked at Campion, who for the first time smiled at her. His face looked soft and warm; no longer did she see his fearful eyes and creased forehead. Gone was the angry sneer and look of menace that could freeze the heart. Without thinking, she smiled back at him, catching his eye with her glance. He covered his face with his fat hand as a deep red blush crossed his cheeks and reddened his neck for all to see.

'Leave this place,' Solomon said gently as he rubbed yet another faux tear from his eye. 'The door to the Citadel stands open – the streets await and you know what is set for your quest. Go speedily and return quickly . . . I will be with you in spirit.' He looked to Campion, nodding for him to follow at a distance. 'I give you these gifts, you may need them in your pursuit of my desire.'

Solomon held out his empty hands and then, with a subtle twist of the wrist and turn of his right arm, a small silver egg seemed to appear from nowhere. It was banded with a rim of bronze and etched with gold thread. The closer Tara looked the more she could see the deep, thin gouges that criss-crossed the surface like a million tiny furrows. In that instant, Solomon twisted his left hand twice around and a dark waft of Chinese powder burst from his fingers and hovered before her like a silver angel. There, in his hand, was a small silver wand, again etched in gold with the finest of inlaid thread.

'Take them for your journey. Your mind is prepared, you will know what to do with them,' Solomon said as he pressed them into her hands.

It was as if the east wind stirred inside her chest. Tara could feel a sudden rush of her heart and a tingling ripping through her bones. Desert dryness gripped her throat, draining the moisture from her, and a desire to run exploded in Tara's feet. She set off at a pace, rising to her tiptoes as she ran, hardly touching the ground. She charged from the room, down the spiral staircase and skipped along the halls and passageways of the Citadel towards the large black doors that guarded the sanctuary. Gone were all thoughts of Jonah, Tersias and Maggot. All that filled her swooning mind was Solomon and his glinting tear-filled eyes.

Following the transformation of her heart, everything around her glistened with hopefulness and joy. The walls of the passageway shouted out her presence as her feet flitted across the cool marble. She ran faster, gulping at the air and taking in the first taste of the cold night. It was as if she was in the belly of a gigantic whale that gently roared as it spewed her onto some foreign shore. There was no doubt in her mind; her thoughts became crisp and bright, striking through her like shafts of pure lightning. They tingled in her brain as each impression darted back and forth. Gone were all daily fears and troubles, gone were the mindless games she played with herself, the tortuous self-doubt and fear that her secrets would be found out. Nothing mattered. In that silent and holy night, locked away in the stillness of her sleep, all her heartache had been laid to rest. She had been set free.

Tara chased along the hallway that led to the landing where the choir had sung its welcome. The lights appeared to burn brighter, reflecting from the walls with the light of the sun. The stones beneath her feet glistened, urging her forward to the night. With every step, her eyes absorbed the glorious beauty of the place. Minute details were brought to life: before her were magnified the tiny details of the gold-encrusted locks and silver door-linings that edged the entrance to every room she passed. Even candles burnt brighter, as if the flames were alive and danced and flickered just for her.

She was in a place of beauty beyond the imagination, and she knew it was now her home and the sanctuary to which she would return. And as she looked at the infinite detail of the ornate ceilings and lattice-tiled floor, every stone spoke of Solomon. In her mind she pictured the man: slight, thin, with deep blue eyes that understood everything about her. With every footstep her mind churned with the possibilities of new life as she raced towards the two large doors that heralded the start of her journey.

It was then that Tara saw his face – the face of the small boy who had offered her a lighted candle as he had sung in the choir on the great landing. He hid in the thick black shadow cast by the door. The boy gripped the fine brass handle with one hand; the other was buried deep in the pocket of his oversized purple coat. He looked at her as she came to a sudden halt before him. There was something about his face that she thought she knew; his eyes reminded her of someone close. She dug deep within her memory to match this boy's face to one she knew, but her mind resisted, closed to anything from the past.

'What is your name, boy?' she asked, panting out the words.

'I have no name, I will only have a name when I die and I am reborn,' he replied. His eyes were downcast as the words stumbled from his mouth.

'So – you are to climb back into your mother's guts and start life again?' Tara asked mockingly as a thick throbbing suddenly started in her head. 'How can someone be born again?'

'You have been reborn, so I am told. You died and Solomon brought you back to life. The outsiders poisoned you and Solomon found you, but you died and it was only because of him that you now live. That is what the master said.' The boy saw Tara grasp the top of her head, pressing the purple bands that covered her skull to try and ease the pain that now beat like a skin drum. 'It'll pass. It always does. The elixir burns and blisters and then bursts out of your head before you will be well. I saw it happen to my mother.'

'How do you know these things?' Tara asked. She held on to the door as her mind swam and eyes burnt with pain.

'It'll pass, always does,' the boy said again as he took her by the hand and led her to the steps of the Citadel. 'I am the door-keeper. I eat and sleep upon these steps. I will always be here, seeing pilgrims come and go on their journeys. Some go and never return, then Campion goes to find them and brings back their purples and they are seen no more. Will you come back?' he asked as the tower bell rang out nine times.

'I will soon return and we will be friends.' She smiled, the pain easing as the linctus ebbed from her body. 'I have a journey to make for Solomon, nothing will stop me doing what he desires and all my wits tell me to run from this place . . .'

'And run you will – run and don't come back. It is not as you now see it, your eyes are blinded by the elixir, they all chant alike but this place is as bad as the streets.'

'You sound like a boy I once knew . . . ungrateful to the one who kept him.' She began to run on her quest, jumping from the steps and landing ankle-deep in the fresh London dirt. 'I will tell Solomon what you have said upon my return and then we will see how grateful you can be to your master,' she shouted as she crossed the street towards the inn.

'Then I will pray that you never come back to this place,' the boy said under his breath as he went back into the Citadel and slowly pressed his slight body against the great doors, pushing them to close with all his might.

Tara hobbled through the dirt as Solomon's words echoed again and again through her mind. Outside the inn a gang of drunken sailors ridiculed her as she passed. They chivvied at her purple coat and banded head, mocking her with catcalls and spits of phlegm. Like a London rat, she turned left and then right through the narrow streets, back and forth, keeping close to the walls, her eyes fixed to the ground. She counted her steps as her heart led her on, foot by foot towards the Bull and Mouth. With every yard of street muck through which Tara trod she thought of what she had to do. Into the inn, up the stairs into the room, clear the bed and find the box. Those had been Solomon's words: *Find the box, bring the knife.* She had seen them both and now would get them for Solomon. A small chink in Tara's memory allowed her a glimpse of the green alabaster. Such a fine thing, beautiful and mysterious and holding within it a sea of quicksilver. It was a memory that flickered on her face as warm as the fire that had burnt in the hearth that night. Yet in her mind she was alone in the room – no Jonah, no Maggot. Even Old Bunce was just a dark shape in the corner of her thought.

Whatever had taken place in her mind had cut from her many recollections of the past. All that was now left were dark ghost-like figures, faceless and black with no thought or character. Her wits stumbled, hoping to bring to mind a name, a place, a pleasant moment, but all she could see were dark spectres that floated across her mind's eye and said nothing.

The pilgrim coat began to rub the back of her neck and the thick bands around her head dug into the shaved skin, itching like a fresh crop of lice. Hart Street was empty, the market stalls had gone and the shop fronts were boarded with planks of wood to cover the dirty glass. The stillness was broken by the wailing of three milk-heifers penned against the wall of Bloomsbury Market. In the cold night air they steamed and panted, breathing spurts of fire-breath that glowed brightly against the cold grey walls of the warden's house. As she passed by they stirred and jumped in the pen, grinding their teeth and churning the cud in their throats in a loud growl as they raised their tails and dunged the walls.

Tara kept her eyes to the ground. It was a habit that went beyond thought. What you didn't see couldn't hurt you. It was dangerous to catch the eye of someone, anyone who lurked the streets at night. Look to the floor and they left you alone, as if you were invisible.

From the dark shadow of the portico that stood against the side of the fish market a pair of red eyes stared at her as she crossed the empty road. They followed each step she took towards the Bull and Mouth. They were hunter's eyes that watched the heated flesh of their victim. Eyes that could find you on the darkest night and follow you through murk and mist as if it were the clearest day.

Tara shivered, feeling she was not alone but fearing to turn and see who or what spied upon her. She quickened her steps, hoping that the inn door would be open and that Old Bunce – that dark shadow in her memory – had not locked out the night. She looked down and saw upon the cobbles drops of blood, deep and red, the blood from the dog she had shot, the dog that had attacked Maggot. In her mind the scene was danced again: Jonah, Maggot, the mist rising from the mud-died street, all was there, and the flash as the pistol exploded, the ringing of the shot as it burnt into the beast's flesh and sent it spinning. All this was remembered in the moment of a quick glance at several drops of dried blood that clung to the stones.

Three steps to the inn door. Tara knew she had to turn just once and check the street behind. She fought with her own mind, not wanting to turn in case someone was there but knowing that this was what she had to do. The irresistible urge to see the one who stared at her from the darkness came upon her like a childhood game. Turn and look, said the voice in her head. Turn – look – run. She skipped warily across the cobbles to the steps of the inn.

The desire was too strong. As she took hold of the door handle to the inn, Tara turned and cast a glimpse from the corner of her eye to the dark portico.

The Court of the New Moon

Tight-lipped, Jonah ran the last few paces through the dark yard off Cheapside to Malachi's stables. He had never dared to look behind as he raced through the empty streets from the prison along Pater Noster Row and into the labyrinth of dark alleyways that he knew so well. Jonah had only stopped once to gather his breath, his eyes drawn to the top of St Paul's and the broken dome. In that moment he had thought of Tara. It was a dark thought, torn from the depths of his soul, as if he were being told by a hidden voice that their friendship had been taken from them and handed to another. Then he had quickly snapped from his dream and set off at a pace, catching the shadow of his legs running before him like a sackcloth figure dragged through the mud.

In the stable yard he felt safe. There was no sound – no one was there, he could tell. It was an instinct, the nous of a thief: nothing in the air spoke of people hiding. It was still and empty, dark and cold. All he could think of was the knife and his promise to Malachi. He couldn't rid his mind of the promise – foolish words, he thought to himself, and only to be broken.

Jonah stopped and looked to the patch of sky that peeped between the roofs of the cluster of buildings that huddled together, propping themselves up like old men in fear of falling. There, in the deepest, darkest depths of space, was a bright star. It caught his eye as it sparkled in the cold black of the night.

'Never swear on a star,' he said as he gazed and gazed. 'Star promises have to be kept, and promises aren't for keeping.'

It was then that he found himself repeating the words of his promise: 'Not goodbye – but till the morning. I will come back.' The words rolled from his lips and fell in the cold night air. It was as if they became real – each word had life, power and control of his soul. In his mind he saw Malachi being hauled from the roof by the militia and placed into the hanging cart as Mrs Devereaux scalded the back of his neck with her hot tongue.

'Not me,' he said out loud to the star above him. 'I am not made for things such as this . . . Don't ask me to do it,' Jonah begged, his eyes fixed to the heavens. 'Find someone else to save him, I am just a poor boy and my story seldom told – don't ask Jonah. My heart tells me one way and my desire another. Tell me to go to York and I will take you to Pimlico – that's Jonah.'

The star shone brilliantly, brighter than all the others above him, piercing the darkness from the edge of space.

'Malachi would know your name,' he said as he stared ever upwards. 'He would know how far away you were and how you were fixed to the heavens and why you only ever dared to be seen by night. You are a candle, a lesser light lit by a giant's hand, and yet I feel you call me to do something I would never want or wish to be a part of.'

As he turned and stepped back into the shadows he wiped his lips with his hand, hoping to brush from them the remnants of his promises. A dark cloud sped across the sky, blocking out the lesser lights and bathing the city in thick velvet. Jonah walked deeper into the shadows as a sudden gasp of breeze shuddered his spine, raising the hairs on his neck like a devil's footstep. He clicked the door lock and dropped to the floor, then crawled into the stable and across the room to the altar table. It was still there – the knife, stuck to its hilt in the soft plaster.

As he touched the handle, it sparked against his skin, hot to the touch and thankful for his company. Taking it in his grip, he twisted the blade back and forth. When he felt it to be free he pulled it from the wall and quickly slipped the blade into his frock-coat pocket, nestling it against the old dried ring finger.

For several minutes Jonah sat in complete darkness, crumbling lumps of dry plaster between his fingers. The building groaned and moaned about him as if it were breathing, snoring. High above his head he could hear the crackling of timbers as the thick slates scraped against each other and the eaves creaked and shivered. There was a cinder glow in the fire-grate, blown bright by the river breeze that was sucked down the chimney. He felt as if he was being told to leave, that this was the time to go quietly into the night. Jonah rolled from under the altar, got to his feet and began to search every jar he could find before him. He went quickly from the table to the shelves, fumbling his way around the room. In the corner of the stable he found what he searched for.

There, in a small cotton sack, was a pound of coarse grey powder. Jonah dipped his hand in, cupping a palmful and holding it to his nose. He smelt the sulphur and saltpetre. 'Gunpowder,' he said as he took the sack and pushed it into the game pocket of his frock coat.

He slipped from the stable and into the alleyway, keeping to the shadows and never looking up, hoping to be free from the gawping star and the promise he had made. At the entrance to Cheapside he stopped and looked around him. The street was empty. He thrust his hand into his pocket and felt the knife; it was warm to the touch. Jonah began to walk faster, laying a hand on every building he passed and keeping his fingers crossed in his pocket.

The street was silent, nothing stirred. The coming of the comet had emptied the town of all but the drunks and the fool-hardy and those who dared not leave behind their chattels and would rather die than lose them.

Jonah scurried through the streets towards Westminster. The alleyways and yards that edged on to the river gave silent passage as he crept through the night towards Vamana House. The knife seemed to urge him on, pointing the way to go. He knew not what he would do. All he could think of were his words to Malachi, words that he had to obey, sworn on a star in a clear black sky. From the river a thick mist filled the streets to waist height. It oozed around the corners of the houses like white syrup being poured out upon the land. Jonah hesitated, unsure of what lay beneath the fog that boiled like the wisps from a witch's cauldron.

Jonah ran through Scotland Yard and turned into Whitehall, then behind the chapel and across the Privy Gardens into Parliament Street. He paused on the corner of Channel Row, unsure if he could make out a distant sound of cartwheels turning against the mud and a faint murmur of singing.

Slowly, surely, the sound grew louder. It echoed from the fronts of the buildings and flew into the myriad of yards and alleys that honeycombed the bankside. It was a cackling, a wailing that pitched itself back and forth, higher then lower as it stumbled the octaves, a mumbling and groaning like that of a dying banshee. From around the singing came laughter, grue-some and cruel.

Jonah stepped into the doorway of a milliner's shop and sunk into the fog, peering out from the murky shadows. Along Parliament Street the mist swirled as the feet of the militia stirred the ground with their marching and laughter. Then came the hanging cart, strapped with two oiled-rag lanterns that lit the path of the donkey. And in the cart, dragged over the cobbles, was Malachi. He stood above the militia, flagon in hand, swigging from the neck as he gulped between each line, drunkenly wailing the half-forgotten words of an old song.

From his hiding place Jonah watched as the procession passed by. Twelve militia, the donkey, Malachi chained to the cart and Skullet, tapping out the beat of the pageant with his long staff. Jonah dipped himself deeper into the bubbling mist, curling himself against the wooden shop door and holding his breath as he counted their footsteps along the road. Malachi wailed even louder as he dropped the wine flagon to the ground as the carriage clattered into Bridge Street. He grabbed a standing post with one hand and shouted at the donkey to stop as he lurched from his song to the babblings of a beggar offering curses that would fall upon the heads of all who passed him by.

'Let me sing . . . Donkey, stop, my wine has gone . . . Sing the call of the bonny lass . . . Skullet, you're an ass . . . You would make a wife for this poor beast of burden. Listen, listen!' he shouted even louder. 'All who take part in the Court of the New Moon will be dammed. Lice will crawl your skin and murder shall be always in your heart.'

'Give him more wine,' ordered Skullet as he whacked the donkey across the rump with his staff. 'I will not listen to his ranting and would rather he be drunk than foul-tongued. He will wake the dead if he continues.'

'The dead!' Malachi screamed, holding his heart as if pierced through by Skullet's words. 'We are surrounded by the dead, they are everywhere.' He moaned as he fell to his backside with a loud thump that rocked the carriage from side to side. 'I shall be one of them, wrongly killed by Lord wart-nose Malpas and his even uglier servant and bottle-washer who breakfasts with the murderous tart of Fleet Prison. Isn't that right, Skullet?' Malachi's ranting went on, descending into a spitting rage.

'If I had my way I would cut your throat here and now,' Skullet said as he lashed his staff towards Malachi. 'Witchcraft alone is a hanging offence, that and theft should see you gone from this world. Now, SILENCE!' His words rang out and echoed through the empty streets.

Jonah followed at a distance, keeping to the shadows and hiding himself in the fog that rolled in from the river. The mist turned New Palace Yard into a lake of soft white, as if the city had been built in the clouds. The buildings stood without earthly foundations as the light from the windows of Union Street danced across the clouds like the wingbeats of angels as the carriage and a silent Malachi paraded along, escorted by a troop of ghostly collaborators.

In two turns they were in Thieving Lane. Vamana House stood before them, the fog cutting the building in half and covering the donkey so it could not be seen. Jonah watched as Malachi had his shackles taken from his wrists and was hauled from the carriage, stumbling in the mist as if he had been dropped from the cloud to fall to earth. He could hear Malachi's chains dragging along the stones as two militia dipped into the swirling mist and pulled him up the steps to the open door of the house, a single candle lighting his path. Malachi emerged from the smog like a dark shadow and staggered through the door, followed by Skullet and several of the militia.

To the right of the entrance stood a tall black carriage, its driver wrapped in a thick horse-blanket. He appeared to be sleeping, oblivious to all that had gone before. Jonah crept along the opposite side of the road, his eyes fixed on the door to the house. A soldier peered out, looked nervously up and down the street, then slammed the door shut as he stepped inside. The carriage driver jumped, juddered from his sleep by the crash of the door, then settled back into the blanket and his wintry dreaming.

High above, Skullet pulled the curtains of the leaded window against the dark of the night and turned to Lord Malpas, who sat squally in his fireside chair.

'Bring him in and let's have this farce over and done with. Lord of the realm and even I have to obey the law. Fine for kings and princes to have their dalliances, get rid of their enemies, have their wives murdered in carriage catastrophes, but I, Lord Malpas, have to obey the law.' Malpas picked up a large log and threw it onto the fire. 'I need the Alabaster, Skullet. The life trickles from my bones and I get weaker by the hour. Without that box I will die and you will never be its guardian.' He rubbed the bloodied bandage that was wrapped tightly around his wrist. 'This curse has followed me through life – been with every Malpas until their untimely deaths, but not so with me. I want to live beyond death and be restored to life without this curse.'

'It was a great thing that Homuncule Malpas did for the King, without his bravery you would not have all what you do today,' Skullet said pointedly. He went back to the window, finished closing the curtains, then for a reason he could not understand opened them a chink and peered into the street briefly before turning back into the room.

'Yes indeed . . . I would not have a wife who refuses to live with me, nor would I have a wound that never heals or a King who thinks he's a farmer, what . . . what . . .' Malpas clucked, mimicking the King's voice. 'Some say I have never had it so good. Waiting to die, day after day in a cold lifeless house, ravaged of what joy I once had. I want the Alabaster. I want the knife and I want to leave this world until a time will come when I can be resurrected and cured of this devilish sickness. That, my dear Skullet, is all I want. NOT TOO MUCH TO ASK, IS IT?' he screamed as he sprung to his feet and kicked the burning logs in the grate, sending a shower of sparks cascading about the room. 'Find me the oracle and all will be well. I will have them back and you will inherit all that is mine until I am restored to life.'

'The Honourable Dobson is restored in the Great Hall, my Lord,' Skullet said quickly as he jumped about the room stamping on the firebrands that had leapt from the flames and were smouldering upon the hearthrug. Malpas looked on as Skullet danced from foot to foot, crushing the brands beneath his feet. 'We should', he said between leaps, 'be going to the Great Hall. Malachi is as drunk as a hosteller and ready to admit that he is the King of Spain if we ask him. Once he is out of the way we can go to the Citadel and get the oracle from Solomon.'

'Solomon?' Malpas asked. 'The prophet has the boy?'

'Taken from Malachi in the alleyway just moments before I arrived with the militia. A sensitive task to get the boy back, but one that will be made easier once Malachi has stretched himself in his grief.' Skullet laughed as he took Malpas by the arm and guided him from the room towards the Great Hall.

Together they twisted and turned their way through the house. Down the staircase, through the long passageway and eventually to the fine oak doors of the Great Hall, guarded by the militia. Malpas stopped and looked at Skullet.

'Witnesses?' he asked hesitantly.

'Three. They all saw him steal the spoon.'

'Motive?'

'He is a thief and a liar. I have one man who will say that he was offered the spoon and the contents of your kitchen should he desire and that Malachi wormed his way in here with talk of telling your future. Dobson hates anything to do with fortune-tellers, will hang them just for their name.'

'You have done well,' Malpas said as he nodded to the guard to open the door. 'One thing – how sane is Dobson this week? I

213

have heard that he was found chewing the grass in Parliament Fields and that he believed he was a horse.'

'He is well. Tethered to the table and groomed for the appearance. I should think he will last the trial and he is the only judge we have in our pocket,' Skullet said. Then they entered the Great Hall and walked across the dirty stone floor towards the long bench by the fire.

Malachi was strapped to a chair and surrounded by militia. In the middle of the room sat the Honourable Dobson, wrapped in his ermine robes and garlanded with his long horsehair wig with its fine curls and blue silk lining. He appeared to be asleep; his bottom lip was pressed out to form a thin shelf filled with white spittle that hung from his mouth like crisp icicles. His eyelids quivered as he twitched his nose like a deathly rabbit, sniffing and snorting the air as in his slumber he rubbed his face with the back of his hand.

'The Court shall rise,' Skullet said, announcing the arrival of Lord Malpas. From the deep black shadows at the back of the Great Hall stepped four men who bowed their heads ceremoniously to Lord Malpas, each clutching a black velvet bag stuffed with silver coins.

Skullet breezed across the room, brushing the dust of the street from his long black coat and staring at each of the witnesses one by one. As he passed the Honourable Dobson, he kicked the chair, jollying the old man from his slumber and startling him into the world.

'GUILTY!' Dobson shouted, jumping to his feet and pointing a finger at Malpas, who was just about to take his seat.

'My lord,' Skullet said, gripping the Judge's chin and turning his head to face Malachi, '*that* is the defendant. He is the one on trial, not Lord Malpas.'

Judge Dobson flummoxed his hands in the air, looked about the room, then promptly sat down in his chair, staring at Malpas and muttering under his breath. 'Where is the counsel?' Dobson asked as he peered over the end of his long nose.

'I stand for the plaintiff,' said Skullet, 'and the defendant insists on speaking for himself.'

'Not satisfactory,' Dobson said as he rubbed his face with his hands, trying to wipe away the sleep. 'Can't have a servant representing his master . . . Whatever will the world think?'

'I assure you it is satisfactory,' Malpas shouted as the Judge looked about the room, trying to count those present and nodding to each in turn as if they were old friends.

'If you say so, Malpas,' Dobson said. 'You're paying . . .' The clock above them struck the first beat of midnight.

'Indeed. And time is money,' Malpas replied. He shuffled nervously in his chair, scowling at Malachi.

The magician looked on, trying to focus his eyes on all that was before him as he licked his lips and pulled on his greasy beard.

'INDEED!' shouted Skullet, trying to gain the attention of the Judge. 'In very few words, the defendant came to this house posing as a fortune-teller and stole from this place a silver spoon valued at one guinea.' Skullet stared at Dobson, hoping there would be some kind of acknowledgment that he had spoken. The Judge stared back as if Skullet were not there and he was somewhere other than the room. 'I have witnesses. Several of them saw the event and one was offered the goods. All in all the case can be opened and closed in one breath. Can it not?'

Judge Dobson closed his eyes and pondered as he picked his lips with his fingers. 'And what does the defendant have to say for himself?' he asked, to the surprise of all that were present.

'I say it's a lie,' Malachi replied. He shuffled closer to the Judge as if this were some game and the chair a fat hobbyhorse. 'It was planted upon me by Skullet, never stolen anything in my –'

'WITNESSES!' Skullet shouted at the Judge. 'There are men who stand in the room who were privy to the event – what does he say about that?'

'I say they are straw men, paid by Malpas to stand for him. Liars and cheats who want to see me dead and steal all that I have.'

The Judge sniffed the air, twitching his nose with each snivel. 'I can smell a demon,' he said in a low voice. 'Someone here has been sucking from the bosom of hell – who dares come into this court with *drink* in their bellies?'

' 'Tis Malachi,' Skullet whispered. 'I am afraid that he is a drunkard and cannot contain himself. All that he does is for the sake of gin. He is a wine-bibber of parliamentarian proportions.'

'A fortune-teller, a wine-bibber and a THIEF!' Dobson spat the words at Malachi. Life appeared to have suddenly returned to his body, as if the presence of a demon had shocked him from death and madness. The Honourable Dobson stood to his feet, rummaged in the pocket of his coat and nimbly pulled out a black hood that he placed upon his head. 'GUILTY!' he bellowed. 'Any man who stands before me with a demon in his belly is GUILTY – no matter what the crime. He shall be taken to Fleet Prison and hanged and the sooner the better.'

Malpas jumped to his feet and leapt towards the Judge. 'Fleet Prison? It can't be . . . We have our own gallows and we could hang him now. My men have spent the afternoon building the finest instrument of death London has ever seen – he could be hung, drawn and quartered all at once, and with no cost to the city.'

'Fleet I have said and Fleet it will be,' Dobson said as he got up from the chair, neatly folded the black hood and placed it back in his pocket. He turned and walked towards Malachi, who sat helpless, his head downcast. 'What awaits you should be seen by no man. Hell is a place where you will never die and sprites will pick at your flesh with red-hot pincers. Every day for eternity you will endure the torture of that place, your eyes burning as if being fried like two golden eggs as every hair of your beard is plucked from your chin one at a time. What do you say to that, my friend?'

Malachi looked up defiantly. 'I say the company shall be more honest and decent than that with which I am now acquainted. I say I shall be warmed to the heart and that your heart is barren of any kindness. I say that when you breathe your last, you shall be with me, with no water to calm your tongue, and begging for your poor soul to be extinguished for-ever. Do what you will, your fate shall be thrice my own.'

'There speaks a guilty man,' Malpas said, rubbing his hands and nodding to the militia to take Malachi away. The heat from the fire had reddened his face to a blush. 'Again, Judge Dobson, we have seen your true virtue and skill – who else could have the insight that we have seen this night? What a wonder to behold.' Malpas began to applaud, encouraging the gathering to join with him as Skullet minced by the witnesses, snatching back the velvet money-bags and ushering them from the room. 'Take the man to Fleet Prison and have the sentence carried out at once. There is no place in this world for one such as him.'

The Captain of the Guard untied Malachi and lifted him to his feet. All strength had left him, his legs buckled as he was puppeted from the Great Hall and into the long corridor to the front door of the house.

Malachi stumbled through the doorway and onto the steps, his mind blank, wiped clear by the whirlpool of fear that now sucked him deeper. 'Oh, what wrong have I done? What evil so great that my end should be as this?' he wailed drunkenly, his long magician's coat trailing behind him tattered and forlorn.

At the foot of the steps stood a tall black carriage harnessed to two dark horses with blue head plumes and ermine collars. 'Lord Malpas wants him to go on his last journey in this carriage,' the coachman growled as the militia brought Malachi down the steps. 'Place him inside, lock the door and one of you travel with me – he won't be escaping, the speed I will fly. You all follow on with the donkey cart.'

'But this is Judge Dobson's carriage,' said the Captain of the Guard.

'And I his coachman. Go check with your master as I have with mine. Do as Lord Malpas desires and put the old man in the carriage and we shall be away,' the coachman grunted in his deep brusque voice. 'If he tries to escape I shall shoot him with Old Meg – many a highwayman has had his rump peppered with this musket.'

Malachi looked up at the coachman. A thick blanket was wrapped around his shoulders, his hat was pulled down over his ears and the blunderbuss rested across his lap. 'Gentlemen, gentlemen,' Malachi said quietly. 'Close the door to Vamana House and keep out the night. Is it so bad that my last journey through this city should be in such a fine carriage? Your master is kind beyond belief. Now let me take mount and go to Fleet Prison to meet my end.'

The Captain of the Guard looked up and down the empty street. Only the calling of a night bird in Parliament Street broke the silence. 'Very well,' he said as he pulled open the carriage door. 'I will travel with the coachman and take the prisoner to the Fleet.'

Malachi stepped into the carriage and slid across the leather seat, snuggling into the corner as if it were his favourite armchair. He smiled to himself as the Captain started to climb the steps.

Suddenly the horsewhip cracked and without warning the horses bolted. The coach lurched from side to side, throwing the Captain into the mud. Then the horses took speed, hooves clattering and plumes flying.

There was a sharp crack of muskets as the militia fired upon the carriage, jolting the horses to run wildly along Thieving Lane, skidding round the turn to King Street and into the darkness. Malachi held tightly to the thin black straps as the carriage yawed back and forth, sliding him across the seat. He kept his grip with one hand as he was tumbled against the floor as the carriage bounced out of control along the street.

'I would prefer to die in Fleet Prison than be smashed to death in a judge's carriage,' Malachi shouted as he tried to wedge himself at the back of the coach.

'You will not die at all if I have my way, dear friend,' Jonah shouted from the coachman's seat as he gripped the reins to slow the horses to a canter.

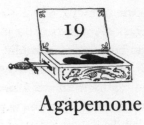

Agapemone

'Quickly!' Jonah shouted as he ran through the marketplace and under the dark portico that towered above him like a stone gallows.

Magnus Malachi hobbled behind, out of breath and out of his mind, his head pounding from the quart of wine that set every nerve on fire and thumped his beating heart. 'I am not a young man,' he shouted as he grabbed hold of a pillar to steady himself against the weakening of his legs and the desire to collapse to the floor. 'I should have stayed to be hanged and then my fate would be sealed and I in a better place.'

Jonah laughed, then stopped in the darkness of the thick shadows and looked about him. The door to the inn stood slightly open, a sliver of brightness slipping through a crack onto the well-trodden mud. There was no sound; the street was empty, eerie and cold; yet it was as if everyone and everything in the world was watching for his arrival. Jonah edged further along the stones of the portico as Malachi went on chuntering under his breath. Legions of will-o'-the-wisps sprung up around him, small twists of fog that bobbed from the mud like fire-hobs twisting over the moor-top. Each one span like a mercury cloud that grasped a shape and then shifted its face, took on the form of another spectre and then faded into the night.

'Water . . .' Malachi groaned as he took hold of Jonah by the back of his coat, expecting to be pulled across the mud and to the inn. 'I can go no further unless I have a drink,' he muttered, then wiped away the spittle from his face, picked his nose and licked the tip of his finger.

'You will have something finer,' Jonah said as he stepped from the cover of the portico and took several quick steps across the mud to the door of the Bull and Mouth. 'This is the place,' he whispered to Malachi, who slowly picked his way through the dirt like a tall black heron. 'Quickly, Malachi, we are wanted men. Malpas will not have you free for long, he wants to see you dead and it is more than I can do to keep you alive until I find a safe place for us both.'

Jonah slipped his hand inside the door and in an instant had vanished.

'Jonah . . .' Malachi whimpered as his head pounded. 'Jonah?' He had blinked momentarily and the boy had gone, plucked like a firebrand from before his eyes.

A face appeared at the door, bespectacled and bearded, with beady eyes that shone like two bright sparks in the shadow.

'You Malachi?' Old Bunce asked as he looked him up and down. Malachi nodded mournfully, his bones weakened and his mind befuddled by the numbing ruin. 'The boy's inside. He says be quick or Malpas will get you.' Old Bunce sniggered to himself as he pushed the door wider to welcome the magician. 'Through the door and into my parlour,' he spluttered. 'We have a guest, a special guest and one that even you will be pleased to see.'

Malachi followed the old man as he led him to the parlour door. The air was heavy with the scent of snuffed candles that blossomed in thick swirls as wisps of smoke spiralled to the ceiling. The room was lit by a single candle that sat snugly in the lips of a fine-stemmed candelabrum on the felt top of a low wine table, nestling by a large leather chair.

Jonah knelt by the fire, staring into the flames, his eyes void as if he was still lost in the London fog, as he listened to the voice of a girl. As Malachi stepped into the room, the girl continued to speak, giving no recognition to his presence. With a flick of her head she turned quickly, looked him in the eye and then cast her glare back to the fire as she told Jonah of her escape.

Tara's tone was flat, her voice slow and measured, with not one glint of excitement. With one hand she itched the bandages that were tightly wrapped around her head. She spoke relentlessly of the Alabaster as her eyes searched the room, hoping to spy some corner of the box and know where it was kept. She knew it was close by. From the time when she had stared at her image in the fine quicksilver a small tendril had entwined her heart for its company.

Malachi waited for her to stop speaking, taking in each word and turning them slowly in his mind. He had seen this girl before, heard her voice, sensed her gluttony for living, but here before him was a wastrel, a soul-less ghoul, dark and empty of life.

'All I could think of was you,' she said as she leant towards Jonah, her eyes unable to rest upon his face. 'We have to get the Alabaster and escape from here, they will be coming for us.' Her hands trembled as she spoke.

Malachi felt uneasy. He sniffed the air, flicking his tongue like a snake trying to taste the sweat of its victim. Tara gibbered on, recounting her escape again and again, asking constantly for the Alabaster.

'Is it here? We need to take it from this place and keep it safe,' she said as she got to her feet and stood by Jonah, her hand tightly squeezing his shoulder as her face burnt bright red from the glare of the fire. 'Tell me, Jonah, tell me where it is and I will take it to somewhere safe and we will all go free – isn't that what you want?'

'I want to find Maggot and get the boy. He has a right to his freedom and Malachi can take care of him. That's what I want, Tara. Nothing more.' Jonah got up from the fire and looked at her. Something had changed. In her eyes there was a distant, faraway look. All that was Tara had gone. Gone the joy, gone the laughter, gone the fire from her heart. Here she stood like a smouldering wick on a wax-less plate. 'Why your obsession with the Alabaster? You've done nothing but moan of it since I came here.'

'Can't you see? It was the Alabaster that has brought all this upon us. Before you stole it we were all just fine.'

'We were penniless and a star was about to crash into the world, that is what we were. You and I have done what we always do – help ourselves. That Alabaster changes nothing. All that has changed in this place is you. It's like Solomon has taken your wits and given you the brain of a donkey, braying his tune.'

'Don't leave her with a cold shoulder, Jonah,' Malachi said as he edged closer to the fire. 'The girl has suffered much and she complains for good reason. This Alabaster is an important thing. I once heard of it many years ago in a coffee-shop in Highgate. It is said to be overflowing with the finest mercury . . . the perfect mirror for seeing yourself. Perhaps the girl would like to see how she now looks?'

'Very well,' Jonah said reluctantly as he stepped back towards a tall suit of medieval armour that hung against the wall next to the stone fireplace. 'If she wants to see her scalded face and washer-woman's tongue then she can. No thanks in being free.'

He turned and lifted the shining breastplate from the wall hinge and took the Alabaster from its hiding place. He held it close to him, his fingers gripping the cold stone. Malachi edged closer, knowing he was in the presence of an instrument of alchemy spoken of in hushed tones.

'The key? I heard talk of a special, delicate key that unhinges the latch and allows you to see the mercury, is that correct?' he slathered, his voice quipping like a young puppy as he jumped from foot to foot with excitement that brought new life to his old bones.

'Not a key, but a knife,' Jonah said quickly, pulling the dagger from his coat and slipping it into the lock for all to see.

The Alabaster opened slowly and Jonah placed it gently on the wine table by the fire. Malachi gasped at its beauty as tiny sparks leapt in an incandescent rain into the room, brighter than the single candle that now paled in its light. 'This is a wonder,' Malachi said to himself, his eyes fixed upon it.

Like the opening of a September rosebud, the Alabaster came to life. The glow of the quicksilver shone brighter than the fire-grate. Tara and Malachi were drawn together by its beauty as Jonah busied himself stoking the fire with a long brass poker and throwing on small lumps of damp coal. Like a giant oyster, the Alabaster opened its shell and gave a ghostly shudder as it lay flat against the table. The mercury quivered with the trembling of the house. From high above them a drop of the whitest candle wax slid silently down the arm of the chandelier and dripped effortlessly through the air before landing upon the quicksilver, sending a spurt of mercury high into the air. Then the Alabaster again lay quiet and still as a shimmering mirror.

Tara was drawn to look at herself. She stared into the looking-glass and there was her face – older, worn and wearisome. A small line stretching across her forehead, invading her youth. And then in the swirling silver-black she saw another creature staring back at her, smiling a red-eyed smile through its pig-eyes. She drew her breath, trying to steal her sight from its glare, but no matter where she looked the creature managed to capture her stare.

Malachi looked into the quicksilver and saw himself. He knew nothing of what was taking place before Tara. All he could see was his fine beard, waxed eyebrows and the distinguished crow's-feet that edged his eyes. Someone had once told him that he looked like a Scottish king, and as he mused on his appearance he realised how right they had been.

It was a different face that enthralled Tara. This was a creature she had known for a long time. This was the mirror beast she had conjured last Hallowe'en. Seven times she had swirled the apple peel around her head, seven times she had chanted the charm and seven times it had glanced at her. Once, on Christmas Eve, in the dark of night she had even seen its reflection in the frosty glass of her room. There the eyes had stared back at her, deep and red, burning like hard coals. This was the price she was paying for making a spell to see her intended in the misted glass.

Now the beast was enjoying her company, eye to eye, searching her every feature. It pushed its hand from deep within the Alabaster and stroked her face. She couldn't move, frozen by its icy hand and by its stare that opened her thoughts like a layered cake, exposing what she had hidden from the world.

Jonah ignored them. He cared not for what they enchanted themselves with. To him it was a stone box sought after by foolish men and only good to be exchanged for a golden guinea. Whatever it did was an alchemist's trick, it was just a mirror that glorified the imagination. He glanced at Malachi, who stood grinning at his own reflection and turning his profile from left to right, smiling and pouting to himself like a Limehouse dandy.

'It is such a clever thing,' Malachi said as he preened his beard again and again. 'The more I stare the more beautiful and younger I become. Look at me, Jonah – are not the years falling away from my face? Does not the alchemy of the box change my visage?'

'If you mean are you getting younger – then no. And if you want to look younger, I would stick your head in a bucket of carriage grease.'

Malachi laughed and threw back his head, cocking his hat and strutting about the room like a beguiled Frenchman convinced his country had finally been victorious in some distant war, sticking out his chest as if it were the resting place of battle silver. 'You are a cruel boy,' he said, pulling upon his shirtsleeves and twisting his beard in his fingers. 'I have the greatest desire to drink chocolate with the King,' he said, thrilled by the sight of his beautification.

Jonah didn't reply. A sound of choking drew him quickly, and he turned to see Tara being sucked inch by inch into the quicksilver, as if the Alabaster were consuming her, pulling her from this world through the narrow portal of the stone box.

'MALACHI!' Jonah grabbed the Alabaster from the table, pulling Tara from her knees as the box suckled itself upon her even faster, pulling her head within. 'IT'S KILLING HER!'

Malachi turned to see the girl being sucked deeper into the stone box, disappearing from sight. The sides of the Alabaster were like the jaws of an invisible creature that had snapped its thick green mouth over the head of its victim. He took her by the waist and began to pull her back as Jonah pushed against the hinges of the box, trying to slam the two sides together.

'The lock! Take the knife from the lock and the box will close!' Malachi shouted as he twisted Tara away from the Alabaster. 'She will soon be gone.'

Jonah pulled on the knife and tugged it back and forth, hoping to free it from the clasp. But the stone gripped the blade as Jonah pulled in vain. 'It's no use!' Jonah screamed as the blade seized against the stone. 'It will not give way.'

'Try from the heart! It was created with hate, the linctus of the alchemist. Try from the heart,' Malachi said as he still pulled Tara towards him while the Alabaster consumed her neck and shoulders. Strands of mercury slid down her back and around her chest like long silver tendrils.

Jonah closed his eyes, trying to calm the beat of his heart, breathing the memories of their friendship and begging for her not to be lost.

There was a sudden lurch as the handle of the knife burst in his grip, burning white hot and scorching the memory of its pattern upon his palm. It jumped from the lock, span across the room and landed in the fire, sizzling as if it were being quenched with spring water.

The Alabaster groaned and spluttered silver across the room as the tendrils lashed out like arms of steel, knocking Malachi to the floor. Tara was spat across the parlour, the bandages that covered her shaved head slithering swiftly through the air and into the deep blackness of the closing case. With the sound of two cavernous rock gates being slammed by a giant's hand, the Alabaster closed and then fell to the floor with a resounding thud that shook the inn.

Tara spewed mercury from her nostrils as she gasped for breath, clawing at her face as if to rid herself of something or someone that grasped at her. 'There is another world,' she shouted as Malachi got to his feet and took her by the hand. 'I saw everything! It wanted me to go with it – to be there and never return.'

'What did?' Jonah asked as his eyes flashed from Malachi to the girl and back again.

'The creature in the box – I could see it clearly, it stared and stared and then I was tranced and it grabbed me by the throat and pulled me through the mercury. It is another world, unlike anything I have ever seen, beautiful . . .' Tara got to her feet and picked the last pieces of crisp mercury from her face, then rubbed her hand over her shaven head. She saw

Jonah looking at her, his eyes following her thin fingers.

'Did Solomon do this to you?' he asked curtly.

'It was part of the transformation, everyone has it done,' she replied without thinking of what she was saying. A hint of anger tinged her words.

'You sound as if you enjoyed it, as if you were part of his family already.'

'I escaped, didn't I? Came back for you like I always do. I could have stayed. I was warm, well fed, and the company was tolerable, unlike . . .'

'And the mark upon your temple, did you agree to that as well? I wouldn't let a madman cut a cockroach in my head.' Jonah touched the side of her head and felt the ridges of a thick tattoo, crusted and bloodied above her right ear. 'Did Solomon give you that?'

Tara snapped his hand away, turning her face to one side to hide the mark from his view. She traced the ink-brand with her finger, following the shape of the creature that felt as if it was burrowing out from under her stubbled skin.

'It isn't a cockroach but a locust,' Malachi interrupted, stepping towards the girl. 'I have seen this before. This is a creature that consumes all before it. The plague of many lands that devours everything. It is Solomon's sign and a proclamation of his power.'

Tara kept silent, knotting her hands together and hunching her shoulders. She tried to smile, but all the joy had been bled from her and all that was left was a half-grimace that hung beneath the black rings of her sunken eyes.

'This place within the Alabaster, was it a reality or just a dream?' Malachi asked, breaking her trance.

'It was as real as you stand there. Like breaking the skin on the water and pushing your head into the deep and watching all that goes on within.' She looked anxiously to the Alabaster that

228

lay untouched before the fire. 'What time is it?'

'Time for us to leave the city,' Jonah said as he got to his feet. 'Our escape continues, and we will have more than Solomon looking for us. We have to get the oracle from the Citadel and leave for good.'

'Tersias is dead,' Tara blurted out, speaking the lie without remorse as she edged herself towards the stone box.

'DEAD?' Malachi asked. 'How can he be dead? We are to help him escape. Why didn't you say before? The boy is gone and all your concern has been about the Alabaster . . .'

'I couldn't tell you before but you have to know. It was the transformation . . . He was weak – his heart. No one meant it to happen.'

Malachi kicked the fire grate. 'So he was killed . . . He was nothing but a child and he was killed. And all you say is no one meant it to happen.'

'At least we didn't keep him in a cage and make him perform like a circus monkey. His last hours were in the warmth and kindness of friends, and not in some dark hole in service to a failed conjurer.' Tara edged closer to the Alabaster, her eyes fixed upon it like her heart's desire. 'The boy died quietly – it happens to us all, none of us will get out of this world alive.'

'You talk of a life, how can you speak of him that way?' Jonah asked. 'Out of all of us it was your heart that was burning with kindness for him.'

'Both of you would have used him for your own gain,' she snapped, ignoring what Jonah had said as she edged even closer to the Alabaster. 'Greed was what kept him in your concerns. Neither of you wanted to help him. You wanted the gold he would bring, and for his condition and well-being you cared nothing.'

'That was before,' Malachi replied. 'Much has happened to us both, and my mind has been turned by what I have faced.

229

Twice I have stared into hell and twice I have been redeemed. I am greatly forgiven and for that I am truly thankful.'

'Then show it – mourn for him, weep for him, tear your clothes in grief, but don't blame me for his death.'

'Did Solomon cut out your heart when he shaved your head and dressed you in his fine gown?' Jonah said. 'We should have let that creature suck you into the box and have done with you, Tara. What changes have been tattooed into your wits? It's you who has changed, not I.'

'That fate would have suited me finely. I didn't ask to be saved. I came for you, remember?' she screamed at him. Then she found the words she had always been too afraid to say. It was as if she had stumbled upon a hornets' nest that nestled deep within her. 'You'll never change, Jonah Ketch. Always a villain, a cheat and a liar.'

'So – she finally fesses to what she really thinks,' he said, spitting the words through his teeth in a low growl. He stepped towards her, his hand clenched in a tight fist. 'It was your heart that caught my eye, and now it's gone.' He laughed smugly, knowing his words were like a kiss upon the lips of death. For the briefest of moments he paused, knowing that he had one last chance to still his maw and pour comfort upon her; but though he knew what to say, he desired not to utter the right words. The insult that festered in his heart was sharper than any dagger and in one quick sentence he could kill their friendship as dead as the blind boy. 'You're a harlot, a cheap slaggart.' He bent and picked the Alabaster from her feet and held it before her. 'Take it, do what you will. Let it leech you dry.' Tara greedily snatched the Alabaster from him and held it to her chest. 'You belong in another world, for in this one you need a heart of flesh . . .'

There came a crashing of timber from the bar of the inn and without warning, Old Bunce was violently bundled into the parlour, spinning head over heels. He landed cumbersomely upon the wooden floor, and gasped a bloodstained breath that bubbled in his mouth. Malachi turned, hearing the clump of gigantic feet and the crashing of the tables by the fireside of the inn. From out of the shadows stepped Campion, bowing his head to step into the parlour. He smiled at Tara, who for a moment stood her ground. Then, seeing Jonah look to her, she began to cower away.

'Come to take you back,' Campion said as he stepped closer, his hand clutching a broken table leg. 'You can't be staying here all night – they could be for turning you back again.'

Tara gripped the Alabaster even tighter as Campion raised the stave in front of Malachi.

'You're still alive?' he asked. 'I thought you had the life beaten from your bones, and you are certainly no ghost.'

'I heal well . . .' the magician said, stepping away from Campion. 'Take the girl – we will not follow. She came to say good-bye and in her own way told us her life was with your company and not in ours.'

'Leave no witnesses, I was told. Leave no one,' Campion said as he took hold of Tara and pulled her towards him, wrapping her gently under his folded arm. 'What do you say, child?' he asked the girl. 'Do I pay him back for my slashed palm and pierced leg?'

Jonah and Malachi looked to her, hoping her words would in some way calm the beast.

Tara squeezed the Alabaster, a true smile returning to her lips. 'I say that servants should do as they are told and make their masters happy . . .'

'Very well, so mote it be.'

Suddenly, Jonah dived towards the fireplace, taking hold of the handle of the knife that lay by the coals. It stuck to his palm like frosted glass, icy cold in his grip. He let out a shrill cry as

Campion lashed down at him with the stave, cracking it against the stone mantel. Jonah twisted from the fire, knife in hand, and lashed out at the giant.

Malachi seized his chance and picked the candlestick from the table and thrashed at Campion again and again. Holding Tara as a shield as he dragged her from the room, the giant thrust the stave back and forth, trying to deal a blow to the magician.

Jonah took Bunce by the collar and pulled him back from the fight. His head fell limply to one side, blood trickling from his ears. Then, clutching the dagger, Jonah sprang across the room, jumping from table to chair, and grabbed the chandelier. He swung towards Campion, kicking him in the chest and sending him scurrying backwards and out of the parlour door.

Tara turned and ran with Campion, one hand gripping the Alabaster and the other clutching the giant's paw as together they dashed from the inn and into the street.

Malachi and Jonah gave futile chase. 'She's gone,' Malachi said as they stood by the portico. The baying of a hound echoed from Bloomsbury Square.

'But not forgotten,' Jonah replied. He looked at the knife, shining with a ghostly glow in the darkness.

20

The Sign of Tironian

Wrapped in a thick blanket, Old Bunce lay deadly still upon the market cart. Its wheels, pulled by Jonah and Malachi, groaned in the silent night of the Tyburn road. Since the coming of the comet, all of the nighthawks had fled the parks and gathering places for fear that another star would come crashing through the sky and splatter upon the earth, and there was an eerie stillness to the streets. A few cattle had taken to grazing on the flowerless waste of Green Park but the horses were gone, they had fled with the dogs when the madness had begun. It was rumoured that they had gathered in a vast herd in the Hampstead valley, whilst to the west the hounds hunted in gigantic packs, preying upon the lost and lonely traveller.

As they pushed the inn-keeper's dying body through the rutted avenues and squares, Jonah could not help remembering the warm smile that Tara had so readily shared on the night that the plot to catch Tersias had been hatched. He could still taste the bitter beef and cock of the forest that they had devoured together by candlelight. They had laughed and she had told tales in the way that only she could, her eyes glinting, her voice suspending disbelief. She had spoken of a king who had been blessed by the gods with the stroke of fortune and all that he touched was transformed to gold. Jonah had never heard such a tale. It was as if it were written for him. Tara had been about to speak of the ending when Maggot had screamed from the street – that was when the dog had attacked. She never finished her story and now she never would, but Jonah knew that such a gift would always bring blessing.

He cast a look to the ground and saw the shape of a man burnt into the dirt. It was as if he had been a human torch, all that was left was the buckle of his shoe. Malachi looked to the sky as he dragged on the cart. They were like two yoked beasts of burden, sharing the labour and knowing that their fates were entwined.

On the cart, Old Bunce stuttered in his breathing. The blow from Campion had crushed the bones in his neck, cutting the life from his hands and feet. Since leaving the inn he had moaned the same word again and again, calling for Tara, begging her to return. To Bunce she had been a daughter, friend and business companion. She had scraped the plates, counted the coins and filtered the dregs back into the barrel, freshening them with a handful of dry hops and a slug of gin. Now she was all he wanted, and he cried out like a small child calling for its mother.

'What do you think Griselda will do for him?' Jonah asked Malachi, hoping to break the long silence.

'From his pallor, I say all that will be done is slip him in the Thames and watch the tide take him away. There comes a time, Jonah my boy, when it is better to give the man to his maker than keep him here on earth. I once read a book that said there was a season for everything, a time to live and a time to die. For this old man his end has surely come.'

'We have to do something, Tara –' Jonah stopped, his thoughts catching his lip and cutting him short.

'Tara, Tara – dining with Solomon, eating oysters by the yard . . .' Malachi sang mockingly, holding out his hands and dancing a jig as he looked up to the stars. 'Her heart has turned; it was not your fault. She is gone. Now you have a duty to your old friend Mister Bunce. In his last hours you can do for him what is right and see your friend Maggot.'

'I don't want to die,' Jonah blurted out unexpectedly. 'Yet sometimes I wish I'd never been born at all.'

'The words of a queen, said before the chopper came down upon her soft white neck.' Malachi laughed to himself. 'There is nothing we can do about it. We are here and the only way of escape is through an uncertain doorway. We are born, we live and we die – that is life.'

'But we never know when our time will be.' Jonah insisted.

'That is the fun of life. Our death waits for us, stalks us, hides behind the bed and lurks in dark places. It is a sprig of hemlock in a friend's glass, a bolt of lightning upon a summer's day, an old rogue waiting in the night, an angel, a devil . . . We never know, nor should we know, for if we did then life would lose its purpose and we would give up our desires and our dreams.'

They talked on as the wheels of the cart turned the yards to Strumbelo and the stars turned the earth towards the sun. Within the hour they had left the broken houses of Tyburn, crossed the Hyde Park and taken the King's Road. Light grew in the east as a hazy sun clawed at the horizon, hoping to pull back the mantle of darkness. A quick wind blew upon them, lifting the taste of the cool dewed grass and spicing it on their lips. Streets gave way to open fields, thick hedges and bare orchards that stretched out towards the river.

In the distance the silver roof of Strumbelo came into view with its multitude of brick-edged chimneys, white plaster walls and black wood lattices. It rose up from a crown of thick sycamore branches and tall oaks, surrounded by a holly hedge that shimmered in the wind, green and blood-red.

Two tall iron gates with gold-painted railings stood before them, barring their way. Malachi rested the cart and checked

Old Bunce. The inn-keeper bleated his breaths, quick and sharp, as he grasped at life's last moments and his gullet rattled like witch's croup.

'He's not got long,' said the magician, looking around him. 'We must get him inside. It would not be good for him to leave us here. Better among friends and by the fire than in the lane by the crossroads.'

To each side of the gate the thick holly hedge stretched into the distance, covering the long stone wall that encircled the estate as far as a lake. Several metal bands formed an intricate lock that tied the portal firmly shut with no visible way of it ever being opened.

Jonah rattled on the gates, and on the other side there appeared a man dressed from head to foot in black and carrying a small lantern on the pike of a staff. His coat was turned up around his neck and his hat pulled down across his forehead so all that could be seen was the glint of one eye and the half-shadow of his broad lips. He appeared without sound, welcome or any herald of his advent.

'We . . .' Jonah said slowly, then looked to Malachi to continue.

'We have a sick man and we need your help. A young friend rests here and we presumed the lady would give us welcome.'

'Magnus Malachi?' the man asked in a rich dark voice that spoke of a far-distant place.

'Yes,' Malachi replied in his bewilderment. 'And –'

'Jonah Ketch?' the gateman asked, raising the lamp higher so that it helped the dawn light their faces.

'It is I, and –'

'Mister Bunce – bring him quickly. She said you would come and you're late. We have waited for two long hours and your feet have dragged every yard. Now, quickly,' he chided as his hand lifted one metal strand and then another, unravelling the lock. He lifted the gate from its keeper, allowing it to swing open by itself.

Without a word, the gateman thrust his staff into Jonah's hand, took hold of the market cart and set off at a pace towards the house with a frantic step. Bunce was rattled along the gravel drive and through the neat flowerbeds that led to the main door of the house. Behind them the gates swung shut and as Jonah looked back he saw the lock weave itself together, pulling the metal strands and quickly forming a tight, impenetrable seal without the aid of human hands. Several sheep huddled close as they grazed the lawn that fronted the large Tudor house. A door-lamp gave its last, as the long shadows of the growing sun slowly lifted the light of the sky and rendered the flickering candle useless.

Malachi and Jonah trotted behind the gateman as he pushed Old Bunce ever quicker to Strumbelo House. It was as if they were expected, and all was prepared for their arrival. The two large blue doors swung open by themselves and the light of the hallway flooded out into the shadowed frontage, lighting the neat brickwork of the wall that edged the building.

Griselda stood in the doorway, her arms wide open as if she welcomed long lost friends. She wore the same suit as when Jonah had first seen her, but this time her hair flowed freely, long and scarlet, tinged with flecks of silver, looking every inch a commander of the guard. She smiled, her soft face breaking the trepidation that Jonah had felt with every yard he had trod from the city to Strumbelo. He could hear the shite-hawks circling over the river to the south as they broke free of their roost and took off towards the Chelsea midden heap.

'Jonah, Magnus Malachi – we have waited for you. Bring him quickly and we will see what can be done,' Griselda said, an urgency squeezing her throat.

'My fear is that it is too late,' Malachi said as he pulled the hat from his head and scrunched it to his chest in the presence of the lady. 'A cure will be impossible, that I know.'

'Nothing is impossible for those who trust. There is a time for everything, and this illness will not end in death, that I know.'

'More faith than sense,' Malachi whispered under his breath as he raised an eyebrow of disbelief, hoping she would not hear his words.

'More faith . . .' she replied as she turned and followed the gateman, who by now had lifted Old Bunce from the market cart and carried his limp body through the fine doors and into the large hallway of the house. Jonah and Malachi followed without invitation, dragged in by the same curiosity as to what presence dwelt in this place. 'Stay here by the fire. You have no concern in what we do,' Griselda said curtly, pointing to the large brick fireplace fronted with two large leather chairs and a welcome table of porter and meat-cakes.

'I think we go no further,' Malachi said as the door to the inner room was slammed in his face by Griselda, striding purposefully on behind her servant. He saw Jonah looking around the hallway with its dark wood, twisting staircase, panelled walls and fine-weave carpet. 'This is Strumbelo – have you not heard of it? One of the finest yet strangest houses in the whole of England,' he said as he walked towards the fireplace and slumped in the chair, picking at the meat-cakes and pouring himself a large glass of porter. 'We'll be safe here. Neither Malpas nor Solomon would ever dare come to this place, she is a charmed woman and protected by the King.'

'You know much of this woman, Malachi. Until the other day I had heard nothing of her. She dresses like a man and carries a bag like a witch and yet you say she is protected by the King.' Jonah knelt at the table, warming his sore back by the fire.

'That's how she would like it to be. Always works in secret, never lets the right know what the left is doing. And yet all the time she is scheming and conjuring. Nobody knows what she is up to. All I know is that she is up to something.'

'And the King?' Jonah asked as he stuffed a meat-cake into his mouth and gulped the porter.

'She is said to have taken the Prince from the gates of death and cured him of his bleeding. He was the King's favourite and Griselda Malpas stepped into the court, spirited him away and brought him back a week later as if he had been born anew. No more sickness, strength in his bones and a jest on his tongue. For that the King will always be grateful,' Malachi said as he looked at the flames and settled back into his comfort.

'*Malpas?*' Jonah gulped as the meat stuck with surprise in his crop. 'Did you say, Griselda *Malpas?*'

'She is the wife of Lord Malpas. A lady in her own right, an arranged marriage of course, but marry him she did. Though many have said that as soon as he spluttered out the words of agreement, it was a marriage in name only. Strumbelo is her mother's house, given to Lady Malpas on the day she died.'

'The history of my family should be left to those who know and not to the ramblings of some old magician,' Griselda said as she jumped the last few steps of the staircase and stood before them. 'What a time you both have had. I hear you have half of London after you and wanting to kill you.' She stopped and looked at Jonah who knelt before her gawping, wide-eyed, his mouth full of food. 'Don't listen to Magnus Malachi, he is an alchemist and it is well known that any magician makes up that which he doesn't know.'

'Bunce?' Jonah sighed as if she had come to tell them the worst. 'Is he –?'

'BUNCE! COME OUT!' she shouted as the doors to the room opposite the stairs slowly opened. 'Your friends are concerned that you are dead.'

'Don't joke with us. We brought him here to die. The man had a broken neck,' Malachi said, getting to his feet and stepping towards her.

'Then you will be grievously disappointed. Bunce, come out!' Griselda commanded as she walked to the door.

It was then that Old Bunce stepped into the hall, scratching his face and ruffling his whiskers. Malachi held the back of the chair to steady his frame as Jonah got to his feet and ran to the old man.

'Touch him not!' Griselda shouted as the gateman stepped from the room, picked Jonah from his feet, swung him around and sat him back in the chair in one quick movement. 'The healing still goes on. You can make your embrace in the morning when all is truly well.'

'Is it really you, Bunce?' Jonah asked as he again tried to get to his feet, only to be pressed to the chair by the gateman's firm hands.

'It is I, Jonah. It is I and I am well. Oh, if you had seen what beauty I have endured in these last hours! You were wise to bring me here. I have never felt better. What wonder, what glory there has been in my dreaming.'

'And you will be even better once you have dried out and eaten your first meal in years,' said Griselda. 'Man cannot live by beer alone, Mister Bunce. Follow Abel, and he shall show you where you will rest.' The gateman gripped Bunce by the sleeve of his coat and led him up the long flight of stairs in front of a large window of leaded glass that let in the first rays of the November sun. 'You'll be wanting to see Maggot. I find he cannot wake much before nine so I let him rest. He has a life of work ahead of him, so what is an idle start when he has been so sorely treated?'

Jonah scowled and looked to the floor. Malachi sensed his tension. 'Strumbelo is a very different place, Lady Malpas,' the magician said as he picked up the porter and poured himself a small glass.

'What happens in the world doesn't happen here and what happens here doesn't happen in the world – is that what you mean, Magnus?' Griselda asked. She went to the oak panelling, pushed upon a wooden square and waited as the wall slid open before their eyes. 'Who has the Alabaster?' she asked as she bent into the darkness and picked up an apothecary's bag and carried it to the table. The wall slid tightly shut behind her.

'Campion took it and he will give it to Solomon the prophet,' Malachi answered like a chastised child.

'And the key? Do you still hide it from the world, thrust in the darkness of your pocket?' she said, looking at Jonah.

'It is here . . . And as you said, it has brought me much lament.' Jonah couldn't look at her as he felt the handle of the knife. It was then that he realised it was cold, lifeless, and gave no warmth. The dagger no longer tingled his fingertips with its touch nor gave him the desire to draw it forth and watch it spark through the air.

'Then keep it, for it still has work to be done and you are the one who will carry it to the place it desires.'

'You know much of what we do, Lady Malpas. It is as if we are the pawns in your game of chess.' Malachi sipped from the porter, which warmed his gullet and loosened his tongue as the fire blazed contentedly behind him.

'I am an onlooker to the game you are entangled in. I have no useful part other than my interest in all of your lives. As for chess, then I too am a piece played by a larger, wiser hand.' Griselda stopped and looked at them both. Malachi stood proudly, his leg straightened. He looked out of place in his long magician's coat that he had kept wrapped about him for the past nine years. Jonah sat wide-eyed, rapt in the tranquillity of all that was around him. It was as if the bricks and timbers spoke of peace, as if the house lived and breathed contentment. 'The future is in your hands and not mine. See how you have been changed, and in that you will bring change to others.'

'What must we do?' Malachi asked, taking both of their thoughts and giving them a single voice.

'Go back to London. Find the girl and the Alabaster. Give the dagger to Lord Malpas,' Griselda said.

'Then you are with him in this?' Jonah snapped.

'I have been with him for many years and have broken my heart over this man and all he has done. There are those around him who would see me dead, and but for the protection of the King that would have come to pass long ago. What troubles him is not of flesh or blood but of powers and principalities our mortal minds have not beheld.' For the first time, Jonah sensed her deep concern, as if her confidence had some hidden chink. 'Malpas has never set foot in this house. He has carried that Alabaster since our wedding day and thought more of it than the covenant we made. In it is his curse, passed from one to the other, father to son. It eats him like the plague and he has turned his back on all that is true. Strumbelo could set him free, but he wants none of its beauty.'

'I saw his life in a dream,' Jonah said quickly, getting up from the comfort of the chair. 'There was a wolf, and the dagger saved the King . . . Look!' He held out the sleeve of his blood-stained shirt.

'More than a dream, a living nightmare – I saw it myself,' Malachi said as he pulled back the sleeve of Jonah's coat to show the rough bandage that he had wrapped around Jonah's arm.

'Then there will be no terrifying chimeras for you. Dread has lodged itself in your heart, and perfect love will cast out all fear.'

Suddenly Griselda grabbed him by the arm and tore the

242

bandage furiously from his skin. The wound exploded in thick gore that bubbled and stank as it was exposed to the air. Malachi put his hand to his face. The teeth-marks in Jonah's flesh quickly festered in the new light of the morning that rainbowed into the hallway through the colours of the stained glass. Griselda took the wound and covered it with her hand, squeezing the skin as she spoke words that Malachi had never heard before.

Jonah screamed as he was thrown to the floor, but Griselda kept her grip and twisted his arm back and forth. As he writhed in pain the air around him slowly filled with a green haze that grew thicker and changed in mass as it formed into strange shape. It seeped from every part of Jonah, flowing from his nostrils like volcanic sulphur. It percolated around their feet, cold and stinking, as the skin on his arm blistered further, bursting open in thick green wounds as Griselda kept her grip upon him, muttering, her eyes fixed upon his. The mist cowered by the fire and piled upon itself, slowly taking the contours of a beast. It began to snarl and growl as it turned into the presence of a translucent wolf.

Malachi leapt from the creature as it crawled about his feet. He hid behind the leather chair, grabbing his curse bag, looking for a charm to protect him. Two large red eyes formed in what could clearly be seen as the creature's long, thin head. They peered in the firelight, looking at each one of them in turn as if to judge who would be the best one to possess.

'You have no place here!' Griselda shouted at the beast as it stepped towards Malachi. 'Lycaon, be gone! Your curse is done and time is ended. Go to that place appointed to you and await your judgement!'

The creature flexed and convulsed with each word. Jonah lurched forward, open-mouthed, trying to gasp a morsel of the mist and give it lodging within his breath.

243

'It is finished Jonah – it has no home with you. What started as a child is gone . . . You have been set free.'

'*Free?*' muttered a voice that hung in the room without form and spoke as if it came from several places at once. 'He will never be free, his kind never are. Their only hope for sanity is to be my lodging house.' The voice whispered like the wind as it gave a deep childlike sob that sent shivers through Malachi. 'Let him take one more breath, he knows he needs my companionship – who else would give him such . . . pleasant . . . dreams?'

Malachi looked to the fireplace as the beast grew in size and darkened to the deepest purple, the hair on its ridged back standing on end. It bared its teeth and growled, its two long fangs matching the wound on Jonah's arm, as it flattened its long black ears close to its head and prepared to strike.

'Jonah, it's me,' it said, mimicking Tara's voice. 'Don't make me go away. You shouldn't listen to this woman, she will stop everything that is planned for your life. Give me sanctuary . . .' From all around them came an echoing sobbing that rang out throughout the house, as if Strumbelo had been filled with a multitude of grieving children.

'GO NOW!' Griselda shouted as she stepped towards the creature, her arm outstretched as if about to grab hold of its mane.

It cowered back, settling itself in the flames that burnt through its body as if it were not there. 'This is your last chance, Jonah . . . It's your mother who speaks,' it said, gin-soaked and careless, just how she would have uttered the words. 'You know I never meant you any harm, boy.'

Jonah threw himself to the floor and covered his ears, hoping never to hear another word from the beast. 'Leave me, leave me! I want nothing from you.'

'BE GONE!' shouted Griselda for the last time. She stepped

into the large fireplace and was consumed in the creature's mist as it gathered about her. 'I will invoke the *name*, so be gone . . .'

There was an ear-splitting call as the creature burst into a thousand pieces, exploding across the room. It knocked Malachi to the floor, tumbling the furniture about it as it spun round before being sucked in upon itself in an ever-greatening darkness. The curse bag pulled tightly around Malachi's neck, choking the wind from his body as it too was sucked into the air towards the black hole. The force lifted the magician from the floor, and he could neither breathe nor speak as he tried to call out to be saved.

Griselda quickly pulled a thin dagger from the top of her boot and lashed out at the cords that twisted themselves around Malachi's neck. Instantly they snapped, and the small leather sack flew through the air and disappeared into the ever-decreasing black hole. There was a sudden gust of wind that shook the house as if it were the voices of a thousand dead souls being dragged to Hades.

Then in an instant all was calm, the storm had been stilled and the creature gone. Lady Malpas looked down upon Jonah and Malachi as they both lay helpless upon the hearthrug, worn out and dishevelled. Jonah tried to speak, many questions filling his eyes.

'Now is not the time,' she said softly as she made the sign for silence upon her lips. 'This is not the end of your journey, but the beginning.'

The Great Remonstrance

In the tower of the Citadel, complete blackness filled the room. The disciples had blackwashed the high windows and stripped the chamber of every candle. Sprigs of yew and holly had been placed by each ledge and seven mistletoe berries circled each one. By the high table was placed a square and compass and a white chalk line led away, cutting the room in two precise halves, measured and re-measured by Solomon and several of his disciples.

From the blackness of the twisted stairwell Campion swaggered up, in his hand a large candelabra holding six crooked red candles that gave off a meagre glow. He walked slowly to the high table between two small stone pillars made of cut marble and entwined around with twisted oak.

Solomon walked behind, slowly chanting to himself as with each step he scratched at his hand nervously, unsure as to what was to come. He stood in the centre of the room, a piece of fine silk cable noosed around his neck, his shirt cut away on the right side and a black feather mask covering his face. By his feet was the wicker coffin, garlanded with fresh flowers.

Tersias sat in the shadowland, the helmet upon his head blinding him from the Wretchkin. Campion had shown the strength of his arm and his disregard for all that the creature had spoken through the boy – there had been no safekeeping, no warmth of heart, as he had doled out his misery with great glee. In his heart Tersias had steeled himself for what he knew would come, for all that he would have to endure. In his muteness he had decided that he would no longer beg like a dog licking for morsels, and would never again do the will of ungracious men.

Solomon dragged Tersias from the chair, which was held upright by Campion. The bruise on the boy's cheek glowed in the candlelight as Solomon then scurried back and forth, lighting the small mounds of incense that he had piled on seven golden plates and placed in a small circle around the room in the height of the tower.

'We need the boy to speak,' Solomon said as he goaded Campion to make him utter the meekest of words. 'We are protected from the demon, and I want to know if he can hear other spirits through which we can be wise.'

Campion twisted the boy's fingers and whispered in his ears. 'Will you speak to us, boy?' he asked. Then he grabbed him by the scruff of his coat and shook him back and forth.

'Don't shake the life from him,' Solomon protested. 'Well, not yet – let him at least speak to us before he dies'

Tersias remained silent, his mind filled with thoughts of Malachi. Something turned in his heart as he thought of the man, something that made him conceive of all that was different in the magician's life. All that Tersias truly wanted was to be free from the curse that had brought him to this place. He had heard the desperation in Malpas's voice as he had struggled to know what was to come; Solomon had felt the same, and it was a desire that Tersias knew he could never satisfy. Both had lusted to know the future, yet even in their grinding voices Tersias had gleaned the chilling sound of fear.

Blinded and double-blinded by the helmet, Tersias sat in his darkness and waited, his thoughts running free. Deep within him was the thread of compassion that he held for Tara. As he listened to the distant comings and goings of Campion and Solomon, with their threats and lonely curses, he thought of the girl. He remembered the sweet voice and soft skin that had led him onwards through the night from captivity. But then Tersias had sensed the subtle change in her voice as he listened drowsily to her transformation.

He began to babble and call out to the Wretchkin, hoping that the creature would come and see his bruised face and seek restitution for all that had been done to him. Nothing came in reply – no sound of the beast's wings, no chilling of his spine, nothing . . . He was lost, lonely and alone, left in the blackness of his imprisonment. But though he yearned for the creature to come, his stronger desire was to be free of its control, never to speak again on the demand of covetous men.

'Come, boy,' Campion said, lifting him higher and placing him in the wooden chair. 'We need you to speak to us . . .'

'Don't call upon the creature,' Solomon babbled. 'We want to listen to *other* spirits – kinder, more gentler oracles that will lead us in to all truth.' Solomon shook Tersias back and forth. 'Speak, boy, speak . . . I have heard it done by other Sayers.'

'I understand,' Tersias said dreamily as he gripped the seat of the wooden chair, his hand searching for a splinter to bring him pain and cause him to find reality again.

'Very well,' Solomon said. He crouched before the boy, examining him for any sign of the presence of the creature. 'To whom will you speak?'

'What is your desire?' Tersias asked. 'I can hear many voices wanting to come to counsel you.'

Solomon wrung his hands in great hope, a thin smile across his lips turning the anguish of his face to a moment of pleasure. 'Of what shall we speak, Campion? Guide me, you oaf. I wish not to waste one word of the oracle's precious breath.'

'Ask him of my future and not that the Wretchkin shall return, another spirit will suffice.'

Tersias heard his words and bowed his head. He thought for a moment and called upon the spirit to hear his voice. There was silence in the heavens, not a word was spoken, no creature heard his call. Tersias panicked, panting, unsure what he was to do, but then a peace came upon him, all-consuming and perfect in its abundance.

'What would you know of me?' he asked in a voice that was deep, lifeless and beyond his years. 'Tell me, the creature is near,' he said, knowing he was alone.

'Is it the . . . Wretchkin?' Solomon asked feebly as he stood behind Campion.

'Another spirit, wiser and more willing to know the ways of man.'

'Speak, spirit, speak,' Solomon said, pushing Campion towards the boy.

'What is it you seek to know?' Tersias said in an altered voice, shaking himself as if deeply chilled and flopping his head from one side to the other.

'You can hear us though the boy is bound within the helmet?' Solomon asked warily.

'Your words come clear as the desires of your heart . . .'

'And what are those desires?' Solomon asked.

'To know what is to come and your place in the history of mankind.'

Solomon gulped as if the voice speaking through Tersias knew his heart. 'How do you know this?' he asked, looking closely through the candlelight to the boy.

'It is written upon your heart. I can hear it with every beat,' Tersias lied.

''Tis true, Campion, that *is* my desire, the oracle knows my mind. Loosen his bonds so that he may speak more, the wreaths will keep the Wretchkin from our door. There are other spirits with which the boy may converse.'

Tersias took in a deep, mournful breath, his lungs burning from the linctus that pulsed through his veins like hot wire. The boy knew Solomon's heart, it was the same as every man's who had stood before him and asked questions of the oracle. It was always the same: people fearful of the future, not content with what was given to them and always wanting more. Once a woman with a screeching voice had asked him what dress she should wear that night. The Wretchkin had laughed when it spoke through him, telling her it would be best to cover her rump in a sail-breadth of sackcloth to hide it from the world. Another had pleaded to know if the sickness he carried would end in death. The creature had spoken boldly that he should dip himself seven times in a vat of finest wine and that he would be cured. The man had rushed away heartily and happy – and when he was a way down the road the Wretchkin had whispered to Tersias that the enquiring pilgrim would be dead within the hour, drowned by his own foolishness and his family indebted to the vintner, to be cast in prison until the sum was repaid. Yet they still came to listen to the truths, half-truths and more often bold lies that the beast would speak. They would believe all in their desperation and discontent, holding out palms to be read by blind eyes.

Tersias grappled with his thoughts. Though his mind was drunk with bitter gall, he knew that this was his chance to speak for himself, to be more than a puppet with coarse strings pulled by men and demons. His mouth had been forced to the shape of men so often that in this hour he sought recompense, a great remonstrance to change his world and bring to an end the war that tore his soul apart. Through the eyes of spirits he had spied the distant glint of dancing and laughter that lived outside his cage of meagreness and cruelty. The face of

Malachi haunted him, churning from within, pushed on by the gall to inhabit his mind's eye like a grey ghost.

'So what is it you would say to me, spirit?' Solomon said as he waited impatiently for the word to come from the boy. He looked around him, listening for the slightest sound at the window, hoping that the Wretchkin could not invade their presence.

'Your future sits before you, but there is another that will seek what you crave. As for your desires, those are written in the lines of your face.'

'And this other,' Solomon asked urgently, 'who shall it be?'

Tersias rocked from side to side, the linctus and gall gripping his throat and twisting the breath from him. 'I will speak no more,' he said in his own weak voice. 'I have done with being an oracle, get away from me, spirit, get away . . . Someone help me, save me!' he shouted at the emptiness.

'Make him speak, Campion,' said Solomon as he pulled a vial of linctus from his pocket. 'Hold him and we'll give him more, no one gets to keep their mind with the sap of the poppy rattling in their bile.' Solomon unscrewed the lid from the bottle and held it to his nose, sniffing the thick, trickling syrup that clung to its edges. 'One day, Campion, when I am the Divine Protector of this land, I shall give this to them all. I will have a spout placed in each house so they can sup of what they wish. There will be no thoughts of revolution, no murmuring of discontent, all will yield to it as the boy will now yield to me. They will be so deluded they will call good, bad and bad, good, and in all this I will be victorious.'

'NO!' screamed Tersias, attempting to speak in the voice of the spirit. 'He needs no more for he will not be able to tell of what is to come . . .'

Solomon looked at Campion and then back to the boy. He held in his eyes a look of apprehension and distrust. 'Tell me, Tersias, who speaks through you?'

There was a long silence. Tersias battled within himself, knowing that for Tara's sake that he must keep a grip on his thoughts and not allow the gall to take from him his speech. The boy could feel the heaviness seeping through each limb, numbing as it went with heavy deadness. His hand trembled as each sinew and nerve died as the linctus spread inch by inch.

It was then he heard a whisper in a far corner of his mind. It was not a demon's voice. It had no words or commands, it called him not to speak for it or beg his reverence. All it said was spoken in feelings of peace that fell upon him like golden waves, wrapping him in bonds of finest charity and grace. Though the poppy linctus numbed the side of his face and the spit slathered from his mouth, his head became filled with a bright pure light that burst through his mind, lifting him from the constraints of his blindness.

Tersias sat bolt upright, his heart quickened by the pulsating radiance that shuddered deep within. Solomon saw the sudden and changed expression on his face: gone was the gall-induced grimace, his cheeks were blessed and rosy red, his dull eyes bright and glistening with fresh tears that spoke of the rush of gladness as the gall and linctus were banished from him.

'He's transformed, Campion, the spirit has entered into him again,' Solomon said, mistakenly taking the sudden change as being the coming of a dark presence. 'Speak child, tell me what the creature has to say – what of my quest? Will I accomplish greatness?'

'I serve you, but I am not your servant, you call me yet I can do what I please,' Tersias said. 'What will you give the boy for my knowledge? Pay the player or the music will remain silent.'

'What do you need for your utterance?' Solomon asked as he fumbled in his pockets, looking for some trinket to appease the ghostly presence.

'Safe passage for the boy, and no more linctus to cloud his

mind.' Tersias pretended to twitch and moan as if some spirit was within him. 'For that I will tell you all you seek to know – that and one thing other.'

'Speak, ask, if it is within my will then I will obey your command,' Solomon replied anxiously.

'There is a girl, give her safe passage.'

'That I will gladly do. It has always been my intention. Upon her return she will be set free like a London dove.'

'Then I will speak,' Tersias said in a deep dark voice as he contorted his face. 'What is it you wish to know?'

Again Solomon looked at Campion as if he were lost for words. 'You . . . you said there was another who would challenge me for what I wanted who shall that be?'

Tersias thought quickly, racking his mind for a name to pick as a threat to Solomon. It was then that within his mind he heard the voice of Lord Malpas, moaning by the Charing Cross.

'His name is Malpas. He seeks power and wants to control the boy. He searches for him and his keeper, Magnus Malachi.'

'And Malpas searches for the oracle?' Solomon asked.

'As you stand here, his men run and listen at the corner of every street, they question men to speak of what they know. Soon they will be here. You must strike at him before he strikes at you. Let the creatures you keep do the will of Solomon so there is no blood on your hands.'

'You know of the locusts?' Solomon asked.

'You will set the girl free?' Tersias asked, his voice disguised in the grunts of the spirit.

'I have promised. But how do I trick Malpas?' Solomon asked.

'Give him a gift of insects. Allow him to open the box and he shall no longer be a problem to you.'

Solomon clapped his hands and jigged from side to side. 'If

I had thought of it myself it could not have been better. You speak well, spirit, you may come again. But now, boy,' he shouted, 'now your task is done I must have you under my control, I cannot allow your mind to be entered by any spirit that would deceive me through your fickle lips. Campion, hold him fast. He shall drink more of his share of linctus.'

Solomon gripped the boy by his face and squeezed open his mouth, then poured the linctus down his throat. Tersias spat back at him but Campion grabbed the boy, engulfing him in the grip of his arm and crushing the breath from him as Tersias slowly weakened, his body giving way to the sudden, powerful force that swept through him.

'He may have lied to us,' Solomon said as Tersias slumped to the floor. 'But to trick Malpas would leave the day open for what we desire. To catch a rat you need good bait. Bait to the trap, Campion, bait to the trap.'

The Opprobrium

The clock struck the half hour as Magnus Malachi strolled down the stairs in Strumbelo House and into the hall. The fire glowed in the night, flashing and sizzling as it consumed the dried hazel and the sprinkling of powdered apple blossom that Abel had scooped upon it. He was alone, but the house was full of sighs as the old timbers contracted and wheezed and the fragrance of hot apple scented the rooms.

Malachi looked to the clock that sat on the long oak case by the front door, its brass face and thick hands pointing clearly to half past nine. He had slept the day and the evening. His bed had been soft and warm with fresh linen. Its posts and curtains rose up from the floor like Corinthian columns, set like a fine temple to a god with no name. For the first time in thirty years he had taken a bath; it had been hot and steamy with French soap and the finest drying cloths he had ever seen. Malachi had been too afraid to spoil them upon his dirtied limbs, so he had rubbed himself dry with the old floor mat by the fireside tub. Then he had changed into the suit of clothes that had been left for him. Fresh boots, a gentleman's coat and a pair of sturdy breeches made of thick oiled cloth. These had been set against a crisp white shirt and yellow waistcoat.

As he had soaked, Malachi had clipped away the years of grime from his fingernails and etched their outline against the skin, clipping each claw back to that of a human hand. He admired his fingers as he walked slowly down the stairs, affording himself every opportunity to gaze upon his clean skin as, with a sly gawp, he looked at his reflection in the tall window.

Malachi smirked like a child caught with cream on its face and fingers wrapped deeply in warm chocolate. 'Oh! What joy!' he muttered in a bold but quiet exclamation as he fought back a rising sense of excitement that filled him to the brim. He danced the last three steps and settled himself in the fine chair by the fireside, then poured the remnants of the porter and stared into the flames. His eyes devoured the room as if he saw the world with a new light. Malachi thought of the creature that had been cast from Jonah that very morning before the hours of sleep had overtaken him.

It was as if he had been freed from a moribund goal that had kept him bound for so long. The poverty of mind and desperation to serve himself had vanished from him. He had sought that which was not of this world, yearned to have his desires for the incredible confirmed with evidence that had long eluded him. Here, in Strumbelo, he had seen all that he needed to give him hope. In the banishing of the beast he had been witness to a power beyond his imagination, magic beyond magic that was filled with the force of creation. The internal struggle that had gripped Malachi for so many years was now over, and he felt no need of magic and alchemy. His mind was now gripped only with a desire to find the blind boy and the girl and set them free.

Like a content old owl he snuggled in the chair and warmed his boots by the fire as he closed his eyes and dozed, delighted in his surroundings. He continued to snooze as approaching footsteps echoed along the high landing. When he felt a gentle breeze from the opening of the door waft upon his face he ignored it like a pleasant irritation, until, slightly opening one eye, he saw Griselda crossing the hallway from the door to the room where Old Bunce had been healed.

The footsteps raced high above them, the sound of the chase getting nearer. Upon each landing, Malachi could hear the echoing squeal of bright laughter. The pounding upon the oak boards beat like a soft drum, warm and welcoming. Griselda sat opposite him, settling back into the chair and folding her arms to match his as she crossed her legs and lay back happily.

'Jonah has found Maggot,' she said, smiling at Malachi. 'They have searched the attics and the cellars and now they chase each other across the landings.'

'You did a good thing for the boy,' Malachi said quietly. 'I have waited many years for such a display of magic and found it here.'

'My dear Magnus, that was not magic, alchemy or any other mad ranting. Nor was it the guile of some secret society. In all truth, it was an honest gesture of love, and there is no greater power than that.'

'Then of that love do I want to share and in its path shall I follow,' Malachi said boldly as the footsteps echoed overhead.

'Those are words that could cost you dearly, for this love was bought at a great price and its acceptance should be highly honoured,' Griselda said as she listened to the stillness that had suddenly descended on the house.

'Then its honour shall be worn upon my heart, and for its purpose I will turn my life.' Malachi smiled at her, his heart warmed by the presence that filled Strumbelo and was impossible to ignore. It was as if the air itself was infected with joy, and the walls themselves gave out the centuries of charity which they had absorbed from generation to generation.

'They are hiding,' Griselda said with a nod as she cast her eyes to the ceiling. 'Maggot has seen much in his short life. No one to care for him. A child who had to search in the squalor for his food until Old Bunce found him. Not a life for one so young.'

'We are a wicked and cruel generation,' Malachi said. 'I fear that the water here may have washed away my good sense. I feel that my heart now bleeds for such as him, and the fate of Tersias and the girl brings me deep distress. Yet even in such great concern I cannot keep the smile from my face.' He rubbed his hand over his smooth chin, his beard now gone, his hair neat and trimmed around the ears and plaited into a precise pigtail. He looked away from Griselda and then back to her face, catching her eye with his smile. 'I want to go and find them, but I can't go alone. The girl, Tara, told me that Tersias was dead, that in the transformation his weakened heart had given in. I need to know if that is true, to find out for myself, and if he is dead then bury him with the dignity he deserves. I beg that you will let me take Jonah and together we will make aright all the meddling and scheming that we have entered into in our old hearts.' Malachi gulped nervously as he sipped the porter. 'Solomon has the city in fear. Every man-jack thinks he was behind the coming of the comet and the night when the sky went black and the earth shuddered. Whatever it is that he seeks to do, I will stop him.'

'Many have tried, Malachi. The churchyards of Poplar are littered with their corpses. What makes you think you could succeed?' Griselda asked as she got to her feet and stood by the firing, warming herself against the flames.

'It's the boy, Tersias. If you knew what I had done to him you would not have me under this roof. My cruelty is tattooed into the lines on my face. For my own sake I have to make amends, even if I were to die in the endeavour.'

'And I will join you Malachi,' Jonah said as a trap door opened in the panelling by the fire and both he and Maggot sprang into the hall. Then a sudden and surprised silence fell upon him. Jonah stared at the old magician, looking him up and down, examining every stitch of fine clothing and every single trimmed hair. 'Malachi – is it you?' He looked upon him as if he stared on the countenance of a stranger.

'It is I, Jonah. Magnus Malachi. Your companion and friend.' A tear welled in his eye as he panted his breath, his lip quivering with joy. 'It is good to see you, and this – this must be your friend, Mister Maggot?'

Jonah lifted Maggot to his feet and brushed the dust from his tunic. 'Not but three days ago his leg was broken – now he is as strong as me. He is completely healed and filled with life. What do you think to that, Malachi?'

'Magnus has thought much this night and he cannot take in any more than his mind will allow. Isn't that right, Magnus?' Griselda asked as she stoked the fire. She filled the grate with a bundle of logs, scooped a cup of apple blossom and watched the sparks dance up the wide chimney.

'So when can we go to London and conquer the Citadel?' Jonah asked. 'I am an outlaw and a fugitive, I have nothing to lose, and my friend to gain.'

'It isn't a game, Jonah. You are fighting more than men and there is more at stake than meets the eye.'

Jonah laughed. 'We fight old Solomon and Lord Malpas,' he said merrily. 'We sneak into the Citadel and find Tara and the boy, kidnap them and bring them to Strumbelo . . . Surely you can shake the devil from Tara's mind and put aright all that Solomon has twisted in her head?'

'If only it were that simple,' Griselda said as she walked from the fire and pushed the secret panel on the wall until it slammed shut. 'She must want to be set free. You had sought to be rid of your fear. It had held you since childhood and now was your time. The dog that picked you from the cradle was a doorway to your soul that allowed the terror to grow. Now it is gone. I can promise nothing for the girl.'

'But you would try?' Jonah asked anxiously, unsure of how

she knew of the beast that had picked him from his cot. 'Whenever I feared the most,' he went on, 'I would see the beast that came from me. In the night by the inn when Maggot was in the street and the dog attacked him, all I could see in my mind was that creature. It stared at me through red eyes, laughing, scolding me for being frightened.'

'I will not stop you going, Jonah. You needn't fear it any more. But be aware that Solomon and Lord Malpas want you, and you will face the militia and the disciples. Are you still prepared to go?'

'Of this I am certain,' Jonah said as he looked at Maggot and then to Malachi. 'In my life, Tara stuck by me no matter how I treated her. In this hour I will stand for her whether she wants me or not.'

'Then the matter is resolved as I knew it would be. You haven't disappointed me, Jonah, nor you, Magnus Malachi.' Griselda turned to Malachi. 'My carriage will take you into the city. It is upon you and Jonah as to what you do then. Bring Tara here and watch for Lycaon, that old wolf has perhaps not said goodbye to you for good.' Enfolded in the brisk scent of apple blossom, she stopped and listened to the silence of the house. 'One thing I know – the oracle is not dead. The boy, Tersias is still alive. If he were dead then the demon that speaks through him would have left the city. My companions tell me that its presence has been felt all these last days. Tread carefully, for it grows in strength and power and soon will be able to speak for itself and do away with the boy for good.'

'We shall go this very hour and make the night our mantle of disguise,' Malachi said as he stood and faced the door. 'Whatever awaits, I know I go into the night with a new heart. I came here a drudge, a broken man wrapped in rags, and in the sleep of the morning I awoke anew. For that I shall always be grateful to you.' Malachi bowed in front of Griselda. 'But one thing . . .'

he said nervously, wringing his hands together. 'It has been on my mind all of the time I have been here and of your consideration I need to be assured.'

'Whatever you said about me before you came is of no concern for me,' Griselda said, reading his mind.

Malachi looked to Jonah as if he had been betrayed.

'I said nothing,' the boy replied.

'You talk in your sleep,' Griselda said. 'Abel prepared your bath and heard your mumblings – but I forgive you, whatever words you spoke of me.'

'I didn't know you and yet was so willing to destroy your repute to the boy,' Malachi said, his eyes still downcast.

'That is the way of the world. Every day we slaughter with our tongues as if our head is inhabited by the foulest of fiends. We can control our sword arm, but we cannot control the smallest muscle that inhabits our body. But for that, Magnus, you are forgiven.'

Malachi smiled, catching a glimpse of himself in the looking-glass that hung by the door. 'Of one thing I am sure – I will not be recognised, not in these fine clothes and with my chin that shines like two fresh orchids.'

'What weapons shall we take with us Malachi?' Jonah asked excitedly as he began to follow.

'Take nothing but the Mastema,' Griselda said. 'You will need nothing more but the dagger. Keep your wits and seek the impossible. Lord Malpas will grow more desperate for the knife. A time is coming when he must have it. I am not sure as to what will be the best for him. I have offered the cure to him many times, but the true cost of his redemption is too great for him to bear. He is a proud man and his pride blinds him from what is gracious and good.' There was sadness in her voice as if it was tinged with grief, and yet she spoke firmly, steadfast and resolute. She looked down at the palms of her hands as if she read a book before her.

The door opened and Abel stood there dressed in a coach-man's jacket that stretched to the floor. He carried a long horsewhip and a cutlass in his hands. He nodded to Malachi for him to follow as a sharp wind blew through the opening, fanning the log flames and scattering the burning apple blossom across the room in tiny yellow sparks.

'Quickly, you can be in London by midnight,' Griselda said. 'There is no moon and the city will be quiet. I hear there is a circus in St James's Field – it will keep Malpas amused and his thoughts away from you.'

Griselda ushered them to the door as Abel opened the carriage and helped Malachi to his seat. Jonah jumped upon the leading wheel and slithered through the open window, sliding across the leather seat and falling into the footwell with a pleasured grunt.

Malachi lifted him to the bench as Abel slammed the door and jumped to the driving plate. He cracked the whip above the horses' heads as they broke trot towards the gates. Jonah looked back towards the house, the red-brick chimneys rising from the roof towards the night. It was then he noticed that Strumbelo shone with an iridescent glow that shimmered from each stone, brick and slate. As they sped along the gravel drive, even the small box-hedges that neatly enclosed each flowerbed gave off a strange, eerie light as if illuminated by the dawn sun.

Abel said nothing as he sat above them wrapped in his thick blanket, his whip and cutlass across his knees. Ahead they heard the gates creaking open, again pulled by unseen hands that worked the lock and allowed the carriage to leave unhindered. As they trotted by, Jonah saw the gates close again and the lock snap shut, weaving itself together as if charmed. He said nothing, his mind reeling from the vain promise he had made to save Tara from Solomon. Grave doubts now clutched his throat, twisting in his gullet as they sped past tall oaks that bowed majestically with their passing.

In the brightness and hope of Strumbelo, all had seemed possible. Bravery came easily when amongst friends and in a passionate light. But here in the trembling darkness of the carriage Jonah's thoughts found their old pattern. He was alone, unable to see more of Malachi than a dark, ghostly outline. The horses dragged him to face an old foe, one he had secretly never hoped to see again. Good intentions had seized him whilst in Griselda's presence; now in her absence he allowed himself to dread what was to come and he was seized by waves of self-doubt.

'Malachi,' he said feebly, and the magician sensed the weakness of his words. 'Will we succeed?'

'We escaped from Malpas and fought with Campion. We have been beaten, imprisoned, cheated, and now we sit in one of London's finest carriages and wear clothes our bodies think are the vestments of a dream – is that not success?'

'But we are going back, and we haven't even got a plan. We can't turn up at Solomon's door and ask for her to be set free.'

'Every castle has its weakest point and even the Citadel can be breached.' Malachi stopped speaking and listened to the steady trundling of the wheels over the broken road. The constant pounding of the horses' hooves reminded him of the clock at Strumbelo that even in the most distant room of the house could somehow be heard, far way, marking out the time like a heartbeat. 'Do you want to see Tara again?' he asked as he reached out a hand in the blackness to steady himself as the carriage rocked from side to side.

'One part of my heart cries out for her, the other cares not for what she has become and tells me to leave her to her fate with Solomon. Yet I know that if it were I trapped in that place dressed in purple and with a cockroach painted on my head, she would be beating down the doors by herself to set me free.'

'Then we shall do the same for her. Too much of my life is left behind in that place. Tersias calls to me, his fate unknown, but my heart was gladdened by the words of Griselda. Perhaps he is still alive and all that Tara said was a lie. Perhaps . . .' Malachi thought for a moment as the carriage turned into the King's Road and passed a row of tiny houses that lined the street with lit windows and pulled curtains.

The coach rattled on into the countryside, carrying them towards the Knight's Bridge and Hyde Park. It slowed in its speed as it left the good going of the country roads and entered the cobbled mud of the London streets. Tallow lamps lit Piccadilly, where a snapped rope dangled tantalisingly from Mister Hatchard's bookshop, the remnant of a failed circus trick.

Abel pulled the horses to a tight rein as he walked them through Leicester Fields and along the dirt track past St Martin's Church. The smell of Covent Garden filled the air, and the towering Citadel rose up above them from the grime-filled streets.

23

The Quotidian of Drury Lane

Far away, the clock of St George's church struck midnight as the carriage ground slowly to a halt at the corner of Drury Lane. Abel jumped from the driving plate and opened the carriage door whilst keeping his cutlass at the ready. He nodded to Malachi, who slid across the leather bench and slipped quietly from the carriage to the road. Jonah sat in the seat corner, his head in his hands, as if shielding himself from what he would have to do.

The coachman looked at Malachi and then to the boy. Then he quickly reached in, took Jonah violently by the scruff of his neck, pulled him from his place and dumped him in a heap on the ground. He slammed the door to the carriage, mounted the footplate and doffed his cap as he lifted the horsewhip and cracked it above the beasts' heads. The carriage started to roll forward with a slow clatter as it pulled away from Malachi and Jonah, who now stood marooned and stranded as if upon a foreign shore.

Together they looked on as the carriage ebbed its way into the night, consumed by the darkness and the thickening fog that rolled into the streets with the advance of the deepening tide.

'Not the best way of getting from a carriage,' a voice said suddenly, coming out of the shadows. 'Couldn't afford to pay the fare, could you?'

It was a rich, warm voice, full of heart and cheer. The man stepped forward. He was as tall as Malachi, much younger and dressed in the finest blue coat and breeches. He smiled at Malachi, looking him up and down, admiring his dress.

'A master and servant abandoned in Drury Lane, falling into the lap of Thomas Danton, the quotidian of this glorious stretch of the King's turf,' the man said as he held out his hand to Malachi, hoping that this gesture of friendship would be received warmly.

Malachi obliged, tenderly gripping the man's fingertips and gently wafting their hands up and down.

'If you can't afford to pay for your carriage then you can't afford to buy me a drink,' the man said as he held his grip on Malachi, and began to draw him down the street as Jonah followed on like an attentive hound. 'I shall treat you to some chocolate – you look like a chocolate man to me – and the boy of course. We cannot have our servants left to starve in the streets whilst their masters dine sumptuously. I know an inn nearby that imports the finest chocolate from the north, made by Mister Bonnet, and so fine a cup you will never find anywhere in the world.' As Danton led them along the lane, Jonah's heart sank as he realised the direction to which they were drawn. High above him the tower of the Citadel loomed like a gesture of dereliction to the city and all those who didn't fall under its spell.

'It's kind of you to give us such a treat, but we have been well fed,' Malachi said as he tried to get away from the man, whose grip had suddenly tightened upon his hand. 'I have visited with friends in the country and now we go back to my business in Cheapside. So we will take your leave.'.

'*My* leave? You will take *my* leave and refuse the hospitality of Thomas Danton? Do you not know that the most privileged of men desire my company? I am sought after by people from around the world for what I do.'

266

'Then you will have to do it alone,' Malachi said, snatching his hand from the man and plunging it firmly into his pocket so it could not be grabbed again. 'My friend and I go to our home, we have much business to attend to and drinking is not one of them.'

'I beg you both earnestly to reconsider, since I will be offended easily. It is just midnight and the pot will be warmed and the nectar oozling, a delight that can be sniffed fragrantly throughout the district.' The man paused for breath, making much of taking the air as he lifted his nose towards the sky.

Jonah looked at Malachi, who without speaking showed his concern as he furrowed his brow and screwed up his face.

'Follow,' whispered Jonah as he pushed Malachi to walk on. 'We need to think, and an hour in the coffee-house will give us that time.'

'Wait!' Malachi shouted to the man, who by now had strolled ahead of them, eyes closed, following his nose and unaware that they dragged behind. 'We will come with you and sample some of Mister Bonnet's fine chocolate, I feel that is all my stomach can take and my young friend is in need of a rest . . .'

Danton stopped and turned around, unaware that they were so far behind and that he had strolled alone gibbering to himself. 'Ah . . . Then if we are to dine together our introductions must be complete and formal as anyone with good manners deserves. Thomas Danton, impresario and owner of many of the finest theatres in London.'

'Magnus Malachi and Jonah Ketch, horse dealers and stable owners of repute,' Malachi said as he gave a genteel bow and a wave of the handkerchief he had found in his pocket. 'Lead on, Macduff, and take us to this sanctuary of the night.'

Danton took Malachi by the hand and led him through the streets. They twisted and turned through small dark alleyways, drawing ever closer to the tower of the Citadel. The streets became squeezed together, uncomfortable in the narrowness of the roads and the height to which the houses rose from the mud, meeting high above their heads and shutting out the night.

The aromatic smell of fine coffee and of thick, dark chocolate filled the air, as murky as any London smog. Several yards ahead of them, the door to the coffee-house lay open. A warm, gentle light illuminated the dry cobbles that had been meticulously swept and polished with linseed. Each of these fine stones had been etched with the curls of a snail so that they resembled a herd of these tiny beasts emerging from the road and crawling towards the open door. The babbling of heated conversation spilled from the house. It echoed in the narrow street excitedly as voice grew on voice, all wanting to be heard above the other.

Danton stepped forward, letting go of Malachi and placing one hand in his pocket, the other in the air as he made his entrance into the room. Suddenly there was silence, and taking this as a warning of unwelcomeness, both Malachi and Jonah edged around the door and peeked inside.

To their complete surprise, the whole room had got to its feet, every man there standing in complete silence as Thomas Danton nodded to each one in turn. As he walked to a table in the darkest corner of the coffee-house, the whole crowd burst into a spontaneous applause, as if they had been witness to some great event.

'Mister Danton,' a tall, neatly-dressed man said as he opened his arms in welcome. 'Your table is ready and your nightcap prepared.'

'I have guests, Mister Mitchell. Two strangers that I have rescued from the night air.' Mitchell looked about him.

'Guests, Mister Danton? I see no one.'

Danton looked about the room and saw Malachi peering in from the street, his fingers clutching the side of the door and his white face mantled by the dark of the night. 'Bring them to me,' Danton said to Mister Mitchell as he warmed his hands on the large cup of steaming mocha that had been placed at his table. 'They are to have what they want and not to pay for a thing. In fact, Mitchell, let everyone in the house celebrate with us.'

There was more loud and rapturous applause as the gathering jumped up wildly and stood at their places, toasting their benefactor. Jonah and Malachi picked their way quietly through Danton's grateful audience and took their seats as the applause finally abated. Mitchell dashed to and fro in the dim light, between tables each lit by a single candle.

'Now, my friends,' Danton said, smiling warmly. 'Of what shall we converse on this dark and troublesome night?'

'We are your guests, surely we should listen to you and enjoy all that you have to say.' Malachi spoke quickly before Jonah could say a word.

Jonah wasn't listening, he was in another world. His eyes darted and flashed around the coffee-shop and glared upon the painted faces and fine clothes that surrounded him. He knew many of these faces, whose caricatures were much doted over in the *London Chronicle*. Actors, playwrights and adventurers adorned every seat as they gossiped in the twilight, sipping lightly from fine china cups, heads buried in deep conversation. Mitchell scurried from table to table, sharing in the conversation and offering them all a well-cut piece of hilarity.

'So,' Danton said as he tapped the boy on his shoulder to gain his attention. 'What shall we discuss?'

Jonah looked to Malachi, unsure what to say.

'Have you come far?' the man asked, hoping to glean a word from the boy's tight lips.

'Far?' answered Jonah as he took the china cup and slurped the treacly black chocolate into his mouth and across his chin.

'As far as Strumbelo?' the man asked, this time in a whisper loud enough to be shared only with those gathered around the table.

Jonah spat the drink back into the cup and stared anxiously to Malachi, whose gaze had suddenly found the most interesting piece of cobweb floating across the ceiling. He had lost the ability to speak.

'Griselda is such a fine host and Abel a man of few words,' the man went on.

Jonah tapped furiously on Malachi's arm, hoping to bring his mind back to earth and a voice back to his head. '*He knows, Malachi,*' Jonah said through gritted teeth.

'Of course I know. Do you think I lurk in doorways waiting to pick up the first vagrants dropped from a carriage? I was waiting for you. It was arranged.' Danton laughed to himself as he took a napkin and carefully wiped the chocolate from the edges of his mouth.

'How can we be sure? You could work for Solomon or Malpas and be tricking us for what we desire,' Malachi said, keeping his eyes fixed on the ceiling.

'Then I would have not brought you to within a cat's hair of the Citadel and have had arranged a door to be left open this very night.' Danton looked at Malachi, suddenly grabbing hold of his ear and giving it a sharp twist. 'I expect to be looked at. I am not a man without influence.'

Jonah giggled as Malachi squealed in pain, and Danton laughed out loud as the heads of those at nearby tables turned to share in the amusement.

'I am a companion of the woman whose house you shared,' Danton said. 'There are many of us in the city living out our ordinary, mundane and commonplace lives, waiting for the time when we can be of service to the greater cause . . . and it would seem that Malachi and Jonah serve a cause which is the greatest of them all. Whatever you have done or are about to do is of vast importance, for ordinarily *I* would not be asked to share in such a task or put myself in danger.' Danton laughed unnecessarily at the end of the sentence, as if to continue the revelry of those around him and disguise the nature of their conversation.

Malachi cackled like a Limehouse hag as he attempted to titter and giggle in appreciation of the merrymaking. 'And when shall we make our move?' he asked as he drank from the cup placed before him.

'It'll soon be one o'clock and the night-watch shall pass by. When he does, we will follow and that is as far as I go. I will take you to the door and no further. Not even service to the cause would induce me to enter the Citadel. The smell of lavender sticks in my throat and I have never liked the colour purple, it makes me look bilious . . .'

'Are there more companions ahead or do we go alone?' Jonah asked.

'That I cannot tell, but none of us travel alone, for goodness dwells in all who seek the truth.'

The coffee-shop slowly emptied of its guests, who one by one spilled into the darkness, merging with the night's silence. The three sat at table and drank more chocolate and shared conversation of London life. Jonah sat transfixed by Danton's tales of the theatre and the secret lives of those who trod the limelit splinters of the bawdy houses. Their table candle slowly ate of itself and dripped its common wax in thin dribbles along the seam of its holder and down to the tablecloth.

Without request, Mister Mitchell refilled their cups, bringing hotter and stronger brews as the hour passed until the time when the night-watch ambled down the alleyway.

'One of the clock and London sleeps well, no comet or quake to keep us from our beds . . . All is well, all is well,' the night-watch sang as he tapped his staff in time with the music of his voice and changed his tune with each change of news. 'All is well, all is well . . . Safe in your bed you shall dwell . . .'

'It's time,' Danton said. He rubbed his fingers and got to his feet, then looked to Mitchell. 'My friends and I retire from your gracious company, Mister Mitchell. I shall see you again.'

Mitchell nodded. He furiously scribbled numbers on a slip of paper and handed it secretly to Danton, enclosed within their leaving handshake. 'Would you like me to find you a sedan?' he enquired as they made their way past the empty tables. 'Or a lamp carrier to light your way?'

'The darkness is a kind veil to protect the innocent from my feverish good looks,' Danton jested as he returned a golden coin into the palm of Mitchell's hand. 'My friends and I will take the night air – there is a breeze from the river that will blow away all that clouds the mind.'

It was Malachi who was the first to step into the cold night air. There was indeed a breeze, stiff and cold, that rattled through the narrow streets like the venting of a dark cave gushing its draught from the depths of the earth. In the distance he could see the torch of the night-watch turning the corner as his song echoed up and down the alleyways, calling for peace and calm to reign over the city.

'Follow on,' Danton said as he pushed Malachi onwards towards the Citadel. 'We mustn't lose sight of him, he is the key that will unlock the door and you will find what you have been waiting for.'

They pressed on, huddled together as they walked in close file, Jonah in front and Malachi and Danton arm in arm and in deep conversation, their words lower than a whisper.

Jonah clutched the dagger in the pocket of his frock coat. Its handle glowed white hot in his hand. It was as if it had come to life, and whatever had conquered its power whilst at Strumbelo no longer could charm it. Touching it made Jonah feel sick. Thoughts of how it was made churned in his mind, flashing scenes of its long existence through him. In one glimpse he clearly saw Hiram Abif, the creator of the Mastema, his head shaved, the tattoo of a snake emblazoned across his cheek. Jonah looked down upon him from a great height as he lay in a shallow grave, the skin cut from his forehead, his dead eyes staring into the night sky.

Jonah let go of the dagger and the vision flew from his mind. He slowed in his pace, snuggling next to Malachi and trying to listen to the words he exchanged with Danton. The two men smiled at him as yard by yard they followed the distant lamp-light that led them towards the Citadel. Jonah suddenly noticed that Malachi no longer had a limp in his gait, and he walked fresh-legged. He dare not voice what he had seen for fear of being stupid, but the thought came to him again and again.

'You don't limp,' he whispered to Malachi, pulling upon his sleeve to remind him he was still there.

Malachi stopped and turned to him, a smile upon his face, and gestured to Danton to walk on alone. 'I know,' he said as he rubbed his hands together gleefully. 'It happened yesterday as I slept. I have had the damp-sickness for twenty years. My bones have ached and stiffened with each winter, but when I slept at Strumbelo, all had gone. I was like a new-born lamb.' Malachi whispered the last words and hopped along the alleyway to catch Danton before he disappeared in the darkness.

They followed on as the night-watch stopped on every corner and gave out his cry, shouting out the quarter of the hour with a loud bellow and giving the good news of peace within the nation. He then turned into a long dark alley and the three followed, a chain's length behind. They huddled in the shadows as the night-watch suddenly stopped, looked back and forth, and then took a key from his pocket, pressed himself against a small door and pulled it open. The man then took out the key from the lock, lifted his lamp in the air three times and turned and went on his way, humming like a fat old bird that had just ruffled its feathers as it sat to roost.

'That is the signal,' Danton said as he took out a silver whistle from his pocket and gave it to Jonah. 'Take this. All the companions know its pitch. If you are ever in danger blow as hard as you can and surely if one of us is nearby we will come to your aid. Now be gone. The door you saw opened is to the cellar of the Citadel. From here you are on your own. The resolution of your fate is in your hands.'

Malachi looked along the alleyway and pulled on Jonah's coat to follow. Then, remembering Danton's kindness, he turned to give him thanks. But the alleyway was empty, their companion had melted into the night.

'Did you see him go?' Malachi asked as Jonah stealthily crept along the darkest shadows to the doorway ahead of them. The boy didn't reply, his mind fixed on what was to come. A sudden and glorious urge swept through him as he remembered the warm fire of Griselda's house and all that he had seen. It was as if his fear was being melted like butter before the fire as excitement grew in his heart. He crept to the door and looked in, seeing along a long narrow corridor tiled from floor to ceiling in bright white, every yard lit by a heart lantern.

'We cannot wait here,' Malachi said quietly. 'Danton said that we would be safe only for a few minutes. We must press on – but to where and for what purpose I still do not know . . .'

Wastrel

'You have come alone?' Solomon asked as he poured himself a drink from the cabinet of his private room in the Citadel just below the tower. He held the glass to the candle and with his eye measured the depth of the golden liquid that sparkled against the crystal of the fine glass.

'I thought Solomites didn't drink the fruit of the vine?' said his guest, who sat in the silk padded chair without being asked.

'They don't, but *I* make the rules and can do as I like,' Solomon replied. 'I find brandy is a good way to end the day, especially if it can be combined with business.' He walked to the empty fireplace that filled a wall of the room. It was carved with interwoven deities and sprites that twirled and flew around each other, taking the eye to the cornice of the ceiling and the minstrel gallery that ran along the upper wall at the back of the room. 'I am glad that you responded so quickly to my messenger and that what I have is of interest to you.'

'Anything of beauty is always of interest,' the man replied as he shuffled uncomfortably in his seat, wanting to dispense with the pleasantries. 'But how did you know I would be interested?'

Solomon looked to his hand and the thick gold ring that had been freshly placed upon his finger. 'Someone special told me, someone very special,' he said, smiling to himself.

'Then they are very gifted. Did they tell you that what you offer me was mine in the first place and that it was stolen from me by a wastrel on Conduit Fields but several nights ago?'

'Sadly, that part of the story was omitted from the tale, but as you say, possession is as good as ownership and I think we can come to some sort of *arrangement*.'

'You can give me what is mine, or I will have the militia pull this place down stone by stone and cart you off to the Fleet Prison. To me that would be a more profitable arrangement, and save me paying you for the privilege of having back what is rightfully mine.'

'Lord Malpas, who said anything about recompense? What I was to suggest was more along the lines of a partnership. I know not why you desire such a stone box or what you will do with it,' he said as he walked across the room to the window. 'My understanding is that it is a gateway to another realm, but my efforts to open it have been in vain. So it is useless to me.' He paused and looked out of the tall window to the scene below. A fine black coach with four horses blocked the narrow street as three coachmen, armed with muskets, stood guard. 'Tonight, Lord Malpas, I will show you something that could change your mind as to what kind of man you think I am.'

'My thoughts are firmly set, Solomon. I have heard much of your gatherings, the abductions of the innocent and the weak and your *transformations*. If I had my way I would make sure there were no cardinals, bishops or anyone else who dressed up in fine robes and twittered about the depravity of my life whilst their own sank into a mire.'

Solomon looked at his glass of brandy and without taking a single sip placed it upon the window ledge. 'What would you say if I told you I could help in your desires?'

'My desires are kept to myself,' Malpas replied, his temper beginning to fray.

'Your desires are as well known as mine,' Solomon snapped back. 'We are both the talk of the coffee-houses and I know more of you than you would think. The man who would be King, isn't that what they call you?'

'My family have always been loyal to our monarch . . .'

'And then they imported one like a fat German sausage and the monarchs that you had supported were left out in the cold in some distant ramshackle manor house in the far north.'

'A quirk of fate that could be remedied by a fading heartbeat,' Malpas replied, unsure as to what treachery he was being led to.

'Imagine a royal accident,' Solomon said quietly, not wanting to be overheard. 'The King gets into his carriage fat and hearty, to be driven to Windsor, and when he arrives there is nothing but a skeleton picked of all its flesh. You could even blame God, say it was a divine retribution, and install yourself as our gracious leader.'

'And how would such a plan be put into effect?' Malpas asked. He got to his feet and crossed the room to look out of the window and check his guards were in place.

High above, the door to the minstrel gallery slowly opened as inch by inch Jonah crept into the room upon his hands and knees. Malachi kept watch in the passageway that led to the stairs and the cellar door through which they had entered. The sound of distant voices had led the two upwards through the stone chambers and constricted staircases that spiralled in an ever-growing maze inside the Citadel. Jonah had recognised those voices – the never-forgettable whining of Lord Malpas, and the crow-like gullet of Solomon that rattled against the cold stone walls.

Solomon spoke again. 'I have at my disposal, certain . . . *creatures* . . . that given the right conditions would do the job for us. I have it in mind to have a spring trap made that would fit under the seat of a coach and when the time is right the canopy would open and my *creatures* would enter the carriage and devour the King completely.'

Malpas started to laugh so loud that it echoed back and forth from wall to wall until it built into a multitude of voices. 'What beasts do you have that could do such a thing? Trained killer mice, or vampire chaffinches perhaps? I have heard you were mad, but a liar as well? Solomon, I am a busy man and the hour is late. Tell me what you want for the Alabaster and let me have done with it.'

'I assure you, Lord Malpas, that I am not mad, and the creatures of which I speak are in this very room.' Solomon crossed the chamber to a large wooden chest pushed against the wall by the door. 'Come and see for yourself. I have a sample of the creatures here and it is time they were fed.'

'This I must see . . . What delight it will truly be to have you ridiculed before my very eyes. How far do you want to take this game, Solomon?'

Solomon opened the lid of the case. 'This is not a game,' he replied as he wiped his sleeve over the thick glass plate that sealed the chest. 'Come closer and see what I have created, it will be a delight to behold.'

'A trick of the light or some strange game, no doubt,' Malpas said as he yawned to himself, the glare of the bright candlelight making his eyes ache.

High above in the minstrel gallery, Jonah held his breath as he listened eagerly to every word. Malachi squatted by the door, eager not to be caught as he watched the corridor for any sign of the Solomonites.

'See for yourself, regard the beasts that are here.' Solomon tapped the side of the chest and pulled a small brass lever that released a catch to one side. Within the chest a door sprung open and several locusts tumbled into view. 'Here they are . . .' Solomon said proudly as the strange beasts crawled back and forth, looking for something to devour.

Lord Malpas stepped back, unsure whether what he could

now see was really true. Before him, one large locust hooked itself to the glass case and stared at him eye to eye. It was as large as a blackbird, and its mandibles scraped noisily against the glass casing as it chirped like a foreign songbird waiting to be fed.

'See, my locusts are real, they exist and soon they will be well known,' Solomon said proudly. 'And as a measure of the importance I attach to our partnership, I would be happy if you would accept as a gift some choice specimens from those you now see.'

'They are fine beasts but are no more frightening than the ravens in the Tower,' Malpas said as he looked warily at the creatures.

'My locusts do not eat grass, but flesh. Look again, Lord Malpas.' Solomon flicked yet another catch and pulled out a hidden drawer. Inside was a pair of thick leather gloves, each finger lined with a jointed metal sheath, and also a thick black bag with drawstring and a white enamelled pot filled with blood-soaked meat. Solomon slipped on the glove and scooped up a handful of meat, then he quickly opened another door on the side of the chest and put his hand inside, bearing both the meat and the black bag. There was a sudden and fretful screaming as the locusts danced in a great frenzy back and forth, pouncing upon the meat and tearing it from the glove.

'They are hungry,' Solomon said as he quickly pulled his gloved hand and the bag from the chest, dropping the remnants of the meat inside for the creatures to gorge themselves upon. Seven of the locusts now squirmed inside the bag.

'And what of living flesh?' Malpas asked as he stepped back from the chest, turned and walked to the window.

'For that they have an even greater desire,' Solomon replied. 'So much that if I were to let them go into the city, a swarm could pick the streets clear within the day.' He put the bloodied glove back into the drawer, sliding it tightly shut.

279

Malpas picked up his brandy glass and took a long hard swallow. 'I cannot talk here, but what I have seen has deeply intrigued me.' He looked about the room for fear that there were hidden witnesses and this were some plot to have him hanged for betraying the King. 'Bring the Alabaster and the dagger to my house at Thieving Lane in two hours and I will look kindly upon our partnership.'

'The Alabaster I have, but of the dagger I am not aware,' Solomon said.

'Then you waste my time. One without the other is of no use. The dagger is the key, you must have known that.' Malpas spoke frantically as he finished the glass and threw it to the floor, smashing it about Solomon's feet. 'YOU SAID YOU HAD ALL THAT I DESIRED –'

'I thought I did, and more.'

'But what of the dagger,' Malpas said again as he tried to calm himself. 'Where is it?'

'It is held by the one who stole it from you,' a soft voice said from the doorway.

Malpas turned as Tara walked slowly towards them, holding out a hand to Solomon. Her head was wrapped in thick purple bands and her eyes were etched in dark kohl.

Solomon beamed, his eyes bursting from his head and his hands trembling. 'This is my wife, in whom I am well pleased,' he said to Malpas. 'She is a great testimony to our process of transformation. But a few days ago she was a common thief, now she is the wife of the prophet.'

In the gallery, Malachi heard the fateful words. Without giving Jonah time to draw breath he quickly grabbed him by the ankle and pulled him back through the doorway and into the cold stairway. He forced his hand over his lips to stop him from speaking and pressed his mouth to Jonah's ear so that what he said could be heard only by him. 'Control your anger,

Jonah. In this moment we have found our answer. Go from this place and hide in the alley. We may just be able to save Tara from Solomon and find Tersias after all.'

No one in the room below heard the slithering across the gallery and the whispering from behind the door. Lord Malpas could not take his eyes from the girl.

She smiled politely and gave him a gentle bow. 'I am sorry that I was part of your trouble, Lord Malpas. The thief didn't mean to steal your knife, in fact it was you who embedded it so deeply within his arm that he had to take it,' Tara said as she embraced Solomon.

'Should have been his heart, then I would have the knife in my possession . . . Does he still have the dagger?' Malpas asked as he strutted back and forth, his face reddening with the anticipation of finding the Mastema.

'I saw it last night, when I stole the Alabaster from him,' Tara said softly, her voice changed to suit her new countenance. 'He used it as a key to open the stone.'

'And does this villain have a name that I might search him out and find him?'

'Jonah Ketch . . .' she replied dreamily. 'He thinks he is a highwayman and you can find him hanging on the bar at the Bull and Mouth.'

'Ketch and Malachi, they are in this together and they will hang from something higher than the table of an inn. I had them both and through stupidity they were lost to me.' Lord Malpas stopped and looked at Tara as she smiled vacantly towards him. 'I take it then that you also know the whereabouts of the boy, Tersias.'

'He is dead,' she said quickly, as if his words had stung her heart.

Malpas looked to the armed guards outside the Citadel and then at Solomon, who, seeing the consequences of any lie, realised that this was not a moment for deception. 'Well, not quite . . . dead,' he said. 'More . . . *sleeping*. He is in the process of transformation. In fact he is above us as we speak.'

'Then he is part of our deal,' Malpas said as he strutted angrily about the room. 'The oracle and the Alabaster, and I will find the dagger. Bring them with you in two hours and the transaction will be complete. When I am Lord Protector, you will have all the disciples you need and all the brandy you can drink.' Malpas stopped suddenly as a viciousness crossed his face. 'I would like the girl to come with me. I have a way to lure the boy Ketch to my house. I have enough guards to keep her safe and I promise I will return her into your safe keeping.'

'I fear, Lord Malpas, that it is a request too far. We are newly wed and our nuptials await us. We have been man and wife for just three hours,' Solomon whined like a dying hound.

'Let me go, Solomon,' Tara said. 'Perhaps Lord Malpas will show me the Alabaster and all that it contains. I would love to look into the mercury again.'

'Again?' Malpas asked. 'You have seen inside the stone?'

'Not once, but twice,' she replied, smiling at him. 'It was the most beautiful thing I have ever seen . . . Apart from my dearest Solomon . . .'

'And what did you see?' asked Malpas, his heart intrigued by the sudden realisation of her desire.

'Everything . . . The land beyond the looking-glass, the keeper of the stone. I saw it all – taken through the quicksilver, pulled against my will, and yet when I opened my eyes and looked at that beauty, I didn't want to return. Look,' she said, holding out several round filings of quicksilver. 'These I picked from my hair, they are my only memory of the other side of the stone.'

'My wife is a great dreamer, the elixir of the transformation has not yet fully released her from its grip.' Solomon spoke nervously, hoping that the words Tara spoke would not inflame Malpas further.

'You may have drugged her into marrying you, but what she says of the stone is true. I too have seen those things, but my time for leaving this world has not yet come. One day I will have the courage to allow the keeper to pull me through the quicksilver, and in that land I will stay for ever.' Malpas held out his hand to Tara. 'Come, girl, we will look upon the stone together and who knows, it may open itself for us to dream.'

Tara stepped forward to walk with Malpas without even turning to Solomon.

'I don't think that will be a good idea,' Solomon said, quickly grasping the sleeve of her coat. 'My wife should stay here. This is between you and me, Malpas,' he said arrogantly.

'Would you like to discuss the matter with my men? They could soon come in and see you, I am sure they would enjoy the exchange,' Malpas said curtly as he took Tara by the hand, pulling her from Solomon's feeble grip.

'If it is put in such an eloquent manner then I cannot refuse,' Solomon said begrudgingly. He looked at his trembling hands.

'I will swap the dagger for Tersias!' A sudden voice shouted from the minstrel gallery above their heads, taking them by surprise.

'Who in –' exclaimed Solomon as he looked up at the shadowy figure leaning on the stone balcony high above them.

'*Who* I am is of no consequence, *what* I have is of importance. In a distant place, far away from here, is a dagger that is the key to the stone that you crave, Lord Malpas.'

'How did you get in?' shouted Solomon, caring not for the man or his words.

'Quiet, you fool!' Malpas said as he jerked Tara towards him, pulling a small dandy gun from his jacket and aiming at the dark figure that peered down at him like an old vulture. 'What would stop me from killing you and taking the knife?'

'You would be a fool. If I die then the knife is to be cut into fragments and melted down and the gold given to the poor. I am sure you would hate that, for charity is not one of your virtues. I am a messenger, a harbinger of good news. Fear not, I say, and good will to all men, for that is the only thing my heart desires. My good will to you, Lord Malpas is to give you the dagger in exchange for Tersias, and you will never see him again. In return I promise to take him far from this city and never allow another word of fortune to come from his lips.' Malachi spoke boldly, the strength of his words shivering his spine.

'And those are your terms?'

'Bold and true,' Malachi replied.

'What is to stop me from capturing you and torturing you for the secret you hold?'

'Honour is not completely dead in your heart and you need the Alabaster and the dagger more than I need life. I am no stranger to death, it is a friend I welcome heartily. So, do what you will.' Malachi gripped the cold stone of the balcony, feeling its icy grasp trickling up his arms and shivering his fingers. 'What's it to be, Malpas? Name a time and a place and I will be there.'

'You know of my house? There is a fayre, a small circus encamped in the gardens of St James. I will meet you there in two hours. There is an elephant, Ozymandias. He stands every night chained to a large elm tree. Meet me there and we will give our exchange.'

'But . . . but . . .' quibbled Solomon behind him.

'Then it is done?' Malachi asked as he stepped into a strand of light, his face seen for the first time.

'Tell me, sir, to whom shall we speak? Your face looks familiar.'

'That, Lord Malpas, is impossible, for my life in this land has only just begun,' Malachi said as he slipped silently through the door to the stairs, his words echoing in the chamber.

'Quickly!' Solomon shouted as he ran to the door of the room. 'He has gone to the back stairs. Your men can find him, my men –'

'Leave him,' Malpas said irately as he pulled Tara behind him. 'He is better left alone until he comes with the dagger. I have built a gallows in that place where we shall meet. They are for the fayre hangings, and he shall be the first to try the noose upon his neck.'

The Elephant and the Elm

Malachi ran from the Citadel and into the alleyway. It was cold, dark and filled with the Thames mist that had crawled like a drunken tramp through the streets of Covent Garden, bringing with it the stench of the sea. He could hear the slamming of carriage doors at the front of the Citadel and the protests of Solomon as Tara was taken away with Lord Malpas for *safekeeping*.

'I will be there soon, Tara, don't fret,' Solomon said quickly, his voice shrill and filled with worry. 'Campion, my coat – disciples, follow on . . . We must follow Tara to Thieving Lane. Bring the Alabaster, Campion . . . CAMPION!'

Malachi leant back into the shadows and sniggered as he listened to Solomon barking orders to a night that wasn't listening. There was a sudden and doleful thud of the front door of the Citadel and the scampering of many feet across the fine white stone steps and into the London dirt. Then all was silent, nothing stirred but the mist about his feet. He waited for Jonah, hoping that his companion would soon be with him. Malachi listened to the chiming of a distant clock as it beat the quarter of the hour, its peal of muddled notes dancing across the silvering rooftops of the houses as the first fingers of frost fell crisply.

Malachi waited . . . The shiver of cold chilled his bones and numbed his fingers as he stood alone in the alleyway. He bit his fingertips, pulling at the quick with his teeth as he constantly looked back and forth, nervously waiting for the boy. Again he heard the sound of the clock chime, its deep bell resounding two long strokes that sent a huddle of pigeons flying from a nearby rooftop, then dropping into the alleyway as they skirted the fog before rising quickly into the clear star-lit sky above.

In the depths of the alleyway came a sudden and bitter creaking as in a distant wall an old iron door swung heavily on its rusted hinges. A dark figure crept slowly from within, falling into the fog as it disappeared from view, then rising to its feet as it kept to the shadows and scurried like a long thin rat along the wall. Malachi froze back into the darkness as he crouched down, hoping that he would not be seen by whatever stalked him from the Citadel.

'Malachi . . . Malachi,' came a thin whisper, as the shadow man got closer.

Magnus Malachi raised his long thin hand from the mist, beckoning for Jonah to cross the alley to his hiding place. The shadow ducked into the fog, then like a jack-in-the-box Jonah appeared by his side, a broad smile emblazoned across his face.

'Where did you go? I told you to wait,' Malachi scolded the boy.

'I couldn't resist . . . I saw something in the room and as I was making my escape from the Citadel I found a door and waited until Solomon and Malpas had gone, then I sneaked into the room. Honest, Malachi, I only went in to look – and then I saw them, they were so beautiful, I had to take . . .'

'And what did you take?' Malachi asked, despairing of the boy.

'Creatures . . . Seven of the finest creatures you have ever seen and wrapped in a thick linen bag and ready to be set free . . . at the right time.'

'I heard Solomon talking of locusts that will kill. Is that what

287

you have?' Malachi asked cautiously as Jonah dangled a black sack in front of his face.

'The same – locusts the size of nightingales . . . And they have teeth that could chew your arm off given half the chance.' Jonah stopped his excited chatter and looked at Malachi. 'I heard what you said to Malpas,' he said quietly. 'We will swap the dagger for Tersias?' he asked, his tone changing as he slumped back against the wall. 'I don't know if he's worth the knife . . .'

'So you would let him rot with Solomon?' Malachi asked as he got to his feet, picking the boy up from the mist. 'All for a knife that will destroy you like it has done to everyone else who has kept it for too long? We meet Malpas in an hour at the circus on St James's Field, an elephant called Ozymandias shall be at the place tied to an elm tree. This is our chance to get Tara and the boy.'

'She would rather stay with Solomon, her days with me are long gone,' Jonah said, his heart laden with anger.

'Tara is bewitched, she has no mind to think for herself. We will take a decision for her life and carry it through until the end.'

'And you know how we shall do all these things?' Jonah asked as he looked to the clear night sky.

'Somehow . . . somehow I am beginning to believe that all our days are foretold and that if we push at a door it shall be opened. All I know is that *this* is the right thing to do – and in that I have my peace.'

'Then in peace, let us go and make war upon Lord Malpas and bring an end to these troubled days.'

'And to Ozymandias, king of kings, let his greeting be upon us all . . .'

'We meet again,' a voice said, and a man stepped from the darkness of a small ginnel that lay unseen by their side. 'Your job is not yet done? I see no boy – does he still await rescue?' Danton asked.

Malachi almost jumped from his skin. 'You are like a ghost that rattles its chains on Christmas Eve . . . Do you lurk everywhere, or are we the victims of a conspiracy of the companions?'

'I was taking the air, freshening myself for a day ahead. My carriage is nearby and in this chance meeting I would offer you a lift to anywhere I could take you at such an unpleasant hour . . .'

'You spy upon us, Mister Danton. You take away my free will and stalk me as if I am a stag to be shot before the first light of dawn.'

'No, no . . . Think of me as a friend whose life is crossing your own and our paths are suddenly intertwined.' Danton laughed as he urged them to walk on with him, putting his hand to Malachi's back.

'I sense a wiser hand in all of this, Jonah. It is the game of chess, and she said that she was a pawn and not the player.'

'Then you will take my carriage to the circus?' Danton asked.

'If we were to refuse then the sky would open and a hand lift us from this alleyway and drop us in that very place, methinks,' Jonah said as Malachi laughed. The three turned from the alleyway and into the street outside the Citadel, where a large barouche stood silently waiting, its four gleaming black horses standing stock-still.

'You travel well, Mister Danton,' Jonah said as he took to the footplate to step upon the high seat at the back of the fine carriage with its shining black panels and silver handles.

'And tonight, Jonah Ketch, you will travel inside with Magnus Malachi. I will be your coachman,' Danton said as he opened the door to the carriage and gave a genteel bow like a servant to his master.

289

Jonah stepped into the carriage and sank into the soft leather seat as Malachi pushed in behind and slumped to the bench opposite.

'Never travelled in one of these all my life then suddenly twice in one night, Jonah. Things must be looking up for old Malachi,' he said with a relieved sigh as the carriage lurched forward and rattled off through the night.

They never spoke as the carriage twisted and turned through the labyrinth of narrow roads that led to the Strand past Jenvey's gin house, where Jonah's mother had pawned all to sniff the apron of the most infamous drunkard in London – who would stand in the street, ladle in hand, and scoop from wooden casks her home-made Geneva, laced with arsenic to give it a bitter taste that would hang on the tongue and curdle the mind.

Onward the wheels rolled as they trundled the long mile from Covent Garden to St James's Field. Jonah clutched the dagger as he fought with himself to give up this prize in exchange for another. He looked around the carriage with its fine silk blinds and glass shutters with their lacquered handles. A small candle-lamp lit Malachi's face as he stared at the passing streets. Jonah smiled to himself – an unlikely friend, he thought, but a friend he had become. Their shared adversity had drawn them like two melting rods smashed by a smithy hammer. He wondered what had touched the old magician's life at Strumbelo and melted his bitterness. Whatever, Jonah said to himself as the carriage rattled along Parliament Street, it had been for the good and not only for Malachi but for him as well. He settled back into the soft couch and felt the locusts crawling feverishly about the sack that he gripped tightly shut with both hands.

The smell of the circus hung over the streets that surrounded the park as the coach went through the large stone arch of De-La-Hay and out onto the fields. Suddenly an encampment of brightly coloured tents surrounded them. All had long, narrow flags strung from high centre poles and streamers that billowed and blew on the fresh breeze; black cast-iron braziers lit each doorway, keeping out the chill of the night and giving light to the horses, gazelles and the multitude of strange creatures that had been gathered from the four corners of the world. They turned not a head as the carriage went by. A large beast that looked to Jonah as if it were a gigantic goat hung its head pitifully. Around its neck a thick leather strap had worn away both coat and dignity with years of chaffing. The beast rocked from side to side in perfect rhythm with an old tiger that stared out from its tiny gilt cage, moving quickly from one foot to another and shaking its head as if to cast off the collar that held it tightly in its madness.

'Look at the creatures, Malachi – have you ever seen such a sight?'

'No, and nor do I want to again,' Malachi said remorsefully. 'What they do to brute beasts, I once did to that boy.' He covered his face with his hands. 'Oh, to never be reminded of my guilt again! What if we could free these beasts?'

'Then all shall be free . . .' Jonah said as he put the locust bag on the seat and banged on the carriage roof with his clenched fist. 'We have seen enough, Mister Danton – take us from this place.'

The carriage turned and drew slowly to a halt as the horses pulled it the last few feet towards a large elm that towered high above them. Under its empty branches a hefty grey lump of a beast sat in a thick putrid pile of straw that was scattered about the tree trunk. Its shaggy wrinkled skin that had once fit tightly now dangled in swags from its heavy bones. Two longs tusks scraped the ground, rubbing back and forth, as a long purple tongue drooped over a pair of worn brown teeth.

Jonah reached to open the coach door to glimpse the beast at close hand. It was then he realised that there were no handles on the inside.

Danton nimbly jumped to the ground and twisted the door latch. He saw the look on Jonah's face. 'Gentlemen should never have to open a door – so all my carriages have handles on the outside. When you travel with Mister Danton, you travel in style. Kudos, esteem and reputation are what my fortune has been built upon.'

'It has been an undoubted pleasure and you have been a true friend,' Malachi said warmly as he held out his hand to the man and smiled. 'I take it that the chess will continue and you will appear again in our future?'

'I thought I would peruse the circus – I am always looking for the next starlet to grace the stage and who knows, perhaps Ozymandias will dance for me tonight?'

'Then we are in good hands, and the pawns shall be on their way,' Malachi said sprightly. 'There is something useful in my new life. I cannot say what it is, but I experience feelings that have not shared my thoughts for many a year. I suspect I once called it happiness, and even in what is to come I can find an ounce of joy.' He looked to Jonah. 'We have a deal to keep and a life to save, Jonah. It is time I took the knife.'

Jonah dug his hand deep into his pocket and clutched the handle of the dagger. It felt warm and soft; the gold seemed to mingle with his fingers. He looked to the ground and then to Danton.

'It's often hard to give up that which we feel we will never have again,' Danton said softly. 'The great thing in giving up is that it is always replaced, overflowing in abundance.' He smiled as he nodded to Jonah, his kindly stare telling the boy to hand the dagger to Malachi.

Jonah hesitated, his hand clasping then releasing its grip on the hilt of the knife. It was as if it spoke to him, chided him for even thinking of handing it willingly to Malachi. He tried again to pull the blade from his pocket, but it was no use. His arm stuck fast, his fingers gripping tight to the point of snapping.

'Willingly . . .' Danton said. 'Think of Tersias – the dagger for the boy.'

Jonah thought of Tersias and Tara. He thought of them dressed in fine purple, full-bellied and shaven-headed with cockroaches cut in their foreheads. He saw Solomon fawning over them and Malpas grinning like he had on the night when this madness had started.

'Give me the dagger,' Malachi said again as he held out his hand.

Jonah looked at him eye to eye. From the depths of his soul he pulled the blade from his pocket and slowly and hesitantly held it towards Malachi.

'Willingly . . .' Danton said again as he stepped into the shadow of the coach and tethered the carriage horses to a tent post. 'It has to be willingly or else it will follow you all of your life and you will always want to have it back.'

'Willingly,' Jonah replied quietly as he handed the knife to Malachi, who grasped it firmly in his hand.

Ozymandias gave a long, loud moan that quivered the elm tree as the beast got to its feet and turned towards them. A thick leather strap cut deep into its neck, chaffing the skin away to a deep sore that exposed the raw flesh beneath. It looked at Malachi with eyes that tried to speak, a single tear hanging from the coarse grey wrinkles of its skin.

Malachi turned quickly, the blade cutting through the cold air and sending sparks splintering towards the night sky. 'It has to be done,' he said, stepping towards the elephant, dagger out-stretched. 'You can't leave a beast to suffer, it's better off dead than tethered to the tree.'

'NO!' shouted Jonah as Malachi plunged the blade towards the creature, and with one swift blow the leather strap fell from its wide grey neck and was pulled to the ground by the heavy chain that had kept it prisoner for so long.

'I'm not for killing the beast,' Malachi said as Jonah took his hands from his eyes.

The elephant swung its trunk back and forth excitedly as it got to its hind legs and raised itself from the ground, walking upright towards them and gurgling the spit in its throat.

'See!' said Malachi with the freshness of a youth in his voice. 'It is the first. My chains have been taken from me and so shall it be for this creature, then Tersias and Tara will follow.'

'I never said anything about the girl!' Malpas stepped towards them with the captain of the militia by his side. 'I was only going to deal with the boy. Now I have you and the knife and Tersias into the bargain. In fact, I now have everything I desire. Take them,' he said to the guards, who drew their swords.

'You agreed, Malpas,' Malachi said as he stepped towards Ozymandias. 'The knife for the boy.'

'Oh, I remember some foolish words that fell from my lips . . . You would call them lies. I would call them getting what I want. Guards!' Malpas shouted loudly. 'Take them all away until I can decide what to do with them.' He took one step forward and looked at Malachi. 'Well, well, well. If it is not Magnus Malachi. The look suits you – if it hadn't been for the smell I would never have recognised you.'

Galloglass in Galligaskins

'Skullet, Skullet!' shouted Malpas as he walked proudly along Thieving Lane at the head of the militia as they dragged Malachi, Jonah and Thomas Danton along the dark streets. 'Open the door, Mister Skullet, we have even more visitors.'

The door to Vamana House opened slowly and Skullet peered suspiciously out into the night. 'More people?' he said angrily. 'The house is full of strangers, why do we need more?'

'These are no strangers,' Malpas replied as he stepped joyfully up the stone slabs at the front of the house. 'These are the ingredients for the broth of life, the cream sauce and brandy butter. Oh, the bittersweet touch of fate! I know we will see great things, great things, dear brother.'

Skullet opened the door as Lord Malpas strode past him, dagger in hand, rolling it in his palm as the metal glowed with the brightness of a divining lamp.

'They are in the Great Hall,' Skullet said. 'I put them with the girl. They have brought a coffin, dragged in by several lunatics and the biggest man I have ever seen. Solomon wants to go now, but I have insisted he waits until you arrived with the knife.'

Malpas walked on, dagger in hand, his eyes fixed on the doors of the Great Hall. 'Let them be a party to what we do tonight. Guards, bring them here and keep them by the wall. If one of them but twitches, run them through.' He pushed open the doors and stepped into the room, holding the dagger aloft as if it were a power beyond all powers. 'Hear me, Solomon, hear me. I have the key to the future. We will change the world. One day I will escape death and you will have all the madmen you need to fill a thousand citadels and give you all their money.'

Solomon shuddered as he slowly crept towards Tara, who sat like a queen in a tall stone throne built upon a marble plinth. She was wrapped in a heavy woven swath of finest red cloth that fell from her shoulders, covering her to her feet, the tips of her purple shoes poking through the folds of material. He bristled that she should be enfolded in something other than purple – it would take the glory from her, the transformation would not be complete. It would offer no protection from the plague.

At Tara's feet was the wicker coffin, the lid shut tightly and bound with straps of leather that bent the willow whips out of shape, twisting them together.

Jonah was thrown into the room and slid across the wooden floor with such force that he sprawled face down at Tara's feet. He looked up and saw her smile, her eyes enjoying all that she encountered as her heart abounded gleefully in his misery.

'You like what you see, my lass?' Malpas asked as he stepped beside her and ran his cold hand across her cheek. 'You were once good friends, conspirators and highway robbers, but you, my dear girl, are forgiven. Honourable Dobson,' Malpas cried out. 'Can I hang him?'

'Calmly, master, calmly,' warned Skullet, concerned at the excitement of Lord Malpas.

Dobson was tied by his hands and feet to a small door at the side of the Great Hall. He dangled from his wrists by bands of thick felt that kept his feet suspended an inch above the floor. 'If you stop hanging me you can quarter him for all I care,' Dobson screamed as he kicked to be free.

'See, Solomon, even the Lord Chancellor agrees that we should hang the boy. What say you, Dobson, about Magnus Malachi and the impresario Mister Thomas Danton?' Malpas shouted with great enthusiasm.

'Hang 'em all,' Dobson shouted like a small child deprived of their favourite toy. 'You will pay for what you have done with me and hang with them.'

Malpas turned to Skullet and whispered in his ear. The servant laughed and rubbed his hands together as he signalled to four militia to cut the Judge from the door and take him away. 'Let him swim for his supper,' Skullet laughed as he gave the command to the guards. 'Take him to the sewer and let him float on the tide, fill him full of gin so he sinks like a stone and wakes on the shore at Rotherhithe.'

Dobson screamed in dire protest as he was roughly cut down with several sword swipes that missed his fingers by the shortest of breadths. 'I will not be done for,' he cried loudly, sobbing like a small boy. 'I curse you, Malpas, and your children's children.'

'Then you are too late, for I am already cursed by the vilest affliction, my blood never stops and for this life I have no more care.' Malpas looked at Solomon and then to Campion, who stood like a giant ogre behind his master. 'You have the Alabaster?'

'Yes,' Solomon said, and he nodded to a disciple who clutched the stone box.

'And the boy?' he asked.

'By your feet, wrapped in death and awaiting new birth.'

'Good.' Malpas giggled as he ran his finger along Tara's forehead down her long thin nose and to her lips. 'Shall he perform for us tonight?'

'If it is your desire. That is within *my* power.'

'POWER!' Malpas screamed. 'Such a beautiful word and one so seldom used! Do you have the power, Solomon, do you?'

he begged as he began to slather with excitement. 'Come then, get the boy, quickly. Bring him to life, give him whatever so that he will live.'

Jonah crouched by the coffin within an arm's length of Tersias as Campion strode boldly from behind his master and untied the lid. He saw the boy as the giant lifted the woven strands from him and unwrapped the purple gauze from his face. His lips were icy blue, his face white as if in true death.

Solomon walked unsteadily towards the coffin, bent towards the boy and put his hand to his lips as he sprinkled several drops of thick liquid from a small pyx hidden in his hand. 'Wake, child,' he said as he rubbed the linctus back and forth, dribbling more into the boy's reviving mouth and gibbering above him as he shook and jerked.

'Just give him the linctus and not the act, Solomon,' Malpas said, jaded by the performance. 'You are amongst the educated and he is no more dead than I. We are all aware of the poisons you use to drug your disciples when you give them birth.'

Solomon looked at Malpas, aware he had been found out. 'He will wake soon,' he said as he stepped away from the boy and held out his hand for Tara to take.

Tara didn't move. Her hands rested in her lap and a sullen smile was upon her face.

'She will stay near to me, Solomon. Don't you think she would make such a nice queen?' Malpas asked as he again stroked her cheek with his now trembling hand.

Tersias stirred as the liquid brought his heart to life. His tiny hands gripped the sides of the sarcophagus as he began feebly to pull himself upright.

'Tersias,' whispered Jonah, holding out a hand to the boy and touching his fingertips. 'Call your Wretchkin, he will save you.'

'Boy!' shouted Malachi as he tried to press himself past the militia. 'Do no such thing! Leave the creature be, it doesn't need you.'

Tersias sat up in the wicker coffin and stared blindly before him, his lips muttering quietly as he called for the Wretchkin. There was a sound of scurrying and from every doorway flooded a mass of long-tailed rats. They ran into the room, covering every surface, and then as soon as they appeared , they were gone. And then the doorway rattled with three long, loud thumps that echoed through the house and into the Great Hall.

The door burst open and a chilling stench rolled into the room as the Wretchkin walked towards them in long bounding strides. 'What brings me to this place, Tersias?' it said in a voice loud enough for all to hear. 'Finally I am called by such a great council,' it said mockingly, Tersias mouthing every word as if possessed.

Malpas gasped as the creature stepped into the room, visible for all to see. There before them was a half-man, half-demon, its skin dry as parchment and pulled tight over its old bones. Jonah looked at the forehead of the beast on which a strip of skin had been torn away to reveal its bare bone skull.

'I see that you take a great interest in me, boy,' the Wretchkin said as it walked towards Jonah, speaking through Tersias.

Jonah didn't reply, struck dumb by the sight of the creature as it smiled at him through dry dead lips pulled tight across its charred black teeth. He noticed that the beast had an old dry wound to the side of its head.

The creature spoke as if it could read his mind. 'I have carried this for many years, boy. Once I was a man, I lived upon this earth. It was my hand that forged the knife's blade, my fingers that scraped the Alabaster and smoothed it to a perfect shape. Then it was taken from me, ripped from my hands as I was smitten, to be a curse.' The creature looked at Malpas. 'From generation to generation it was handed from the devious to the dangerous and I looked on, unable to be seen or dabble my hand in the doings of men. Then I found Tersias, and my strength grew as his faded, I grew in life as cruelty and shame burst forth in his. The more he suffered the stronger I became, his cruelty became my overwhelming joy.'

'So what do you say to us?' Malpas asked as he gripped the chair.

'I say I am done with human life and answering your futile questions of what is to come. Who shall I marry, what dress shall I wear? – is this the sum of human knowledge? Is there not one who will ask of me something that will tax my understanding?' The creature roared at the gathering as it paced up and down. 'Look at you, look at you – magicians, charlatans and politicians. All of you corrupt and bankrupt, all of you self-seeking. You, Malpas, wanted the boy to tell of your future plans to steal the life of a king and take what he had for your own whilst in your body your death stalked you with each incurable day. What a man you are, filled with such love that your own flesh and blood waited upon you and emptied the slop from your privy. And you, Solomon, slaving away with the name of a king and not a jot of his wisdom, fooling the world with talk of the end times and being a saviour. Oh, how many will come like you, shouting and quivering, fooling the poor and gullible, taking their money and twisting their minds.' As Tersias shouted the words that came from the creature, with each breath he grew weaker and weaker. 'Your fate will come sooner than you think, and from your own desires will death pick your bones.'

Tersias began to grunt and groan. The Wretchkin walked towards him as everyone stared at him.

'Leave him!' Malachi shouted in anger. 'What has he done to you but been your servant?'

'How dare you?' screamed the beast as it looked at Malachi

300

eye to eye. 'You were the cruellest of all. Many a night I actually pitied the boy when he was in your care. Kept in a cage, starved and threatened with burning pokers. He saw it all. Blind you thought him to be, but through my eyes he saw *everything*.'

Malachi bowed his head in shame as the grief welled from him. 'Leave him, and harm me. Whatever wrong he has done to you I take it upon myself. Take my soul and set him free.'

'Grace has touched your life,' the Wretchkin said scornfully. 'Fine, sentimental grace. I come to set him free, he needs me no longer as his death hovers above him. That is the nature of possession. I pass from life to life, but this time I have chosen wisely for I have seen what is to come and my victim stands open-mouthed and gasping . . .' And on those words the Wretchkin leapt towards Malpas, taking him by surprise.

Malpas clutched the back of the stone throne, unable to stand. His right hand bent upwards to the shape of a claw and the side of his face dropped, his lips numb and and eyelids quivering as a palsy gripped his body. The Wretchkin spun around him, transformed into a dark winged beast that clutched upon his neck and prised open his mouth – and then it buried its head deep within and crawled into his throat and in an instant had disappeared.

'SILENCE!' Malpas roared as several drops of deep fresh blood suddenly issued from his lips and fell to the floor. The militia, seeing his distress, formed a tight flank around him, swords drawn to protect their master.

'Skullet,' Malpas mumbled. 'It is time . . . I am dying, but it is . . . too soon.' Malpas stuttered his words through failing, fumbling lips that refused to be moulded by his desire. 'The Alabaster – take the knife and open the doorway. It will do the rest. Have it near to me . . .' Malpas slumped to the floor and lay helpless like a wounded dove, broken-winged and shot from the sky. He looked to Tara. 'Will you join with me in another land?' he asked as blood trickled from his ears and nose and his eyes blurred, swollen and full of tears.

Tara's heart stirred as the memories of the Alabaster welled up within her. She looked at Solomon and then to Malpas, blind and helpless on the cold stone floor. His eyes stared blankly to the high ceiling as he held out his hand towards her. At once she stepped from the throne, throwing the blanket from her shoulders and wrapping it around his trembling body.

Solomon reached out to grab her by the arm and pull her from the peer's side. He was pushed brutally by the captain of the militia, sword outstretched, ready to lash out. 'Back!' he shouted as Campion stood to guard his master.

Skullet ran for the Alabaster. He grabbed it from a disciple and stabbed the dagger into the lock. As the box began to open he took it to Malpas, who now lay gasping out his breath by the throne, surrounded by the guard and held tightly by Tara.

The stone opened, and a cold blast of quicksilver filled the room like the first flood of mist from the river. The candles trembled as the air was sucked from the chamber towards the heart of the Alabaster, dragging the fading light deep within the stone slabs. Then a ghostly hand reached out into the world from deep within and grasped Malpas by his throat and began to drag him slowly towards the oblivion of the mercury.

The guards fled from the Great Hall, covering their eyes as their master was consumed, their screams echoing down the long hallway and into the cold night of the street. Solomon's disciples cowered in the corner of the room, hiding behind the thick calico curtain that covered the great window to the east. Everything appeared to be suspended in the air as the Alabaster cast its spell over the gathering. Particles of fine dust fell like silver rain, shimmering before the eyes. A dark gloom consumed the light as if the sun would never lighten the room again, and above the fireplace the painting of Lord Malpas was stripped of every piece of colour, leaving only the blank frame and an empty canvas that seemed never to have seen the touch of paint.

'My brother – NO!' screamed Skullet, holding tightly to the ankle of Lord Malpas as he was dragged closer and closer to the shivering mirror, the crown of his skull beginning to disappear within the moving silver.

In his last breath, Malpas reached into the pocket of his frock coat and pushed a folded paper into Skullet's hand. His hand that passed the will to Skullet waved feebly before disappearing into the Alabaster. 'It is all for you . . . Everything . . . I go to see our father,' he said weakly as he was consumed by the mercury. The dandy gun fell from his pocket and dropped down the two steps from the throne plinth to the dirty wooden floor.

In that moment Lord Malpas was gone from the world, taken by the Alabaster into the mercurial land of the quicksilver.

A blast of pure light burst from the stone box and showered the chamber, dowsing all who stood by in shards of dew. The doorway between two worlds stood open, and an array of spectral creatures swirled about the room with ghostly green and sightless eyes, singing in voices at the very edge of hearing. Hair billowed from each one like long strands of seaweed as they flew and all in the room were unable to move, transfixed by the voices of the choir that floated before their eyes. Solomon covered his face as the flowing creatures reached out to stroke his cheek with long thin hands that were tipped with bone, fleshless fingertips

The dance quickened, the choir swirled faster and faster, mingling to become a mass of sea-green that filled the chamber and hid the Alabaster from view. Tara got to her feet and

303

reached out. She was lifted from the floor and taken up by a hundred hands to join the dance and swirl amongst the creatures. They churned the air into a spinning vortex that rattled the windows and doors, pulled the curtains from their tracks and cascaded plaster and horsehair from the walls. From the mass darted spindly fingers that ripped the clothes of the watchers and scratched their faces and sought to pick their flesh with jagged bones.

Jonah looked up as Tara floated high above him. By his side, Tersias somehow got to his feet, knowing that she was being taken from them. He jumped for the creatures, not seeing nor understanding but blindly following the desire that grew like holly bindings around his heart. 'Leave her!' he screamed as he spat the mucus from his throat. 'She is not to be taken.'

A sea-green creature formed instantly before him, its face smiling, its hair swirling in eddies and whirlpools, its sightless eyes staring into his. With one blow it slapped him suddenly across the face with its hand of bone, spinning Tersias across the floor to Malachi's feet. He lay silent, unmoving, three thick, deep scratches across his cheek.

Jonah cowered to the ground as the same creature lunged for him, hands outstretched and grasping to pick his eyes like chestnuts from the fire. Instinctively, he lashed out with his arms, beating the fingers away as they ripped the weave of his coat, pulling through each cut strips of shirt and skin from beneath. Then it spun around him, pulling back his head and grabbing his throat and ripping the collar from his coat and shredding it in its fingers.

All this time Tara was being pulled closer to the Alabaster as if the voice of Malpas was drawing her in.

Malachi lifted Tersias from the splintering floor and held him close, breathing life into his mouth, as Danton thrust his hand to the boy's chest and gabbled in a tongue that Malachi had never heard before. Tersias opened his eyes as death let him rest, cast from him by the deep concerns of his companion.

Two strides away, Jonah watched in fear as Tara was pulled by the sea-creatures towards the widening green jaws of the Alabaster. He grabbed her ankles with both hands and tugged her back to him, his feet braced against the stone. But she was wrenched ever closer to the mouth of the abyss.

'Jonah – the knife!' Malachi shouted as Tara was about to be consumed, the struggle heightening towards completion.

Jonah grabbed the dagger and, with one hand still desperately holding on to Tara, attempted to pull it from the stone. It was as if the dagger had melted within the lock, fused by the heat and a desire to keep the portal from closing. Jonah pulled again and again, but the stone refused to let its hold slip. All around him the sea-creatures swirled and twisted as they were sucked back within the stone. He cleared his mind of all thought and concentrated all his effort into pulling the blade. It juddered in the lock, then sprang back. Again he pulled the burning handle but it sealed itself even deeper in the stone.

As Tara slipped closer and closer to the mercury sea, one by one the sea-creatures fled the room and hid within the shimmering quicksilver, their hands outstretched from beyond the veil, tearing at what was not theirs and pulling her to oblivion.

'Again, Jonah, again!' Jonah heard Malachi's words as if they were rantings in a dream, just cutting through the mournful singing of the sea-creatures.

Jonah pulled even harder, forcing his fingers under the small hilt between the dagger and the stone. The handle of the dagger burnt in his hand, scorching his skin to black, as Tara willingly allowed herself to be pulled closer into the Alabaster.

'Let me go!' she shouted to Jonah above the crowing of the creatures that grabbed at her from the Alabaster. 'There is nothing left for me here.'

'Help me, Malachi!' Jonah shouted as he struggled to keep his grip of the girl. With one last effort, Jonah pulled at the dagger – and suddenly it snapped rom the lock and fell to the floor, spinning across the wooden boards and landing at Skullet's feet.

The Alabaster slammed shut, evaporating the hands of the sea-creatures that were left hanging onto Tara. Jonah fell back against the stone plinth as Tara struggled to free herself from his grip. She grabbed the Alabaster and scraped her fingers into the smooth stone in the hope of prising the two sides apart and following Malpas to the other side.

'Give me the knife!' she shouted at Skullet. 'Let me go!'

No one spoke. The room was now silent. Malachi, Solomon and Skullet looked at each other, unsure what would happen next. It was as if the cause of their struggle had been taken from them and now they searched each other for a reason for enmity. Skullet fumbled with the folded parchment, given to his hand by Malpas, his eyes scanning the lines again and again. The others watched silently, no one daring to move, as if the Alabaster still held them in its charm.

'Give me the knife,' Tara said again, holding out her hand for Skullet to give it to her.

'Stay my dear,' Solomon said as he crossed the room, his face set coldly in a long scowl.

'I want nothing of this world,' she screamed, the effects of the mind-numbing linctus gone from her body. 'That is where I want to be. I have seen it. That is what I desire.'

'But you are here with me, you cannot leave me,' Solomon whimpered as he walked towards her.

'I want nothing of this world,' she said again as she got to her feet, clutching the Alabaster.

'Then I cannot let you go,' Solomon said, and he grabbed the dandy gun from the floor and aimed it at the girl.

'NO!' Jonah screamed as he ran towards Solomon, grabbing his hand, forcing the gun towards the ceiling. Tara ran to Skullet, reaching for the dagger with one hand, as Campion pulled Jonah from his feet and threw him at Malachi.

Tara stumbled as she ran, falling headlong towards Skullet, taking him in her embrace and dropping the Alabaster to the floor. She gave a sudden short cry as if in delight as together they fell to the floor, Tara lying motionless as Skullet struggled to be free.

'Let her go!' Jonah screamed as he got to his feet, held back by Malachi.

Solomon turned and aimed the dandy gun at Skullet. 'Give me back my wife,' he cried as he stepped towards them.

Skullet pushed her from him as he got to his feet, realising that the life had left her and clutching the dagger that now dripped with Tara's blood. He stared at Solomon, who raised the gun and pulled back the hammer.

'She's dead . . . It was a misadventure, an accident . . .' he pleaded as Solomon pulled the trigger and a shot exploded from the gun, hitting Skullet in the chest.

He held his hand to the wound and smiled at Solomon. 'Not a fatal wound,' he said. The colour drained from his lips, leaving them icy blue, as blood seeped from beneath his coat and dripped slowly to the floor.

He staggered to the throne and sat against the cold stone as he looked at the wound, unable to take his gaze from the sight of blood. 'Malpas and I were brothers,' he said slowly. 'My father was his father. I was born below stairs and he above . . . on the same day, at the same time. Now I know this is a cruel earth, for he is in one world and I shall go to oblivion.' His breath wheezed through his teeth as his head fell to his chest and he said no more.

Jonah ran to Tara's side and stared at her face. A small trickle of blood seeped from the corner of her mouth. He took a hand-kerchief from his pocket and gently wiped it away, his heart broken. Solomon began to step back pace by pace, and he gave a sign to Campion to steal the Alabaster and escape.

Malachi looked and saw them turn silently, no words to say in mourning. 'Leaving so soon, Solomon? Nothing to utter for all you have done?' Malachi asked as he looked to Danton, who nursed Tersias in his arms.

'We are to avoid death . . . It pollutes us with uncleanliness. The dead are the dead and I am concerned with the living.'

'You are concerned with yourself. The writing is upon the wall of your Citadel, Solomon. You have been held in the balance and found wanting.'

'Don't make me laugh, Malachi. A haircut and a fresh set of garments do not make *you* so righteous. A failed magician, that is all you will ever be.'

'That is true, but through Jonah I have found a new life and one that you'll never know. Be gone from this place, we will take care of the dead. The Alabaster stays here and we'll fight you for it.'

'Very well, Malachi,' Solomon said as he stepped back through the great door and into the hall, fleeing from the house with Campion close behind and a straggle of disciples scurrying like frightened mice. 'But leave the city if you know what is good for you. A plague is coming that may cut short your new life and then we will see who will be king. Come, Campion – they came in a carriage fit for a king and now we shall depart in one.'

27

Veritas

Jonah Ketch looked up from where he held Tara close to him. Tears streaked his face as he sobbed and sobbed. His mind was overwhelmed by the loss of his friend. He stared into her eyes that looked back in death and he thought how she had been changed. Gone was her red hair and raucous smile, no longer would she chide him with words only half-meant. No more would he feel the warmth of her hand held out to him in friendship. In his arms he cradled her chilling body as with every second the blood drained from her face.

Jonah pulled her closer, trying to warm the death from her, hoping against hope that she would look up and speak to him just one more word. It was a moment that he hoped would last for ever, never wanting to let her go, not knowing to what place she had gone.

Soon anger as well as grief welled up within him as thoughts of Solomon running like a scalded cat filled his mind. He looked to Malachi, tight-lipped to hold back the sobs. 'He flees the murder as if it were nothing . . .' Jonah said coldly as he gently lay Tara against the side of the throne and wrapped her blood-soaked body in the blanket that she had worn. 'I cannot let him go, I have to get due payment for this –'

'Leave it,' Danton said as he cradled Tersias in a sleep from which he would not wake. 'Revenge is not for you, it belongs to another.'

'Then I will go about his business and do what he should have done so long ago. I let her down so often in life, that in death I *will* be the man.' Jonah pulled the bloodstained dagger from her chest and wiped it on his breeches as he strode from the room, his mind burning red, eyes blurred with tears. 'Quickly, quickly!' he called to the remnant of the militia who had hidden from the sea-creatures. 'They have killed Skullet and they make their escape.'

From the darkness of the stairway, the captain of the guard ran into the room and saw Skullet dead by the door, the bullet wound to his chest like the mouth of a charred volcano that had burnt a neat hole in his waistcoat.

Jonah faced him, man to man, anger filling his every inch and shaking him as he stood. 'Solomon shot Skullet – and now I go after him, he cannot escape,' he said as he stepped by the guard and ran to the door. The captain hesitated, not knowing what to do. Malachi turned to follow his young friend, only to be grabbed by Danton.

'What he does, he must do alone,' Danton said as the large wooden doors to Vamana House crashed open.

In the distance Jonah could hear the scrambling of feet scraping against the stones that stuck from the rough mud. Far to his left, he glimpsed the purple swirl of a long frock coat as it turned into the alleyway that led from Thieving Lane into St James's Field.

He ran as he had never run before, dagger in hand, breath choking, heart pounding. A vision of Tara plagued his wits. Two steps behind, the captain kept pace, sword drawn and ready to avenge his master. They spoke not, their minds fixed on the chase, pounding through the mist-filled dark streets, chasing the shadows of the disciples that wove in and out of the darkened footways.

As Jonah ran into the opening of St James's Field, quickly

followed by the captain of the guard, he glimpsed the giant frame of Campion far in the distance, lit by torchlight from the encampment. Ahead of the giant he could see the carriage by the elm tree, the horses loosely tied. The elephant lay in a ruffled hump of sagging skin, basking in the glow of the moon, snuggled in the thick straw.

'Ozymandias, Ozymandias!' Jonah cried loudly as he ran, coughing out the words through his tears. He saw Solomon turn as Campion mounted the carriage. A disciple threw back the reins from the tether, another opened the carriage door for Solomon to sneak inside out of the night. The elephant heard Jonah's calling and hungrily pulled itself to its feet, turning towards him. 'Stop them, stop them!' Jonah called as he ran.

The carriage set forth slowly, its wheels sticking in the rutted mud of the field as the horses dug their hooves deep into the ground, frightened by Campion's screaming. Ozymandias stirred like a tired old king rising graciously from the mercy seat, swinging his long trunk back and forth as the growling of caged tigers and the howl of mad monkeys filled the air, bringing half-dressed clowns and mountebanks from their beds.

Campion screamed loudly as Solomon banged on the windows of the carriage for him to drive on. Slowly, as if pressed by an unseen hand, the coach sank deeper into the soft earth, the weight of the giant tilting it to one side as he jumped up and down on the driving plate. 'Come on, you beasts!' he screamed, lashing at the air with the whip he had picked from its stand.

Jonah heard his screaming and ran like the wind, chased by the captain.

Solomon saw the boy as he bobbed in and out of the myriad of tents, leaping the lines and pegs as he sprinted, with every second getting nearer to the bogged carriage. 'Quickly, Campion, the boy comes with the guard,' he shouted loudly, banging frantically on the window frame as the carriage rocked back and forth and the horses pulled against the leads, trying to drag it free.

It was then that Solomon looked to his feet. There by the soft purple leather of his finest boots was the black sack taken from his chamber with the locusts inside. A sharp thought of horror flashed through his mind. That somehow a locust could have been taken from the Citadel and set free was surely, he thought, impossible. He slumped onto the leather bench and looked up. There, hanging like bats to the roof of the carriage, were seven black locusts. They dangled by their hind legs, their complex eyes shining in the blackness, staring at him. One by one they bristled their long scaly legs, rubbing them excitedly and filling the carriage with their baroque song.

Solomon froze in the night, reaching out his fingers for the handle to the door so he could slip from the carriage and make for freedom. His hand slithered over the lacquered wood as he attempted to find the missing latch. He gulped, long and loud, his tongue swelling in his gullet as beads of sweat bubbled from his forehead. The dark realisation of imprisonment came quickly to his mind. Solomon had no lavender to scent himself, and in the darkness his robe could not be seen for its fine purple that would, in daylight, ward off the creatures. He was trapped, and the locusts were awake in their roost.

From every corner of the circus gathered the strangest people Jonah had ever seen – a man so tall that his neck stretched a yard from his shoulders, a girl with two heads and three arms who talked to herself. As they watched Campion struggle to free the carriage the screaming from inside grew louder and louder. Ozymandias prowled around the carriage, standing on his hind legs and bellowing at Campion.

Hearing the screams from inside the carriage, Campion jumped from the driving seat. The captain of the guard broke through the encircling crowd of circus monstrosities with

Jonah close behind. There was a sudden crack as Campion flicked out an arm that pierced the air like an arrow, and the captain fell to the floor before he could raise his sword an inch.

Jonah stood before the giant, who looked down at him and glared. He felt the elephant close by him. 'Do it for me!' shouted Jonah as he held out the knife. 'Ozymandias, the carriage . . .'

The elephant raised itself again on its hind legs and stepped towards the carriage, crashing down upon the drawing pole and cracking it in two. The horses bolted to freedom through the crowd and across the field.

Campion looked back and forth. The screaming of his master to be free and the desire to destroy the boy tore his thoughts into strands of hesitation.

'He's going nowhere and neither are you,' Jonah shouted. 'Come on, fat boy. Do me like you did the Captain, one punch on the chin and I'll be yours . . .' He danced back and forth on his tippy-toes, glinting the knife in the moonlight. 'Solomon doesn't need you and you'll never get the chance to have me again. Come on, you lily-liver – hit me like I know you can . . .'

Close behind, Ozymandias pushed against the carriage, lifting it from the mud and spinning it to its roof. The screaming stopped as Solomon was rattled like a broken eggshell in the tumbling coach. The elephant lifted it again, rolling it to its wheels and then back to its roof as if it were but a blown feather on a summer's day.

Campion lashed out at the boy, his fist snapping the air just short of Jonah's face as he leapt backwards, somersaulting to his feet to the applause of the crowd.

'Make a fool of me, boy?' Campion said, drooling snot from his chin in long green strands. 'With one hand I could pull your head off and with two your ears as well,' he snarled.

'Then I would be as ugly as you,' Jonah taunted as he danced back and forth.

A hand flashed from the darkness, hitting Jonah in the arm and sending the knife spinning from his grip. Then another and another as three blows beat home double quick, taking the breath from his body and the life from his legs.

Campion stepped closer, towering over the boy who lay beaten on the damp ground. 'Now I have you and you will not jest with me,' he said, raising his hand above his head to rain down one last fatal blow on the boy's chest.

Time stood still for Jonah. The noise of the circus, the cry of Ozymandias and the cackling of the crowd faded into the expanse of night sky. He looked up at the giant and saw his hammer-like fist high above him, about to fall. All he could feel was the cold damp earth and the smell of winter grass mixed with the sobering fragrance of London dirt. Somewhere very near he sensed the vapour of old gin and stale beer. In his last living glance he caught the eyes of the two-headed woman who smiled two soft smiles and mouthed a word that he could not hear.

Jonah looked back to Campion, knowing what was to come. Soon, he thought, he would be with Tara.

With a snap, a loud crack and a sudden flash the elephant's trunk wrapped itself around Campion's neck and jolted him from the ground as the beast choked his throat. Ozymandias dangled the giant above the ground. Campion grappled with his large, weakening hands, struggling to breathe as he hung like a puppet.

No one dared move. The crowd was silenced. The elephant turned. Campion was carried like a limp doll as the beast strode from the encampment and into the dark night, screaming and bellowing as it disappeared into the blackness.

Jonah got to his feet, gasping in the cold night air that burnt his lungs and chilled his spine. The carriage lay broken and trampled, its door hanging loose. He walked slowly forward in the flickering torchlight and moon shadows. A wall of faces surrounded him, whispering to each other, one calling his name.

Jonah stepped closer and lifted the handle, pulling the wood from the frame. Then he leapt back, stumbling, falling to his knees as he scrabbled madly to free himself from the horror his eyes had allowed his soul to perceive. Solomon's bones fell from the carriage, picked clean by the locusts that now gorged themselves on each other as their greed brought their own demise.

As the boy grabbed the dagger that lay beside him, the prophet's bald and gnawed head rolled across the grass towards him, its one remaining eye staring wildly from the mantle of its socket, its mouth half smiling.

A hand reached down and took Jonah by the scruff of his neck, pulling him to his feet and tugging him close in warm embrace. 'Come, my friend,' said Malachi. 'We have nothing here. The morning comes and we have a woe-day to endure . . .'

The procession snaked through the long dead grass of Conduit Fields, leaving the dank smoke-filled smog of London far behind as the tall houses of Queen Square faded into the distance. Far to the front, Jonah pulled the horse that in turn dragged the flat cart. Rocking gently on the stark wooden boards of the wagon, the lifeless forms of Tersias and Tara lay together, wrapped tightly against the chill air, their faces taking the breeze that sped across the common.

Malachi walked with the cart and Danton stepped slowly behind, head to the ground, counting the paces as he walked. 'Two dead, Mister Danton,' Malachi called behind him as he pressed on towards Black Mary's Well. 'Was stopping Malpas and Solomon worth two young lives?'

'That we will never know,' Danton said heavily as he stumbled along the cart track. 'Sometimes in life we will never understand until we too have gone the way of our friends.'

'Once I thought there was a light at the end of the tunnel – now all I see is a boy in despair,' Malachi replied as he looked at Jonah. 'I thought Tersias would live, but then he slipped from us in his sleep. Gone with Tara, that is my hope. He'll no more be troubled with his second sight. No more prophecies, no more Wretchkin and begging for him.' Malachi wallowed in melancholy. 'I would have taken him for my own. The change in me would have been a change for him, but he was stolen from me.' He sighed as he walked, looking at the bright blue winter sky. 'If only he could have seen this place – to be buried by the well and the King's Cross, such a fine sepulchre, away from the dirt and grime of London.'

'And the dagger and the Alabaster – what will you do with them, Magnus?' Danton asked.

'They will rest with Tara. She will keep them guarded. They are not for this world, and we shall be sure that Malpas does not return. Do you not think?'

'Do you mark the grave, Magnus?'

'Only with the pain of my heart,' Malachi replied, quickening his pace to catch Jonah as the outline of three shapes broke the horizon by the well stones. 'Someone is already there before us . . . The gravedigger should be long gone. Who can it be?' Malachi anxiously bobbed back and forth, shielding the sun from his eyes as he looked towards the dark figures. He watched as Jonah raised his hand and waved, and the smallest visitor broke free from its companions and came running along the track towards him.

Maggot ran to his friend and flung himself into his embrace as he wiped the tears from his face with the back of his hand. 'Dead?' he asked Jonah, disbelieving the shrouded bodies that lay before him.

'Sleeping to wake again,' Jonah replied as he pushed back a shudder from his lips, not wanting Maggot to see him cry.

'There's a grave made ready, lined with lavender and sea grass,' Maggot said as he gripped his hand.

'A resting bed until they wake. Warm and cradled in soft earth to face the rising sun and wait for that splendid day.' Jonah coughed as he cleared his throat and put his hand to his lips to silence the boy. 'Words have no more place here, for words started this death upon the heath and I have nothing left to say, my young friend.'

They travelled on, hand in hand, the breeze breaking the silence as it whirled through the branches of the hedges that lined the lane to the well. It was two coats colder than the night as clouds raced across the darkening sky, the last rays of sunlight stealing through them before the sun was blotted like dark ink from the heavens.

Waiting by the well, Griselda held on to Old Bunce, who trembled in his thick coat, shivering more through anticipation than biting cold. He bit his fingers, nibbling skin and nail, as the procession drew closer, wanting to see the face of his little girl.

The horse stopped, its feet bathed in cool clear water that spurted from the well, hastened by the strong rains. By the ring of stones a neat, deep pit had been carved from cold earth. It fell away into the depths of the dark, rich peat, the faint smell of lavender and sea grass gently scenting the grave.

Jonah stood, gripping the horse, burying his face into its neck, feeling its sharp coat against his skin. He closed his eyes, not wanting to see Danton and Malachi lift the bodies of Tara and Tersias from the cart and clumsily place them upon the earth. Old Bunce stepped towards him and took Jonah by the arm. He turned his face towards Tara as she lay quietly upon the grass.

'We do this for them . . .' he whispered, for once not smelling of gin.

'They should not be dead,' Jonah sobbed. 'If I had been the man I should be I would have saved them both. It is I who should lay there and they should mourn me.'

'Not meant to be,' Griselda chided him gently. 'Your death waits in another place, far in the future, hiding behind a doorway or sleeping away, old and well fed.'

'You . . . you could do something . . . Some magic, a charm, what you did to me . . .' Jonah said as he scraped the ground with his feet.

'Do you want to do this?' Malachi asked as he held out the Alabaster and dagger to Jonah. 'The deeper it is buried, the more we will know that it will never be seen again.'

'I wish I had never seen them, that the night had never happened and we had never met you, Malachi. She would have still been in the Bull and Mouth and Tersias locked in his cage.'

'Would that have been life for them or us?' Malachi asked as he threw the Alabaster into the depths of the grave.

'I still have the finger I stole from you, Malachi. We could make a charm of life and cast off death,' Jonah said, rummaging in his pocket. He brought out the withered ring finger with its dark gnarled nail.

'Give it to the grave, Jonah. It is of no use to me now. I walk a different road.'

'So you give in to circumstance and won't even try?' Jonah cried as he hung on to the horse's neck. 'A doormat for dirty feet to walk upon, is that what you are?'

'Say goodbye to them, Jonah, give her one last kiss and let us lay them down to sleep,' Malachi said.

Jonah turned and saw Griselda kneeling by the cold bodies of Tara and Tersias. 'Come, Jonah. Sit with us,' she said softly, beckoning him with her thin white hands. 'For friendship if not for love.'

He looked to the well and the babbling of the water that gurgled from the spring and over the cold grey stones. With one hand he took the horse bag and dipped it deeply into the well, then walked to where Tara lay and gently wiped her face. A penny piece lay on each of her eyes, and her blue lips were tight and lifeless.

In the grief and sadness of the moment, Jonah looked towards the sky and saw the dark clouds brighten before him as a jolt of lightning cracked from east to west. He wiped a finger across his face, pressing the tear from his cheek and smearing it upon Tara's lips. He did the same to Tersias, not knowing the reason, only that it should be done. Griselda smiled, knowing what stirred in his heart.

He looked up at Malachi, Maggot and Old Bunce. They all stood silent as if frozen in time, the clouds hanging above them, motionless and still. Jonah took Danton's whistle from his pocket and put it to his lips. The cold burnt his skin as he blew the note once, then again and again, louder and louder. It called like the sound of a shrill summer bird flying high, higher than the clouds, higher than the sky. A creature you hear but never see, as if it was never really there. He remembered Danton's words that if he was in trouble then he could use the whistle to call a companion, a comforter, and he would come.

Jonah waited in the silence, hoping for the promised miracle. At the top of the lane he saw a dark figure standing by the hedge, cowering like a golem in the long grass. In his heart he knew it to be Malpas, back for one last look and gloat in his contentment. He looked again and the shadow had gone. All around him, ice gripped the ground and enfolded each crease of Tara's grave clothes in crisp white seams – and then, like the sudden changing of the season and passing of winter, it was gone.

By Tara's head a sprig of snowdrops burst through the dry, barren earth, shooting forth their buds and bursting white. The sky burnt bright as another shard of light cracked the heavens, then again and again like canes of blue light beating against the sky.

Jonah's heart raced. 'This will not end in death,' he thought to himself, not daring to believe, as the thought came again, spoken on his lips.

Tersias stirred from his sleep, his eyes opened and stared at Jonah. 'It is you . . .' he said, smiling at him. 'And Magnus Malachi . . .' The boy laughed as he struggled to be free from his bindings.

Choking back his fear, Jonah tore at the cloth that held the boy fast. There was a sudden crack of thunder, and Malachi was jolted from his dreaming.

'Tersias!' he cried as he saw the boy twisting to be free.

A frenzy broke out in the gathering as Danton and Malachi pulled the boy to his feet and pulled open the bindings.

'Tara . . . It is time,' Jonah said, knowing that she could hear his every word. 'Wake up – the winter is over, the spring has come . . .'

Tara opened her tired eyes as the blood flooded her soft cheeks and Jonah ripped the purple bandages from her head.